THE

WIZARD SLAYER

- Book One of the Wizard Slayer Saga -

Franklin Roberts

CONTENTS

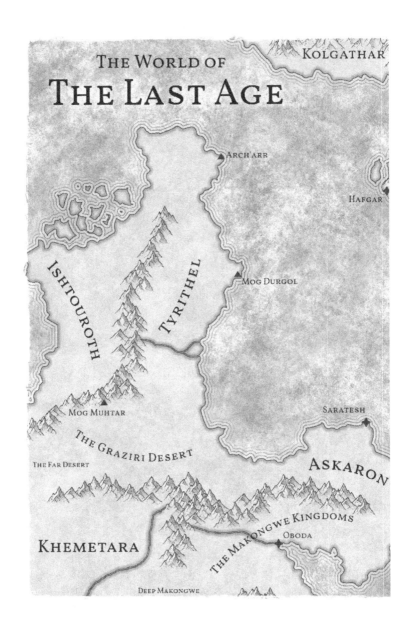

THE WORLD OF

THE LAST AGE

KOLGATHAR

ARCH'ARR

HAFGAR

ISHTOUROTH

TYRITHEL

MOG DURGOL

MOG MUHTAR

SARATESH

THE GRAZIRI DESERT

THE FAR DESERT

ASKARON

KHEMETARA

THE MAKONGWE KINGDOMS

OBODA

DEEP MAKONGWE

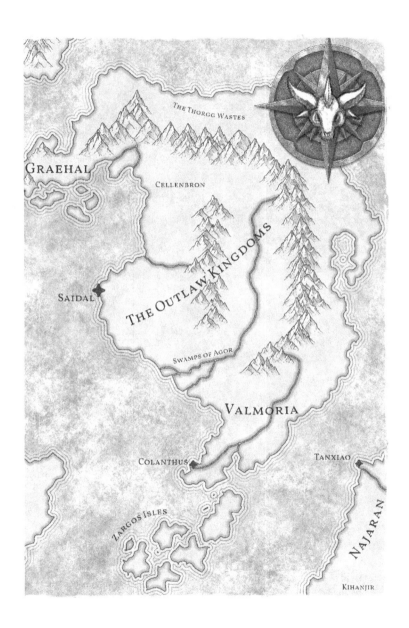

PROLOGUE

Screams of agony went unheard as they echoed amidst the crumbling spires of the timeworn structure. The skeletal ruin had been constructed in an earlier age of great machinery, but like the civilization that had created it, all that remained was a husk of former glory. Any winding paths that once led to the place had long been abandoned, covered by avalanche or rockfall, making the site truly isolated.

The sorceress Shar-Khetra had made this place her home, able to work her dark magicks without interruption from the outside world. That night she stood in the central hall, whose vaulted ceiling had long since crumbled away, revealing the ominous black sky. The wind whistled amidst the craggy peaks of steel-imbued masonry, and in the distance, thunder boomed, echoing amongst the great stone walls of the steep mountains. Behind an altar, she stood reciting a dark, blasphemous tongue. The feeble flames of candles flickered in the wind as the sorceress's midnight robes flung about her seductive form. From behind luscious lips, her teeth gnashed, uttering the dark incantations that would invoke the power of her malign masters.

In the shadows lurked Shar-Khetra's minions: disheveled mountain men that had been entranced by the sorceress's beauty. Their worn, bearded faces stared in fear at the clouds above, whose changing forms twisted and writhed unlike any storm they had seen before. For a moment, they saw faces in the tumultuous sky. Maniacal grins and sneers, along with piercing eyes, shone in the shadows of crackling lightning. The mountain men wanted to believe the faces were just a trick of the light and imagination, but they knew deep in their hearts that these were the visages of deities that best remained unknown.

A finger, tipped with a long, curving black nail, pointed to one of the cowering thralls. "Bring them forth," said Shar-Khetra with a sinister glow in her dark cat-like eyes.

Knowing what this vague command meant, the minion left the hall and returned with a chain in hand. Along this chain were shackled nine prisoners. They were a motley band varying in race and age. While they hailed from many different realms, they were all oracles in their own cultures. Each able to foresee the fates that awaited them, the prisoners fought against their chains. Visions of a single man were conjured by their prescience. He was not just a man of evil design, but the very fulcrum of dark fate. In his hands would lie the world, and by his hand, it all could end. The oracles' struggle proved futile as their hungry, thinning bodies could do little to resist the strength of the mountain men.

The sorceress held aloft a dagger, whose jagged edges and irregular curves would make any cut from it agonizing. The first of the oracles, an Askarian woman, was brought forward and tied to the altar. She thrashed against the stone table not out of fear of death but of knowing what the ritual would lead to.

One by one, Shar-Khetra plunged the sinister blade into the flesh of the oracles, chanting as their blood collected in pools on the altar. As the victims thrashed in agony, the cruel edges of the dagger tore their bodies apart. The process was slow, for the pain was just as important to the spell as the death it accompanied. Flesh tore and bones splintered. High above, the clouds continued to clash, folding and tumbling about each other. In the chaos, the vile faces could be seen.

The lifeless bodies of the oracles were pulled from the grisly altar. Blood and entrails of the nine victims lay on the stone table, illuminated by faint candles and lightning from above. The sorceress's claw-like nails waved over it all, and her thralls trembled. The wind began to rise. Elevated by the whistles and howls was Shar-Khetra's chanting, which sounded like no mortal voice, but a chorus of otherworldly screams.

The mountain men began to flee at a full sprint. They scrambled out of the chamber, an umbral fear gripping their hearts with claws of ice. Shar-Khetra did not care. The wind whipped about her pitch-black hair as the very walls of the forsaken structure shook, threatening to bury the whole room in a torrent of crumbling stone and rusted metal. Still, she continued, as this was expected, for there was powerful magick at work here. Soon, the gore began to slither. Blood flowed of its own accord. The remnants of the nine oracles gathered at the center of the stone table, quivering and congealing. Flesh reformed about itself, making something entirely new.

The wind died down. The clouds above no longer swirled. Shar-Khetra dropped to her knees, shaking. On the table lay a wailing newborn. Gathering her strength, the sorceress lifted herself to see the product of her endeavor. The blood was gone, and the baby lay on the cold stone naked. His skin was pale, and a fine, silvery hair had already begun to grow from his tiny head. As the sorceress loomed over him, he opened his eyes, revealing two vibrant jade irises.

Shar-Khetra picked up the child, who still cried. He was *Nihaya Azgaad*, but in his youth, he would be called Prince Eledrith Calidign. She held a boy destined to defy all of Creation. He would not know it for many years, but he would have the power to bring reality to its knees.

The Dark Gods laughed.

1
AN IRREFUSABLE OFFER

A single lantern did little to illuminate the cramped cells of the prison, and no windows allowed the reek of sweat to leave the stone-walled chamber. Rusted iron bars ran from floor to ceiling, separating the rabble of prisoners from the guard that rested his back against the locked door. Clad in a simple jack and flat helm, the man may not have been the most formidable, but he could at the very least keep watch over the convicted men. The area behind the iron bars was a festering assemblage of unwashed bodies and hushed voices that, in gruff and vulgar tones, talked ill of each other and the powers that imprisoned them. Dark eyes glared contemptuously at the single guard and the cudgel hanging from his belt.

One prisoner, named Dorgar, was an obvious sailor. A plethora of blue-black tattoos was scrawled across his weathered skin, and a thin white beard ran down from his old, scarred face. He said in a seafarer's dialect, "Ye hear about the poor bastards that got killed down in the Sailor's Quarter? One of the brawls at the Squid and Spear got outta hand."

"As to be suspected from that hive of scum, I suppose," said another.

"What do ye mean, Ludwen?" said Dorgar. "That's a must-stop place for anyone docking in the port o' Saidal."

"Coming from the likes of you," said Ludwen. Unlike his counterpart, he was a merchant and spoke with a more formal vocabulary. Whatever crooked dealing that had landed him in that cell went unknown. "But I'll have you know that, yes, I have heard that rumor. Was it not but one man that killed eleven?"

"Aye, it was, and a monster of a man at that!"

"I suppose it takes a monster to win a fight when outnumbered."

The guard's eyes wandered amidst the prisoners, and his attention fell upon one who sat in a shadow-shrouded corner, or at least what little of him could be seen. The elusive figure had yet to utter a single word, and both the sailor and merchant were oblivious to him.

Dorgar said, "He be more than a monster, though. They say he's a Wizard Slayer."

Breaking out into laughter, Ludwen said, "You can't be serious!"

Drowned out by the merchant's outburst was a deep, growling chuckle. As the hidden prisoner smiled, canine teeth too ferocious to be human glinted in the feeble lamplight.

"Aye, I am serious!"

"You sailors are all superstitious fools. Whenever something comes along that you can't wrap your rum-addled mind around, you blame the workings of gods or magick."

A solemn look filled Dorgar's eyes. "Gods may not be real like some say, but ye best believe in magick. I've seen things in my time that'd make ye abandon reason as well."

"Like what?"

"I've heard tales of crews turning against each other. One moment, they're brothers in arms, the next, they act like rabid dogs clawing at each other's throats."

With a dismissive smirk, the merchant said, "Tales, say? Alright, I'll play along. Let's say magick is real."

"It is."

"Then how could someone possibly fight against it? If a spell can compromise someone's will, there's simply no hope."

Running a hand through his tobacco-stained beard, the sailor said, "I guess it takes the same kind of man that can win a fight eleven to one."

A rapping came upon the reinforced door, and the guard opened it in response. Eight Saidalian soldiers clad in long mail hauberks and conical helms marched through the arched frame. In their hands were hafted mancatchers, their mechanical crescent heads lined with dull spikes. Leading them was a government official marked by his elaborate dress and lack of practical armor. His thin neck sprouted from amidst the frills of his blue and purple doublet, although not far enough to rival the stature of the soldiers that accompanied him. The official spoke. "We are here for the Wizard Slayer. His Majesty's orders."

Before the prison guard could open his mouth, a letter sealed with the royal crest was thrust toward him. A soldier picked the lantern up and brought it to the edge of each cell, examining the prisoners within. As the wavering light danced across the scowling faces and slouched forms, the official paced just beyond the bars, hands behind his back and thin chin held high.

The official found who he was looking for. Sitting in the corner cell was a man that no civilized society could produce. Corded, predatory muscles covered his towering frame, and beneath untamed black hair glared two cold gray eyes. The man's strong jaw was clean-shaven, but that was the only mark of domestication about him. He rose, and the chains that bound his hands and feet rattled. No other in the cell necessitated such binds. As his pupils caught the lantern's light, they seemed to reflect like a nocturnal animal's, if only for a split second.

"Everyone against the back wall!" barked the guard.

The mass of men receded, leaving the hulking prisoner alone. "That is him, no doubt," said the official. "I want no less than four men restraining him at a time."

As the lock on the cell door clanked open, four mancatchers latched around the Slayer's neck. The barbarian did not resist, and as he shuffled forward as best as his manacles would allow, he glared at the tiny man in the lavish doublet. They were stark opposites, one a monolith of primal ferocity, the other a weakling hiding behind the immaterial power of a nepotistic society.

"Let us make haste," said the official, averting the Slayer's gaze. "We still have yet to fetch his companion."

With mancatchers pulling at his neck, the barbarian was escorted from the chamber into the winding passages beyond. Long after the shuffling of feet and clinking of mail faded, Ludwen muttered, "By hell…"

———◆———

Steel rang against steel. High above the winding corridors of the city below was the garden terrace of the Calidign Palace. Flowered bushes grew amongst crystalline fountains and white marble statues, and an expansive courtyard stood in its midst. On the intricately patterned stone, two sets of feet stepped in the delicate dance of swordplay. To one side of the garden stood the walls of the palace, which ascended high with its narrow spires and buttressed walls. To the west, over the forest of towers and buildings of the massive city below, was the sea. The fresh wind that blew across the turbulent waters for countless miles reached the palace and rustled through the brightly petaled flowers.

The two swordsmen that fought in the garden were not evenly matched. Sir Garrick, Knight and Captain of the Royal Guard, was considered a master of swordcraft, but even he found it difficult to hold his own. The man was in his late fifties, and his short gray hair was testament to this. No longer relying on the virility of his earlier years, Garrick instead utilized the decades of battlefield experience and honed technique to ward off the flurry of strikes that came toward him.

The swordmaster's feet slid backward across the marble as he warded off the incoming blitz of slashes. Try as he might to capitalize on his opponent's overaggressive onslaught, he couldn't seem to find an opening. Garrick's weapon was parried to the side with a sharp clang, and his foe's blade came down toward his exposed neck, halting an inch away from a killing blow.

The opponent that had bested the swordmaster was nothing short of a prodigy. He was but a youth, just shy of eighteen years of age, yet he wielded his sword as if he was born with it in his hand. The ocean breeze sifted through his long, silky silver-blond hair, and a cunning smile came to his handsome, pallid face.

"Well done, Your Majesty," said Garrick, gasping for breath.

The young princeling lowered his blunted practice sword. "I learned from the best."

Garrick chuckled, wiping the sweat from his scarred, bearded face. "I'm sure you'll want to have at it again, but I'll need a quick breather here if you don't mind."

"By all means, take your time. It's a gorgeous day, and every second spent out here is a blessing to me." The prince hadn't so much as broken a sweat during the sparring match. He looked to the sky with vibrant jade eyes.

Garrick took a seat on one of the many carved benches in the garden and loosened his padded vest. Sometimes the prince's good nature irritated the old mentor, and he couldn't help but roll his eyes.

"I really do appreciate this practice, you know."

Garrick looked up.

"Everything I know about swordplay," continued the prince, "I owe to you. Natural talent be damned, you taught me a life's worth of technique in the span of… what is it now, four years?"

"Aye, about that long, yes. Don't let your skills get to your head, though."

"I'll try not to," said the prince with a laugh. "Come now, I yearn for another round! Do not hold back, Garrick."

To the old knight's relief, a third voice said, "Prince Eledrith, your presence is requested in the throne room at once."

"Damn it all," cursed the prince, hand falling away from his sheathed weapon. He turned to the servant. "Tell my father I'll be there soon."

Eledrith rushed through the ornate halls of the palace and into the throne room, now wearing an elegant black doublet. Two great braziers lighted the massive hall near the throne, and the natural light drifted in through the many arched windows along the walls. Red carpet covered the center of the checkered floor, and the walls were of smooth dark marble. Lining these walls were royal guards, each protected by a coat of tightly linked mail and sporting a halberd. Hanging amidst the chamber were the colors of House Calidign: a round golden sun rising from a blue sea into a purple sky. Sitting on the throne was the King of Saidal himself. He was Torvaren Calidign, and upon his reddish brown, bearded head sat a gilded, ornate crown. His form was plump, and his large eyes were fixated on the concubine leaning against his throne.

The prince grimaced at his father but held his tongue.

"Eledrith, my boy," the king said, almost startled, "how was your morning training?"

"Excellent," said Garrick, who had just entered behind the prince. "His skills are as sharp as ever, Your Majesty."

The old mentor looked odd in formal dress, for his face was that of a veteran warrior. A scar ran through his right eyebrow and down his nose, deforming his nostril and upper lip. Despite this deformation, he exuded an aura of respect and authority greater than King Torvaren himself. No one would have suspected he had been beaten in sparring by the slim youth that was Eledrith.

After the king whispered something into her ear, the concubine slipped away from the throne and left the room. A servant called out from the opposite end of the hall, "The Wizard Slayer is here, my lord."

"Bring him in!" said Torvaren. "I am eager to see this living legend myself."

Eledrith and Garrick exchanged confused looks. Slaying a wizard was a feat of legends indeed.

As the doors at the far end of the hall opened, the sound of many footsteps and the clanking of heavy chains came. Four guards entered, holding mancatchers to the neck of a figure who stood at least one head taller than all of them. An untamed mess of black hair hung past his massive, muscular shoulders. The Wizard Slayer was a man by appearance, but there was a certain animality about him that was immediately apparent. He did not have the healthy physique of an ordinary warrior, but instead, enormous, jagged muscles ran underneath a tapestry of pale scars that was his skin. His sunken gray eyes peered out with predatory intensity.

Garrick muttered, "If anyone would be able to kill a wizard, it'd be someone like him."

From behind the first group followed another, smaller prisoner. He was likewise bound and escorted, although only one guard held his arm with an iron grip. This second prisoner went unnoticed by those in the king's hall, for all eyes stared at the barbarian.

The Slayer continued through the room until he came within twenty feet of the throne. Once close enough for conversation, the king said, "Greetings, Wizard Slayer. You stand in the hall of Torvaren Calidign, High King of Saidal."

The guards surrounding him kneeled, but the Slayer simply bowed his head, resisting the pull of mancatchers on his neck. Perturbed, the fat king shifted in his throne before continuing. "By what name should I call you?"

"Krael," he responded in a deep, almost growling voice.

In the short time it took to say his name, Krael's mouth had opened to reveal long canine teeth more like a hound's fangs. Torvaren's eyes grew wide. After recovering his composure, he said, "Greetings, Krael, and forgive me for these... precautions." He gestured to the heavy chains and small army of guards that surrounded him. "But your reputation precedes you. I understand it was but a month ago when you killed eleven men in a tavern brawl."

"But they were trying to kill us!" shouted a voice from behind the Slayer.

"Compose yourself," ordered Garrick. "You will speak only when spoken to!"

"Sorry," said the voice.

The second prisoner that had been brought forth was a far cry from his companion. He looked young for his age. His handsome elfin face was youthful, and his light frame and shorter height didn't help. A mop of tawny hair was contained by a headband, which also hid the pointed tips of his ears, a telltale mark of true elven ancestry. In these days, there was seldom a full-blooded elf left after untold generations of crossbreeding with humans, and the actual traits of that fair race were shrouded in mystery and hearsay. The elf-blooded hid his heritage for a good reason, for there was rampant superstition about the alchemical properties of his race's blood. More than once had his life been threatened by those wishing to sell his corpse to the highest bidder, as there was a severe demand amongst those considered witches.

"Who is this companion here?" asked the king.

"He is Darreth," said Garrick, "and from what information I could gather, he is a sort of assistant to the Wizard Slayer. He killed one of the eleven you previously mentioned. Am I correct?"

Darreth nodded.

"He goes where I go," said the Slayer.

"Very well," said Torvaren, "but let us get back to the topic at hand. Is it true, Krael, that you killed those eleven, er, ten men that night?"

Eledrith bit his lip, wondering what his father was scheming. *Torvaren would not go to this length for a mere confession, so why bring him here?*

"Yes," said Krael.

11

"And is it true that you and your companion made no effort to resist your arrest when the city guard arrived at the scene?"

As Darreth nodded, Krael said, "Yes."

"Sir Garrick has undergone a thorough investigation of you after rumors that a Wizard Slayer was held in the dungeons. I'll now allow him to tell you what he found and verify that his information is correct."

Torvaren's crowned head nodded toward Garrick, who then stepped forward. "Thank you, my lord," he said. "As far as I can tell, Krael, you do not work for coin, but instead by a personal vendetta. In no account of your dealings has anyone ever said you asked for compensation."

"It is why I live," said Krael with grim conviction.

Garrick continued. "Supposedly, you're a man of honor, and you wouldn't kill eleven men without good reason. I can only assume that, as your companion here mentioned, you were acting in self-defense."

"Unfortunately, the system of justice we have here in Saidal has already found you guilty of murder," said the king, "but I, out of kindness, wish to make you an offer."

"Travedd is a small village on the moors to the south. I have reason to believe my traitorous nephew, Count Thalnar Calidign, has sought refuge there. After being found guilty of conspiring to have me assassinated, he could not risk staying in Saidal where the whole city guard was prepared to kill him on sight."

Eledrith knew this to be familiar and public knowledge, save where his treacherous relative had exactly fled. Still, he listened, eager to understand why a Wizard Slayer was needed to bring Count Thalnar to justice.

"Upon learning his whereabouts, I sent a small force of fighting men to Travedd. There were over fifty in their number. Only one returned."

The king called out to a previously unseen servant, who brought in a husk of a man. He came shuffling through a side door, helped along by the guiding hands of the king's servant. His emaciated form was garbed by tattered, torn clothes. Any vitality that the young man should have had was gone, replaced with an unnatural, exhausted aura. His face was unnervingly gaunt, and at his sides, his hands trembled. Two sunken eyes stared as if in fear. "He has been like this since we found him on the side of the road just outside Saidal. In all the time since then, he has said little except mentions of speaking to a wizard after he escaped from wolves."

At the mention of "wizard," the poor man's eyes grew even wider, and a horrible moan came from his throat. Trembling hands rose to protect from unseen threats as he sank to the floor. Turning away from the cowering wretch, the king signaled for him to be sent off. Two servants had to drag the former soldier, screaming, from the king's hall.

"I cannot imagine anything other than foul sorcery bringing someone to such a lowly state. I know little about the situation and even less about magick. That is why I have searched for someone like you, Krael. I ask you to learn the truth of what is going on in Travedd, bring Count Thalnar back here to face his punishment, and, as your title suggests, kill a wizard if need be. In return, I shall offer you a full pardon of your crimes against Saidal."

"And if I refuse?" said the Slayer, his dark, slow voice resounding off the marble walls.

The king chuckled at this. "Well, given your crimes of murder—"

"Murder? But he even agreed it was self-defense!" Darreth cried out, looking to Garrick to back him up.

"Mind your manners, dog!" said the guard attending to the elf-blooded. "You're speaking to the king."

"Yes, murder," Torvaren continued. "The penalty for murder is death, and without the pardon I have so graciously offered, the city guards would have the authority to strike you down on sight.

If you wish to accept, Garrick will accompany you on your journey. If you defy his orders in any way, he will send you to your grave."

Garrick's hand drifted to a broad dagger sheathed on his belt, whose large metal scabbard preserved the poison that covered its razor edge. Krael saw this and recognized such a scabbard. "This is no offer. It is coercion," he said.

Eledrith couldn't help but smirk. The courts of Saidal were riddled with amoral plots and schemes hiding under the guise of benevolence. Where most wouldn't dare call out the king for what he had done, the Slayer had not hesitated to speak the truth. For this, the prince looked upon the Wizard Slayer with admiration.

Darreth, on the other hand, stared wide-eyed at his friend. Quickly putting his silver tongue to use, he said, "Call this whatever you like; we accept and will bring to light whatever is happening in Travedd, Your Majesty. Be it wizard or some other strange foe, I'm sure Krael here will make short work of it."

"Your assistant is eager to accept, but what say you, Wizard Slayer?"

After a pause, Krael said, "I agree."

2
BEYOND ANCIENT WALLS

Eledrith stowed his ornate blade onto the back of his white stallion. It was of cruciform shape, and a sweeping hilt offered additional protection to his hand. He had wielded the sword for years, and no other would be as comfortable in his possession. The journey through the Outlaw Kingdoms to Travedd would take three days, and the saddlebags were just large enough to stow the necessary supplies. As he fastened his last things to the saddle, he heard his mentor's voice from behind. "If it were up to me, I wouldn't allow you to come on such a strange mission."

The prince turned to see Garrick's scarred face. His graying eyebrows narrowed in concern. "Don't worry, I've had a good teacher," said Eledrith, laying a hand on the veteran's shoulder.

"There are far more dangerous things out there than an old man with a sword," said Garrick.

The prince rolled his eyes. Frustrated with his student's naivety, Garrick asked, "Whatever convinced your father to send you with us?"

"Publicity. I'm apparently considered a 'spoiled and sheltered brat' by some powerful officials. To prove them wrong and bring respect to my name, I'll help bring a wanted traitor to justice myself."

"Damn it all," Garrick muttered. "I have no choice but to allow this, but you better be careful, you hear me? Regardless of what His Majesty thinks, I care about you too, Eledrith, and I won't be able to bear the guilt of knowing you've perished under my watch."

"Something tells me I'll be the one saving your old hide," said Eledrith, smirking.

When the young prince wasn't looking, Garrick cracked a smile.

A servant brought forth two more horses from the stables, one each for Darreth and Krael to ride on. They weren't of the same stock as the prince's, but they would serve their purpose. As the small party made their final preparations, Garrick asked, "Are you sure four of us will be enough, Wizard Slayer? I have a whole regiment of fighting men at my disposal."

"No," said Krael, "magick turns allies into enemies. We have too many already."

"I see," said Garrick. He scratched his gray beard, imagining the grim implications of the Slayer's words.

Krael's gray eyes wandered to the poisonous dagger sheathed on the knight's hip. Upon noticing this, Garrick said, "Fear not, I have no desire to use this."

The barbarian's face twisted in confusion, so Garrick elaborated. "From one fighting man to another, you have my respect. If the rumors about you are true, you are no cutthroat vagabond, and I have no reason to worry. That being said, I am sworn to the king's service and must enforce his orders."

Onward the four went from the gates of King Torvaren's palace and through the narrow cobbled streets of the city-state of Saidal. Even at midday, the alleys and avenues were shrouded in an eerie twilight. What little light shone directly between buildings was like the rare rays that break through the canopy of an old and choking forest. Despite the gloom, crowds filled the streets, slowing the riders' pace to a crawl.

Krael attracted a great many eyes. The Slayer was massive, sure, but the enormous sword stowed on the saddle warned on-lookers of his fighting prowess. Borrowed from the royal armory was an executioner's sword. Far too heavy and unbalanced for even an experienced soldier to wield correctly, the long two-handed blade ended in not a pointed tip but a square head. It was a tool specialized for beheadings, but it was perfect for the likes of the Slayer.

Saidal was vast, as it was the largest city left in the world. The sprawling metropolis stretched miles across, and it was all pro-tected by an encompassing exterior wall. Black stone served to construct this imposing barrier, and the crenels atop its battle-ments ascended to a sinister point. This wall was out of necessity, as the lawless outside realms were dangerous, and its denizens would not hesitate to strike out at settlements not so heavily guarded. The region surrounding Saidal was known as the Outlaw Kingdoms, for it was a land fought over by a feudal collection of unorganized states. Warlords declared themselves kings once they had amassed enough wealth and territory, and noble blood was little more than the lineages of these brutal conquerors.

The mighty black wall of Saidal extended a hundred yards out into the sea, where it opened and made a sheltered port. From here, ships sailed carrying cargo from every corner of the known world and beyond. Inside the walls, the city was crowded. Instead of ex-panding across more land, buildings stretched skyward. In the first years of this construction, the towers had been sturdy and safe, but the foundations weakened and crumbled with time. Generations after the architects dared to reach new heights, the whole city was a jungle of teetering towers leaning against one another, new structures erected atop old ruins, and once-wide streets narrowing to thin alleys that were only graced by the sun when it reached its zenith. The shortest buildings were three stories high, while royal palaces came as high as twenty.

Folk of all sorts could be seen in the crowded streets. The fleet of ships that sailed to and from the megacity connected continents from other hemispheres, making Saidal a microcosm of the wider world. From dark-skinned Askarians to pale Graehalians, people of all types gathered there. While culture and dress separated them, the common High Tongue, spoken by those from Cellenbron to the northern reaches of Valmoria, allowed the populace to do business with each other.

In an earlier age, the first inhabitants of Saidal revered the sea-god Atlor. Statues resembling a bearded man holding a spear crumbled in the empty halls of repurposed temples. While the folk of Saidal still remembered and invoked his name, this was out of habit rather than heartfelt devotion. It was a hollow corpse of a religion, the genuine tenants of which were long forgotten. In the mercantile, cutthroat chaos of the city, materialism swelled with each exchange of coin. The true god of the city was money, and even the most potent bureaucrats bowed before it.

It was late afternoon when the four came to the Southern Gate. A twenty-foot wide and tall portcullis was raised above the entryway, through which crowds of merchants from the Outlaw Kingdoms brought their crops to sell to the hungry population of the metropolis. Wearing tightly linked chainmail and conical helms, the guards searched the belongings of every person wishing to pass through the gate. Garrick nodded to the armored men. The guards immediately recognized the scarred knight, and the group was let through without question.

Leaving the city was like entering another world. Instead of cramped, almost cavern-like alleys, the Outlaw Kingdoms were rolling hills dotted with farmsteads, forests, and rusted ruins. Even though the sky was now covered with dark gray clouds, Eledrith couldn't help but smile. He could count on one hand how many times he had been outside of the city's walls, and those times were some of his most cherished. No longer enveloped by the crooked, crowded buildings of the city, he was able to see for miles around.

The outer wall of Saidal climbed high, almost one hundred feet, and was decorated with gibbeted bodies of criminals. Black crows swarmed the wall, picking flesh from the rotting corpses. The naive prince knew little of the infamous type that these corpses were meant to deter, as his only experience outside the city was under the protection of the royal guard.

Darreth wrinkled his nose as the stench of the macabre decorations wafted by on a gentle breeze. "I was about to say it's nice to finally get out of the city, but—"

"It'll get better once we hit the open road," said Garrick.

The ruins of unknown ages were a common sight in the lands around Saidal. Strange, featureless slabs of concrete and remnants of arcane technology were scattered across the wilderness. None of the travelers were surprised to see the husk of an old machine of war crookedly planted on the side of the road. Its thick steel shell had rusted to a dull brown. Sprouting from holes in the surface were the rifled barrels of ballistic weapons, which stood like grave markers of years long forgotten. While the dominant technology of war in their age, the knowledge of manufacturing their ammunition and how to operate them were secrets well guarded by time.

Scavengers had left a negligible mark on the metal remnants, for superstition guarded and preserved them. Tales spread of sicknesses exuding from the weathered steel. Seemingly without cause, those with prolonged, regular exposure to the old machines would grow tumors and bleed from their gums. The arcane alloys themselves were also notoriously hard to forge with. Whatever heat source had given them their shape greatly outmatched the contemporary blacksmith bellows of even the greatest Saidalian metalworkers. For these reasons, the broken triumphs of civilizations forgotten were left to wither.

What entrapped the riders' attention hung from the greatest of the rusted gun barrels: a crucified corpse. Sickly yellow arms were bound to the gun with hempen rope, and the rest of the body hung grotesquely low, both shoulders long since pulled out of each socket. Crows had feasted voraciously, and little flesh was left on the face. About the slumping neck was hung a banner of the Calidign flag.

"I see the feelings between us are mutual," said Eledrith, gazing up at the grisly display.

"What do you mean?" said Garrick.

"We hang criminals outside of our walls. This isn't that different, is it?"

Garrick shook his head. "Those are, or at least used to be, clothes of a diplomat. Unlike them, we don't kill the messengers they send us. The folk out here are a different breed. Less civilized. Less forgiving."

Eledrith stared at the corpse, realizing his mistake, and tried his best to keep from imagining what would be done to him if the powers of the Outlaw Kingdoms figured out his true identity.

"Let's hurry up," said Darreth, shielding his nose from the corpse's stench. "I've smelled enough death today."

———◆———

As the Wizard Slayer and his companions rode on, the dark clouds that had gathered began to let down a light shower. It wasn't enough to slow their pace, but all four had donned their hoods and pulled their cloaks about them. The Slayer and Garrick rode at the front while Darreth conversed with the prince and took up the rear.

"So, who exactly is this Wizard Slayer you accompany?"

Darreth scratched his head and gazed into the rolling fields. "He's harder to explain than you'd think."

"Then unwinding his tale may help pass the time on our journey."

After a sigh, Darreth caved in. "He was raised in this place called Mog Muhtar, though I doubt you'd recognize the name."

"I do not."

"Neither have I or anyone I've asked about it."

"So, what did Krael learn there? How to fight wizards, I presume?"

Darreth lowered his voice, parodying the Slayer's deep, slow speech. "The Way of Mog Muhtar."

Snickering, Eledrith said, "Your impression was pretty spot on."

Darreth chuckled and leaned to one side of his saddle, looking to see if the Slayer had heard him. "Krael doesn't like it when I do that, but I don't care."

"So," said the prince, "what exactly is this Way of Mog Muhtar?"

"Some sort of ancient religion. I never really understood it, but then again, Krael has never excelled at explaining complex things. The discernment between good and evil is a big deal, though. Trust me, Krael takes that kind of stuff very seriously."

"Like when someone is being given an offer when in reality it's a threat?"

"Yeah," said the elf-blooded, laughing, "For a moment, I was worried that he would try and fight back then and there in the throne room. He's done that before, and you know it's coming when he gives someone that glare."

Eledrith laughed with Darreth, albeit with some nervousness in his eyes. Looking at the hulking figure at the head of their company, he thought, *Could that man really be so bold?*

Darreth said, "He wouldn't have actually done that. But there have been times when we've had to team up with some... well, less than moral people."

The prince, whose fear had been replaced with curiosity, raised an eyebrow.

"We were working with some highwaymen," said Darreth, "because we needed their help to find where a sorcerer was hiding. He had been kidnapping children from nearby towns, and after

Krael killed him, we had over twenty kids on our hands. The high-waymen insisted on raising them in their criminal band, but Krael wouldn't let them. Instead of walking away, he fought all of them off."

Eledrith's jade eyes were filled with admiration. "How did he fend them all off? Is his strength great enough to best an entire group at once?"

"Actually, no. I can't remember how many wounds I had to stitch back together. He only managed to get two of them, but the way they died..." Darreth nervously chuckled at the thought. "It was enough to send the rest of them running. Not to mention the nightmares it undoubtedly gave the children we saved."

"So, if he despises evil so much, why does he go after magick users and not just criminals?"

"Magick is so much worse," said the elf-blooded, a solemn look on his face.

The prince wished for him to elaborate, but seeing his companion's expression, he decided not to push further. Instead, he asked, "So, how did you come to follow the Slayer? Surely, it's a tale worth telling."

"It's also a very long one."

"You've piqued my curiosity, Darreth. If you don't answer me now, I'll be asking about it all the way to Travedd."

"Alright," he said, making sure the pointed tips of his ears were covered with his headband, "I guess I have to tell you. A while back, two or three years now, I think, I lived in the Swamps of Agor. I didn't ever know my family, but other outcasts took me in. We somehow survived off what little game lived in that horrible marsh."

Eledrith interjected. "You mean to say you lived off the land?"

"Barely, but yes."

"Living in Saidal, I've never hunted anything. It sounds exciting!"

"It's not when you don't actually kill anything. That's what happened, and we were all starving, so my friends sold me to a witch."

It took the prince a moment to come to terms with what Darreth had said. Seeing his look of confusion, the elf-blooded nodded and continued. "They blindfolded me when I least expected it, and the next thing I knew, I was in a witch's hut with a knife to my neck."

"What did she look like, this witch?"

"Gross. She looked like she was hundreds of years old, but she didn't have any eyes. Just empty sockets filled with maggots."

"That's... fascinating," said Eledrith, at a near loss for words. "Do you think Thalnar will appear as terrifying as that witch?"

The elf-blooded shrugged. "I've seen quite a few spellcasters. Not all of them were that gross, but there's something about magick that changes a person. Anyway, right before she could slit my throat, Krael burst through the door and ran her through with his sword. That wasn't enough to finish her off, though, so Krael ended it with his bare hands."

Eledrith looked at the Wizard Slayer. He seemed perfectly capable of such a feat.

Darreth said, "And from then onward, I kind of just stuck around. It's not like I had anywhere to go. And since he's not the conversational type, I usually act as Krael's spokesman."

The prince nodded. "Why were you given to the witch? Wouldn't it have been easier for your former friends to find a poor wayfarer and hand him over?"

Darreth had prepared to avoid this question. Without hesitation, he flashed a smile and said, "You tell me. Maybe it's because of my good looks."

Eledrith let out a short laugh. After shaking his head at the stupid joke, he said, "It sure is a relief to leave the city, even if the weather is dreadful."

"I don't know. The room in the palace that Krael and I stayed in was quite nice. Much better than the prison cell from the other night."

"I'm sure it was, but for me, those walls just remind me of the king. I yearn to get away from that."

"What do you mean?"

"His Majesty is often more concerned with concubines and drink than anything else. Honestly, it's repulsive. I find comfort in the fact that I look nothing like him."

Eledrith's fair, silvery features were far from King Torvaren's plump face. The way the prince's chin came to a narrow yet strong point and his silvery-blond hair had to have been inherited from his mother. His jade eyes burned with a ferocity that the dull brown of his father's never could. Darreth would never have guessed that the two were of the same blood.

"I have no love for him," Eledrith continued. "He is neither a good father nor a good king. Sir Garrick is the one who truly raised me, not Torvaren."

"I'm sure His Majesty was busy with, you know, king's business and all."

"If a king's business is a harem of concubines, then yes, he was. He loves power for the respect and wealth it brings but is unwilling to shoulder its responsibility. He has delegated most of his duties to the petty counts of Saidal, who in turn only use the duties to leverage their own ascension in the hierarchy of rulership. Meanwhile, criminals swarm the streets, feeding off the decent folk. The whole of Saidal is a festering cesspool of corruption, and the king embodies it well."

Darreth was caught off guard. The prince's tone was firm as if coming from someone already king, not the boy who rode beside him. "Sounds like you're ready to rule yourself."

"I'd like to think so," said the prince.

"Your mother, then, the queen," said Darreth carefully, knowing he was most likely bringing up a tough subject for the prince, "she, er..."

"Died when I was young," said Eledrith.

"I'm sorry."

"No, no, it's alright. How could I miss someone I never truly knew?"

The elf-blooded did not know how to respond to this. To his relief, Eledrith continued. "I do have one memory of her, though. Weirdly enough, it was on a beach. This is strange, mind you, as we seldom leave the protective walls of Saidal. I remember she helped me make a sandcastle. It had this great tower in the center, too – I can still see it now. Then, as the tide came in, it was washed away. I must have cried so much because it still makes me feel sad. Strange, isn't it?"

"Yeah," said Darreth. "At least you have one memory. I have no idea who either of my parents could be."

"Yeah," replied the prince.

There was something sour about the way Eledrith held himself. His lip subtly curled, and his gaze lowered to the back of his mount's neck. It was as if something had reopened when he shared the single surviving memory of his mother. One could assume it was a hidden wound. To Eledrith, it was a yearning to know the full truth of his forgotten childhood.

Hoping to lighten the mood, the elf-blooded said, "I'm sure your mother would be proud to see who you've become."

The prince turned to Darreth, who had a good-natured smile. Eledrith wanted to tell him how he looked up to his late mother, Queen Elisia. Stories were told of her kindness and inner strength, but the prince couldn't shake the feeling that these were idealizations of a flawed human. Instead of trying to articulate things that not even he truly understood, Eledrith simply said, "Thank you, Darreth."

3
THE WITCH AND THE ELF-BLOODED

Three years ago...

A line of three horse-drawn wagons rolled through the soft, fetid soil of the marsh. Knobby, twisting trees sprang up from the gray-brown muck, and a cold, overcast sky made the whole land seem even bleaker. Countless creatures lurked in the murky water, which lay stagnant save when the wagon wheels or horses' hooves came crashing through it. The horses moved as fast as possible, given the unstable terrain. Twice already had one of the wheels completely sunk into the earth, and only after an hour's worth of sweat had the travelers managed to pull it free.

The driver at the front of the caravan urged the steeds on despite their apparent hesitation. They fought against the reins and weight behind them as best they could, but the ground began to give way beneath their mud-covered hooves. The driver commanded the horses to halt, but it was not this that caused them to stop. As the wagon sank into the earth, the axle began to act as a brake.

Cursing to himself, the driver hopped down from his seat to assess the situation. His fine blue traveler's clothes had long since been tainted with the dull brown of mud, and he tread through the muck without concern for his garments. One of his companions called from the wagon, "We should've never taken this route, Baltor! It may have been a nice shortcut in autumn, but the springtime melting has damn near flooded this place."

The companion, Feldorano, stayed in his own wagon, crossbow on his lap. His skeptical eyes scanned the surrounding marsh. His fears were more grounded in reality than he knew.

A fair, golden-haired head popped out from the side of the wagon. "Is everything going to be alright, Baltor?"

"Don't worry, darling," he said. "We've gotten out of this twice before. At this point, we're experts."

Fellow travelers from the rest of the caravan aided in whatever way they could to free their leader from the swamp's grip. Feldorano, being a hired bodyguard, kept watch. The hairs on his neck began to stand straight as he realized how helpless the caravan was.

An arrow hissed from behind a tuft of tall, dry grass and found its mark in Feldorano's chest. He had no chance to let out a cry of warning as he fell. His companions, busy trying to lift the wagon's side, didn't notice as he feebly gasped on the ground.

The bandits were suddenly upon them. Clad in furs and pelts, they could've been easily mistaken for some savage tribe who made their home in the swamplands of Agor. Forward they charged, brandishing falchions, maces, and whatever else they had taken from foolhardy travelers in the past. At their head was a woman with blazing red hair and a face covered in warpaint. She hollered like a crazed ape, paralyzing her prey with shock and rallying her brethren.

The travelers, already exhausted from lifting the wagon, never stood a chance. To call it a battle would be far too generous. Bones broke as weaponless hands rose in defense against the onslaught of steel. At the sight of this, shrill cries of horror erupted from the wagons behind. Crimson mixed with dull, muddy brown as the men were utterly slaughtered.

From behind the fray came the archer who had shot down Feldorano. He looked small, young, and handsome, and poking from his mop of tawny hair were the tips of two knife-like ears. Staying clear of the battle proper, Darreth nocked an arrow, searching for any other guards that could become a problem. He tried his best to ignore the sounds of carnage behind him. The canvas coverings of the wagons hung ominously, for there was no telling if someone was hiding on the other side, waiting for the right time to strike.

A flap of the cover flung open, and with a flinch response, Darreth pulled back and let loose his bow. The shot burrowed into its target, and only then did the elf-blooded realize his mistake. From such a close distance, the arrow had easily made its way through the child and the mother who desperately held him. Her brown eyes were wide in shock, and tears formed in the final moments when she still lived.

Darreth's blood ran cold. He had been part of this bandit gang for months, and many had died by his hand, but they held weapons, not children, in their hands. His slim form began to tremble. Trying not to think, he continued to the last wagon. He moved for no other purpose than to move.

Not bothering to nock another arrow, the elf-blooded walked forward. He was helpless to defend against the cudgel that came for his head. Darreth's face fell into the mud, and the gray-brown of the marsh faded to a cloudy black.

⸺◆⸺

"Look who's finally awake!"

Darreth stumbled from his tent, feeling the bump that had formed above his brow. Sitting around a fire were his fellow bandits, some already drunk even though the sun still shone as a low red disk beyond the shelter of the swamp trees. A dozen small tents sat near the firepit, and most of the camp's denizens sat near the stack of crates and barrels, chewing on dried meat and other trail rations.

The red-haired woman sat on a tree stump, holding a rusted steel helm in one hand. "We got this for you, elf-blooded," she said, snickering at Darreth.

Trying to ignore the pain of a splitting headache, Darreth sat on a log. "Thanks, Ragna," he said as he caught the helmet.

"And here's your share of the earnings," said Ragna, tossing a leather pouch into the helm.

Darreth emptied the bag into his hand and frowned at the few silver coins that rolled out. "This is it?"

"Yeah, those people weren't hauling much. Even their supplies won't last us a day or two. That being said, feel free to chow down on what little we do have. If you didn't take out that man with the crossbow, I'm sure one of us would've been killed."

Smiling to himself, Darreth walked to the pile of stolen goods.

"You also made that two-for-one shot, didn't you?" said one of the bandits, laughing.

Darreth instantly lost his appetite. He grabbed a strip of dried beef and walked back to the fire, idly gnawing at the salty meal and staring into the flickering tongues of flames. He had hoped that the woman and her child were just a nightmare, but this confirmed that they were real.

Ragna recognized Darreth's change of behavior. Usually, he ate more than everyone else, contrary to what his size might suggest. She sat next to him, putting an arm around his shoulders. "You don't feel bad about that, do you?"

Darreth shook his head.

Ragna chuckled. "Normally, you're a much better liar."

The elf-blooded avoided the woman's gaze, but she would not relent.

"Listen, this world is a dangerous place. Some people have lots of money, and they, or their ancestors, killed someone to get it. That's just how the world works. We don't have the luxury of choosing who to kill. When there are more of us, and we have better weapons, maybe we could, but we take whatever we can for now. You understand?"

He nodded his head.

"You did what you had to do, elf-blooded."

Still gazing into the flames, Darreth was unconvinced. The throbbing pain in his head kept him from protesting, and he remained silent.

The sky turned from maroon to black, and countless stars shone through the leafless trees with their pure, cold light. The gang of bandits sang their out-of-tune songs, too affected by drink to care about who may be listening. There was little other than a single unkempt road for miles around, and there was no need for secrecy. Throughout the Swamps of Agor echoed their vulgar chanting. Darreth mumbled along with his comrades, but neither drink nor camaraderie could lift his spirits.

The bandits celebrated their meager victory nonetheless, stumbling around the fire, wrestling with each other, and laughing. They were an untamed lot and reveled in the freedom that lawlessness provided. So free were they that they lost sight of anything other than what the whim of their will demanded. As the flames withdrew to red coals, the brigands laid down to sleep wherever they wanted. Some, entranced by the stars, drifted off looking to the open sky. Others wandered in a drunken stupor, sleeping wherever they had tripped and fallen. Darreth, coming to terms with the weight of his eyelids, retired to the warm bedroll of his tent. There, alone in the darkness, he wept.

Over the next few months, word had spread of the hazardous nature of the swamp. Fewer and fewer caravans dared risk the shortcut through Agor. This was terrible news for Ragna and her gang, to whom the taste of sparse, unseasoned swamp meats had begun to grow unbearable. Their usual plan of following a caravan until it became stuck on the dangerous road was totally abandoned, and instead, they ambushed any traveler they came across. This only worsened Agor's reputation, and the single road passing through was nearly deserted.

Darreth had kept himself busy with hunting. A sort of peace came with solitude, and it kept the ruminations of guilt at bay. His skills as a marksman only improved, and he grew to become one of the more valuable members of the group. Each night he returned, it would be to appreciation from his mates. This was not to last.

One autumn evening, Darreth returned later than usual. A sloppy shot on a deer led to its slow death, but not before it had stumbled into the deep of a cold, murky pond. Hauling the relatively small stag back was difficult enough, but pulling it from the near-freezing water resulted in all of the elf-blooded's clothes being soaked. The dagger he kept in his hide boot rubbed against his ankle as the wet leather clung to his leg. Balancing the kill atop his shoulders, he marched back to camp, hoping the blood flow would warm his fingers and toes, which rang with the pains of cold. His joints ached as he made the arduous journey across the uneven terrain. With the added weight of the stag, he sank deeper into the spongy earth than usual, and many times he had to drop the carcass, pull his feet from the mud, and pick up the heavy load again. He didn't dare leave it behind to get help from camp since no doubt some scavenger would claim the meal for itself, and Darreth had worked too hard to leave this bounty behind.

At last, shivering, he made it back to the camp. As he set the stag on the ground, he met eyes with Ragna. There was no warmth or welcome in her mannerisms. Instead, she looked at him, almost sadly. Hoping to change this, Darreth smiled and said, "Look what I got!"

"Thank you, Darreth," she said.

Darreth was even more unnerved. Ragna seldom used his real name, instead calling him elf-blooded or some other informal insult.

"Is there something wrong?" he asked.

"No, I just feel off today," she said.

He would have pushed Ragna further, but Darreth was in a hurry to warm his aching bones. He stood on the edge of the fire-pit, finding relief in the heat.

"Need a blanket, elf-blooded?" said someone from the camp.

Darreth nodded, waiting to strip from his damp clothes until protection from the night wind would come.

It never arrived. Half a dozen bandits came upon Darreth, pulling him to the ground and binding him with rope. A blindfold and gag were constricted about his head, silencing the elf-blooded's curse-riddled protests.

"Let's hurry this up. I don't want to keep her waiting," said Ragna.

Darreth was picked up and carried. As he writhed against his former friends, they struck him hard. These sharp pains were enough to get him to comply. The elf-blooded heard whispered apologies from the bandits more than once, which didn't help soften the blow of betrayal. They offered no explanation as they went.

The group came to a halt, and Darreth was set on the ground.

"Where is she?" asked a voice.

"Shouldn't be too long," replied Ragna.

Only the night's breeze could be heard as they waited in silence. The barren limbs of skeletal trees could be heard clacking together. Hoarse croaks came from creatures hidden just below the surface of the cold mud. Darreth kept quiet, hoping to listen to any sound to get some clue about what was going on.

Before any approaching footsteps came the cackling of an old woman. Its shrill reverberances seemed too loud for an average human, and Darreth's imagination was alight with terrifying images of what could've created that dreadful sound.

Apparently, the bandits were just as scared as Darreth was. Ragna, who typically was fearless and laughed in the face of death, stammered, "N-not another step, you c-crone. Not until y-you've paid up."

A shaking, aged voice responded, "Let me see him first."

The sounds of the bandit's boots receded from around Darreth, and a faint shuffling approached. There was a smell like moist, festering rot. "Haven't seen one this pure in a long, long time."

Coins clattered together. "Here's your payment," continued the crone, "three hundred silver pieces, as promised."

That was no small amount. Given what the crone had said, she had to have been interested in Darreth's elven blood, which confirmed his suspicions. Because of his lineage, he was first ostracized from normal society, and now it would prove to be his downfall.

Ragna, less obviously scared now, said, "Take him and be gone, witch."

"Pleasure doing business with you."

A vise-like grip closed around Darreth's ankles and he was carried upside-down through the night. As his blindfold was removed, he found himself inside a thatch hut. The conditions were squalid at best, and the most expensive thing, other than the elf-blooded himself, was a large black cauldron. A thin, skeletal hand held the blindfold, and as he turned his head, Darreth was met with the face that caused Ragna to be so afraid.

Instead of eyes, the witch had deep, dark sockets on her pale, leathery face in the depths of which writhed what looked like a squirming swarm of maggots. Thin white hair draped down from a skull-like scalp. Her smile revealed long, twisting yellow teeth rising up from black gums. "Don't look so afraid," she said. "When you're over three hundred years old, you'll look far worse."

Darreth tried to panic, but his binds only allowed him to do so much. He was picked up with inhuman strength and hung by the rope that bound his feet. Below him sat the cauldron, whose dark opening seemed like the mouth of a hungry beast ready to devour its prey.

The witch turned away and began rummaging through a small box, which would perhaps be the elf-blooded's only chance at escape. Mind racing desperately for a solution, he remembered the dagger he kept in his boot. His former comrades, in their hurry, had forgotten to check him for weapons. Ecstatic, Darreth pulled himself up. Under normal circumstances, the knife was difficult to pull out, but the elf-blooded was sure that if he reached hard enough, he'd be able to cut himself down and have a fighting chance. He hunched his body upward and bent his legs, fighting against both gravity and the restrictions of his binds.

As his fingers found purchase on the small iron pommel, an unrelated thought found its way into Darreth's head. The woman and child he had shot, the gasp of horror, and sorrow in her eyes played again in his mind. Suddenly he felt fatigued, and he swung down, the knife no longer in reach. *Perhaps it's for the best*, he thought, *that I end here. It's what a murderer like me deserves.*

The witch turned back around, and Darreth's window of escape closed. In her hand was a hooked dagger, and the smile on her face grew unnaturally wide. "I'm going to look very young thanks to what you'll give me."

Darreth closed his eyes, hoping the end would be swift and painless. He could sense the crone moving forward, breathing heavily as she went. The scent of decay exuded with each of her hissing wheezes. A strange feeling of comfort came with knowing that justice, albeit at the expense of his life, would be achieved.

A sudden crash sounded to the elf-blooded's surprise, followed by a blood-choked wail. Darreth opened his eyes to see the gleam of sharpened steel jutting from the witch's crooked chest. Maggot-infested blood poured from her wound and mouth as she tried to scream, dark eye sockets gazing in horror. Standing behind her, amidst the shattered remnants of the wooden door, was the savage, corded form of a natural predator. Thick black hair blew about his head, moved by the wind that howled through the open doorframe. With a thrust of his boot, the crone was sent tumbling forward. As she stumbled about the floor, blood spilling from her chest, the intruder readied his broadsword for the final blow.

Still prone, the witch extended a gnarled hand to the barbarian. The knobby joints of her fingers folded backward and sideways, resulting in a gesture no human could naturally perform. As if on command, jagged tendrils of metal sprouted from the man's blade and lashed toward his flesh with whip-like speed. He cast his weapon aside as if expecting this while ducking away from its hostile growths. The silvery, angular tentacles slowed to a halt as the sword fell to the dirt.

The nigh-bestial figure in the doorway needed no weapon to continue his dirty work. As the witch let out a vile hiss of anger, the barbarian charged forward and plunged both hands into the gaping wound in her chest, palms outward as if to rend her in two. The witch clawed at the hulking arms to no avail, and with a literal roar no human could muster, the man tore her body open. Brown-red ichor splattered across the room as maggot-infested entrails spilled onto the floor. Lacking intact lungs needed to scream, the witch could do little more than gnash her crooked teeth in agony. With an unnatural vitality, her body still moved, trying to pick itself up despite no longer resembling its former shape.

The scene was gruesome enough to sicken the most hardened of warriors, but Darreth still watched in amazement. He had doubted the existence of spellcasters, but seeing the witch be brutally mutilated yet still live showed how real and inhuman her kind was.

Ending the battle once and for all, the heel of the man's boot came crashing through the witch's skull, sending shards of bone and gore scattering in all directions. It was then that the fearsome warrior looked to Darreth. The sunken hunter's eyes looked out from the rugged features of his face. With some ease, although nowhere near how easily the witch had done, the fearsome barbarian brought Darreth down from the ceiling and untied him.

"What was that thing?" said Darreth, finally able to find words.

"Witch," said the barbarian in a slow, deep voice, emphasizing the word as if it were a vulgar curse.

Following his rescuer out of the hut, Darreth found himself on a lone hill rising above the wet marsh, hundreds of pools reflecting the light of the moon and stars. He turned back to take one final look at the strange corpse, and to his horror, he saw it still moved. Ever so slowly, the splayed limbs began to rise and stand once again. With the erratic, swaying posture of a string puppet, her mangled body rose. "She's still alive!" he cried out.

The barbarian was in no hurry. He picked up a lantern that he had previously left outside and brought it to the dry thatch that was the hut. Within a minute, the place was alight, and everything inside, all the scattered gore and squirming insects, were consumed by fire. For a short time, the witch's screech could be heard piercing the inferno's roar. As the flames grew, the screech's pitch wavered and fell.

Darreth sat on the relatively dry hill, watching the flames reach higher as the hut walls collapsed. The barbarian did so as well, breathing heavily. After the fire, Darreth asked, "Who even are you?"

"Krael," the Slayer growled.

"I'm Darreth," said the elf-blooded awkwardly and to no reply.

Krael was obviously not conversational, but Darreth pressed on anyway. "You arrived just in time. Another minute and I would've bled out like an animal."

The Slayer nodded.

"My friends betrayed me, you know. They sold me out to her."

"Your friends are dead."

Darreth's eyes widened. "How?"

"Magick."

They waited in silence for some time, staying near to the warmth of the flame-engulfed hut. Once they had rested, the two marched through the swamp toward the nearest place of civilization. By chance, they came upon Ragna and her accomplices. They lay dead around a scattered pile of coins from which sprouted knife-like protrusions not dissimilar to those from Krael's sword. The gleaming silver wove through the corpse's bodies, piercing their flesh. Even though they had betrayed him, Darreth felt sorrow at the passing of what were his only friends.

"Do you think we should give them a proper burial?" he asked.

The Slayer shook his head. "We keep moving."

Nodding solemnly, Darreth shut the lifeless eyes of the group, making their final rest appear slightly more peaceful. Grabbing a pair of swords from the dead, he said, "Don't think they'll need these anymore."

Krael received one of the blades and fastened it to his belt. "We should go. Their stench will attract wolves. Or worse."

With little more than the light of the moon and stars to guide their path, the two stumbled through cattails and mossy bogs for hours before they came to a village's edge. The sparse buildings were no more than collections of sticks lashed together in the vague form of huts, the spindly limbs of which stretched upward toward the moss-draped canopy of trees above. Flickering torches seemed to cast more shadows than illuminate, and Darreth was hesitant to step within the orange light. From the reaches of the crude huts hung bone charms that clicked in the light breeze. The scent of the swamp, a mixture of wet soil and earthy decay, became more potent in that horrible place.

The Slayer's savage features twisted into a look of contempt. "I've been here before."

"What do you mean by that?"

Darreth's question was answered for him when a voice called out, "We told ye not to return, dog-tooth!"

From one of the many shadows approached a man in a decrepit tunic. While he was of the stock that populated the wider Outlaw Kingdoms, his unshaven beard, slouched posture, and missing teeth gave him a much more uncivilized appearance. In a hand, he carried a spear, the rusted tip of which only faintly caught the torchlight.

"You know these people?" asked Darreth.

Krael drew the falchion from his hip and snarled. "They pointed me to the witch. They knew her well."

More men, the likes of the first, appeared from the crooked frames of the huts. In seconds, ten-score spears were aimed at the barbarian's broad chest. Most of the men could not even rival Darreth's height, who himself wasn't very tall. However, they still posed a threat as their mud-caked arms were covered in knotted muscle bred by a life in the wilderness. One said, "We saw the fire at the Mother's home. Did ye do this?"

"Mother?" Darreth asked himself, turning his head to where they came from. Sure enough, the smoldering embers of the witch's hut could be seen from where they came.

"Did ye do this?" the man screeched.

Krael, with a sardonic smile on his face, said, "Yes."

The collection of stunted swamp dwellers let out a chorus of horrible wails.

"Get 'em," shouted one, "for killin' the Mother!"

Darreth saw the inbreds' eyes harden as they readied their spears. For as mighty as Krael was, there was no way he could fend off all the cretins at once. His body was unprotected, and as the elf-blooded's mind raced for an answer, the men encircled the barbarian.

"You think you fools stand a chance?" said Darreth, arms crossed and sword sheathed. "I mean, I saw him kill your mother. She didn't stand a chance."

The many spears then faltered. Krael shot Darreth a desperate glance, and the elf-blooded instantly knew that even the mighty Wizard Slayer figured the odds were against him. With their spears, they had the advantage of reach in addition to superior numbers. Still, Darreth continued. "Oh, by all means, go ahead and try. I'll enjoy watching you all get your entrails torn out."

One of the swamp men froze. Another began to tremble. Fear was on all of their asymmetrical faces. One of them whispered, "What is a en-trails?"

Krael had caught on. Baring his pronounced canines, he let out a growling chuckle. The curving steel of his falchion flashed as he brandished it above his head. His pupils, reflecting the fire-light like a wild animal, glowed yellow. At this terrifying sight, the swamp dwellers began to lose their morale. Some shuffled back into the safety of their crude dwellings. The few that stood stoic numbered too little to pose the threat they once did, and within seconds even their stunted minds realized this. Snarling and gnashing what few teeth they had, the men backed away.

"We're gonna get you later! Really, don't come back!" cried one from the depths of his dwelling.

Darreth covered his mouth to keep himself from laughing at the empty threat. Krael was not so lighthearted. With the swamp men out of earshot, he whispered to the elf-blooded, "I could not have killed them all."

"But they didn't know that."

"They could have attacked."

"But they didn't," said Darreth, smirking.

The Slayer's cross face became even more disgruntled. "It is not good to lie."

The orange of eyes glimmering in firelight began to show in the shadowy entrances to the huts, and Darreth noticed this. "Maybe, but we should probably continue this somewhere else."

Nodding, Krael led the way back through the swamp's shadowy groves and muddy pools. As they went, Darreth constantly looked back over his shoulder, fearing the approach of the men they had so narrowly escaped. Ahead of him marched Krael, whose long, powerful strides snapped any branches in his path.

By morning they had reached the northern edge of the Swamps of Agor, and in the glow of dawn, they espied upon the rolling green fields a village far more civilized than the one they had come across the previous night. The two weary men made their way toward the place, sighing in relief at the log walls and thatched roofs. A cozy earthen-floor tavern served as a haven, and soon after the two had shoveled food into their mouths, they sat in a state of half-sleep at the table.

"I suppose this is where our paths diverge," said Darreth, fidgeting with his spoon and empty bowl.

The Slayer only grunted. All around the room, people stared at the hulking barbarian. More fear than admiration was in their eyes. Krael seemed to not care.

"Unless you want me to follow," continued the elf-blooded. "I mean, everyone I know is dead, so it's not like anyone is waiting on me."

Krael's eyes looked up to Darreth, and a chill ran through his body. There was a predatory aspect to his gaze that the more civilized races of men lacked. At the same time, the Slayer's face showed trust.

"And when you think about it," continued Darreth, "if I hadn't spoken up to the swamp men, you might not have made it."

After a moment, Krael said, "You may follow."

4
FANGS IN THE NIGHT

The weather continued to be dreadful as the four riders pushed on toward Travedd. A steady downpour turned the dirt road into a river of mud. A small cluster of torchlights could be seen piercing the gloom just after dusk. Seeking shelter, Garrick led his companions to the small town.

Around the settlement was a moat of mud which would have been a dry trench if the weather was less dreary. Piercing the murky surface were dozens of sharpened wooden stakes, making what would have been an inconvenience to potential intruders a deadly defense. Over a rickety drawbridge came the riders. Its small width necessitated single file, and after a short conversation Darreth had with the guards at the gate, they were let in.

The town wasn't much – if it could even be called a town. A handful of shacks for houses sat around a moderate inn. Their horses trotted between the log-walled and thatch-roofed dwellings, whose windows glowed with a warmth that made the travelers envious. The stench of animal dung and smoke pierced the downpour and hung about the place. The rain had been unrelenting, and their cloaks were thoroughly soaked. Relief came in the form of the three-storied inn at the heart of the settlement.

With no room left on the crowded hitch posts, the group's horses were tied to a nearby tree. "This place is going to be packed," observed Darreth.

The elf-blooded was right. Inside were the usual traveling merchants and couriers, but amongst them were a hardier sort. Muscular men, drunkenly chanting toneless songs, filled the room. A few of them still wore loose chainmail and ragged splint armor. On their hips were arming swords, axes, and poniards. Seeing the crowd, Darreth made sure his headband covered the pointed tips of his ears.

"Mercenaries," Garrick muttered. "Keep your guard up. I don't like the look of them."

"We have no need for strong drink, and I'm perfectly happy to snack on rations in bed," said Eledrith. "Let's just rent lodging and call it a night."

"Good plan," responded the old veteran.

The four weaved through tables, careful to avoid the rambunctious swords-for-hire. As Darreth bargained with the owner of the establishment, Garrick, Eledrith, and the Slayer stood waiting behind him.

Garrick whispered to Krael, "I have a bad feeling about this."

"As do I."

"These may be mercenaries, but don't forget we're in the Outlaw Kingdoms. In my experience, their kind often acts like outlaws themselves."

Eledrith shifted his weight from foot to foot as the elf-blooded continued to haggle. From his side came an unknown voice. "That's a nice sword."

Hoping he had accidentally eavesdropped, the prince kept his eyes forward. Unfortunately, the same voice continued to press him. "Hey, green-eyes, you hear me?"

Eledrith turned to see a long-haired and bearded man twisted around in his chair. "I said that's a nice sword," he said.

"Er, thanks. Likewise," said Eledrith, nodding toward the moderately decorated blade on the man's hip.

"No, no, yours must have been really expensive."

Wishing to end the conversation, the prince nodded and broke eye contact.

"I want it."

"Sorry, no," said Eledrith.

"How about this, we go outside with our weapons. Whoever draws first blood wins the other man's sword."

A coy smile came to Eledrith's face. The mercenary spoke with the telltale slur of inebriation, and even if he were sober, the prince knew he would surely win in combat. Despite his advantage, he said, "No. Get lost."

The mercenary began to rise out of his chair, but his eyes widened at something behind and above Eledrith's hooded head. A low, slow voice growled, "Get lost."

Eledrith only then noticed Krael, who loomed over them both, pointed canines bared. Taking the Slayer's advice, the now wide-eyed mercenary retreated to his seat and kept quiet, not even speaking to his comrades.

"Thanks for that, Krael," whispered Eledrith.

At last, Darreth turned back to his companions, a key in hand. As they walked up the stairs, Garrick remarked, "What took you so long? We have my liege's funding. There's no need to pinch pennies."

"My alias doesn't have funding," said Darreth.

"And who might this alias be since we all accompany him?"

"I am Caedorn, a downtrodden merchant of Saidal," said the elf-blooded, changing his tone slightly to fit his role. "My bodyguards and I have run on a bad string of luck and just need a place to sleep for the night."

"Alright, Caedorn," said Garrick, "let's get to sleep. We're not even halfway to Travedd."

That night, the four men stayed together in the same cramped room. While the accommodations were meager, the rooms were warm, and the beds were soft. The clamor of the common room below was a distant murmur behind several walls, and the patter of raindrops against the glass was soothing. While these conditions were perfect for Garrick to sleep in, the old man could not help but remain awake. Long after Darreth and Eledrith had dozed off, Krael began to shift in his bed. The large Kolgathian's breathing became rapid, and out of panic, the knight reached for the poisoned dagger that waited on his belt. He did not dare wonder what nightmares plagued the Wizard Slayer's mind.

⸺◆⸺

By midday, the ceiling of clouds broke, and what little heat came from the late autumn sun began to dry the puddle-riddled road. That day they passed more travelers than the previous. Most were peasant farmers garbed in torn, roughspun garments. These folk kept to themselves and stayed out of the way of the cloaked and armed strangers.

One group of passersby was unlike the rest. Given the ragged secondhand armor, they could have been either mercenaries or highwaymen. As their eight-strong party approached, they did not move to the side of the road, forcing Krael and his companions to ride single file. Darreth looked out from beneath his hood to see their leader sneering back at him. The man's face was gruff and weathered, but the most jarring feature of all was his missing left eye. No patch or bandage covered the wound, and the sagging remnants of the fleshy lid were on full display. Darreth couldn't help but shudder.

Hands may have crept toward weapons, but the thugs passed by without a word.

⸺◆⸺

As they passed through a small forest, Garrick decided it was best to make camp under the cover of the trees. Darreth quickly got to making a fire, and soon smoke rose through the upper reaches of the thin, leafless branches.

"I'll take the first watch," barked Garrick, "then Your Highness will take the second."

Eledrith opened his mouth to protest but stopped before he could complain about how tired he was. He realized this was what life was like outside the castle, pulling your weight and the weight of others if need be. With this thought in mind, the prince was almost eager to watch over the camp.

"I'll stay up for the rest of the night. Krael can become grumpy if he doesn't get his beauty sleep," said Darreth, snickering.

The barbarian narrowed his eyes, but before the elf-blooded could crack another joke, Garrick said, "Good idea. At this pace, we'll make it to Travedd by dusk tomorrow. We'll want our Wizard Slayer to be well rested."

The fire waned from an orange blaze to a red pile of coals. With Garrick standing against a tree, his companions gradually drifted off into a shallow slumber.

Eledrith awakened as he felt something grab his arm. Adrenaline shook off the sluggishness of sleep immediately, but before the prince could reach for his sword, he heard a voice say, "I'm heading to bed. It's your watch now, Your Highness."

Leaving the warm comfort of his bedroll, the prince got up and took Garrick's place. A light breeze drifted between the trees, giving the smoldering remnants of the fire a renewed glow. Other than the gentle rustling of dying leaves, all was silent. With time Eledrith's eyes adjusted to the darkness, giving the tree line a more defined form. However, the shadows beyond were too thick, and the prince struggled to make out whatever could be lurking just a few yards away in the feeble combination of fire and starlight.

A rapid, heaving breath came from within the camp, and the prince's head snapped around to meet it. Eledrith's nerves had gotten to him, as the sound was only Krael emerging from his bedroll, face glistening from a cold sweat. The barbarian stood up and tilted his neck to the side, letting out a series of loud cracks.

"Trouble sleeping?" asked Eledrith in a whisper.

"Always."

The prince knew the inefficiencies of law enforcement in Saidal, and while he knew Krael most likely wasn't to blame for the crimes he was sentenced with, Eledrith still felt nervous being in the presence of a convicted killer. To ease the tension, he said, "You're welcome to stay up and tell stories of wizards you killed. Darreth recounted how you tore open the Witch of Agor, and I found it thrilling."

The barbarian grunted. Before Eledrith could figure out what his companion meant by this, the Slayer sat next to the fire and answered more eloquently, "I'm no storyteller. Ask Darreth when he is awake."

"Alright then. How does one battle a wizard? Have you studied magick to learn its flaws and possible counters?"

"No." Krael gazed into the fire with dark gray eyes. In the glow of the embers, his hard-featured face somehow grew even more stern. "It is evil. I do not study magick; I destroy it."

"But isn't magick just science that one does not yet understand? How can it be evil?"

The Slayer, who was already speaking slowly and choosing his words carefully, took even more time to answer this question. "Magick turns men into gods. Men were not born to be gods."

"So like tyrants corrupted by power, wizards are but mortal men with abilities they cannot truly control."

Krael nodded.

"Surely someone noble and pure of heart could wield such power properly."

"No one is that pure," said the Slayer, glaring at the prince with a dark fanaticism.

In the distance, a wolf howled.

Krael's change in demeanor went unnoticed by the naive prince. "Then what truly is magick? Undeserved, unwieldable power is hardly something that is exclusively supernatural."

"Not even wizards truly know, though they think they do."

Eledrith ran a hand through his silver-blond hair, trying to unpack the vague answer. "All this makes me eager to hear stories of your battles. I've heard that with magick, wizards can control minds, raise the dead, and change reality itself, and I can't imagine how I would stand a chance against it."

The teachings of Mog Muhtar, the trial of the Pit and the Candle, and Krael's own mental breaking and rebirth are things that someone skilled with words would have trouble describing. Krael, whose barbaric mind had not learned language until late in adulthood, didn't even bother to attempt an explanation. Instead, he simply said, "It's not easy."

Eledrith laughed. "I'd figured as much."

Krael didn't have the same lightheartedness as the prince. Wanting to avoid awkward silence, Eledrith asked, "I'm sure you are asked this a lot, but why are your teeth so...?"

"It's a trait of my people."

Eledrith raised his eyebrows. He had never heard of a race of men that looked so monstrous.

"In Kolgathar, there were once many that looked like me."

"I've never heard of that place before."

As the embers waned, the Wizard Slayer slowly opened up to the young prince, whose curiosity seemed to know no bounds. Krael told of his homeland, Kolgathar, and how its desolate glaciers were melted by volcanic fire, allowing life to exist in a realm that should have been a frozen wasteland. It was a land of utter savagery whose inhabitants became beasts, of whom only the most ferocious survived. Before Krael could give his account of how the Kolgathians were enslaved, he became silent.

"You were saying?" asked the prince with a yawn.

With the frenzy of a wild animal in his eyes, Krael stared out into the darkness. "Wake the others," he said.

Eledrith followed the Kolgathian's eyes, which were fixed on multiple vague forms in the blackness. As he struggled to make them out, Krael yelled, "Now!"

The prince scrambled to Garrick and shook the old man awake. Without the need for explanation, the veteran grabbed his battle-axe and shield. Much slower to rise was Darreth. Only after seeing Krael raise his massive sword did he prepare himself. From his pack, he produced a bow and quiver.

Krael couldn't hear or see the pack of wolves per se, but with a primal sixth sense, he knew they were completely surrounded. The horses, hitched to a tree, sensed this too, and they began to tremble and pull against their reins. From the darkness, a beast leaped toward the Wizard Slayer, who stepped backward and tore the wolf in two with a single stroke of his heavy sword. Its yelp of agony was cut short as its innards spilled onto the dirt. Another one of the creatures came forward, and its fangs clenched tightly onto the barbarian's forearm. Krael gritted his teeth and shoved the wolf backward, pinning it against a tree. Upon having its skull collide with the solid trunk, the wolf let go of its enemy and staggered. That time spent trying to regain its bearings proved fatal, as the Slayer's boot came crashing down onto the beast's head, resulting in a sickening crunch and the bulging of its yellow eyes.

Krael and Garrick fended off most of the wolves, who snarled and howled as they met their gruesome fates. The royal captain used his shield in offense as well as defense, slamming its edge onto the skulls of his enemies. Unlike the more reserved veteran, the Kolgathian charged into the midst of the pack, swinging his oversized sword with one hand and grabbing at the wolves with the other. He was a beast amongst beasts, baring his teeth as steel tore through flesh. The wolves' dark yellow eyes flashed as they leaped toward their prey, showing more than just a carnivorous appetite, but instead true malice.

One of the wolves charged toward Eledrith, who raised his guard to fend off the creature. To the prince's surprise, the beast did not waver in its assault, and it pounced upon him, knocking him to the ground and getting too close for his weapon to be of use. Eledrith could feel the creature's hot breath as its fanged maw snapped shut only a few inches from his throat. He strained against the wolf's weight, keeping the voracious jaws just far enough from his jugular to remain alive. Furiously the fangs snapped, unrelenting, until an arrow pierced the creature's side. Hot blood trickled down the manged gray coat, and the prince's hand followed it until he felt the arrow's shaft, slick with the gore of the animal. Eledrith grabbed this and shoved it deeper into the wound, causing the canine foe to contort and relent in his attack.

As the wolf tumbled off the prince, Darreth sent another arrow into the creature's head from only two yards away, killing it instantly. The elf-blooded helped the shaken prince to his feet. When he had sparred for a minute at a time with Garrick, Eledrith seldom broke a sweat. However, when fighting the wolf, he became as tired as if he had been training for half an hour straight. Each of his gasping breaths drew in the stinging cold of the night air, which was already tainted by the stench of blood and sundered intestines.

They could not hold back the entirety of the enemy, who had long before surrounded the encampment. From the darkness, a set of fangs buried itself into one of the horses, and soon the mount was taken to the ground by a swarm of gray-black predators. Eledrith and Darreth slew the few they could while desperate hooves cracked bone, but the wolves were too numerous, and the horses' wounds could not be undone.

The air was so cold that Krael's heavy breaths could be seen as plumes of steam. In the darkness around him prowled yellow eyes, reflecting the firelight. Though more subtly, the Kolga-thian's eyes glowed likewise. They came upon him like a horde, and the Slayer did not relent as he met them, sometimes cleaving two with a single sword stroke. On the other hand, Garrick was far more accustomed to fighting in a proper battle line. The veteran felt uncomfortable with his flanks so exposed, and whether con-sciously or not, he slowly moved backward to keep the enemy at his front.

Eledrith, Garrick, and Darreth stood in a circle around the fire, fending off the pack. It was not an offensive fight; instead, each of the men vied for a moment to breathe and regain their strength. Having run out of arrows, the elf-blooded wielded a brand taken from the embers in one hand and his trusty dagger in the other. He plunged the red-hot stick into one of the wolves, but it did not give in to the pain even as the smell of burning flesh and hair became apparent. Darreth quickly realized that the enemy he faced was no normal animal, but something urged on by a motivation other than instinct.

While the three men around the fire felt overwhelmed, their Kolgathian ally drowned in wolves, both living and dead. Even the creatures' simple minds could tell that Krael was the most sig-nificant threat, and they ran toward him without fear. The executioner's sword arced and cleaved, rending its foes apart and sending trails of blood flying in all directions. Fast as it may have swung, it could not cover all directions of attack.

"We've got to help Krael," said Darreth, half-surprised he was saying such a phrase.

Eledrith, across the fray, noticed this as well. He gritted his teeth and let out a battle cry of sheer anger. The fear and hesitation that had gripped him since he was knocked to the ground were washed away in a tide of vigorous, adrenaline-fueled blood. For-ward he charged, almost foolheartedly, to the Slayer. With an elegant pirouette, he avoided the jaws of one beast and decapitated it with the false edge of his sword. This kill only fueled his battle lust, and forward he ran even faster than before.

Silver hair waved about as Eledrith spun and struck at the wolves. His blade pierced their hides with what seemed like no resistance. Each strike and thrust had excellent form. Although he had learned to place them on a human body, he quickly adapted his techniques to the shorter statures of his current adversaries.

The beasts had fought to their last. Soon, Eledrith and Krael were surrounded by carcasses. The rush of triumph came to the prince's head, and he couldn't help but let out a cry of victory. At this, Krael smiled. "You fought well."

"Thanks," said the prince as he wiped the already-coagulating blood from his blade.

"Atlor damn them!" cursed Garrick.

The old veteran stood above the horses. It was too late for them. Eledrith's white stallion lay in a pool of dark ichor, gasping its final breaths. "Not one left alive," grumbled the old man.

"At least we saved our own skin," said Darreth, struggling to raise even his spirits.

After scanning the darkness for any sign of a second attack, Krael approached the others. The hand that held his sword was utterly covered in red.

"They fought without fear, and that was the largest pack I've ever seen. Do you think this could be the workings of magick, Krael?" Darreth asked.

Garrick spoke up before the Wizard Slayer could answer. "It could very well be, but I have a more mundane explanation. There has been a war between the barons and warlords of this land for a long while. Lately, the battles have died down, given the large number of casualties. The rulers have grown wearier of open conflict."

"And what does this have to do with wolves?" interrupted the elf-blooded.

"I'm getting to that. With less fighting, there are fewer corpses that litter the fields. I think the wolf population may have grown because of abundant food, and now that their food source is gone—"

"They are banding together, becoming bolder," finished Dar-reth.

"Exactly, but I wouldn't rule out magick just yet. I'm simply offering another perspective."

"It's still too strange..." added the Slayer.

While the elf-blooded was responsible for keeping watch for the rest of the night, his companions didn't dare lower their guard. The wolves were a burden on their minds, and a good night's rest would be worthless if it were interrupted by the beasts' return. In silence, the four waited, and every odd noise carried and distorted by the wind conjured waking nightmares of the pack.

The sun's warm rays pierced through the line of thin, twisting trees. In the cold air of dawn, the companions rose and determined their next course of action. They took as much of their supplies as they could carry themselves and began the long walk to Travedd.

5
REMNANTS BENEATH

A thick, ghostly mist wafted between the hills of the barren moor. Thin grass sprouted up from the dense soil, and dotting the pale green were jagged black boulders and the occasional rusted monolith of twisted metal. The wind howled across the open land and into the faces of the Wizard Slayer and his companions, making the journey all the more difficult. The saddlebags they carried were manageable for a time, but soon they truly felt nothing like a burden designed for human shoulders. The road itself also proved troublesome, as the uphill portions demanded much from their legs. Going downhill was no relief either, as the travelers spent much energy trying to keep themselves and all they carried from tumbling forward.

By midday, they were exhausted. The exertion of battle the night before and the lack of proper rest were slowly beginning to show their true cost. Krael, who led the group, paid little mind to his aches and fatigue, but more than once, he turned around to see his companions trudging more than twenty paces behind.

"Glad to see last night hasn't taken its toll on you, Slayer," said Garrick as he caught up with the barbarian.

Instead of making conversation, Krael simply grunted. In his mind, the longer they tarried on the open road, the more chances their enemy had to stop them. Oblivious to this, Darreth let his saddlebags slide from his shoulders, saying, "I'm hungry."

Eledrith and Garrick slowed as well, but the Kolgathian continued his march to the crest of the next hill. Only then did he see it. In the distance, atop a tall and rocky hill, was a fortified town. From over the sharpened palisade, the thatch roofs of many buildings could be seen, most elevated of all a modest stone castle on the hill's crest. The gray, weathered walls betrayed its age, and while the four squat towers may not have rivaled the mighty spires of Saidal, they stood high and opulent over the surrounding lands.

"There it is," called Krael to his resting companions.

Reluctantly they ascended the hill and gazed upon the supposed haven of Thalnar. "Aye, that must be Travedd," said Garrick.

"From here I go alone," said Krael. "The wizard should not be taken lightly."

As he was used to traveling with Krael, Darreth nodded in agreement, wanting to be as far away from the wizard as possible. Garrick was not of the same mentality. "I'm sorry, but that goes against my orders. While I trust you, I serve His Majesty, and it is my duty to accompany you and ensure that you return after this task is completed."

"No."

Garrick's eyes flashed with a blaze of anger as a hand went to the hilt of the poisonous dagger on his hip. "I wish it hadn't come to this," he said, "but you'll have to cross swords with me if you wish to leave by yourself. Know full well that if you try, I will show you no quarter."

The two men glared at one another, each waiting for a sign of yielding. After what seemed like a whole minute had passed, Krael gave in. Through gritted fangs, he said, "Fine. But if you are bewitched, I will kill you."

"Who goes there?"

The guard had to shout from atop the parapet. His ragged gambeson and fur-lined cap were not for protection from blows so much as the chill autumn wind that howled about the high hill. Darreth shouted back, "I am Caedorn, merchant of Saidal. I was waylaid by bandits on the road and robbed of my goods and horses. We only seek shelter and wish to purchase new mounts."

The guard rubbed his bristly chin skeptically. "And who might these armed men be that accompany you?" he said as he pointed specifically to the huge cloaked figure with an oversized sword.

"These three are my bodyguards."

"They must be lousy bodyguards indeed if they couldn't fend off highwaymen, but that's your affair, not mine. Open the gate!"

Ahead of the travelers, a reinforced double door swung open, revealing the streets of Travedd. "I think the guard's suspicious," Garrick said in a hushed voice. "Perhaps your alias isn't as convincing as you think."

"Doesn't matter, he let us in without further question. Just leave the talking to me and we'll be fine."

Other than the four outsiders, the muddy streets were barren. There was no evening bustle typical of the alleys of Saidal. While no one would have expected Travedd to be as overcrowded as that metropolis, the town seemed unnaturally quiet. Even the howling wind of the moor died away, whether that be because of the shelter of the palisade or another, less rational, explanation. From the crest of a thatch roof, a raven cawed. Startled, Eledrith peered up at it, and the bird's dark eye met his. The prince knew something felt wrong, and to soothe his nerves, he let his hand casually rest on the hilt of his sword. Still, the bird cried out its shrill, monotone song.

Engraved on a wooden sign was a goat holding a flagon. The picture had long lost its comedic charm with years of wind and rain slowly removing paint. Below was engraved "The Happy Goat."

"Seems like a good enough place to stop," said Darreth, whose facade as the group's head effectively made him their leader, at least for the time being.

The others nodded, and without another word, the outsiders made their way into the small tavern. As the sign's condition suggested, the interior was far from well kept. The earthen floor was uneven in places, spilled drinks lay in stagnant pools, and not even the owner noticed as the four made their way to a table in the back corner. Few others sat in the underlit room.

Darreth approached the owner standing behind the bar. His conversation with the beer-bellied and balding man was just out of earshot of his companions.

"I don't like the feel of this place," said Garrick.

"That means we're close," Krael responded, almost smiling.

As Eledrith made himself more comfortable, he reached to pull his hood back but saw Garrick's scarred face nonverbally warn against it. The prince realized his mistake and kept his hood close. While the others may have passed for regular travelers (as long as the Kolgathian didn't bare his teeth), Eledrith's countenance was difficult to forget. The flowing silver hair and piercing jade eyes, along with fair and noble features, were known far outside the mighty walls of Saidal.

"What is your plan now, Krael?" asked the prince.

"We wait."

"For what?"

The Slayer looked over to his elf-blooded friend and then back to Eledrith. "He's not getting drinks. He's getting information."

The owner of the Happy Goat was intentionally more focused on polishing a mug than listening to the outsider, and Darreth could tell. His fat lips, surrounded by gray stubble, were pulled into an indifferent frown. The elf-blooded decided to use the man's dislike to his advantage. "No offense, sir, but my men and

I would prefer to be out of here as soon as possible. Is there anyone selling horses?"

Just as he intended, the man's eyes left the mug and met his own. "Aye, there's a stable on the east side o' town. Owned by Lordon, or maybe one of his sons now. Can't guarantee the mount won't be swaybacked or lame, but it'll be better than on foot."

"The worse they look, the less likely they will be stolen again, right?"

It was a bad joke, but the bartender nonetheless let out a humorous snort. "That's one way to look at it."

With the man somewhat opening up, Darreth took his chance. He slid half a dozen silver coins across the bar top with a deft hand. "So, you see many people come through here lately?"

Their weathered edges and tarnished faces reflected little light, but the coins were currency nonetheless. They caught the barkeep's suspicious eye, and whatever semblance of a smile on his face disappeared. "What's it mean to you?"

Darreth froze. He expected the bribe to be taken without question. Thinking quickly and careful not to reveal his group's motives, he said, "For your time, that's all. I understand the last person you'd want to speak with is nosy outsiders."

The barkeep pocketed the small pile of coins. "My time's not worth that much, though I appreciate the thought."

"So, as I was saying," said Darreth, wishing he would've counted the coins in his pocket before handing them over, "do many people stop here?"

"Seldom normally, and even less so in the past few months. Somethin's wrong with the animals around here. Gettin' real aggressive, they are."

"What do you mean?"

"Well, there was that whole bunch o' soldiers from Saidal. There weren't no room for 'em in town, so they camped outside the walls. Then, in the middle of the night, they got torn apart by wolves."

57

"Wolves," said Darreth, primarily to himself. The previous night's encounter was still fresh in his mind, and he now concluded that it was no coincidence.

"It's not just the wolves, you know. When the old baron resigned and let that drunken vagabond take his place, a few people got ready to storm the castle. Before they could, a bunch of crows swarmed at 'em. Never seen so many in my life! We all took it as a bad omen. Never bothered with the whole affair since."

"You mentioned a drunken vagabond?"

"An outsider from Saidal showed up in this very tavern a few months ago. He looked highborn, but there was something off. There was a desperate look in his eye, and he ordered quite a few drinks to help him forget whatever was on his mind. Once he relaxed, he got a little too handsy with a girl, so I kicked the bastard out of here myself. Later I learned he was causing some more ruckus, so he was thrown out o' town."

"And now he's back running everything?" asked Darreth, although he knew perhaps how he had managed this: magick.

"No one knows how, but yeah, and damn near running things into the ground. I don't bother dwellin' too much on it, given that there weren't nothin' to run down in the first place. That's the nice thing about small towns; most o' the warlords and kings leave you alone as long as ye pay 'em yer taxes and such."

After ordering a round of drinks and paying for lodging, Darreth returned to the group and, in a hushed tone, relayed what the owner of the Happy Goat had said.

"That's Thalnar," said Eledrith, "no doubt about it. He's a highborn from Saidal."

"We go now," said Krael.

"Patience," said Garrick. "We only just began to rest our feet."

"Fine, then I go alone."

Garrick's voice took on an aggravated tone. "You won't be going anywhere without me. Besides, what even is your plan? To knock on the front gate?"

Krael sat in thought, considering his words carefully. "Fine. We go on your command."

From how his friend narrowed his gray eyes and gritted his fanged teeth, Darreth could tell that Krael was holding back. To relieve the tension amidst the group, he said, "You know, with an hour's rest and a good meal, I think I'd be alright."

Their whispers were faint enough to be drowned out by the clinking of mugs and crackling of the hearth, but to one intent on reading lips, the nature of their conversation could be ascertained. This was the case for the thin-haired man at the opposite end of the room, whose sunken eyes peered over the top of his long-since dried cup as he pretended to take another sip. Rigfeld was his name, and he was easily mistaken for a vagrant given the dirty rags he disguised himself with. He watched the four with great intensity, and while he couldn't determine their true identities, he did know they had come to Travedd seeking his master.

Before he attracted any unnecessary attention, Rigfeld slipped from the Happy Goat and headed toward the old castle atop the hill.

———◆———

Count Thalnar sat with his feet resting on the long, ornate oak table that ran the length of the main hall. A golden goblet filled with wine was in one hand, and the other was around the slim figure of the former baron's wife, Nettra. She giggled, running a fair hand through her master's blond hair. Dancing throughout the vaulted hall were other women the exiled noble had taken a liking to, bewitched on a whim, and brought to his newly acquired castle. While he may have only been the ruler of a small town, his court was decorated like an emperor's palace. Incense drifted in the air, mixing with the smell of roasted meats. Dozens of candles danced, giving the room a vibrant glow. The sound of a harp set the pace of the dance, its elegant, slow melody bringing a calming, serene feel to the place.

Nettra's hand slipped down the lord's face, coming to his jaw. She readied her lips for a kiss, but as she gently pulled her master in, his face came away from his goblet, spilling dark wine on his scarlet and purple silk robe.

Thalnar's handsome face twisted in anger, nostrils flaring at his concubine's impudence. As he stood up, Nettra recoiled. Her master did not need to physically strike her, however, and instead met her with a terrible gaze. Compelled by no will of her own, she looked into her master's eyes. It was then that she felt a sickening fear swell up from the depths of her imagination. Like an illogical paranoia, she couldn't help but scream terror. The harp still played from across the room as Nettra let out cries of utter horror. Amidst screams, the dancers continued to dance.

Nettra's torturer grinned. Tears ran down her face as she scraped her nails on the stone tiles of the floor. Once he had his fill, Thalnar ended her fear, rendering his favorite concubine a weeping wreck on the floor. Satisfied, he sat back in his throne and beckoned to the woman. "It's alright, sweet Nettra," he said in his warm, soothing voice. "Come close and show me your devotion."

Still sobbing, Nettra crawled onto her master's lap and began kissing his neck. The sorcerer couldn't help but laugh. He had complete control over his thralls, and he relished in it.

As Nettra began to slip her hand into her master's robe, the doors at the end of the hall opened, and a cold breeze pierced the air. In crept Rigfeld, whose hunched posture, mottled face, and long, thin hair stood in contrast to the maidens that danced and swayed throughout the room. "Ah, Rigfeld," said Thalnar, "what news does my favorite human spy bring me?"

The man kneeled and brought his eyes to the floor out of respect for his master, who allowed Nettra to continue kissing his chest despite holding counsel with his minion.

"My lord, the group from Saidal has just arrived in town," Rigfeld said. The tone of his unpleasant voice was like the croaking of a toad. "It's as you thought. They're coming for you."

"You mean the travelers that slew my wolves?"

"The very same."

Thalnar took another sip of wine, contemplating. "What of their identities?"

"The youngest was asking many questions, especially about you."

"I see. And the others?"

"Another kept his hood up and did not speak. There was also a brute. Huge man, but talked slow."

"Hired muscle, perhaps," said Thalnar, who was oblivious to the rumors of the Wizard Slayer of Mog Muhtar. "If he is as half-witted as his speech suggests, I'll have no trouble bending him to my will."

"The last was a man with a scar on his face. Ran from his brow to his lip."

"Sir Garrick," said Thalnar out of surprise, more to himself than his servant. All nobles of Saidal held respect for the seasoned knight, whose skill in battle was something not to be taken lightly. "He's the one we'll need to watch out for."

"They're planning on making their way here at dusk."

"Let them come," Thalnar said with a coy grin. "My power waxes by the day, and I've been hoping for a chance to test my abilities."

The sorcerer rose, pushing Nettra to the side. He was taller than average, and as he stood amidst the debauchery and splendor of his hall, he seemed god-like. Golden blond hair tumbled to his shoulders, and his handsome, noble visage was one not easily forgotten.

Rigfeld began to chew his thumbnail, torn between speaking against his master's plan and allowing Thalnar's hubris to go unchecked. Before the sorcerer could leave the room, Rigfeld called out, "There may be only four, but perhaps they are more formidable than we know."

"Oh, dear Rigfeld," said Thalnar, laughing to himself, "if only you knew what terrible sorcery I have in store."

Through a small side door, the sorcerer himself left. Unlike the main hall, the underlit side passage was cold and callous. Between unadorned masonry walls was a narrow staircase that wound down until it opened into a repurposed cellar. Instead of stacked crates and barrels, the floor was covered with complex runes and sigils. In its center was a wooden pedestal, and atop it, illuminated by candles, was an ancient grimoire.

Even stranger was the corpse that sat in the corner of the room. Without both legs and an arm, it leaned upright against the wall, head tilted at an unnatural angle. White skin stretched tight across the skeletal frame of the body. Its lips were pulled back in a twisted mockery of a smile, showing two rows of jagged teeth. One of its eyes, despite the condition of the rest of the body, seemed healthy and hydrated. The other socket was covered by a black metal box from which sprung wires and tubes that burrowed themselves into the pallid corpse flesh. As Thalnar entered, the living eye followed him into the room.

Paying no mind to the unliving thing in the corner, Count Thalnar paged through his tome and began muttering the dark language that had granted him so many things before.

———◆———

Thunder crashed in the sky, and for a moment, the rocky hills of the moor were as clear as day. Rain rushed through the thin grass, making the climb up the hill for Count Thalnar even more treacherous. Still inebriated by drink, he wandered over the barren lands like an old dog looking for a place to lay down and die. Only a week ago, he had fled Saidal, and just before that, he had been a respected count from one of the wealthiest ruling families of the massive city-state.

A mile behind lay the town of Travedd, whose denizens had rejected him as well. Instead of ending his life outright, they had sent him into the wilderness to perish. He would not even be granted a decent burial and was doomed to be devoured by the carrion birds, wolves, or other degenerated creatures that stalked the land. Thalnar continued to drunkenly crawl with this thought in mind, shivering in the downpour. His hand slipped, and he tumbled forward, head meeting a jagged rock. Between the cold and alcohol, he was utterly numb to the pain, and he continued on. Blood mixed with the rain that poured down his face. Near blind, he could only put one hand in front of the other.

By chance or fate, he came upon the cave. That night the elements had weathered away the side of a rocky hill, revealing a crevasse that had been long since forgotten. The thin layer of soil had eroded, revealing a small gap between two boulders that would be difficult to find even by day, let alone on a storming night. Guided by something he did not know, Thalnar crept forward into the aperture.

After bracing his weight against a stone, his hand slipped again, but this time with greater consequence. He fell to the side, slamming his shoulder against the unforgiving rock, then began to slide forward. His handhold, unbeknownst to Thalnar, was the precipice of a tunnel that shot nearly straight downward. Through shadows, he tumbled, the slight angle of the cavern wall slowing his descent enough to avoid any significant injury. The tunnel was far from smooth, however, and as he fell, the many craggy edges of the rock battered his flesh.

Hours later, he awoke, sore from the innumerable wounds gifted to him by his less than graceful descent. They were overlooked the previous night, but now that he had come to his senses, he could feel the pangs of every bruise and scrape. The storm had subsided into a drizzle, and the gray light of the dreary morning shone on only the shallowest depths of the cave, which was to Thalnar but a faint light hundreds of feet above. Just barely distinguishable from the sound of rain outside was a low hum. Its steady drone went almost unnoticed by Thalnar.

The exiled count preferred staying in place rather than investigating the ominous sound from deeper in the dark. He sat there, thinking, but it seemed to get louder as he ignored the hum. It was not the rhythmic breathing of an animal that dwelled in the cave but the persistent sound of something far less natural. Considering his circumstances, Thalnar touched a hand to the rugged cavern wall and began feeling his way deeper into the earth. That was his only sense of bearing, since there was no light to speak of in the depths of that place.

The tunnel wound and contracted, with Thalnar needing to crouch in places, but the cavern opened after what had to have been over a hundred paces. The air in the chamber was stagnant, but the hum was louder than ever. Following the wall around a corner, Thalnar was startled to feel that it became smooth as it opened. He concluded that no natural process made this part of the cavern. His eyes, which had long since adjusted to the blackness, could barely make out the faintest of lights on the far side of the room. Hesitant to take his hand from the wall, he walked into the midst of the chamber.

With arms outstretched toward the lights, Thalnar made his way closer. In the darkness, he felt a cold metal wall that vibrated with the loud, droning hum. Intrigued, he felt the strange machine. Guided by the same hand of fate that brought him into the cave, his finger grazed a switch that brought hundreds of devices whirring to life. The flickering lights multiplied, and the metal casing of the great machine resembled a starry night sky.

From Thalnar's right came a metallic, monotone voice. "Welcome, trespasser. Who dares awaken me?"

The disheveled count froze in fright. While stammering for words, he turned to see a terrifying amalgamation of machine and man. A corpse, whose head was half composed of ancient technology, stared at him with a single living, lidless eye. Its lipless maw did not move as it spoke. "Speak up, wretch!"

"C-Count Thalnar of Saidal," stammered the horrified man, who used his former noble title out of habit, forgetting his pseudonym out of fear.

"Saidal... where is that?" said the half-machine.

The old metropolis was known in realms on the other side of the world, and the fact that the thing before him did not recognize it told Thalnar that the corpse was ancient indeed. The corpse said, "Answer me!"

"It's, er, to the north. On the coast. The largest city-state in the known world."

After a short silence, the metallic voice asked, "What of Ashkazanar, of fair Zatraenor?"

"I've never heard those names before in my life."

After a silence, the machine-man let out an agonizing, monotone wail so loud that Thalnar had to shield his ears with his hands, which did nothing to reduce the noise. "How long have I slept? How many years must pass for the Empire of Ashkazanar to die, even in memory?"

Thalnar looked to the room's exit: a crack in the otherwise rectangular chamber. He wondered if it was worth it to flee from this thing. If so, to where? The climb out of the cave would be difficult, if not impossible, and how would the corpse react? These questions came to an end when, out of nowhere, the machine-thing asked, "Do you desire power?"

"Yes," Thalnar found himself saying.

A monotone, inhuman laugh echoed. "What do you know of the Dark Gods?"

"Are gods naught but superstition? Things meant to explain that which is not understood?"

"You and those of your generation are fools if you believe that!" shouted the machine corpse. "To think you can know all with your own reason... how painfully naive."

Thalnar opened his mouth to protest but remembered that he was talking to a thing that, all things considered, should be lifeless.

"If you wish to become a god amongst mortals," the corpse continued, "you must open your mind. Forgo the confines of reason and morality."

"Alright then, what are these... Dark Gods?"

"They are the infinite horde of passions and principalities, things unseen that whisper thoughts into the minds of men. They no doubt led you here to awaken me. Be grateful that they favor you."

The exiled count felt anything but favored, yet he recognized the corpse's point. It was against all odds that he stumbled upon such a strange place. "And they can grant me power, I assume."

"Beyond your feeble imagination."

Seeing this was his only hope for living as anything other than a wretch, Thalnar asked, "What must I do?"

"Call me master. Forsake your past and become the apprentice of Akhred the Eternal, Last Sorcerer of Ashkazanar."

Over the next few weeks, Thalnar studied the ways of magick under the tutelage of Akhred. In the cavern's depths, he toiled over the pages of his master's tomes, opening himself to knowledge no mortal was fit to know. He learned to understand the dead tongues of Ashkazanar in which the grimoires were written. Instead of living on food and water, the dark power of Akhred's machines sustained him. Time in the ancient cave seemed to pass like a dream without the rising and falling of the sun. The light of Akhred's devices glowed incessantly, being powered by energy darker than mere electricity. Count Thalnar's past life was a distant memory. The bustling life in Saidal became a naive, wasted existence in light of what secrets Akhred had to offer. Even the might of the great city-state, which was the most powerful of all civilizations at the time, was but an unlikely flame in the dying pile of embers that was mankind.

"Tell me of your home empire, master," said Thalnar.

"It was vast and beautiful. Metal towers pierced into the sky, and machines served the needs of all. So comfortable was life in Ashkazanar that even the beggars were fat and long-lived."

The count struggled to imagine such a standard of living. That kind of place seemed paradisal, yet not too dissimilar from Saidal. While well-fed beggars baffled the count, the high towers invoked memories of the city-state's skyline.

"But as you can tell, it was not to last," said the mechanical voice, coming as close to sorrow as an unliving tone could be. "Those who first built the machines that allowed such a world had died away, and their descendants knew little of their complexities. Instead of fixing the old machines, new devices were invented to make up for the shortcomings of their predecessors. This cycle continued, systems struggling to maintain themselves. As these things began to fail critically, those who relied on them were helpless to repair them. They were not subject to the disorders of one generation's work but dozens simultaneously. My people were utterly doomed.

"The silvery spires of Zatraenor rotted from within. Spreading from there, all of Ashkazanar withered away. Barbarians and degenerates plundered its riches and squandered them, not knowing their true value. It pains me to imagine the vastness of what was lost. So much innovation and wisdom, utterly destroyed. The coming of the invaders is what drove me into the depths of the earth. Have you noticed that this place was built with no entries or exits?"

Thalnar nodded. He was very familiar with the chamber he had spent innumerable hours within.

"This place was meant to house my corporeal form so that I would not perish at the hands of the uncivilized invaders but instead live forever."

"It's almost terrifying knowing that a land far greater than my own had fallen so far as to be forgotten."

"Thus is the cycle of time, my apprentice. Great men build empires, which are only doomed to fall when their children are raised sheltered and ungrateful. No one can truly know how many empires like Ashkazanar, or perhaps even greater, rose and fell in the forgotten past. The plight of man is a doomed one, for all his efforts are subject to the unceasing decay of entropy."

———◆———

Akhred the Eternal watched as his student prepared spells for the coming of Sir Garrick. If the corpse could still manipulate his facial muscles, it would have smiled. Thalnar, in reality, was a puppet of the ancient sorcerer. Ever since he had awakened him from his slumber, Akhred had been prying and controlling the young man's mind. When they communicated, it wasn't truly spoken word but a telepathic connection that Thalnar only rationalized as sound, hence why Akhred could speak the language of a foreign time. Through this connection with Thalnar, Akhred could experience the pleasures of life. Every taste of food or touch of a concubine was shared by both the exiled noble and the corpse machine.

6
CONFRONTING THE SORCERER

Against a crimson sky stood the black silhouette that was Castle Travedd. Circling the towers were swarms of black ravens cawing their shrill song. Weapons at the ready, Krael and his companions made their way toward the fortress. Along the street, shutters were closed and doors were locked. The people of Travedd had learned what happens when the usurper sorcerer is crossed, and the gathering of ravens was a warning that his wrath would fall once again.

Krael hated that he had to be accompanied. There was little that Garrick, Eledrith, or Darreth could do to aid him in this fight. Yet, they followed at Garrick's behest, thinking that staying together would increase their chances of survival. Unlike the Slayer, they all wore armor, Garrick in his chainmail, Eledrith protected by a shining breastplate of steel underneath his cloak, and Darreth in a padded jack. Krael knew that armor did little to stop the effects of spells, so he wore nothing more than a sleeveless vest. Even his cloak had been forsaken so as to not constrict his movements while fighting.

Atop the hill, the castle sat, and a single narrow staircase led to the front gate. Eyes cautiously watching the cloud of ravens, the companions continued up the stone steps. There were no guards on watch, at least any that could be seen. As if on cue, the wooden double doors swung inward, and from within came an orange glow and the echoes of laughter. Krael halted, tightening his grip on his massive sword.

Garrick said, "I don't like this. It's as if he wants to face us."

"What do you suggest we do, Wizard Slayer?" asked Eledrith as he tried to catch a glimpse of whatever lay inside.

"Stay out of my way."

After the four had entered, the heavy doors slammed shut. At the far end of the hall sat six concubines, poised leisurely in their seats and shrouded by flickering shadows of the dim candlelight. In their midst was Count Thalnar himself, whose cocky smirk only served to put the Slayer and his companions even more on edge. "Come in, make yourselves welcome. It's a pleasure to see you again, Sir Garrick. And do my eyes deceive me, or is that the Prince of Saidal? How long has it been, dear cousin?"

Krael paid no mind to the wizard's words. The whole table rumbled as the Slayer leaped onto it and dashed toward Thalnar, executioner's sword raised and teeth bared. Garrick and Eledrith followed on either side, hoping to cut off any possible escape routes.

In the face of the charging Kolgathian, Thalnar at first merely chuckled. The sorcerer gazed into the eyes of the barbarian and began whispering the eldritch incantations he had studied so fervently. Unlike the many people Thalnar had bewitched previously, Krael's mind was impenetrable. It was not that the Slayer merely resisted the spell, but instead, there was no way for the magick to manipulate him. His will was as steel, and Thalnar's sorcery was helpless to stop it. Upon realizing this, the wizard's handsome face drained of color. Scrambling out of panic, he flung himself out of his seat, barely avoiding the five-foot blade that came whistling down and buried itself deep into the chair's wooden back.

Garrick and the prince were still many paces behind the Wizard Slayer, but what they saw caused them to stop dead in their tracks. The concubines were not as innocent as they seemed mere moments ago. In their hands were knives and shivs, and with a shrill cry, they charged forward to defend their master. One concubine held a dagger poised for the Slayer's heart, but she was knocked back with a swing of his massive arm. Krael would stop at nothing until Thalnar was dead, and he followed the fleeing sorcerer through the small door that led to his study.

Left behind, Eledrith, Garrick, and Darreth hesitantly raised their weapons to the concubines, who showed no sign of yielding despite being outmatched. "Don't harm them!" said the prince. "They're slaves to the wizard's will, no doubt. If we can just hold them back until Krael kills their master, we can save them."

Darreth, who still stood by the door, nocked an arrow. "Easier said than done."

"I believe we can do it," said Eledrith, who adjusted his grip on his sword so that he would be striking with the flat of the blade.

The wizard's thralls, garbed in little more than silk dresses, quickly closed in on the three men. Instead of human war cries, they uttered bestial shrieks that sent a chill down even the veteran Garrick's spine. With no thought of self-preservation, they came in for the kill.

Thalnar leaped down the stairs and flung open the yellowed pages of his grimoire. His trembling fingers stumbled and struggled to turn the withered corners of the parchment fast enough. The spell that was to be his last resort was a dangerous one indeed – not even Akhred dared use it unless necessary. The corpse machine himself sat against the cold stone wall, aiding the young Thalnar with his psionic manipulations. The puppet had become a proficient sorcerer in his own right, but without Akhred's assistance, he was a fraction of what he believed himself to be.

Just behind Thalnar came the Wizard Slayer in his unrelenting charge. It was more than the fury of a predator or territorial beast, for there was no hesitation or wavering. He was machine-like in his persistence. Every step, every small motion, closed the distance between him and the sorcerer. In the face of this inhuman focus, Thalnar's face once again smirked. He had found the page, uttered the forgotten tongues, and the forces he invoked from realities beyond had already begun to send their umbral servant.

The shadows in the cracks of the floor began to quiver. An ethereal ooze crept forth, and as it rose, it took the form of a dark, stunted ape. Its shape was asymmetrical and its limbs irregular. In its black maw were equally black fangs, sharp and jagged. While it stood no higher than an average man's shoulder, the sheer bulk of its odd and knotted muscles made it rival the Wizard Slayer himself in mass. On the creature's head were two short horns, sharpened to a stout point.

Krael did not hesitate to swing his blade in a wide arc. It crashed into the demon's side, but it did not pierce as deep as the barbarian had anticipated. It had sunk into the flesh less than an inch, and as he pulled his weapon free, the gouge closed itself as fast as it had opened. The demon, unfazed by the Wizard Slayer's attack, let out a roar far too low for a creature of its size. It dashed forward, flailing its arms, grabbing its opponent's off-arm and blade. Whether unfamiliarity with steel weapons or well-backed confidence in its own otherworldly fortitude, the misshapen hand had closed on the blade without hesitation. Krael roared to meet it, and while the Kolgathian's battle cry was far from truly human, it was nothing compared to the creature tearing away at his guard. The grip of the beast's hand was unrelenting, both on the Slayer's arm and weapon. His hand was numb, and the bones in his forearm felt like they would shatter. With no other option, Krael raised his leg and planted the heel of his boot onto the creature's throat. This strike proved to be as effective as the last, and the grip on his arm only became more agonizing.

Seeing the Wizard Slayer in agony was a relief to Thalnar. As Krael struggled with the otherworldly beast, the sorcerer brushed the hair out of his face and smoothed his robe. "I see there is more to you than I first realized. I don't think I've ever had such trouble with someone before. So, if you would be so kind, what is it that makes you so hard to entrance? Is it a spell you yourself have cast, or are you just so dim-witted there is almost nothing to control?"

Krael didn't respond. He had begun to stomp with both legs simultaneously, and he was only becoming more fatigued by the second. The rush of his kicks was just barely holding back the gnashing maw of the demon's teeth.

"I'd answer sooner than later if I were you. There's no telling how long you have."

<hr />

The concubine wailed as a bashing from Garrick's shield sent her to the floor. The attack hadn't been strong by intention, but the knife held by the now prone attacker had come far too close to the old man's face for comfort.

The sorcerer's thralls had forced Garrick and Eledrith back toward the door that was the entrance to the castle. Darreth, armed with his bow, had been there the entire time. He grew more anxious as the enemy pushed in. Try as he might, the elf-blooded couldn't force the doors open. They did not so much as shake as he slammed his shoulder into them, for it was magick that held them shut.

The flat of the prince's blade struck the brow of one concubine who had moved in too close and too quickly. This didn't deter her, and she pushed forward, not caring for her own safety. A kick to her hip sent her staggering back, but not before the razor edge of her dagger sliced at the prince's exposed arm.

"Dammit, Eledrith, your chivalry will be the death of us!" said Darreth.

"Just hold them back," barked Garrick. "If what the prince says is true, we only need to buy Krael more time."

Eledrith and his mentor struggled to fend off the unrelenting enemy. They were out of room to continue backing up, and sooner or later, they would have to go on the offensive. Darreth, armed only with a bow, could do little but wait until he was given permission to use lethal force.

Above, hidden in the rafters, Rigfeld went unnoticed. Crossbow in hand, he watched wide-eyed as the men struggled against the bewitched women. His master had ordered him to kill Garrick at the first chance, but he had taken his time, waiting for the perfect opportunity to strike. The old knight moved with surprising vigor, and amidst the commotion, a clean shot could not be made. What worried Rigfeld more was the one with the bow. If the spy were to be noticed, the man in the headband would surely fire back. *He'll die first, then the knight*, thought Rigfeld.

Darreth heard a mechanical click somewhere above his head. Startled, he twisted his body, and a crossbow bolt whistled past his ear. Above him, garbed in dark clothes and hidden out of plain sight, was the assailant, who had since forsaken his ranged weapon and reached for a shortsword. While Darreth could dodge the incoming missile, he was not quick enough to fire a return shot and was knocked to the ground as Rigfeld dropped on him with all of his weight.

Eledrith noticed the assassin fall, and after sending a concubine back with another ferocious kick to the hip, he whirled around, changing his hands to a lethal, and because of practice, more comfortable, grip. The slash was very telegraphed, and Rigfeld could block it with his smaller blade even as he recovered from the over ten-foot drop.

Sidestepping to fill the hole left by the prince, Garrick struggled to hold back the wizard's servants. He had no choice but to allow some attacks to come through, hoping his mail would do its job. The concubines wielded surprising strength thanks to Thalnar's sorcery, and the knives that plunged into the rings of Garrick's armor, while failing to pierce his flesh, knocked the wind out of the soldier. Despite the agony, he fought on, trying to strike soft targets with the blunt side of his axe and not fracture the skulls of the enslaved women.

Eledrith parried Rigfeld's counterattack with ease. His sword arced toward the wretched assassin's neck, but out of habit, he wavered. The prince had never killed a man before. Taking advantage of his hesitation, Rigfeld pushed the sword out of the way and slashed at Eledrith's face. The attack was sloppy, and with a simple step backward, Eledrith avoided the blow. With renewed vigor and mustered courage, the prince sent his blade into his enemy's shoulder. When fighting, Eledrith learned to watch the eyes of the enemy, for they betrayed the intentions of attack long before any footwork would. In Rigfeld's bloodshot eyes, he saw surprise, then terror. Taking his eyes off the enemy's, Eledrith brought his sword up again and cleaved his skull to end the man's suffering. A rush then came to the young prince, and with it, his emotions of fear and sorrow were washed away.

———◆———

The crooked black fangs of the ape-demon snapped with a terrifying strength. The Wizard Slayer kicked and writhed, but its unyielding grip would not be shaken. As the creature's hold of the blade tightened, the steel didn't so much as pierce the umbral flesh. With no other options left, Krael picked both his legs up, but instead of kicking the foe, he dropped his weight and pulled on his sword. Down through the ape-demon's hand it slid, and if the grip wasn't as tight, the injury may not have been so severe. As the blade sliced, the fingers that held onto it so tightly were severed, falling to the floor and freeing the Slayer's weapon.

The demon let out another impossible scream, but it was cut short as Krael hacked into its neck with his newly freed sword. The beast backed away, letting go of its foe's arm, never having felt such grievous pain before. The Slayer gave it no time to recover and came flying toward it, heavy sword cleaving left and right with terrifying speed. These slashes, each of which would normally rend a man in two, did little to the summoned creature, but as the lacerations grew in number, they also slowed in healing.

Thalnar noticed this and was terrified. Summoning that dark creature was his last resort, and he did not know what else he could do. Even Akhred the Eternal, whose living corpse sat unnoticed in the corner of the chamber, felt fear upon witnessing the Slayer's resolve.

Faster and faster, the Kolgathian swung his blade, with each strike hewing off a small piece of the summoned monstrosity. Its ape-like head snapped in rage, but it could do nothing to stop its mortal foe. Black muscled arms lashed out, but Krael sidestepped their strikes. The beast's mindless swings were easy to see coming, and the Wizard Slayer made sure not to fall into its grip a second time. In the fury of his onslaught, the Slayer's sword hit the flat by accident. The weapon, under much stress already, bent and broke in two. One end clattered to the floor, but the other continued to dig into the demonic flesh of the beast. With a shorter and lighter weapon, Krael could strike twice as fast as he had before, much to the lament of Thalnar and his demon. With a final two-handed swing, the baboon-like head of the monster was cleaved from its body. The husk slumped to the floor, and the midnight fangs ceased to gnash. It was slain.

The Slayer's heaving breath wavered. It had been a full minute of swinging his weapon against the enemy without ceasing, and given the sword's weight before it broke, it was a feat that few men could push themselves to. The Kolgathian's hair stuck to the sweat that beaded on his face, and the half of the sword he still held trembled with the remnants of adrenaline.

Thalnar stared, mortified, and out of habit turned to his corpse-machine master. Krael saw this and immediately understood. Marching straight for the remnants of the ancient sorcerer, his hate-filled gaze met the single living eye of Akhred the Eternal.

"What sort of man are you to be unaffected by my powers?" asked Akhred's metallic voice.

Krael shoved Thalnar to the ground with a single arm, intentions now on the corpse machine.

"Answer me, barbarian cur!" Akhred continued.

The Slayer did not respond. He only stalked forward.

"Don't lay your hands on me. I command you!"

Krael picked up the helpless corpse by the neck with a single hand. Lying on the floor, Thalnar was powerless to defend the master. With one quick motion, Krael smashed the machine corpse's head against the stone wall of the chamber. The ancient bone gave little resistance, and from the skull poured a cloud of dust and sparks. Akhred the Eternal, the ancient sorcerer, born three thousand years ago in the Empire of Ashkazanar, finally died. With him ended the last living memory of that advanced empire and the fair city of Zatraenor.

———◆———

In an instant, the wizard's concubines ceased their attack. They held their heads, confused as if awakening from a slumber. Some reacted to the pain of wounds they had been oblivious to only seconds before.

Eledrith let out a holler of celebration. "It's over! Krael's done it!"

The concubines looked confused, and while they had sustained wounds, none of them had perished. The prince's celebration was cut short when Garrick cried out, "My lord, you're bleeding!"

Eledrith met him with a look of confusion, but as the thrill of battle and victory waned, he began to feel lightheaded. Garrick had only noticed this thanks to the growing pool of crimson on the flagstone beneath him. "Sit down, boy!" said the veteran as he removed the young prince's cloak.

Much of the silvery-blond hair was tainted red from the wound. A steady stream of blood came from a deep gash on Eledrith's upper back, just to the left of his spine.

"Damn, it's deep," said Garrick. "You sure you didn't feel this?"

"I remember getting hit there, but I didn't think it pierced the skin."

"Well, it definitely did," said Garrick, who fashioned a makeshift bandage from a strip of the prince's cloak.

Darreth was busy trying to deal with the newly conscious concubines. Nettra, who had a severe bruise forming on her arm from Garrick's shield, was otherwise unharmed. "Where is my husband?" she asked.

Darreth bit his lip, thinking. Afraid that the wizard's spell may not have genuinely ended, the elf-blooded nervously asked, "You're not talking about Count Thalnar, are you?"

Nettra looked not just confused but insulted. "My husband is the baron of the castle in which you stand, idiot!"

Darreth gulped. Instead of addressing that matter, he changed the subject and asked, "Are any of you seriously hurt?"

After seeing that the elf-blooded had his hands full, Garrick looked the prince dead in the eye. "Don't you dare move. That bandage will stop the bleeding, but we'll need to get that properly fixed up soon. In the meantime, don't make it any worse."

"Yes, sir," said Eledrith.

"Now, where's Krael? He hasn't taken off yet now that the job's done, has he?"

Eledrith furrowed his silvery eyebrows, thinking, then pointed to the side door at the end of the hall. "Last I saw, he went that way after Thalnar."

"I'm going to go check on him. For all we know, he could be in worse shape than you."

Garrick turned, hustled to the side door, and descended the narrow staircase.

———◆———

"Get away from me!"

Thalnar squirmed about on the hard stone floor with his back against the wall. There was nowhere for him to run; the Wizard Slayer stood between him and the door. He looked to the pile of twisted bone and wires that had been his mentor. With Akhred finally dead, the count was at a fraction of his power, and Thalnar could feel it. His hold over the servants upstairs had dissipated, and he could no longer see from the eyes of his bestial thralls. All he could do was stare in horror at the barbarian that stood before him. He was taller than most, and the sheer muscularity was of a kind that the coddling fires of civilization had burned away from domesticated man long ago. His arms were covered in twisting, jagged veins that still bulged from the exertion of killing the demon. In a hand, he held the remnants of his executioner's sword, of which the rough, broken tip seemed just as menacing as the Kolgathian's carnivorous fangs.

Krael raised the sword, ready to send the broken steel deep into Count Thalnar's skull.

"Krael, wait! I demand you take him alive!"

The Wizard Slayer turned to see Garrick out of the corner of his eye. Through gritted fangs, he asked, "Why?"

"His Majesty ordered that we take him alive if possible. Count Thalnar should be tried in the courts of Saidal, so justice can properly be served."

Krael scowled. "I do not care," he said as he turned to kill the sorcerer.

Thalnar was trying his best to influence the mind of Garrick, who only by luck had been ordered to bring the exiled count back to the massive city. Silently he whispered the ancient tongues that, without Akhred's assistance, could only make the Captain of the Royal Guard more assertive in his already existing notion.

"Hand me the sword," commanded Garrick.

Reluctantly, Krael handed over the shattered weapon. "Thank you, Krael, and I hate to be like this, but I am first and foremost a servant of His Majesty. Now I—"

It all happened in a fraction of a moment. Before Garrick's eyes, the barbarian whipped around to meet the terrified sorcerer. There was no time for Thalnar to scream as the Wizard Slayer's knee came crashing into his head. A deep crack reverberated as his skull was crushed between his assailant's strength and the stone brick behind him. Blood poured from his nose and ears, and he slumped to the ground, unmoving.

"Damn it, Krael!" roared Garrick. The veins of his temples were easily visible as he fumed.

"He cannot be trusted to live."

"And why is that?"

"He used magick."

With a sigh, the veteran calmed himself. Handing the Slayer his weapon back, he said, "I suppose it doesn't matter now. Let's just get going. Eledrith is hurt."

After the Slayer left the room, Garrick took one last look at Thalnar's corpse. Beneath the bloodstained blond locks of hair, it was obvious that the skull did not retain its ordinary shape. The sorcerer's head uncannily sagged, and the sight made the knight shudder.

7
DARK MACHINATIONS

Countless stars shone in the sky above the terrace courtyard of the king's palace. What were colorful flowered bushes by day were vague black forms. Perambulating between these forms was King Torvaren, wrapped in a warm cloak. In hand, he held a candle, which offered little light to pierce the gloom.

From the shadows came a strong, low voice. "Your Majesty."

King Torvaren jumped, and the candle he held came close to falling out of its stand. Straightening the candle, he said, "Damn, Ordric, you startled me!"

"Forgive me," said a tall man wearing a slim silk tunic and black cloak. "I did not mean to."

Count Ordric of House Maumont naturally blended into the unilluminated foliage given his dark garb. His face was easily recognizable given the full beard, widow's peak, and aquiline nose. With long strides, he approached the king and came to the edge of the candlelight.

"Well, you have my attention now. What's the purpose of this secretive meeting?"

"It concerns the man you sent to hunt down Count Thalnar."

"Krael, the Wizard Slayer? What of him?"

"I think you underestimate his worth."

Torvaren sat down at one of many stone benches placed around the courtyard. "How so?"

Ordric, without sitting, continued. "It's not what the Wizard Slayer himself can do, but those he kills. Are you aware of how many wielders of magick exist in the lands surrounding this city?"

The king shook his head.

"More than you'd imagine. In the Outlaw Kingdoms, they sometimes serve as advisors to the petty warlords. Others live as hermits, but even they hold sway over territory."

"I've heard of no such thing. I know there are wizards out there, but don't they just sit in ruined towers, studying their old tomes and experimenting with magick?" asked Torvaren.

"Oh, far from it. These wizards wield a great deal of power in the literal sense, and it's only logical that they have political power," said the count, who fidgeted with a peculiar signet ring beneath his cloak.

"What does the Wizard Slayer have to do with all this, then?"

Ordric realized the king wasn't going to make the connection himself. He sat down on a stone bench opposite the man and looked him in the eyes. "The Slayer is leverage against these wielders of magick."

Torvaren understood, and his eyes grew wide. "You're suggesting a dangerous game, Count Ordric, and for what reason? What can this lead to?"

"My eyes can see beyond the crumbling walls of this city, Your Majesty," said Ordric, whose tone became harsher despite the maintenance of manners. "I've read tales of empires that have spanned beyond all that the Outlaw Kingdoms encompass, from north of Cellenbron and reaching beyond Valmoria in the distant south. You possess an asset that can bring this about, even if you don't know it."

The king's eyes were wide in shock at the zeal of the count. "Don't you hear what you're saying? You sound mad!"

Sighing, Count Ordric arose. With a wave of his arm, his cloak was unfurled, and he set a firm hand on the king's shoulder. On that hand was the signet ring, whose silver band resembled a serpent's skin. The signet itself was a three-eyed skull, an emblem seldom seen in the courts of Saidal. "Come now, Your Majesty, just try to imagine it yourself. The Outlaw Kingdoms and beyond, all part of your empire."

Torvaren's eyes drifted away from the count and gazed blankly into the black horizon. "My empire..." he muttered.

"The hedge wizards and warlocks will all serve their purpose. With the Wizard Slayer under our control, they'll bend the knee or suffer at his hands."

The king continued to stare into the distance. After a short pause, Count Ordric took his hand from the king's shoulder and sat back on the bench opposite him. "So, what do you think of my idea?"

"I think it's quite brilliant," said King Torvaren without irony or doubt.

<hr>

Garrick, followed by Krael and Darreth, made his way through the massive king's hall. The sun shone strongly through the eastern windows, and images of the arched panes lay glowing on the red carpet. Over these walked the travelers, and down from his dais came King Torvaren to meet them. Arms spread apart, he said, "Behold, the heroes have returned, but where is my son Eledrith?"

For a moment, Torvaren's face turned somber, fearing the worst. Garrick answered, "He was wounded in battle, Your Majesty. Darreth here was able to fix him up, but the prince managed to tear the stitches before we got back. Don't worry, he's here safe, just in the infirmary for now."

"Ah, that's good to hear."

The veteran kneeled before his king, and Darreth followed suit. Krael refused to the ire of Torvaren, who did not betray his irritation consciously but clenched his jaw and refrained from chastising the barbarian. After the formalities, the king sat back on his throne. "So tell me what has become of my nephew, Count Thalnar? Could he not be brought back alive as I had requested?"

Garrick's eyes wandered to the Slayer. "As per Krael's request, we had his body burned before leaving town, but I suppose I am getting ahead of myself. Allow me to explain what happened."

As the knight recounted the details of their mission, Torvaren's eyes wandered to the Wizard Slayer. At that moment, Count Ordric's plans were at the forefront of the king's thoughts.

"We then burned everything Thalnar possessed. His body, spell book, and his clothes were thrown into a bonfire just outside of town," finished Garrick.

The old knight had left out the detail of the strange corpse machine, which even he struggled to understand the significance of. Whatever that pile of dust, wires, and bones had been, it was a secret that had died with Thalnar.

"How did my son suffer his wound?" asked Torvaren.

"In the fight with Thalnar's concubines, he demanded that they not be hurt, as they were but pawns against their will. He took a knife to the back, saving Darreth's life, actually."

Darreth nodded, verifying what Garrick had said.

"What a truly virtuous man my son is! Shame I can't congratulate him here now," said the king, "but I was thinking, to celebrate your victory and my son's safe return, a ball will be thrown in your honor. You three and Eledrith's honor, that is."

Darreth's jaw dropped, eyes wide. His mouth watered at the idea of all the food that would be prepared for the celebration. Krael, however, groaned. As subtly as possible, the elf-blooded kicked his barbarian friend in the ankle.

"Is there something wrong?" asked Torvaren.

"No, Your Highness," said Darreth, "we'd be grateful."

"When will I be pardoned?" said Krael.

The king considered his words carefully, his face showing a good-natured grin while he panicked internally. The Wizard Slayer was still considered a murderer under Saidalian law, and the pardon was the only control Torvaren held over him. "In time, my friend," the king said, "but don't fear, you are under royal protection and in no threat of execution."

Krael glared at Torvaren but didn't say a word. The king shifted in his throne, feebly adjusting his robe to comfort himself. Still, the Slayer watched him like a predator would a wounded animal. Torvaren again flashed a smile, to no effect.

Darreth nervously watched Krael, knowing full well what his barbarian friend was thinking. To break the tension, he asked, "So, the ball, when will that be, Your Majesty?"

"I see you're as eager as I am," said the king. "Soon, if all goes well. There have been no formal plans made, but I'm sure the nobles of this city will be eager to attend such an event, regardless of the short notice."

With that, Krael and Darreth were dismissed, leaving Garrick to discuss the finer details of the mission with the king. Once the two left earshot, the elf-blooded whispered to the Slayer, "What were you thinking? I haven't had a nice meal in weeks, and you treat the king like that?"

"He thinks me a slave."

"We'll be eating like kings if you stop being such a…"

Darreth clenched a fist, trying to vent his frustration. To his relief, a royal servant stopped them before he could admit he was at a loss for an insult. They were led through the mahogany double doors at the end of the hall and from there to their quarters in the palace.

As the closing of the heavy doors rang throughout the room, king Torvaren shifted the conversation. "What do you think of the Slayer?"

"He's very straightforward. Every action Krael takes is to bring himself closer to his goal."

"Which is?"

"Well, killing wizards, of course."

"But why?" asked the king. "Is it an oath of vengeance?"

"It's ideological, as far as I can tell."

The king rested his plump chin on his fist. After considering his words, he said, "I think Krael may prove to be an important asset in the future."

The words were not considered carefully enough, and Garrick raised a scarred eyebrow. "What do you mean by that? Are wizards truly that great of a threat to Saidal? If they are, the Slayer would be happy to dispose of them on his own terms."

"I'll discuss this with you at a later time, I suppose. I'm sure you're exhausted from your travels."

Garrick nodded. "That I am. Thank you, Your Majesty."

With a bow, the old veteran began the long walk through the carpeted hall. As he came halfway to the door, he turned and said, "Be careful with the Wizard Slayer, my lord. I didn't mention this earlier, but he went against my orders and refused to take Thalnar alive."

Torvaren straightened his posture and said, "I see."

Before the king could dismiss his warning, Garrick continued. "I took his weapon, but the minute I looked away, Krael killed Thalnar with his bare hands. I consider myself fortunate that I did not put myself between the Wizard Slayer and his prey."

Nodding dismissively, the king avoided the intense look in Garrick's old eyes. "Thank you, Sir Garrick."

Hoping his lord would heed his warning, Garrick saw himself out of the hall.

The servant's hands quickly glided over the fabric of the scarlet dress-to-be, measuring and pinning frills in place. By her reckoning, at least, the dress was coming along quite nicely. Not too garish or flamboyant, the simple garment would accentuate the lady's dainty, slim form without too many extra frills or other elaborations. A flowering embroidery would keep the dress from seeming too bland, and a fur-lined overcoat would give her enough presence at the ball where her small size may lead her to be unnoticed. Only in the noble houses of Saidal would such fine garb be worn in that age, and the nobles themselves knew it. They aspired to seem like gods amongst mortals to assert their status, and Lady Morwenna hated that game.

"I'd much rather not go to this ball at all. Besides, it's celebrating the death of the king's nephew. It just doesn't feel right, Idda."

The servant of House Maumont, Idda, rolled her eyes and continued with her work, which she could perform almost without looking. The old woman had served Lady Morwenna since birth and her mother since adolescence. "You know," she said, "the young Prince Eledrith will be there."

Morwenna scoffed. "Oh, and I am so excited to see him," she said, her voice dripping with sarcasm.

"Come now, my lady. I think he's cute."

The lady rolled her large brown eyes. "Sure, he's cute, but all he does is practice swordplay. It takes more than just skill with a weapon to be a man. Besides, isn't he kind of skinny?"

"I admire your prudence, Morwenna, but give Eledrith a chance. There might be more to that man than you can tell. Besides, I heard he helped in the fight against Count Thalnar himself."

"And I heard a hired killer sent the count to his grave."

Idda pursed her lips. She said, "Well, you'll be able to ask the prince himself what happened soon."

Morwenna knew that she would make a good wife for any bachelor that prowled the courts. Her house held great power over Saidal, and her family had especially benefited from King Torvaren delegating much of the responsibility of rulership to the counts. Even the lady's appearance was renowned. Her large brown eyes were captivating and brought out by long, curling auburn hair. Her lips were thin, but the way her cheeks folded and dimples appeared gave her a look of innocent beauty.

"How is my daughter's dress coming along, Idda?"

Both the servant and Lady Morwenna turned to see Count Ordric's imposing stature filling the doorway to the chamber.

"Very well, actually," said the servant.

"Excellent. Forgive me, Morwenna. I'm afraid I'm not going to be present at dinner tonight."

"How come?" she asked. "It seems we hardly ever eat together as a family anymore."

"I must hold counsel with the Captain of the Royal Guard, and tonight was the only time it would work for him."

"Shame. Why not invite him here for dinner?"

"Your mother suggested the same thing. The conversation would be nothing but boring logistics, and I wouldn't want to subject you to that."

"Fine," said Morwenna.

"I'm sorry," said the count, "but this is very important, and while I trust you and your mother, confidentiality is important to the captain."

His daughter chose not to respond, so Ordric left the room with the final word.

———◆———

Krael appeared from behind the changing screen. His bulging muscles seemed precariously close to ripping the black doublet that he wore. His hair had been combed back, and his face was somewhere between a pout and a scowl. Darreth had to cover his mouth to hide his laughter.

"What?" said Krael.

"Oh, nothing. I'm sure the ladies will be fighting for a chance to dance with you," said Darreth, on the verge of tears.

"Perhaps a size larger," suggested the royal servant assigned to fitting the two men for the ball.

Krael walked over to a mirror, and upon seeing himself, his thick eyebrows rose. He tried to raise his arms to tousle his hair, but the small size of the doublet didn't allow it. He turned, baring his teeth. "I don't want to go."

"Relax, Krael. There will be more food than we've been able to get our hands on in a very long time. I know you may not care, but I personally like not going to bed hungry."

The Kolgathian still scowled, so Darreth added, "Who knows, perhaps we'll learn rumors of where another wizard may be."

Krael's eyes narrowed at his friend. "I doubt it," he said, no more enthusiastic about the ordeal.

The door to the chamber opened, and through it came Eledrith. The prince laughed upon seeing Krael in too-small clothes. "You look ready for the ball."

This did nothing to improve the Slayer's mood. Growling to himself, he took off the elaborate doublet and let it fall to the floor. The servant picked it up and prepared to continue fitting the barbarian, but the prince stopped him with a hand. "A moment, if you will," he asked.

The servant bowed and left the room. Eledrith then turned to the Slayer and his assistant, two common outsiders in the most powerful of city-states. "Is something wrong?" Darreth asked.

"No, don't worry, I'm just tired of having to be heard by the king's servants."

"What do you mean by that?" said Darreth.

"Whatever I say will send echoes of whispers throughout this palace, and I'd prefer to be able to speak honestly without worrying about what others outside this conversation may think."

"Who knows what people say about this guy, then."

They both looked at Krael, who said, "I care not what they think."

"That's good," said Eledrith, "because they don't think highly of you."

"For the best," said Krael.

While Darreth rolled his eyes, Eledrith smiled. "I find that quite admirable," said the prince. "The king allowed me on this journey to improve others' opinion of me, but I couldn't care less, either. I've found that perceived virtuousness and virtue itself are seldom the same."

"Well spoken," said Darreth.

"Thanks. And there's, er..." said Eledrith, searching for the proper words. "I hate to sound overly sentimental, but my most cherished memories will be the time spent on the hunt for Count Thalnar. I know that sounds strange, but for the first time, I knew things were genuine. I wasn't a prince. I was more than that. A man."

Krael nodded, recognizing the truthfulness of Eledrith's words. The prince continued. "And I'm sure you two will be off soon, continuing to venture across the world, but remember that you will always have a friend in Saidal."

"Thank you, Your Majesty," said Darreth.

Chuckling, the prince said, "Please call me anything but that."

The two embraced each other. When they were done, Eledrith turned to the Wizard Slayer.

"He's not one for hugs," said the elf-blooded.

Krael and the prince clasped hands and, to Darreth's surprise, pulled each other close. The Kolgathian's large hand patted Eledrith firmly on the back.

"I doubt we'll have a chance to speak much at the ball tomorrow night. There'll be a swarm of counts and nobles trying to kiss my backside," said the prince.

"Well, if they get too unbearable, I'll just send Krael over," said Darreth.

Krael groaned. "I do not want to be there."

"Neither do I, Wizard Slayer," said Eledrith, "but it's necessary, I suppose. Who knows? Something good could come of it."

———◆———

Count Ordric stooped to pass beneath the rickety doorframe of the decrepit hut. The small wooden shack was built in a side alley in the underbelly of Saidal. Hardly a place for a count to be seen, Ordric was dressed in worn-down clothes and covered in a mud-stained cloak. The only thing that could betray his identity was the serpentine signet ring, which he did not dare be without. He spun the metal band to hide the three-eyed skull within a closed fist, gripping it tightly. Many in that dark, secluded place were willing and able to steal the ring without the count's notice, even if they didn't know its actual value.

A single lantern hung in the corner of the shack, and the faded yellow glow reflected off dozens of jars that sat atop the uneven shelves on every wall. Inside the glass were preserved parts of flora and fauna found across the known and unknown world. Strange six-legged lizards floated in a preservative. A ghastly array of pale, bloated organs sat in jars as well. Sitting in the corner, looking over a small cauldron, was an old woman. Thin white hair hung down over a wrinkled face. Her hands were almost skeletal, shaking as they stirred a putrid concoction.

"Ah, Count Ordric," she said with a toothless smile.

"Don't you dare utter that name here, witch!" snapped the count.

"Relax, you're in Stregana's house. You're safer here than if you were in the cozy walls of your mansion."

Ordric wrinkled his nose, scanning the crumbling shack in disgust. Stregana chuckled at the man, then gestured to a thatch mat on the floor. "Come, come, sit down. Did you bring the elves' blood?"

After sitting down, the count reached into the tattered cloak and procured a small vial filled with red liquid. "You have no idea how much this cost me. Your kind have hunted the elves to damn near extinction."

"Well, give it here," said Stregana, holding out an eager spindly hand.

"Not until you prove you have upheld your end of the bargain."

The witch's demeanor hardened. "The scrying requires a small amount of the blood. Give it to me now."

"I'm no fool in matters of magick, crone. Elven blood only has the power to slow aging. Any use for it in your scrying ritual is either superstition or a sign of your senility."

Stregana scowled, the wrinkles on her face deepening. He had called her bluff. "Alright, Count Ordric, you may be right, but Stregana still refuses to provide her services until she is paid."

"Fine," said the count, placing the vial into the witch's hand.

Gripping her payment with surprising strength, the witch offered a disingenuous smile. "Stregana thanks you for your patronage."

Stregana turned to her many shelves, pulling down seemingly random jars. Ordric may have known of elven blood, but the strange assortment of ingredients the witch had gathered was totally foreign to him. Popping corked lids from glassware released pungent stenches that made the already unsettling smell of the shack nigh unbearable. Into the cauldron ingredients went, Stregana measuring each with just her crooked fingers. The color of the concoction turned from a mundane brown to a deep bluish black. With the change of hue came what seemed to be a deepening of the cauldron itself. Though Ordric could not describe how, it was as if the pot contained the fathomless black of night instead of an opaque liquid.

Stregana leaned over the brew, muttering a repetitive incantation. She then looked up to the count, eyes rolled back so far into her head that only the whites could be seen. "What do you wish to know, Count Ordric of Saidal?"

"I wish to know more of Krael, the Wizard Slayer. Who exactly is he? How can he be controlled?"

The witch tilted her head back to the cauldron. After a moment, she shuddered. "The Hound of Mog Muhtar cannot be tamed. You cannot alter his thoughts like you have so many before."

"Then what can force his hand?"

Stregana strained to peer deeper and deeper into the swirling blackness, but after a time, she shook her head. "There is no easy way. He cares not for wealth or the pleasures of this world. The only thing the Wizard Slayer is bound to is his hatred of magick. Only through this can he be controlled, if it is possible at all."

Ordric cursed to himself. This was not the simple solution he had been hoping for. "Not even your powers allow you to know this for sure, witch?"

"This is no man," she said as she stared wide-eyed into the cauldron. "He is something else entirely."

"You're wasting my time," said the count.

"You are wasting your own! I see only death in your future if you continue on this path. If he knew the true nature of that foul ring you possess, he wouldn't hesitate to kill you, Ordric!"

"Save your ravings for your other patrons; they have no effect on me. I have set plans in motion that cannot be undone. I will forge an empire, and a petty witch like you won't stop me."

"Swallow your pride."

Count Ordric laughed. "You have every intention of stopping me! It's the hedge wizards and soothsayers like you that will become my unwilling servants. It's good that you fear the Wizard Slayer, for he will be the knife I will constantly have at your throat."

Stregana kicked the cauldron, spilling its contents onto the earthen floor. Standing up, she shouted, "Out with you! I no longer desire the company of a madman."

The count took a deep breath, then said, "Alright, I will oblige your request."

A contemptuous sneer was on Ordric's face as he left the shack, and Stregana was filled with dread.

8
THE BALL

The day had finally arrived. Servants hustled through the halls connecting to the ballroom, quickly making their final preparations. Enough food lined the many tables to feed an army, and the vast chamber was filled with the scents of golden-brown dishes and expensive spices. Ivory-colored marble columns upheld the great vaulted ceiling, and two glistening chandeliers were needed to illuminate the entirety of the place. No tables were left in the center of the floor, whose black and white tiles nearly reflected like mirrors. All along the walls stood the finest of the king's guard, whose silver plate was for style as much as protection. Per the king's orders, they took their place long before the ball began. Their conical helms hid their faces, and ornate halberds were held in gauntleted hands.

There were two balconies at each end of the hall, and from each descended two staircases. From these came the guests whose styles befitted their dramatic entrances. Saidal was a port city that had connections to cultures on far-flung continents, and these helped inspire a variety of exotic and lavish outfits. Material of every color could be seen, and in time, the dance floor was like a vibrant, flowery garden. Lords, ladies, counts, and countesses mingled, vying for status in their ungenuine conversations.

Darreth and Krael made their way through one of the side hall-ways, taking a final relief of solitude before their plunge into the chaos of the gathering. The Slayer had been fitted into a custom-tailored outfit to account for his bulking musculature. Even with this, he seemed strange in the ornate black clothing. He was a bar-barian, and the very way he walked was in conflict with the sophisticated garb he was forced into. On the other hand, his elf-blooded friend seemed perfectly normal in his blue and gold dou-blet. The only thing odd about Darreth's appearance was his headband, which, to the lament of the servant fitting him, he had insisted on wearing.

"Didn't Eledrith say we were gonna go in with him and Gar-rick?" asked Darreth.

"I thought so."

They came upon a servant whose all-black but plain dress sep-arated him from the highborn guests. Darreth approached him and asked, "Do you happen to know where the prince is?"

The servant turned and looked at something far past Darreth. "I believe His Majesty and Sir Garrick are approaching as we speak."

Sure enough, Eledrith approached in all white. Accompanying him was the old veteran, who wore a decorated military uniform. Smiling, the prince asked, "Nervous, Darreth?"

"No, just wanted to make sure you didn't head in without us."

"Trust me, friend, if I had entered already, the collective lust-ful sighs of the ladies would have been heard throughout the palace."

The two chuckled but gathered themselves as Garrick scolded, "Come now, we have appearances to uphold."

"Are you gentlemen ready?" asked the servant.

The men nodded, and the servant proceeded through the dou-ble doors. The four followed, presenting themselves to the crowd. All eyes were on them. "Ladies and gentlemen," called out the servant, "now entering are tonight's guests of honor: His Majesty

Prince Eledrith Calidign, Captain of the Royal Guard Sir Garrick, Krael the Wizard Slayer, and the valiant Darreth."

An applause came from the crowd that echoed throughout the vast marble-walled hall. As it died away, the four went down the stairs and entered the subtle battlefield that was the ball. Krael felt the eyes of countless nobles watch him, whispering things amongst each other as they stared. The Slayer could do nothing to stop this, so he stood alone.

Eledrith's welcome was much warmer than the Slayer's, and many gathered around to congratulate the young prince on his successful journey.

"You are showing great promise, my lord," said one.

"I'm glad all that time training with your sword has finally paid off," said another.

Yet another said, "You have more courage than most to face a wizard in combat."

As the praise continued without sign of ceasing, Eledrith ceased politely nodding and smiling. Growing cross, he stopped in his tracks. "Please, please, that's enough," he snapped. "Yes, I ventured across the Outlaw Kingdoms and met a great deal of danger, but it is the Wizard Slayer Krael who you should praise. His courage and will are why we all were able to return safely."

The nobles paused, unsure how to react to the prince's outburst. To end the tense silence, Garrick said, "His Majesty is humble, perhaps too much so for his own good. Have you heard of how he refused to harm those bewitched against their own will?"

Garrick recounted how they had fended off Thalnar's concubines, along with the details of Eledrith's killing of the unexpected assassin from above. While he did this, the prince stood by. He looked across the room to see Krael and Darreth conversing with another group of nobles. Relieved that the Slayer wasn't totally ostracized for his appearance, he sighed and faced the crowd with a rejuvenated sense of sociability.

The Wizard Slayer stood next to one of the side tables, using the assorted delicacies to avoid conversation as much as he could. This was to no avail, and the elderly and bald Count Boridron persisted in his questions.

"Are you the same Wizard Slayer that caused the upheaval of the Cellenbron Valley a few years past?"

Darreth looked to his barbarian friend, unaware of what Boridron was referring to. Krael said, "Yes," before sinking his teeth into a disappointingly small poultry leg.

Boridron raised a wispy white eyebrow. To his side, nobles whispered between each other. Tired of being left in the dark, Darreth interjected. "That must've been before I came to follow you. Care to tell me what happened?"

"Alrik the Bear made a deal with a wizard. I killed the wizard."

"Which resulted in a famine that brought Alrik's domain to its knees," interrupted Boridron. "And if rumor can be trusted, it was you that smashed in Alrik's head in full display of his subjects."

Darreth shrugged and nodded. "That sounds about right."

The nobles, however, were horrified. Some let out muffled gasps. Others backed away, their faces pale. "I had no choice," said Krael.

Count Boridron gulped out of nervousness. To relieve the tension, he said, "Well, we should not leave this to rumor. Let's hear your side of the story."

In his slow, straightforward pattern of speech, Krael recounted the tale. Darreth could tell that the nobles weren't totally convinced that Krael did the right thing, so once the Kolgathian was done speaking, the elf-blooded changed the subject. "Did you know that when we were passing through the Outlaw Kingdoms, Krael saved His Majesty Eledrith's life?"

Darreth told the story of the wolf attack, embellishing details to make both the prince and Krael seem more competent. "Three wolves came on the prince at once, and while one was stopped by an expert cut of his blade, the other two brought him to the ground. That's when Krael came charging in, sword held high, and cut down the beasts, saving His Majesty's life."

Boridron and his entourage responded much better to the embellished tale than the harsh truth that Krael had told. The Slayer himself rolled his eyes at Darreth's antics and turned away from the group, making a meal out of minute cuts of smoked meat that were meant to be only an appetizer.

———◆———

From the top of one of the balconies came the projected voice of a servant. "Now entering is His Majesty, King Torvaren Calidign the Third, High King of Saidal."

The whole room turned to see the tall man garbed in ornate royal purple. His doublet effectively hid his plump form, and a grand scarlet cape lined with white fur made his presence imposing. He wore over his brown hair a small golden circlet in place of the top-heavy official crown of the king. As he made his way down the staircase, those around him bowed.

"About time he showed up to his own party," Eledrith mumbled.

"It's intentional," said Garrick, taking the prince by surprise. "What good is a dramatic entrance if only a fraction of the guests are here to see it?"

Eledrith deftly brought a crystal glass of wine to his lips, masking his words from prying eyes. "You know as well as I do that he was busy attending to one of his mistresses."

"That may be true, but not another word. Now isn't the time to address such matters."

With the king's entrance, Eledrith had a window of time to be out of the limelight. After actually taking a gulp of wine, he said, "How I wish we could be practicing swordwork right now, Garrick."

The veteran chuckled. "The last thing you need is more practice with your sword, but I admit I'd rather be doing that as well. One of these days, I will beat you again, boy."

"We'll see," said the prince with a smile.

"My lord," said a voice the prince only vaguely recognized.

It belonged to Countess Sedrana, a cousin of Eledrith's late mother. Only a few times had she spoken to the prince before, despite the close connection. Her blond hair was tied in an elaborate coiffure, and makeup covered the sparse wrinkles of her middle-aged face. "If I may ask, what is he like?" she said, gesturing to Krael, whose black-haired head could easily be seen over the top of the crowd.

"The Wizard Slayer? Krael is his name. He is a good man. Don't let his looks frighten you; that's just the nature of his people. He was born in a land far from here. Have you ever heard of Kolgathar?"

Sedrana shook her head.

"Well, that's where he's from. Krael may look like a barbarian, and he sure fights like one, but there's a deep discipline to him. Killing those who use magick is his only goal. His friend there, Darreth..." The prince pointed to the elf-blooded. "The one in the headband. He told me that Krael doesn't care about gold, fame, or women, only the next wizard to hunt."

"What a sad life he must live," said the countess.

"On the contrary, I think it's the greatest of lives."

Before the prince could elaborate, Sedrana interrupted. "What are you saying, Your Majesty?"

"He lives for justice. Wielders of magick sow suffering and pain, and he brings an end to them. It's perhaps the highest calling one can have. I hope I can somehow emulate that."

"To slay wizards?"

"No," said Eledrith, growing frustrated, "I mean to live for justice and what is good, not for myself. And unlike Krael, I do wish to fall in love and sire heirs, don't worry."

Countess Sedrana laughed. "Good. It'd be chaos if you didn't, given how many counts have viable claims to the throne."

Throughout the night, Krael continued to avoid conversation as best he could. He made his way from table to table, devouring anything that looked like meat. Most dishes were too small and strangely seasoned for his taste. What the barbarian really craved was a massive leg of mutton. Unfortunately, the nobles preferred to graze a variety of expensive foods instead of dedicating time to one genuinely filling meal.

"Don't try those," said Darreth, pointing to a silver tray containing several hard cakes, each topped with a pinkish paste. "I didn't know you could make something taste so bad."

Before Krael could disregard Darreth's warning and try one for himself, someone from behind said, "So, I hear you're the one who killed Count Thalnar."

The Slayer turned to see a smug noble who was reasonably young but seemed experienced given his long beard. "Forgive me, where are my manners? Lord Jarlen at your service," he said with a bow.

"I'm Krael," growled the Slayer with a quick nod. "I killed Thalnar."

"Truly is a shame," said Jarlen, who took a bite of one of the paste-covered cakes and showed no sign of disgust. "Not that he's dead, of course, that traitorous bastard belonged in a grave. I just wish he could've been brought back here to be executed publicly. Nothing against you. I'm sure you had your reasons."

"He was a wizard," said Krael. "He couldn't be trusted."

"Thalnar was the wizard himself? Strange. How does one learn the secret arts of magick?"

"It's a secret for a reason," said the barbarian.

"Come, now. Surely, we can discuss this simply to satisfy my own curiosity."

"I wouldn't push it," said Darreth. "He's a Wizard Slayer: literally the worst kind of person to ask about magick."

"Fair point," said Lord Jarlen, who smiled in a vain attempt to salvage the favor of the Slayer and his companion.

A woman in a vibrant blue dress approached and greeted the count. "May I introduce my sister," said Jarlen, "Lady Viselva."

The noble curtseyed and batted long eyelashes toward Darreth. "It's a pleasure to meet you."

"Likewise," said Darreth.

As the elf-blooded flirted with Viselva, Krael was able to retreat from the conversation. The ball was becoming too much for him. Conversation on its own was difficult enough for the Kolgathian, but the ongoing small talk had worn away at his patience like some cruel form of psychological torture. He understood deeper than before why Eledrith hated life in the palace. As his eyes wandered, they met the jade eyes of the prince, who offered a warm smile and a nod from across the room. This comforted Krael.

———◆———

"How does my son fare this fine evening?" said the king, beaming.

"Good," Eledrith replied with an awkward smile.

"Thank you again, Sir Garrick, for keeping him safe," said Torvaren.

The veteran gave a shallow, polite bow. "Not as hard of a task as you'd think, Your Majesty."

"How is your wound, son?"

"Not too bad anymore," said the prince, testing the flexibility of his injured shoulder.

"Good to hear."

The king's eyes drifted to something beyond the prince. "Ah, Eledrith, there's someone I wanted to formally introduce you to. This is Count Ordric."

Eledrith turned to see the tall count. "It's a pleasure to speak with you, Your Majesty. Your father has told me much about you."

The prince smiled. "Likewise."

Ordric spoke, addressing the king and the prince, but Eledrith's jade eyes drifted to a stunning figure garbed in scarlet. Her deep brown eyes met his, and the prince was frozen in something between adoration and anxiety.

"Eledrith," said Torvaren sternly.

The prince's attention was brought back to the group around him. "Yes?" he said, a sheepish look on his face.

By his tone, it was evident that Ordric was repeating himself. "I was wondering how your journey was."

"It was good," said the prince.

While he conversed, Eledrith tried to steal another glimpse at the girl with auburn hair. To his lament, she had disappeared into the swirling crowd of nobles. The conversation with Ordric had devolved into one of politics, and Eledrith did not bother to contribute.

A soft, bouncing melody resounded from a twenty-strong orchestra, whose delicate instruments easily projected their music to all corners of the hall. The middle of the room opened, and couples began a slow, conserved dance that consisted more of rhythmic footsteps than artistic expression.

Eledrith, by chance, was able to sneak over to Krael. The Slayer's elf-blooded friend had abandoned him to dance with Lady Viselva, and the barbarian stood alone.

"Looks like Darreth is having a good time," said Eledrith.

A snort came from Krael's nostrils, and whether it was a laugh or scoff, the prince could not tell. Together they watched Darreth dance, fitting in surprisingly well with the noble crowd.

"We should spar sometime," said Eledrith, pulling the notion from thin air.

The Slayer turned to him, a thick eyebrow raised.

"Not right now, of course, although I wish we could. We could borrow the practice swords from the armory and have a good go at it."

Krael shook his head. "You would beat me."

"You can't be sure of that unless we try."

"I've seen you fight. You know much."

"Come now, you must know your fair share as well."

"I was never trained."

The prince was astonished. "Really?"

Krael nodded.

"Perhaps I could teach you, then."

The corner of the Slayer's mouth curled upward into a deft smile. "You should."

"Tomorrow then, and if that doesn't work, the next chance I get," said the prince.

From the whirl of exotic, extravagant dress came a figure covered in deep scarlet. Eledrith was immediately captivated by the deep brown eyes of the woman. "I'll be back," he said as he followed her.

Many turned to greet the prince. To avoid being rude, Eledrith smiled and nodded as he hurried across the marble floor. Before he could regain his composure, those same deep eyes looked at him again. "Your Majesty," she said.

Eledrith had, to his discomfort, leaped before he looked. Before him stood, as far as he could tell, the most captivating woman he had ever seen. Beauty to the prince was fickle, as makeup and light can often make all the difference. The girl in red had a certain cleverness behind her eyes, and Eledrith wanted to know more.

Unfortunately for him, he had been more concerned with not losing sight of her than thinking of something to say.

"Would you like to dance?" he found himself blurting out.

Her thin eyebrows raised, and Eledrith could have sworn he saw a dimple form on her cheek. *Is she trying to hold in laughter?* He thought, mind racing in near panic.

"It would be an honor, my prince," she said.

As she extended her hand, he held it, and together they walked into the midst of the ballroom. Many gave way to the prince, who was, at least to public knowledge, undertaking a romantic endeavor for the first time. Immediately rumors were sown in the whispered conversations of the room, and Eledrith figured that would happen. Caring not, he began to dance, slowly stepping and moving to the gentle music.

Riding on the success of his last question, he asked, "What is your name, by the way?"

The girl smiled. "I was wondering when you were going to ask that."

Eledrith could feel himself blush.

"Morwenna," she said, holding him as they danced.

"Well, if you didn't know already, I'm Prince Eledrith," he said jokingly.

"Everyone here knows you," she said with either a coy or mocking tone. At the moment, Eledrith could not tell.

"No, they don't," said the prince. "They recognize my face and name, but they don't truly know me."

Lady Morwenna's eyes drifted away from the prince, disinterested by the egotistical statement. She still, however, held Eledrith's shoulder. They danced in silence, moving to the beat of the gentle song. The prince tried to catch her eye again, and while he was successful once, he immediately felt like his endeavor seemed too desperate.

Morwenna broke the silence. "You're not a very good dancer, are you?"

"What?" he asked, baffled.

"You keep pulling me around. Try to dance *with* me."

"Sorry, I'm more used to swordplay."

"Would you rather be playing with your sword right now?" she asked.

Eledrith was struck, once again, off guard. Laughing off the comment he hoped he was correctly interpreting, he continued to dance without falling into the trap of saying yes or no. As the song ended, Morwenna let go of his shoulder and turned away. Before his chance disappeared, Eledrith asked, "We should dance again sometime. Maybe I'll get a little better at it by then."

Morwenna turned back, a smile on her thin, gentle lips. "Maybe."

With that, she disappeared back into the sea of nobles. Eledrith groaned to himself. *If she at least said no, I'd have some sense of closure*, he thought. Taking refuge in a goblet of wine, he was approached by Sir Garrick, whose scarred face was near laughter.

"She has you like a dog on a leash, doesn't she?" asked the old man.

"It's that obvious?"

Garrick finally broke. A deep, hearty laugh resounded. "Yes, it is, Your Majesty."

"Well, that's a good thing, right?"

"Er, no. The more desperate you seem, the less Lady Morwenna will think of you."

"Is it not romantic to pursue with desperation?"

The knight scratched his gray beard and said, "If there were a simple way to these things, love wouldn't mean anything, I suppose."

"Fair enough," said the prince, struggling to keep Lady Morwenna out of his thoughts.

"Ah, Wizard Slayer, I was hoping I'd get a chance to speak with you."

Krael didn't bother hiding a groan. He had hoped that he could've gone the rest of the night without speaking. This was no childish distaste of social interaction, though, since, for the Kolgathian, spoken language required mental strain to understand. His mind was that of a beast of war to whom battle was intuitive. The complex social games he was being forced to play were simply too difficult for him. Hoping for the best, Krael turned to see King Torvaren.

"Not one for parties, are you?" he said.

An entourage of nobles, primarily young women, stood behind the king. They stood watching and whispering as if they were there to see an exotic animal brought in from a faraway land.

"I should thank you again for bringing my traitorous nephew to justice," said the king.

"No need," said Krael.

"I suppose you would've done this of your own volition, though, had the opportunity presented itself."

That sentence was too complicated for the tiring Slayer. He could at least tell that it was not a question by the rhythm and tone of voice that Torvaren used, so Krael simply nodded.

"Why do you spend your days chasing down witches and wizards? I never quite understood that."

"It's my purpose," said Krael. It was his standard response to that question, however vague it may be.

"Fair enough," said the king.

Krael understood social cues better than speech, and there was something rushed, almost condescending, about that phrase. If Torvaren was genuinely interested in a better answer, he would've pressed further, but, as Krael's skeptical mind deduced, that was not the true motivation of the conversation. From across the room,

Krael caught the eye of Count Ordric and felt that he was watching them.

"So, what do you intend to do after this?" asked the king. "Continue your hunting, I presume?"

"Yes," said Krael shortly.

"Where to?"

"Don't know."

"I was thinking," said the king, "that these sorcerers and witches cause great evil in the Outlaw Kingdoms and, in some cases, within the very walls of Saidal. You, Krael, are the only person I know that can possibly stand against them. Why not stay here in my palace and allow my network of spies to search out the users of magick for you? When you have enough information, you could hunt them down yourself."

After a short time spent interpreting, Krael's eyes narrowed. "Why?"

"I beg your pardon?"

Slowly, Krael said, "What do you have to gain?"

"I'm doing this out of a mutual disdain for the dark arts."

Krael knew this was a lie. "No."

Torvaren and his entourage looked baffled. The king turned his head to somewhere across the room. Krael followed his eyes, which gazed at Count Ordric, who nodded back to the king. The Slayer couldn't articulate precisely why, but he felt like an animal that had just come across a trap, and unseen machinations were closing in from all sides.

"Come, now," said Torvaren. "Imagine what we might accomplish. My network of agents will seek out the users of magick, and once we gather the necessary information, we'll send you in. It's right to the point. No muddling through rumors and such."

"So, I serve you?"

The king chuckled nervously. "No, no! Nothing of the sort. Think of it as us serving you, really."

Krael sensed the politician's desperation but, at the same time, did not feel in control. Beneath the many layers of his garments, a cold sweat formed. His gray eyes shot from the king to the dark-haired man across the room, who still watched him intently. "I fight in the name of Mog Muhtar and no other."

"I beg your pardon? Mawg, uh, what? Now, I assure you—"

Krael had heard enough. He knew he was the target of manipulation. With purpose, he turned his back to the king and strode into the middle of the dance floor. Darreth still danced with Lady Viselva. "Darreth, we need to go," the barbarian growled.

The elf-blooded and his dance partner both looked confused. "But why?" Darreth asked.

Upon seeing the look on the Slayer's grim face, Darreth understood the urgency, albeit not the details of the situation. Leaving Viselva confused, he followed Krael out of the ballroom, the two moving at a brisk walk. Nobles gasped and protested as the barbarian shoved them to the side. The infraction of decorum meant nothing to the Slayer, who felt taken off guard and outmatched by whatever plot King Torvaren and his accomplices had in store.

Before leaving the hall, Krael turned back to see how far behind Darreth had fallen. To his surprise, the shorter elf-blooded had kept up. He also saw Eledrith, who looked understandably confused at the scene. After catching the prince's eye, the two exchanged solemn expressions before the Wizard Slayer and his companion fled from the hall.

———◆———

"What the hell is going on, Krael?" Darreth asked as they ran.

Royal servants and half-drunk nobles gave the barbarian a wide berth as he charged through the ornate halls of the royal palace.

"I do not know," said Krael.

Darreth understood this was a bad thing, not a shortcoming of the Slayer, and continued to follow without question. In their short time inside the palace, they did not have a chance to learn the complexities of its layout. They wandered the halls, turning sharp corners and descending marble staircases. Krael knew the stables meant the quickest chance of escape, and as long as he kept going down, he would eventually end up at ground level. Downward they went, their heavy footsteps echoing off the polished floors and walls.

In time, they came to the stables where many horses stood sleeping. A lone guard approached them as they each woke a mount and attached a saddle to their backs. The guard was at a loss for words, alarmed at the urgency at which the two moved. Before he could take action, the bottom of Krael's fist collided with the side of his conical steel helm. He fell to the ground, dazed, only able to see blurred figures gallop out into the night.

"What happened back there?" said Darreth, struggling to yell over the two sets of hooves clattering against the cobblestone streets.

"They wish to control me," said Krael.

Their horses galloped at full speed, darting around sharp corners into narrow alleys. The crevasses that were the streets between the towering buildings of Saidal could be traversed without trouble since few were out at that late hour. After a great while, Krael and Darreth came to a small, cramped square. A fountain statue of the god Atlor was crumbling, and the creatures at his feet that once spewed water were dry. Only stale rainwater filled the pool that surrounded the statue. Darreth hitched his horse to one of the decorative carvings at the pool's edge. "Alright, Krael, I think we've ridden far enough. I want a full explanation now."

The Slayer hitched his mount likewise and sat on the basin's edge. "Torvaren wanted to find wizards for me and tell me which to hunt."

"Sounds like that will make our lives easier. Why is this a bad thing?"

"I must find them myself. Each I find, I kill. No exceptions."

"And you think Torvaren will selectively tell you which ones to kill to further his own ends? Seems unlikely."

"Not just Torvaren," the Slayer growled. "There's more. More than we know."

Darreth pondered the Slayer's words. As he thought, he walked to the edge of the fountain and peered into the shallow collection of water. In the dark, murky reflection, he saw he still wore the formal doublet. "And is it worth giving up life in the palace? Eledrith is still there, and you know how much he hates the king. We could easily counter his plots!"

"No. I fight in the name of Mog Muhtar and no other. Any other master is a puppet of the Dark Gods."

The dark resonance of that strange name echoed through the square. *Mog Muhtar.* Krael seldom spoke of the mysterious monastery at which he trained, and rarely did he converse with such vigor and ease. Darreth knew his friend had not formulated that sentence himself; instead, he recited a litany he had learned many years ago.

"I just thought," said Darreth, "that things were finally coming together, you know? We were finally fitting in. And Eledrith and Garrick, they seemed more like family than I've ever had, other than you. I just…"

As the elf-blooded's eyes met Krael's, he realized there was nothing he needed to, or could, say. Hidden in the sunken gray stare, there was an old pain that slowly grew over time as friends and companions died. Despite this, there was also a ferocity in the Slayer's look, not temperable or yielding.

"We best get moving," said Darreth, successfully gathering himself in the likeness of his friend. "If we sold these clothes, we'd probably get enough money to buy enough supplies to get to wherever the hell we're going."

The ball was a chaos of rumors and confusion, so much so that even the orchestra had ceased playing. Instead of gentle music, harsh chatter filled the massive hall. Rumors of Eledrith and Lady Morwenna, Krael and Darreth, and fabrications linking the two were the topic of every conversation. For Torvaren, this was a disaster. He gestured for Count Ordric to follow him from the main hall and into one of the side passageways to hopefully have some privacy. Prying eyes watched as two of the most powerful nobles left the room together, but this was a sacrifice the king was willing to make. After checking the hallway for potential eavesdroppers, Torvaren whispered, "That bastard is onto us! What could I have said to make him flee with such haste?"

Ordric remained much calmer than the king, whose bloated face was red with anger. "This is an inconvenience, yes, but a necessary one."

"What do you mean by that?" said Torvaren, still fuming.

"In his haste, he revealed something that he values," said Ordric, a cunning smile forming.

Torvaren searched his memory, replaying the events in his head. Just as Ordric prepared to give the king a hint, Torvaren's eyes widened. "The boy in the headband! That's his ward, I believe."

"If the Wizard Slayer was in enough hurry to cause a scene, why would he waste time telling that boy to follow him? Because, one way or another, he values him, perhaps more than just an assistant."

"So, if we capture this Darreth…" said the king.

"Then the Slayer is as good as ours, and we'll have true leverage over him."

"We should send my guards after him at once!"

Count Ordric shook his head. "We need to be much more sub-tle in this. The more word gets out, the more cracks begin to show in my plan. Leave this to me, Your Majesty."

"Alright, but wouldn't it—"

Torvaren was cut off as the door to the ballroom flung open. Eledrith stood in the doorway, white hair whipping as he rushed forward.

"What the hell did you say to him?" said the prince, enraged.

Ordric curled his lip. "One should compose himself before speaking to the King of Saidal."

This comment only fanned the flames of Eledrith's anger. "Answer me," he said through gritted teeth, glaring at both the king and the count.

"I offered him lodging in this palace," said Torvaren, "but he insisted that he continue to wander the lands outside."

"Liar," said Eledrith.

Torvaren was at a loss for words, so Ordric stepped in, touch-ing his signet ring. "You should know better than most that the Wizard Slayer's ways are esoteric. Perhaps this isn't as out of character as you assume."

Eledrith's jade eyes smoldered. "Damn you both," he said as he turned back to the ballroom.

"Forgive his temper," said Torvaren. "He became quite close with the Slayer, and I fear that he allies closer to him than us."

Ordric didn't respond. Instead, a trembling hand touched the three-eyed skull signet. A cold sweat began to form on his brow as his mind raced to find an explanation as to how Eledrith was utterly unaffected by the magick of the ring. *Did the Wizard Slayer teach him this power?* he thought. His many questions went, for the time being, unanswered.

9
JUSTICE OR DEATH

Deep reds and blues were cast across the circular table of the High Council Chamber, emulating the stained glass windows that the midday light shone through. Around the table sat all fourteen counts of the city, and in a seat higher than the rest sat King Torvaren the Third himself. Even before the council had begun, the counts had already started to discuss the Wizard Slayer and the events of the ball the previous night. Eledrith, having no seat at the table, stood behind his father, watching the politicians with contempt. It was here where the counts vied for control of the city to serve their own ends. Torvaren, having inherited the formidable wealth and power of the Calidign family, did not bother to play the political games. Slowly, however, the counts had, under the precept of delegating responsibility from the king's shoulders, taken more and more of Saidal for themselves.

"Let us begin," said the king, "with what is on all of our minds."

Countess Sedrana spoke up. "Whatever happened to the Wizard Slayer?"

"He wished to continue his life of wandering abroad," said Torvaren.

Eledrith clenched his jaw but held his tongue. The counts who saw the prince's expression found reason to doubt the king's words but did not push the subject any further.

"A shame, really," said the king.

"But to more important matters," said Ordric, rising from his seat and gesturing to a servant on the far side of the circular room.

A map of Saidal and the lands beyond was unfurled across the table. "The reason His Majesty called for this council," said Ordric, pacing around the table as he spoke, "is because of the Outlaw Kingdoms."

"What of them?" asked Count Boridron. "They have been kept in check for the past three hundred years! Even recently, there has been peace between the kingdoms, meaning they have more crops to sell us."

"Ah, Boridron," said Ordric, scratching his dark beard, "let us not mistake peace for safety. Sure, they do not bicker amongst each other as they have in the past, but that is the opposite of what we want."

Count Gilduin, whose house had concerned itself with the Outlaw Kingdoms, provided his own specialized insight. "Aye, what Ordric says is true. Agents of mine have sown discord when one power had grown too large. You see, each kingdom, or warlord, really, relies on Saidal to fund their petty conflicts. When we buy their crops, we fund their wars with each other. If the Outlaw Kingdoms were to unite, they would no longer rely on our trading."

"And they would no doubt extort us for the food our citizens so desperately need," said Ordric.

Many heads at the table nodded. "So, are you suggesting we end the peace that exists out there now?" asked a count.

"No," said Torvaren, "Ordric and I have determined a more… permanent solution."

Gilduin looked toward Ordric, his fair Valmorian features contorted in skepticism.

With a smile, Ordric said, "We conquer the Outlaw Kingdoms."

Even Eledrith was surprised at this, but his gasp of shock was drowned out by the uproar from the thirteen counts around the table. Accusations of madness and power lust were hurled at Ordric and the king, but both men stood unfazed.

As the clamor died away, Gilduin's voice rose above the rest. "This is preposterous! We lack the number of troops it will take to succeed in such a campaign. Even if we could muster such a force, the Outlaw Kingdoms are too fractured and would not declare a single clean surrender. The war would be a long and needlessly bloody one."

Still smiling, Count Ordric leaned forward on the round wooden table, placing his hands on the decorated edge for support. With his signet ring in view of the whole table, he said, "I will admit this may seem overly ambitious, but believe me, it can be done. Know that I already have a plan in motion to bring the outside lands under our rule, but I will need your help."

The table was now chillingly quiet, and Eledrith could swear that the very air of the room seemed to change. Each face of the counts grew blank and apathetic.

"Any agents under your control," continued Ordric, "must be under my command. I cannot give a reason as to why since the nature of the plan is of utmost secrecy."

Everyone around the table, save Torvaren and Ordric himself, quietly nodded.

King Torvaren stood up. "I suppose we can now move on to other matters, then, unless anyone else has something they wish to discuss."

Uncharacteristic of such councils, no one spoke up. Eledrith stood against the wall next to the door, shocked. The prince did not find Count Ordric remarkably charismatic, but even the most seasoned of statesmen would've had trouble convincing anyone of such a lofty plan. The council then moved to more routine matters of discussion. Trade agreements with partners overseas took up most of the talk, and Eledrith's mind couldn't help but dwell on Ordric's plans of conquest.

After the counts had left the room, Ordric turned to the young prince. "And what does my lord think of such a plan?"

At first, Eledrith was silent out of fear, but justice-hungry courage overcame it. "I think it's unnecessary and too ambitious."

For a moment, Ordric's dark eyes narrowed, but they then softened as a smile came to his bearded face. "Interesting observation, but perhaps once you're more experienced in the matters of politics, you'll see the benefits of such an action."

The count's compliment was not enough to dispel the fear that still lingered in Eledrith's mind, but the prince was at a loss for words. Ordric put an endearing hand on Eledrith's back as the two left the chamber. "If I recall correctly, it was you who danced with my daughter last night."

Eledrith's fears multiplied. "Yes," he spat out before he could help himself.

"She's a shrewd one, just like her mother, but you have my blessing to continue speaking to Morwenna."

"Thank you, sir."

In his heart, the prince knew that Ordric had something to do with Krael's sudden departure. *Perhaps I could discuss this with Garrick*, he thought, but after remembering the knight's allegiance lay with the king before the Slayer, and how Torvaren seemed to now serve Ordric, things seemed hopeless to the prince.

Sharp iron spikes of the heavy portcullis loomed over the dark stone arch that was the Eastern Gate. Through this slowly passed merchants coming to and from the city, whose persons and belongings were searched by the mail-clad guards. A line of carts, horses, and disgruntled travelers had clogged the narrow alleys leading to the gate. To congest the place even further, trinket peddlers pushed souvenirs. The merchants were a captive audience, and if they were to leave their spot in line, untold hours of waiting would be for nothing.

Darreth stood in the stirrups of his saddle, looking over the mass of heads, horses, and wagons. Somehow the looming gate looked small in the presence of such a sprawling crowd. With a groan, the elf-blooded plopped back into the seat of his saddle and leaned into a shade-covered alley.

"There's just no way," said Darreth. "Even if we were to somehow get through the gate without question, it'd take hours at least, and the last thing I want to do is stand in the open with so many guards around."

In the shadow of the buildings stood the Wizard Slayer. His hooded face hardened with perturbance. "We must find another way."

"I don't think there is another way. Other than the port, which is on the other side of Saidal, there are just the eastern and southern gates. Odds are the Southern Gate is just as bad as this one."

"Bribe one of them." Krael gestured to the many impatient men driving a wagon. "To get us through."

"That's impossible! The guards will find us instantly, and what am I to bribe them with? We're broke, remember?"

"Our horses."

Darreth looked wide-eyed at the beast between his legs. "Oh, come on!"

"Royal horses," Krael grunted, "good stock."

"Fine, I'll see what I can do," the elf-blooded groaned.

Over the next hour, Darreth wandered the crowd, keeping a watchful eye on the guards. Krael stood against the cold stone wall of the alley, waiting. With his hood up and mouth closed, he passed for a normal, albeit intimidating, man. After what seemed too long, Darreth returned, face strangely wrought with a sense of dread. "I found someone," he said, "but just remember that my options were limited."

"What do you mean?"

"You know I used to run with a bad crowd, and I learned how to spot these kinds of people. You're not going to like him. I don't like him," said Darreth, fidgeting with his headband. "He, er... He's smuggling a girl out."

Krael's lip curled as he grunted, the barbarian's non-lingual form of cursing. In his youth, the Kolgathian had been enslaved, and the cruelty of that institution stoked a personal hatred. Long since had the scars of lashings faded beneath the marks of spells, but their memory remained. In addition to this, the teachings of Mog Muhtar also condemned enslavement. More than anyone, the Slayer had a right to hate human traffickers.

Darreth said, "Just promise me you won't do the thing where you glare at them the whole time like you want to put his head on a pike."

"I want his head on a pike."

———◆———

A brunette man of respectable build whipped his reins, urging the two black stallions from the royal stables to pull a cargo wagon forward. The man himself, despite his unremarkable lineage, had the aura of a Saidalian noble. His face, while unshaven, made his elegant features seem even more masculine. The neck of his red silk shirt was cut low, and the snaking tendril of a tattoo could be seen on his chest. As one of the guards approached, the driver flashed a smile.

"Passing through again, Amris?" asked the guard.

The driver nodded, a pouch of silver at the ready. "Aye, it's been a busy month for me."

With a deft, practiced movement of the hand, the guard pocketed the bag of coins. "Let me just check here quick."

Amris's two armored lackeys, mercenaries of the Outlaw Kingdoms, made way for the guard, their patchwork secondhand armor clinking as they moved. The guard approached the wagon side, where he lifted the canvas cover only so far as to let himself see what was inside. Sitting in the fetal position, a gag tight about her mouth, was a black-haired woman, her dark eyes filled with resentment. This, however, was not what surprised the guard. Also cramped in the wagon was the muscled form of a man whose pupils seemed to reflect what little sunlight made it beneath the canvas.

Surprised, the guard called back to Amris. "Looks like you're hauling something extra today."

The driver's assertive tone didn't match the people-pleasing smile that he still bore. "That pouch was a little heavier than normal, wasn't it?"

Forgoing his casual facade, the guard leaned in and whispered, "Yes, but wasn't that the Wizard Slayer in there?"

"Don't know and don't care," said Amris. "It shouldn't make a difference."

"It's just that I have orders to arrest him."

Hidden in the wagon, Darreth's heart beat like a drum, and the choking, sweat-reeking air seemed more unbearable than ever. He struggled against the canvas cover, bags of supplies, and bodies that trapped him in an awkward squatting position.

"You may have orders to arrest that man," said Amris, "but did you really see him?"

"It's an order from the king himself."

The two men exchanged looks. As Amris's smile faded to a dead stare, the guard gave in and looked away.

"I thought so," said Amris.

Mumbling to himself, the guard backed out of the way of the wagon, allowing it to pass. The two well-bred black stallions pulled the disguised cart, and Amris's mercenary bodyguards followed on foot. With wheels rumbling, the horses passed through the aperture of the wall and out into the open land beyond. Amris took one last look at Saidal, whose tall outer wall loomed. Watchtowers reached up from the parapet, windows gazing out like watchful eyes. The many forsaken corpses of criminals that hung like macabre decorations on the wall made Amris's blood run cold even as he continued into the safety of the wilderness.

The road continued for over a mile, dissecting fields littered with the husks of harvested crops and metal ruins alike. As the season had come to an end, the chill winds of winter strengthened. Dry, dead leaves scraped and tumbled across the hard earth. Naked tree limbs waved in the breeze that ran unchecked across the countryside.

Hours after the small black shape that was Saidal had faded into the horizon, a new, stranger sight stood in the distance. A vaguely humanoid form rose far above the treetops and ruined towers of the land, hunched forward as if in a daze. If the travelers had been closer, they would have seen that the limbs were built of aged metal. Pistons and hinges had rusted into place, their time of motion long since faded away. Like a petrified corpse, the cryptic mechanical titan stood, forever silent. For this reason, the thing was known as the Dead Giant. Many other ruins like it dotted the Outlaw Kingdoms, but no other stood as opulent and preserved as the one that Amris looked upon. The Dead Giant was considered by many to be the edge of Saidal's influence (although many would also argue that the city-state's government didn't even have proper control within its own walls).

Amris lifted the cover of the wagon. Hands shielding from the harsh sunlight, Darreth and Krael stumbled out, joints sore from the journey.

"Well, gentlemen," said the smuggler, "there you are, safely out of Saidal, just as we agreed, although if I'd known the king himself was looking for you, I might've asked for more than just these horses."

Darreth awkwardly smiled but couldn't keep his eyes away from the face of the bound girl who still sat gagged in the wagon. Amris noticed this but didn't draw attention to it. The trafficker said, "This is where we say farewell, my friends. I'd love to let you tag along, but I have places to be and a client to meet. Before you go, though, I can't help but ask, are you actually the Wizard Slayer?"

Krael nodded, his savage eyes glaring at Amris like he wanted to put his head on a pike. Darreth noticed the two brutish mercenaries put a hand on their sheathed swords, waiting for the Slayer's response. Tension hung in the air like static before a lightning strike.

"What kind of money does that bring in? I can't imagine there being much of a market for that sort of thing," said Amris.

"None. I kill wizards because they are evil," Krael responded.

Darreth muttered to himself, "Please don't."

"So, I see chivalry does still persist," jested Amris. "It sure takes a... savage form nowadays, doesn't it?"

Krael's gaze was laser-like in its intensity, and Amris still wasn't catching on. His bodyguards, on the other hand, did. Drawing their weapons, they sprang from the back of the wagon. They were not fast enough to stop the Wizard Slayer, who, in a single bound, leaped onto the driver's seat. With the strength of only one of the Kolgathian's arms, Amris was thrown to the hard ground. The Slayer's rapid onslaught was enough to scare the horses, causing them to buck and storm down the path, wagon in tow. Krael had not expected this, and as mighty as his grip was, the jerking start of the wagon took him by surprise, and he fell to the dirt, although far more gracefully than Amris. As the horses charged, Darreth had to dive and roll to avoid being trampled. The elf-blooded and Amris were both enveloped in a cloud of upturned dust.

The bodyguards, clad in dark, dented armor, charged at the unarmed barbarian. They stopped short, holding him at sword-point.

"What the hell are you doing?" screamed Amris, his voice cracking.

Krael didn't answer. Instead, his eyes were on the two armed and armored men. Darreth feigned defeat, lying on the ground with a hidden hand around the dagger in his boot.

"You think you're a hero for doing this? It means nothing," said Amris. "For as long as men have desires, they'll be willing to pay for them. I'm just making a profit on it. If you really want to 'kill those who do evil,' you'll have to kill everyone."

The weathered faces of the mercenaries sneered behind the noseguards of their spiked helmets, swords raised. Amris was fuming, his handsome face red, flowing hair and elegant clothes covered in dirt. He continued. "Are you seriously willing to die for some naive sense of justice?"

He definitely is, thought Darreth as he drew his knife.

As if to answer the trafficker's question, Krael charged straight toward one of the mercenaries. Taken by surprise, the man hastily swung his blade in a wide horizontal arc, aiming for the Slayer's chest. The steel sank into the barbarian's flesh, blood gushing from the straining muscles. This cut was deep but not lethal, for the Slayer had caught the enemy's sword arm and halted the weapon. Unable to come around for another strike, the mercenary could only struggle against the barbarian's grip.

Red poured from Krael's side. Keeping one hand on the arm of his enemy, he plunged the fingers of his other into the mercenary's eyes. The fleshy orbs popped with unnerving ease, and gore spattered forth. The man screamed, dropping his weapon and falling to the ground, thrashing against the agony that ran deep into his skull.

Darreth had no time to stab the back of the other bodyguard, who within seconds came lunging at the Wizard Slayer with his falchion. Picking up the blade of the man he had just barely overcome, Krael readied his defense. The bodyguard, whose technical skill with a sword greatly outmatched the Slayer's, came in with a blitz of slashes. Only by backpedaling could the barbarian avoid the razor edge that whirled with terrifying precision.

"Behind you!" screamed Amris.

The bodyguard had become too confident in his advantage and continued pressuring the Slayer. Harder and faster, he swung, and with each desperate block, his enemy only lost more blood from his side. Amidst the conflict, he noticed Krael's eyes drawn to something behind him. In that fraction of a second, he remembered his employer's warning, but by then, it was too late. A sharp pain struck his back as Darreth's knife slid into a gap between two plates of armor. Before the mercenary could understand what was happening, Krael slashed open his throat.

Amris backed away, mortified. Nothing he could do would stop the hulking barbarian from approaching. Teeth bared, Krael ran down the human trafficker, taking him to the ground like a lion would a gazelle. "No! Please! I'll give you anything!" begged Amris.

The Wizard Slayer had no sympathy for the man. It took only three punches to send Amris's jaw shattering back into his skull. The only sound the trafficker could make was the gurgling of his own blood.

Darreth examined the scene. Three dead men lay on gore-stained dirt. Much of the blood was Krael's, whose wound only bled faster the harder he fought. Suddenly disoriented, the Slayer teetered to the side. The numbness that racked his body was too strong to be caused by battle frenzy. As he tried to approach his friend, the barbarian dropped to his knees.

"Take it easy, Krael!" said Darreth.

The elf-blooded struggled to tie a makeshift bandage around Krael's torso. "Was this really worth it?" he asked.

As he faded to unconsciousness, Krael wore a sardonic, fang-baring smile.

10
THE PIT AND THE CANDLE

Seventeen years ago...

Cold iron chains tightened around Krael's body. In vain, he struggled against them, veins bulging and teeth snapping as he was slowly lowered into the dark pit. From above came a gray light and the solemn chanting of the monks of Mog Muhtar. Krael had not yet known spoken language, and the words' meaning were lost to him. In defiance of his captors, he roared with inhuman ferocity. His protests were to no avail, and he was lowered into the dark pit, each mechanical click of the winch reverberating through his binds. He swung as his body thrashed, yet nothing would stop what was to come.

From below came a cacophony of hisses that rang about the stone walls of the pit. The sound was overwhelming, drowning out the monks' chanting and Krael's roars. The reverberating hisses grew louder as a heavy steel door closed over the top of the pit, letting in no light. Unseen fangs came from the dark, sinking into Krael's flesh and injecting their foul venom. In utter blackness, the barbarian was submerged, subject to the serpent's bites. Time seemed irrelevant, as there was only the dark and fear. Krael's roaring of defiance turned into primal cries for help. Still, the torture continued, and terror consumed the Kolgathian's heart.

Like a star, a faint light pierced the dark. It was a single candle flame suspended in blackness, whose golden glow barely reflected off twisting scales. Desperately, Krael looked to it. It offered no salve to the pain and agony that the snakes caused, but it was a single point of certainty in a writhing sea of shadows. It was all the barbarian had, and to it, his mind clung. Agonizing days passed, and the serpents continued to torment their Kolgathian prey. He screamed into the dark, the chains still constricting him, and only by the light of the candle did he maintain some semblance of hope.

Then the candle went out, and darkness enveloped Krael. His paranoia quickly went to work, forming hideous shapes from the unseen chaos around him. He began to panic, hyperventilating and thrashing against any slight touch of the snakes, using the last of his dwindling stamina. The barbarian's very mind seemed exhausted, and he ached for death. By some cruel miracle, the venom that now tainted his blood had not done its work, and still, he hung in the pit.

To give himself some certainty, Krael imagined the candle that had failed him. The single point of light, even though it only existed to the Kolgathian, provided hope. While the snakes continued to twist around him and the shadows tempted his mind to give form to demons, the light was a bastion of sanity. To it, he clung with what little strength he had left. There he hung, glaring into the empty dark.

White light poured into the pit as the metal door was drawn back, and the Wizard Slayer arose.

11
THE HUNT BEGINS

Breath heaving, Darreth ran down the road, following the newly carved tracks in the dry dirt. The wagon had tumbled into a small wooded area, the trees of which were thin and spindly. Despite having lost their leaves, the twisting branches blocked sight, and Darreth could only guess as to around which bend the wagon had stopped. As he rounded one of the many corners in the forest, he was relieved to see the horses standing idly. The elf-blooded came to the side of the cart and lifted the cover.

The glinting razor edge of a knife stood less than an inch from the elf-blooded's throat, yet the wagon itself was bare. A woman's voice from behind said, "Don't move."

He complied, freezing where he stood. The voice continued. "Give me your name and one reason why I shouldn't kill you."

"Uh," started Darreth, whose silver tongue had lost its sheen when under the threat of the knife.

The cold edge of steel touched his Adam's apple, which forced the elf-blooded to spew forth the unembellished truth. "I'm Darreth and we paid Amris to smuggle us out of Saidal but then Krael killed him and his bodyguards and now he's bleeding out and we don't want to hurt you."

The knife came away from his throat, and he sighed. Just as he thought he was no longer in danger, the woman behind him shoved his shoulder, sending the elf-blooded spinning. His back crashed into the side of the cart. Still dizzy from the impact, he looked up to see his gorgeous assailant. Her large dark eyes were narrowed in anger, but her equally large lips and slender olive face seemed inviting, at least to Darreth. She was distinctly Valmorian. Midnight hair flowed in luscious curls. She still held a dagger in her hand, but this was no awkward grasp of desperation. Darreth had seen masters of knife-fighting, and the woman's grip, down to the positioning of her fingers, revealed her expertise. "Who the hell is Krael?" she hissed.

"The Wizard Slayer," said Darreth, totally complying.

The woman narrowed her eyes further, looking more confused than angry, although she maintained a hostile posture. After seeing the terror-stricken look on Darreth's youthful face, she lowered the knife. "Whatever," she spat, "just no sudden movements."

Breathing a little easier, Darreth said, "He's just up the road. It'll make a little more sense if we head back there."

The two climbed into the empty cart. With Darreth at the reins, they rode the short distance back to the carnage where Krael slept.

The black-haired woman cursed in her Valmorian language, then in the High Tongue said, "I've never seen such…"

She stared wide-eyed at the three men covered in blood. Amris's face, jaw shoved back into his skull, stared blankly into the sky.

"You get used to it when you travel with Krael," said Darreth.

The Slayer himself lay against a tree, breathing heavily. The bandage about his torso was already stained a dark, dull red. His eyes were closed, and his head tilted to the side, out cold.

"Why did you do this?" asked the woman. "Why would you risk your lives for me?"

Darreth shrugged, stepping out of the cart and heading to the fallen Slayer. "Don't ask me. Ask him when he's awake."

The woman picked up one of the fallen bodyguard's swords, wiping the blood onto the former owner's garments. Standing tall, she held the weapon out, gave it a graceful swing, reversed her grip, then flourished it in a figure-eight motion. "Horrible balance," she muttered, "but it will do."

Struggling to lift the unconscious Kolgathian, Darreth's knees began to shake. All of the massive bulk was now dead weight. While he had helped a wounded Krael before, the barbarian was usually conscious, reducing Darreth's job to providing stability. He groaned, heaving against his friend's bulk. Suddenly, the burden became lighter.

"Damn, he's heavy," said the woman, and together she and Darreth lifted the barbarian, each under one of his thick arms. Slowly they walked, Krael's feet dragging on the ground as they went. They laid him in the cart, where he continued to lie unresponsive.

After catching his breath, Darreth said, "Thanks."

"Don't mention it," said the woman. "Although I am a foreigner in this land, and while I can fend for myself, I'll be as good as dead if I try to survive without a guide."

"You've stumbled upon the worst possible guides," Darreth laughed. "Currently, we're being hunted by King Torvaren. At least I think we are."

"I care not. As far as I'm concerned, my luck has turned around. Mere hours ago, I was bound to be sold to some warlord to serve as his guard and concubine. Now, things have changed."

Despite the brightening of her mood, the woman's face was still grim. Her thick lips were pulled into a frown. "I am called Lorienne. From birth, I was trained as a sword-dancer to serve in the noble courts of Valmoria. Hopefully, I can be of some assistance to you for the time being."

Darreth remembered only rumors of sword-dancers. They were known to serve as bodyguards as well as entertainers, though often as concubines as well. Their fighting style was of grace and subtlety, looking more like a dance than a martial art. So far, she fit the description.

After rummaging through the supplies on the wagon, Darreth found everything he'd need to stitch up Krael's wound. The bandage and clothes were removed, revealing a deep gash in the Kolgathian's sickly pale side. A bottle of vodka, half-emptied by Amris and his men the night before, was poured on the wound. Methodically, the elf-blooded then stitched together the Slayer's flesh. Lorienne couldn't help but look away. While not normally sickened by gore, the pulling of the threads through the skin was too unnerving for the sword-dancer to watch.

"There, good as new," said Darreth.

"You certainly know what you're doing there," said Lorienne, comfortable examining the work in its finished state.

"I've had lots of practice, trust me. See that one there?" He pointed to a broad, jagged scar on Krael's shoulder. "That's one I definitely messed up."

Despite Darreth's casual tone, Lorienne was astonished at the exposed body of the Slayer. She didn't find it attractive by any means and instead marveled at the numerous marks and scars laid over the corded muscle. Amidst the faint scratches and punctures, there were old wounds that seemed burn-like but which shapes were too defined to be the random marks left by heat and, at the same time, too alien to be a brand.

"We best get going," said Darreth. "These bodies will no doubt draw attention, and that's the last thing I want right now."

With a whip of the reins, the wagon made its way down the road away from Saidal, carrying the newly freed captive, the elf-blooded, and the stitched-up Wizard Slayer. The winds proved unforgiving, and Lorienne did her best to distribute the late Amris's meager supplies throughout the group. Winter seemed nearer than ever. Before long, all of them were shivering.

"So, you're from Valmoria?" asked Darreth, teeth chattering.

Lorienne nodded, handling the cold far better than the skinny elf-blooded. "I am, yes, born and raised in the capital of Colanthus. Many ships from Saidal come there, hence why I can also speak the High Tongue."

"What's your homeland like? I've never had the chance to travel that far south."

"A lot warmer than here, that's for sure."

Darreth scoffed, trying his best to keep his hands warm while holding the reins.

"It's far more beautiful, too," Lorienne continued. "Everything in Saidal was made of dark, depressing bricks. Colanthian architecture is far more beautiful. Huge, white marble columns uphold decorated rooftops. Even in the deepest part of the city, gardens of trees dot the boulevards. Oh, how I wish I could be back there amidst the olive trees and warm winds."

"Yeah, those warm winds sound pretty good right now," said Darreth.

"I'm afraid I'll never be able to return there. My whole life, I was trained to be a sword-dancer. For years I dreamed of serving in the beautiful white-columned palaces of Colanthus, but as my training ended, I realized my duty would always be to serve someone else."

"And that's a bad thing because…?"

"My destiny wouldn't be in my own hands. The whims of my liege would control everything I was. Then, like a sick joke, I'm kidnapped and shipped away to that abhorrent megacity, Saidal. I was doomed to serve, but now even the beauty of my homeland wouldn't comfort me. I may be accompanying you for the time being, but remember that this is of my own will, and at any moment, I can turn my back and tread my own path."

Darreth looked to Lorienne, whose focused eyes glanced to the far horizon. Her large, almost hooking nose seemed to compliment her other features, and the elf-blooded reckoned that she would've been the most beautiful woman he had ever seen if her visage wasn't contorted with resentment. Keeping that thought to himself, he focused on the road ahead. Only a few yards away loomed the Dead Giant. Knowing this unmistakable landmark, Darreth found his bearings and began to ride deeper into the Outlaw Kingdoms.

Garrick marched into the throne room, his steps resounding off the vast arched ceiling. His pace was quick, and upon noticing this, Torvaren ended his hushed conversation with Count Ordric and gave the Knight and Captain of the Royal Guard his full attention.

"Your Majesty," said Garrick, out of breath from his hasty walk, "I've just received word that the Wizard Slayer was seen leaving Saidal by the Eastern Gate three days ago."

Ordric, standing behind the throne, raised an eyebrow. Torvaren sat erect in his seat, forgoing his normal slouched posture at this critical news. "Really, now? Why was he not apprehended?"

"Something to do with a bribed guard. He was hesitant to let us know the day it happened. He only came forward an hour ago."

Torvaren said, "Make sure the guard responsible is publicly punished for this transgression."

"That is already being taken care of, Your Majesty."

"So," started Ordric, stepping forth from behind the king, "the Wizard Slayer has fled to the Outlaw Kingdoms."

"So it would seem," said Garrick, resisting the urge to narrow his eyes at the count. *That man spends far too much time with the king. He can't be trusted.*

"As my most esteemed knight," said the king, "I am going to trust you with information you must guard with your life. Are you aware of our plans for the Outlaw Kingdoms?"

"Yes, Your Majesty."

"It seems lofty at first glance," said Ordric, "but the most crucial detail must remain secret. If one knows where to look, the kingdoms are, in fact, riddled with magick users. These sorcerers and mages exert control over the land. While some of the kingdoms will need to be taken by more conventional means, many will bend the knee if we can control the wizards."

"And you need the Wizard Slayer to control them," said Garrick.

"Exactly, and that's where you come in."

The old man swallowed nervously. To him, the plan seemed lofty even in light of using wizards for control. "What must I do?"

"Bring him to us alive by any means necessary," said Ordric. "Capture his companion Darreth if you must since we believe we can control the Slayer through him."

Garrick began to speak in protest, but Ordric shouted over him, "You have investigated and worked alongside both the Wizard Slayer and his companion; there is no one better to hunt him down. As a Knight of Saidal, it is your sworn duty to serve the Calidign line. Have you already forgotten that?"

Defeated, Garrick looked to the floor. "I have not, Count Ordric."

"Good," said the count with a sneer, "and to aid you in this hunt, we will be sending with you some assistance."

Ordric signaled to a servant, who then bowed and left the room. Upon returning, he was accompanied by a figure cloaked in foreign robes. The black cloth was inlaid with many wide steel rings: the light assassin's mail of distant Askaron. His face was unlike that of the Askarians, however, for his bald head was covered with bone-white skin. Purple veins wormed beneath his sickly flesh, and his eyes were small and sunken. His jaw was broad and strong, and as loose as his robes were, his muscular form was visible beneath the dark cloth. As he walked with cat-like grace into the room, the talwars on each hip silently bobbed as he went. Garrick could not ascertain his age, as his face was barren of any hair, and his skin was pulled tight like a dried corpse.

Upon reaching the throne, he bowed deeply. "This is Morgvid," said Ordric, "an assassin of the Serpent's Hand."

"I have heard much about you, Sir Garrick," said Morgvid.

His accent was as hard to determine as his age. He emphasized plosives like the speakers of the northern Graehalic tongues, while at the same time, his tone carried distinct Askarian subtleties. Garrick nodded to the ghoulish assassin out of politeness, although his face betrayed disgust. "Forgive me," said the knight, "but I am unfamiliar with the Serpent's Hand."

"Do not be ashamed; few on this continent would know of my guild. We are considered the best assassins and manhunters money can buy, and I aim to prove that reputation to Count Ordric and King Torvaren."

The king seemed unnerved at Morgvid's appearance, but a warm smile hid his grimace. "It is a pleasure to have you serve me. Forgive my curiosity, but what caused your complexion to become so…?"

Morgvid grinned. "There are many snakes in Askaron, and each has its own distinct venom. While they most often kill, those of my guild have learned that after refining these dangerous substances, they can have more beneficial properties. My appearance is a side effect of this venom alchemy."

"Interesting," said Torvaren.

"I understand you have fought alongside a Wizard Slayer," said Morgvid, turning his dark eyes to Garrick. "I know many stories of his kind but have yet to see one for myself."

"His kind?" interrupted Ordric, intrigued.

"There are many tales of the Wizard Slayers where I come from," said the assassin, "although I think this Krael may be one of the last. Enemies of magick never live long."

"Interesting," said the count, running a hand down his dark beard.

"I had journeyed with Krael," said Garrick, addressing his soon-to-be partner. "He's of a different make than the average man. He cares not for fame or gold, instead desiring to continue his crusade against magick. I'll have you know that he is an honorable, albeit straightforward and callous, person. I would trust him with my life, and in fact, I already had when we journeyed to Travedd."

"Of course, this feeling of trust will not interfere with your duties, will it, Garrick?" asked Torvaren, which by the tone of his voice was demanding compliance rather than an honest answer.

"It will not, Your Majesty."

"As I thought," said Torvaren. "Now make haste. The Wizard Slayer no doubt gains distance as we speak."

Garrick and Morgvid left through the far end of the hall. From the corner of his eye, the old man watched his new partner with caution. The assassin moved with an eerie grace. Hoping to gain an insight into a man he may have to trust his life with, Garrick asked, "What brings you so far from your homeland, then? Count Ordric couldn't have summoned you all the way from Askaron."

Morgvid's chuckle seemed more like a snicker. "My homeland is Graehal, but fate brought me to Askaron. That is a tale for another time, however. What brings me here is a quest of my own ambition. Many in the Serpent's Hand think I am not experienced enough to attain the rank of Al'Katiil, so I have come to the largest city in the world to find a worthy target and prove my abilities. Besting a Wizard Slayer, even if I am not to kill him outright, is a feat worthy of much respect."

"Are you sure you're up to this task? It seems like you might be going after a target you may not yet be ready for," said Garrick.

"Even if I am outmatched, I have no choice but to exert myself to the fullest. A member of the Serpent's Hand is bound to complete any mission he agrees to. My guild does not tolerate failure."

They rounded a corner of the hall. Garrick's nod served as a casual salute to one of the guards, and the subordinate opened the ornate double doors leading outside. Before he did this, he stared wide-eyed at Morgvid's hideous countenance. The assassin did not seem to care.

"What exactly do you mean by not tolerating failure?" asked Garrick.

"It's cunningly simple," said Morgvid. "They kill me, then finish the job I left behind."

The two stood between the palace itself and a defensive wall. Behind them reached the whitewashed spires of the Calidign Palace, and ahead loomed the decrepit city. Guards and nobles paced about the paved walkways, the polished stones of which shined in the midday sun.

Garrick said, "So a mark set by the Serpent's Hand is a death sentence."

"Or a captivity sentence, in the Wizard Slayer's case, but yes. For centuries we have worked hard to build this reputation. Count Ordric could trust no one better for this task."

Before Morgvid could turn to leave, Garrick asked one final question: "If you only came to Saidal by happenstance, then why did Ordric approach you with this assignment?"

"Actually, it was I who approached him," said Morgvid, an eerie smile on his pallid face. "Rumors of the Wizard Slayer's exploits found my ears, and I approached the governing lords wishing to know more. Fortune seems to be on my side, as I did not expect to be tasked with hunting him down."

The knight could see Morgvid's body poising to turn away, and he thought against pushing his inquiry any further. If the assassin had become irritated, there was no telling on his face. "I'll meet you here in two hours' time," said Garrick. "I have some preparations I need to make."

"As do I."

Eledrith's blade sliced through the cool air that whistled about the tops of the towers of Saidal. Through gritted teeth, he grunted, slashing through imaginary opponents as his silvery-blond hair blew in the wind. As of late, the balcony where he preferred to train had become a haven. Ordric's strange plans put the prince's nerves on edge, and the only way he knew to vent was to hone his skills. With vigor, he moved, focusing on every precise step and being mindful of his weight distribution and edge alignment. He had been practicing for far longer than normal, and his lungs were aching for rest. Over the white stone tiles, his feet slid as he recited the techniques Garrick had taught so many years ago. Each movement was graceful like flowing water until it turned into a fiery slash as the prince's sword reached the pinnacle of its arc.

"You sure are better at this than dancing."

The prince leaped back and raised his weapon. Upon seeing Lady Morwenna sitting on the edge of a fountain, he exhaled in relief. "Hello," he said awkwardly, heart still pounding from exertion.

Dimples formed as Morwenna smiled and tilted her head. As he sheathed his weapon, he said, "So, how long have you been sitting there?"

"Long enough."

The prince quietly laughed as he looked at Morwenna. There was trust in her deep brown eyes, and the flowing auburn hair that gently tumbled down her shoulders was captivating. Realizing that he had been silent for perhaps too long, Eledrith brushed his own sweat-damp hair out of his face and said, "So, what brings you here?"

"My father has more business to do with His Majesty. I figured I could tag along, but he insists his work must remain a secret, so here I am, wandering your palace."

"Come upon anything interesting?"

"You could say that."

The two exchanged looks before shyness overcame them, and their eyes began to wander to the flowers and foliage that rustled in the wind. "So," started the prince, "how have you been?"

"Good, but you seem a bit stressed yourself."

"No, I'm not. I'm just…"

Morwenna raised an eyebrow. The prince sighed. He came to the edge of the fountain, next to where she sat, and watched as the sparkling water crashed into the rippling pool. "Ever since the ball, things have been, well, bad, I guess."

"Bad?" asked Morwenna, resting a supple hand on Eledrith's arm.

"I trusted Darreth and Krael more than anyone here, other than Garrick, but now that they're gone, I feel more alone than ever."

Eledrith wanted nothing more than to rage at the thought of both Count Ordric and King Torvaren, who, for all the prince knew, had caused Krael to flee from whatever plots they had formed. The way Ordric had chastised him, along with the king's flimsy lie, were like a slap in the face which made his blood boil. Morwenna saw Eledrith's jade eyes narrow in anger but was oblivious to how her father played into his distress.

"But I suppose life still goes on," said Eledrith, rage subsiding in the presence of Morwenna.

"Well, if my father continues doing so much business here at the palace, I may be here more often."

Eledrith looked to Morwenna, whose hand still rested on him. She was sitting closer than he had realized. So close, in fact, that the soft frills of her pale blue dress brushed against his leg. Not knowing what to say, Eledrith backed away. He immediately regretted the decision, realizing that it may have been Morwenna who inched closer.

The prince felt a hand on his shoulder, and before he knew what to do, Lady Morwenna had pulled him into the midst of the open space of the garden. "What are you doing?"

"I'm going to teach you how to dance," she said.

"But there's no music."

Shushing the prince, Morwenna clasped his hand and began to count. Following her lead, Eledrith stepped with her, gently moving to her cadence.

Alone on the balcony, they laughed together. The clamor of the chaotic streets could not be heard on the high terrace, where the two danced to their own rhythms and the ethereal whistling of the ocean wind. Whatever words were spoken went unknown to everyone but themselves, and a bond stronger than any formal pact began to intertwine the man and the woman. Together they moved like the virgin-white clouds drifting through the azure sky. For Prince Eledrith, no amount of sword practice could give him the feeling of serenity that he felt at that moment.

"You seem rather cheerful," said Garrick.

He stood in the doorway of Eledrith's chambers. The prince was trying on different formal garbs and overanalyzing his reflection in the mirror. "Yes, I am," he said proudly.

"Things are going well with Lady Morwenna?"

Taking his eyes from the mirror, he turned to Garrick. "That would be an understatement. We finally got a chance to talk earlier today, and well, it, I..."

The knight chuckled as Eledrith stammered. While the prince's giddiness had, for a moment, raised his spirits, solemnity washed over his face. Noticing this, Eledrith asked, "Is there something wrong?"

The old man nodded. Taking a seat in a carved mahogany chair, he stared into a distance beyond the walls of the chamber. "Something is very wrong in this palace, Your Majesty."

"What do you mean? Does this have to do with Krael and Darreth?"

"And what Count Ordric intends to do with them. Have you heard what his plans are for the Outlaw Kingdoms?"

Eledrith set down his latest change of clothes and sat across from Garrick. "I haven't been able to stop thinking about it… Until today, that is."

"I was sworn to secrecy by your father, but since my oath is sworn to House Calidign, I have no regrets in passing this information onto you."

Garrick recounted Count Ordric's plan to utilize the Wizard Slayer. Upon hearing this, Eledrith grew nauseous. "He's a madman!" he said. "You remember how Krael acted in front of the king and how he went against your orders to kill Thalnar. There's simply no way."

"You'll need to convince the count and your father of that. I already agree with you."

Eledrith buried his face in his hands and cursed to himself. "I think I'll have a chance to do that sooner rather than later," he said.

"What do you mean?"

"I'll be having dinner at Ordric's estate later this evening. Lady Morwenna invited me."

Garrick kept a stoic composure, holding back a sense of despair that festered in the corner of his thoughts. "Be careful, Eledrith. There's something to him that I don't think either of us truly understands yet."

Eledrith nodded, his eyes smoldering.

"There's one more thing," the old man continued, "and there's no easy way to say this. I'm being sent to capture Krael."

The prince stood up, sending his chair clattering to the floor behind him. "Why, Garrick? Why would you accept such a task?" he said.

Garrick stayed silent as Eledrith paced throughout the room. After cooling his temper, the prince commanded, "Answer me, Garrick."

"It is my sworn oath to serve the king."

"Damn your oaths, and damn that bastard who sits on the throne," said Eledrith through his teeth.

"I'm sorry, Your Majesty, but—"

"Don't bother."

A silence hung in the room like smoke lurking over charred ruins. Standing up, Garrick said, "I was supposed to leave earlier, but I needed to properly say goodbye."

The prince embraced his mentor.

"It's going to be alright, my boy," said Garrick, knowing in his heart that he may have just told a lie.

The two separated, and the prince composed himself, taming the locks of his silvery hair. "Just remember," continued the old mentor, "to stay strong. There's no shortage of people in this city who wish to influence you. Remember what I have taught you."

Eledrith nodded. "It's going to be hard."

"No one ever said your life was going to be easy."

"Yeah," the prince said to himself.

"I should depart soon, for my mission is urgent. Farwell, Eledrith. I hope to return to you soon."

"Farewell, Garrick."

After a moment, the old mentor left the room. As the door clanged shut, Eledrith realized how alone he truly was.

12
GAMES OF THE MIND

Shadows danced and throbbed in the wavering candlelight. Each object and oddity on the many shelves cast a strange projection on the stone wall behind, whether it be the frayed page edges of an old tome, the thin shell of an animal skull, or the abstract structure of an astronomical model. What caught the candlelight the most and held Count Ordric Maumont's attention like a vise was the signet ring on the table before him. Only in privacy was the count willing to remove that ring, and his hidden study assured that there were no prying eyes watching.

The books that lined the shelves were of the occult: a subject which had been a hidden obsession of the count's. While he had little skill in working spells, his knowledge of eldritch powers was formidable. From the Empire of Ashkazanar to the resurrection of the dead, secrets filled the grimoires hidden in his private study.

The signet ring stood unmoving in the warm glow of the single candle. Each diamond-shaped scale on its serpentine band reflected a glimmer of light. What did not shine were the three empty sockets of the skull in the signet itself, each of which possessed a surreal, unfathomable depth. Into these sockets glared Ordric. "What have you done to me?" he muttered, taking a sip of wine from a gilded chalice.

The ring did not respond and instead stared blankly toward the count.

"I owe so much – nay, everything – to you. My wealth, my power, my…"

The count's tongue fumbled, unwilling to confess such a painful truth. "My wife," he managed.

His whole world rested on the manipulative powers granted by the silver ring. A trembling hand caused his chalice to drop, spilling a wave of deep red as the silver clattered on the stone floor. With his mind under such a weight, he struggled even to think. That weight manifested itself to the count, and he clenched his hands against his head. "But this has to stop. It's all getting out of control now."

The ring's effect was noticeable whenever it was worn. The confidence, almost arrogance, flowed through him. Like a drug, Ordric craved this feeling. His very personality was molded by its influence. Without it, the count was reduced to the timid, nervous man he had been so many years ago. Ordric's fingers dug into the skin of his scalp, disheveling his black hair and breaking through his skin. Like a child without a parent, he began to rock back and forth in a vain attempt at comfort.

The ring remained still.

"Damn the witch that gifted you unto me!" he said, spitting as he cursed.

Ordric remembered this witch vividly. She was unlike Stregana, who was revolting at best. The woman from his memory was alluring beyond words, her lithe form striding with grace from the blackness of the alley where they met. Ordric was a younger man then, and her feline eyes possessed his passions. Her lips parted, whispering her name.

"Shar-Khetra," Ordric growled, hating the woman.

Just then, a knock came from somewhere beyond the privacy of the study. The count swept the ring from the table and slipped it onto his finger. Even in his moment of rebellion, he quickly regressed into his old, unhealthy comforts. Leaving the puddle of wine to sit on the floor, Ordric blew out the candle and strode from his chamber through a slim door. Pushing away his heavy winter cloaks, he replaced the false back of his wardrobe cabinet and stepped into his bedroom just as the knock resounded a second time.

"I'm coming," said the count in a relaxed manner.

Upon opening the door, he was met with the warm, aged face of Idda, his servant. She curtseyed. "My lord, His Majesty Prince Eledrith has just arrived and awaits you in the dining room."

Upon rising and seeing his disheveled appearance, she said, "Also, you may want to tidy yourself up before you head downstairs."

Ordric feigned a chuckle. "Forgive me. I just awoke from a nap."

Idda smiled, nodded, and returned downstairs. Sighing, the count turned to his gold-framed mirror and made himself presentable. Before leaving, he looked down at the silver band around his finger. *I've come too far to turn back now. If I falter here, everything will collapse.*

As Ordric descended the staircase of his estate, he saw Eledrith pacing across the maroon carpet, examining the many paintings on the wall. "Your Majesty," said Ordric, "it is a pleasure to dine with you in my own home."

The prince turned, a frantic look in his eyes. Disguising this with a smile, he said, "The pleasure is mine."

The count walked down the remainder of the stairs and examined the paintings onto which Eledrith had been fixated. "The Maumont family," he stated.

Eledrith was nervous in the count's presence, and he did not know if Ordric could tell. He looked to the tall noble, whose eyes scanned the paintings. The way the count composed himself exuded an aura of power. His strong, broad shoulders were in perfect posture, and his chin was held high. Hoping to avoid awkward silence, the prince said, "I can't find any pictures of you when you were young."

"That's because I married into the family. You see this one here…" He pointed to a portrait of himself and a fair brown-haired woman. "This is the earliest painting you'll see of me."

Eledrith read the inscription on the ornate frame, "Ordric and Camelia Maumont."

"Despite what many assume, I am of common birth."

"Going from common birth to count of one of the greater houses of Saidal is no easy feat. How did you manage it?"

"I caught Camelia's eye," said Ordric, smiling, "but that's a story she can tell. She most likely waits in the dining room for us."

"I'd hate to keep her waiting any longer," said the prince.

Atop a patterned rug sat a long wooden table. Its dark finished surface reflected the glistening of the basted roast boar that, in turn, reflected light from the glistening chandelier suspended by a bronze chain. The walls were of dark stained wood, and the whole of the room held a comforting, warm aura that the Calidign Palace somehow lacked in all its grand marble spectacle. At the end of the table sat Lady Morwenna and her mother, Countess Camelia. The countess's features were strikingly similar to her daughter's, save the subtle wrinkles of age around the corners of her mouth and eyes. After exchanging formalities, the nobles began feasting on the succulent ham and other rich side dishes.

"It's a relief to be out of your family's palace for once," said Ordric, jesting toward the prince. "Sometimes it seems like I live there instead of my own home."

Eledrith's perturbed reaction was covered by Countess Camelia saying, "Indeed it does."

"It's for an important reason. His Majesty and I have been discussing foreign affairs more than ever. Rumor suggests that the two petty kingdoms bordering Saidal may ally with each other. As you know, the Outlaw Kingdoms must remain divided lest they become a threat."

"But that certainly isn't in their best interest, now, is it?" interjected Eledrith.

"The best interest of these upstart kings is to leverage an even higher price on their exports to this city," said the count.

"I'm not speaking for the kings; I mean the overall populace. If we were to intervene, we would gain certainty, but they would lose it. Surely there is a way where both sides can live in peace."

Morwenna eagerly looked to her father, awaiting his response and secretly hoping the prince had cornered him. To her dismay, a sly grin appeared on his bearded face. "You're treading the same paths of thought that I had. If you continue this way, you'll realize that total conquest of the outer lands eliminates the outlaw kings, who are the root of the problem as far as I'm concerned, and the common folk are given peace."

Eledrith pursed his lips in defeat. Ordric said, "Thus we're led to my plan that you yourself dissented to."

Camelia had had enough. "No more politics at the dinner table. You two will have enough time to discuss this at the king's palace."

Eledrith found a flaw in the count's last comment, and in defiance of Countess Camelia, he said, "It was the scope of your plan that I had a problem with. The Outlaw Kingdoms are too fractured to wage a conventional war against."

"I wasn't suggesting we ever wage a conventional war," said the count with a spark in his dark eyes.

"Gentlemen!" said Camelia, ending their debate.

Morwenna rested a hand on Eledrith's arm. At this, the prince let her father have the last word. *And using Krael to subdue wizards and conquering through them is your alternative? Foolish. We barely controlled him when hunting Thalnar*, thought the prince.

"Forgive me, darling," said Ordric.

"So, Eledrith," said the countess, changing the subject, "how has your father been lately?"

"Good," said Eledrith, taking a sip of white wine, "good as ever, really."

"That's good to hear." Camelia smiled.

The rest of the dinner continued without incident, and while small talk bored the prince, he enjoyed the time with Lady Morwenna and her family nonetheless. After a few glasses of wine, even Count Ordric seemed less threatening than he had been. The scheming statesman was gone, instead replaced with a loving husband and father. Long after each had eaten their fill, their conversations continued.

Eledrith stood up from his chair and stretched his arms outward, feeling an ache in his back. Instinctively, a hand reached for it, and he felt the stitches and scarred skin where he had been stabbed in the back when fending off Thalnar's minions. The scar was a cherished keepsake of the adventure. Noticing Eledrith's face grimacing from the ache, Camelia asked, "Is something wrong, Your Majesty?"

"Oh, it's nothing," said Eledrith, "just the wound I got while in Travedd."

"How has that been healing up?" asked Ordric.

"Not very well," admitted the prince. "I've been practicing my swordwork, and it keeps opening up from all the movement."

"I don't think you've ever mentioned it to me," said Morwenna.

"I let my guard down. Didn't notice it until after the fighting was done," Eledrith explained.

"From what Garrick said at the ball, there's more to the story than that," said Ordric.

Morwenna raised an eyebrow to Eledrith, who then looked to Ordric. The count then recounted how the prince refused to harm those under Thalnar's control.

"That must've been quite difficult," said Camelia, "to not strike against people that intended to kill you."

"Not difficult for him," said Morwenna, poking a playful finger at Eledrith. "He practices every chance he gets."

Eledrith smiled awkwardly amidst the praise, unsure how to handle Morwenna's tipsy flirting.

Ordric said, "Considering you keep opening that wound, why don't we test your mettle with a game that allows its players to sit still? How good are you at *sakhmet*?"

"Garrick tried teaching me, but I never really got the hang of it," said Eledrith.

"It's never too late to learn," said Ordric. "Besides, I'm sure Morwenna would love to have the first game."

"I'll leave you to your games. I think I'm going to retire for the night," said Camelia.

As the countess left for bed, Ordric, Morwenna, and Prince Eledrith made their way to the lounge, where a *sakhmet* board sat on a small side table between two velvet-cushioned chairs. The board itself was a slab of polished marble tile made up of black and white hexagons. On either side of the board were carved ivory and onyx pieces depicting various types of soldiers, save one. Grand bat-like wings sprang from the largest and most notable piece of each army: a dragon. Morwenna sat in one chair and began setting each piece on her side of the board. Following suit, Eledrith did so with his half of the pieces. Garrick's instructions on setting up the board were a distant memory, and when this memory failed the prince, he copied Morwenna's half of the board.

"That's not right," said Morwenna.

"Pardon?"

"Your dragon and knight should be switched," she said. "Our setups shouldn't be symmetrical."

With a sheepish smile, Eledrith said, "I knew that. I was just testing you."

Fixing his pieces for him, Morwenna shot a playful look.

"Go easy on him," said Ordric. "I'm guessing it's been a while since you last played, Eledrith?"

"You could say that, yeah."

In truth, the prince had never finished a full game, but he didn't let that detail hinder his confidence. Amidst the mundane white hexagons were seven black ones embellished with a trim of gold, and the prince recognized these as the game's objective. The first player to capture four of the black hexes, which were called castles by those who knew the game better than Eledrith, was the victor. After the prince's first hesitant turn, Morwenna brought her pieces into play. Standing with his back to the glowing hearth, Ordric watched quietly.

As Morwenna captured her fourth castle, Eledrith struck his forehead with his palm. "How did I not see that?"

Ordric chuckled. "You did well, Eledrith. Surprisingly well, actually. I don't usually last that long against her. Then again, I usually have more than three pieces left."

"You're too eager to bring out the dragon," said Morwenna. "It can fly to any hex other than a castle, but it can be quickly countered and taken out of play. It's best to only use it when you need to."

Eledrith stood up. "Well, I tried my best."

Before the prince could retreat any further, Ordric said to Morwenna, "Let me have the next game. I'm eager to see how I fare against him."

Sitting back down, Eledrith prepared the *sakhmet* board for another game. Before long, the two miniature armies were poised against one another. The prince was given the first turn again, this time moving a knight piece to one of the castle hexes on the side of the board.

"Bold strategy," said Ordric. "I suppose I should meet it with an equally bold one."

The count similarly moved his knight on his side of the board. "Unless you were trying to bait me," continued the count.

Eledrith kept his eyes on the board to not subconsciously reveal his frustration. The first move was, as Ordric had figured, a bait to pull his forces away from the center of the board. The following turns proved to be as tense as the first, with Count Ordric utilizing his experience with the game to predict each of Eledrith's plans. Adhering to Morwenna's advice, the prince kept his dragon out of the fray, reserving it for the perfect moment.

As the two armies spread across the board, the game began to look like a stalemate. Every one of the castle spaces on the edge of the board was occupied, and only the hex in the center remained. Each player had three castles captured, making the one in the center the focus of their attention. Soldiers of white and black surrounded the space as if besieging it, waiting for the command to attack. Alone in the hex stood Ordric's assassin pawn. The assassin was perhaps the most valuable piece other than the dragon. Its unique ability to move quickly across the board allowed it to be placed in a castle early on, and while it couldn't eliminate another piece, if it was attacked, both pieces were removed.

The most glaring of the assassin's drawbacks was that the castle it occupied was not considered captured. On this technicality, the whole game rested. The small onyx pawn sat there, carved in the likeness of a hooded figure, to the lament of both Eledrith and Ordric.

The count was astonished at how quickly Eledrith had picked up the minute strategies of the game. Sure, he had lost against Morwenna, but if he could be taken at his word, that was the prince's first game in years. "It's your turn, Your Majesty," said the count, irritated that a beginner was so close to beating him.

"I know."

Ordric watched his opponent's jade eyes flicker between different areas of the board. *Now is the time to test his resistance to this ring*, he thought. *With a strong will, my powers can be defied, but an arbitrary decision is far more malleable.* Ordric casually rested his head in his hand, the three dark eyes of his signet ring staring at Eledrith.

It was then that the prince's eyes drifted to the back half of the marble board. A lone spearman piece stood on the castle, otherwise unprotected. Ordric, in his fixation on the board's center, had moved the stronger troops that had reinforced that hex. Eledrith had not yet utilized his dragon, and while it couldn't immediately move onto the castle, it could fly to an adjacent hex and capture it on the following turn. Upon realizing this, Eledrith smiled. It was an obtuse strategy, not easily found amidst the chaos of the game. He picked up the white figurine and moved it to the far side of the board. "You weren't expecting that one, were you?"

The count appeared stunned. "No, I wasn't," he said, looking not at the board but at the prince himself.

"Is there something wrong, Father?" asked Morwenna.

"No," said the count, "I just can't believe I lost out of nowhere."

Morwenna's face hardened. She wasn't buying her father's lie.

"The game's not over yet," said Eledrith. "It's still going to take me one more turn to capture that space."

As expected, there was no way for the count to counter the prince's strategy, and in the following turn, Eledrith captured his fourth castle. At his opponent's victory, Ordric shook his hand and offered a warm smile, but there was still a hint of apprehension on his face. "Good game, Your Majesty. You'll make a fine king with that kind of tactical prowess."

"Thank you," said the prince, growing meek amidst the praise. "I'll probably need a little more practice. Let's not forget how badly I lost to your daughter."

"Then she will be a good queen."

Both Eledrith and Morwenna grew shy at the thought. "This has been great fun," said Ordric, "but this old man needs some sleep after all the excitement."

After bidding the prince and his daughter a good night, Ordric left for his chambers, leaving the two alone in the warm glow of the dying fire.

"I had fun," said the prince with a smile.

Morwenna's countenance was stern. After a sigh, she said, "There's something we need to discuss."

"Is everything alright?"

After glancing at where her father had left, she said, "How about we take a short walk? Enjoy the night air?"

"Sure," said Eledrith.

Surrounding the Maumont Estate was a small yard where sculptures of old bygone nobles stood above a well-kept lawn. The typical green of the grass appeared a metallic blue in the faint starlight. Walking along a winding paved path, the prince held Morwenna close by the waist. "Is this about your father?" he asked.

She nodded. "What you two argued about over dinner just isn't sitting right with me."

"Did I say something wrong?"

"I'd prefer you didn't speak on the subject at all. His plans frighten me. The way he talks about them frightens me. I don't want you to be like that."

"What do you mean? I hate his plans of conquest. Need I remind you I was arguing against them?"

"Yes, you were," said Morwenna, sitting at the base of one of the opulent statues. "It's just that you're both so idealistic about these foreign affairs."

"I'm a prince, Morwenna. I need to have stances on the subject."

Morwenna crossed her arms and leaned against the stone leg behind her. After she remained silent, Eledrith said, "I still don't understand why you're so angry."

"It's because the both of you sounded so power hungry, like you knew what was best for everyone."

"If I'm to rule, shouldn't that be my concern?"

"I guess so. Maybe I am overreacting. It's because of how my father's been lately. It's put me on edge. I don't want you to be pulled into what he's doing."

Eledrith looked down at Morwenna. She was drained. A weight pulled down on her heart, and only now did she show it. Sitting next to her and placing his arm back around her waist, the prince said, "I'm sorry."

Resting her head underneath his chin, Morwenna closed her eyes.

The midnight beak of a raven tore at the dried flesh of the roadside corpse. Long since scavenged of any valuables by passersby, the bodies of Amris and his bodyguards had begun to bloat. The whole area reeked, and out of the hunting party that had approached, only Morgvid seemed unaffected. He squatted down next to Amris's body, shooing away the carrion bird that had delved its entire beak into the corpse's eye socket. With calculating bloodshot eyes, the assassin of the Serpent's Hand examined the dead face, marveling at how the jaw had caved in backward.

Silently, the pale assassin rose. He examined the rest of the scene, twisting his head like a snake's as he fit together each piece of the gruesome puzzle. A cold wind blew over the discolored bodies, and scraps of flesh torn by wolves gently waved like macabre ribbons. The assassin's hairless brow bent in frustration as he struggled to discriminate between pre and postmortem wounds.

A distance up the road, upwind of the bodies, sat Garrick and twenty armored men, waiting as the expert hunter did his work. Noticing his companion's frustration, Garrick called out, "I'd reckon this is the Slayer's doing, given the mess."

Returning to his horse, Morgvid remounted with one graceful motion, sending his armored robes waving like flags as he leaped into the saddle. "Then we should make haste," he said, speaking in his exotic accent. "These men have been dead for days."

A harsh snap of the reins sent Morgvid's horse into a full gallop, and Garrick followed with equal speed. The twenty-strong regiment of Saidalian men-at-arms charged behind, reducing the corpses to unrecognizable piles of gore as the heavy hooves of the mounts fell unrelenting.

13
REFUGE IN THE MOUNTAINS

Darreth nearly fell out of the wagon as Krael awoke with a roar.

The Slayer's black hair clung to the cold sweat on his brow, and the entirety of his body ached. Lorienne, who sat on the wagon's edge, snapped around and drew her falchion. Darreth's face was pale and stricken with surprise. Gasping, he said, "Glad to see you're finally awake."

The Kolgathian poised himself upright and observed his surroundings. After looking puzzled at the woman who still had yet to sheathe her sword, Darreth explained, "She's with us, now."

Krael was still trying to find his bearings. He examined his surroundings, noticing that the coniferous pine forest they traveled through was much different than the thin, leafless trees in the wilderness around Saidal. "How long have I slept?"

"Four days, I think," said Darreth. This statement came casually from the elf-blooded, as he was used to the Wizard Slayer's hibernation after receiving grievous wounds. Perhaps a trait of his race, Krael would sleep for days at a time, replenishing blood and repairing bones. This quick healing came at the cost of scarring and lingering pains, both of which Krael easily ignored.

After nodding and grunting, Krael said, "I hunger."

"We all do," said Lorienne, sheathing her falchion. "We're planning on stopping for supplies at the next town."

The barbarian examined the woman, whose graceful sheathing betrayed her skill. Noticing his stare, the sword-dancer
narrowed her large brown eyes. "What, never seen a woman before?"

"You were with us," said Krael, whose poor lingual skills prevented him from being more precise. "Why do you stay?"

"Why did you bother to save me in the first place?" asked Lorienne.

After a moment to organize his thoughts, Krael said, "Amris
was evil. I kill evil."

Lorienne leaned backward and crossed her arms, puzzled.
"Darreth said you were a Wizard Slayer, though."

Darreth began to talk over his shoulder, stepping in so he
wouldn't have to listen to Krael's stumbling verbiage. "A bunch
of monks raised him, and while they couldn't teach him how to
talk right, they drilled into his head the idea of good and evil a
little too well. That's why he hates magick; it's a pure form of
evil."

Good and evil, it's never that clear-cut, thought Lorienne.

"Why do you stay?" repeated the Kolgathian.

The sword-dancer could feel Darreth's curious eyes glance
back at her. "Purely out of necessity. I would be lost without
someone who knows these lands," she stated matter-of-factly.

As they rode the inclining terrain of the frigid forest, Lorienne
explained that she was a sword-dancer, which was also the reason
she was captured and sold in the first place. Many warlords of the
Outlaw Kingdoms would pay a high price for someone with
beauty and skill like her. As the wagon rolled onward, light snow
began to drift to the ground. While none of the white powder accumulated, the air was still as frigid as winter, and soon the
travelers concluded that they would also need shelter before nightfall.

Ahead, the road forked, and planted at the intersection was a
tall wooden stake that served as a signpost. Most notable was the

severed head atop the stake. Its face was stout and misshapen, likely caused by inbreeding. A thin, straggly beard blew in the wind. Dotting the discolored gums of the gaping mouth were sparse, crooked teeth.

"Raven's Watch, four leagues ahead," said Darreth, ignoring the macabre decoration and reading the sign aloud.

"What is that?" asked Lorienne. "It's too small to be a man's head."

The head was about the size of a child's, but the ugly features and facial hair were uncharacteristic of youth. As he whipped the reins and turned toward Raven's Watch, Darreth asked, "Never seen a dwarf before?"

"No," said Lorienne, staring at the head as they passed, "they're but a myth in Valmoria."

The Slayer scoffed.

"They're not a myth up here," said Darreth. "Krael here's probably killed hundreds."

"So are the stories true?" asked Lorienne. "Do they kill and eat anything, or anyone, they can get their hands on?"

"Oh yeah, they're vicious little pricks," said the elf-blooded, "but it depends on their numbers. One or two, and they won't do much, but when a whole pack is on you, they fight without wavering. Normally they stay in their underground holes, but if food is scarce, they'll sometimes raid towns."

"I heard if you pay them in gold, they'll let you be, but that might just be an old Colanthian wives' tale."

"They're not even smart enough to talk, let alone barter with. Think of dwarves more like animals than people."

As Lorienne and Darreth talked about the stunted, degenerate race, Krael remembered his many battles with the creatures. Their vile maws gnashed as stout arms wielding makeshift weapons stabbed and sliced. They were driven by hunger and anger, too dim-witted for higher rational thought.

"Supposedly, they were once a noble race," said Darreth. "They dug huge cities underneath mountains and mined precious stones. Like all such legends, these cities are long lost, and one calamity or another led to the dwarves' downfall. Some say it was isolation. After being underground for so long, they went communally insane. Others think it was some curse."

"And what do you think?" asked the sword-dancer.

After a short time of pondering, Darreth said, "I don't know. Part of me wishes they were made that way. If noble dwarves can turn into monsters, we humans could, too."

Lorienne then looked at the Kolgathian, who by appearance alone was more monster than man. *If it were not for his training in Mog Muhtar*, she pondered, *how bestial would this man be?*

The great wall of thick pines, now gently frosted white with powdery snow, opened to a wide, clear area where half a dozen farmsteads dotted the harvested soil. Beyond it, the travelers saw the rounded peaks of the Wylderen Mountains. Only at precipices was the granite of the mountains exposed, otherwise covered under the forest of evergreens. Far below these peaks sat the destination of the hungry travelers. Like most settlements in the Outlaw Kingdoms, a thick, spiked palisade surrounded the log-cabin-style buildings of the town. Lining the tops of the pointed timbers were the impaled heads of more dwarves, their asymmetrical faces frozen in a cry of agony. Guardhouses peered above the wall, each perched atop four stilt-like beams. From the center of the town rose a round stone tower, the likeness of which was starkly different from the settlement. Its construction was alien and from a forgotten age. Four solid buttresses ran up its featureless gray walls. Crumbling masonry at the tower's peak, as well as rusted and exposed iron support rods, showed the structure was much shorter than it once was. As the wagon rolled toward the main gate, someone called down from one of the guardhouses, "Hail, there! What is your business here in Raven's Watch?"

"Supplies and decent lodging," said Darreth, seeing no reason to lie.

The guard said, "You'll find rooms at the Raven's Rest, which is just north of the tower. As for supplies, the market is in the southern half of town, on your right."

"Thank you, kind sir!" said Darreth, surprised at the guard's unnecessary hospitality.

As the double wooden doors opened, the black stallions pulled the wagon into the town and turned north toward the Raven's Rest. The small dirt street was becoming muddy with the falling snow, and the log-walled houses made each turn sharp and difficult for a drawn load. To the traveler's delight, they blended into the bustle of the town easily. While some heads turned to examine the newcomers, most were busy with their own business.

The wagon stopped outside the largest of the town's structures, save the tower itself. The Raven's Rest stood two stories high, and the many windows of the rooms flickered with a warm glow. The dancing drone of a hurdy-gurdy was heard alongside clinking mugs and hoarse bellows of laughter. The companions, eager to drive the chill from their aching bones, pushed open the door and strode into the common room.

The three wound their way between crowded tables to a secluded corner of the room, wherein the shadow of the firelight sat an empty table. "You two wait here. I'll get us some food," said Darreth.

Obeying their companion, the two sat down and doffed their cloaks. As the elf-blooded bartered, Krael sat against the wall, scanning the room. Mere feet away, a group of what looked to be woodcutters by their builds and sap-stained garb threw knives at a target on a wall. A gambling game erupted into a roar of laughter as a bluff was called. Sitting next to the fire was an old, hooded man who steadily turned the crank of the hurdy-gurdy, filling the whole place with music.

"So, I've been hesitant to ask you this," said Lorienne, "but what exactly did you and Darreth do to become fugitives?"

"Long story," said the Slayer.

Lorienne raised a speculative eyebrow. "Summarize it," she commanded.

"The king wished to control me."

"That's it?"

Krael nodded, having no desire to elaborate.

"You are one of a kind, aren't you?" Lorienne said.

In time, Darreth returned to the table with bowls of stew and enough beer to last them the night. While everyone was hungry, Krael wolfed down his food quickest of all. Before Darreth was halfway to the bottom of his bowl, the Slayer said, "More."

Struggling not to spit out his mouthful in surprise, the elf-blooded swallowed and said, "Slow down! Keep eating at that rate, and we'll be broke before we go to bed."

"How much money do we have left?" asked Lorienne.

"Not much," said Darreth, searching for a bite of meat in the warm brown broth of the stew. "All we have is what Amris had in his pockets. We need to make some coin if we're gonna buy enough supplies to keep moving."

"Maybe we could win some by gambling," said Lorienne, eyeing the group of men hurling knives at the wall.

"Or some more honest work," said Darreth, the fear of debt collectors lingering over his thoughts.

"Trust me," said Lorienne.

Not bothering to change Darreth's mind, the sword-dancer spun out of her seat and began talking to a man with beer suds dripping from his mustache. He tossed a knife in his hand, clearly comfortable with the tool and eager to put his skills, even when inebriated, to the test.

"I can't look," said Darreth. "Come on, Krael, let's find some real work."

The two walked across the room, and the Slayer's body and face, no longer hidden by his cloak, drew much attention. Wishing to avoid any interaction, Krael kept his eyes forward as he followed his much shorter companion.

"Hello, it's me again," said Darreth to the establishment's owner.

The broad-shouldered man ran a hand through his red beard. "Now what do you want? Any more haggling and I'll have you thrown out of here."

"Actually, I was wondering where a man could find some honest work for a few days in this town."

The owner let out a deep, hearty laugh. As he and the elf-blooded discussed mundane labor opportunities, Krael's attention drifted between conversations amidst the crowd.

"It's too cold for this time of year," said a man.

Another voice from another table said, "Aye, don't see too many of them this side o' the Wylderens, but I'd still keep me eye out."

"You think it could be *magick*?"

Just as Krael's mind was becoming exhausted from listening to spoken language, the word *magick* rang like the snapping of a branch in an otherwise silent forest. Leaving his companion's side, he strode in the direction of the word. His purposeful steps gathered the attention of many, but the Kolgathian continued nonetheless. As he came to the table where he thought the word was spoken, he asked, "You speak of magick?"

Every head at the long wooden table turned to the barbarian. They were well-built men of varying ages, perhaps mercenaries or off-duty guards. Heavy gambesons provided them warmth and protection, and shortswords hung in leather scabbards on their hips. The group's leader, whose dark brown hair glistened with subtle streaks of gray, said, "And what would it mean to ye, my eavesdropping friend?"

"I kill wizards," said Krael, the unwelcoming looks of the men not hindering his straightforwardness.

A smirk came to the eldest's mustached face. "Really, now?"

The dead stare was enough of an answer for the man, who took the hulking barbarian at his word with a shrug. "It's our lord's newborn son, ye see. He's sick, but it's a sickness like no other. Cold as a corpse he is, yet he lives."

"Barely," added another at the table. "I've never heard a newborn wheeze like that. It's a sound that I don't wish to remember."

"The child's parents…" started the Slayer.

"They're the rulers of Raven's Watch," said the veteran guard. "Well, his father, Lord Artreth, still is. His mother died givin' birth to him."

"What caused the curse?" said Krael bluntly.

The men at the table murmured to each other. "We're not even sure if it's magick," one of them said.

"But if it is," said the group's leader, "do ye think ye could save the child?"

Krael spoke even slower than usual, choosing his words carefully. "I will kill whoever caused the curse."

"Perhaps I should bring ye to Lord Artreth himself," said the old guard, pushing himself up from the table. "If yer words be truth, then he'll want to speak to ye."

The man approached, his gait marred by a limp. As he came to the Slayer, he bowed. "Cap'n Galfred, at yer service."

"Krael. Wizard Slayer."

Galfred glanced through a window at the darkening winter sky. "We best be off to the tower soon, then."

Before the men could turn to leave, Darreth approached, confused. "Krael, what's going on?"

"I'm hunting."

The elf-blooded stammered, forming half-words in frustration. After gathering himself, he managed, "Right now? For all we know, Torvaren's men could be but a few leagues away!"

Krael remained silent, disregarding his friend's warnings.

"I guess I'm not stopping you," said Darreth, remembering not to come between the Slayer and his prey. "But I wasn't able to find any short-term work for us. How will we pay for supplies?"

As Galfred beckoned him to hurry, Krael turned to Darreth and said, "I'll be back."

"When?"

"When the wizard is dead."

With that, the door to the Raven's Rest opened, and a spray of white snow billowed in, chilling patrons who sat nearby. Fighting the sudden blizzard, Krael and Galfred wrapped their cloaks about them and strode into the night.

Darreth returned to his table in defeat. Head in his hands, he stared at the bottom of his empty wooden bowl, the last few drops of lukewarm broth sitting stagnant. *There's still the question of money and supplies*, he thought.

The elf-blooded's pouting ended when a sudden clamor erupted from the table next to him. The drunken band Lorienne had been gambling with had thrown their hands up in surprise, cheering like a pack of baboons. Their attention was fixed on the wall, where a sketch of a wanted criminal had been nailed. A dagger was stuck just to the side of the slash-riddled face. In the center of the sketch, still vibrating from impact, was the blade that Lorienne had thrown.

Money changed hands as the bets were paid out. Lorienne stood with one hand on her hip and the other outstretched, coin after coin clinking into her palm. "And you boys thought women didn't know how to throw knives," she boasted.

Upon seeing Darreth, Lorienne returned to the table, letting her winnings clatter onto the wooden surface. "So, how did I do?" she asked, a cocky smile on her lips.

"Not bad at all," said the elf-blooded.

Darreth counted the silver coins, each minted with various designs. Some bore crowns, sigils, faces, and coats of arms. The only commonality between the currencies was their material and weight. Countless warlords of the Outlaw Kingdoms stamped their faces on coinage, hoping to prolong their legacy. While their names were quickly forgotten, their likenesses continued.

"Thirty in all," said Darreth.

"I'm not from around here," said Lorienne. "How much is that, exactly?"

"Enough to buy us some more food and maybe – if we're lucky – enough supplies for a week."

"Then I should get back to throwing," said the sword-dancer. "It took me a couple of games to get used to their knife's weight, but now I feel warmed up."

Darreth shook his head. "I wouldn't risk it. We should try to keep a low profile as much as possible."

"You're no fun," said Lorienne, leaning back into her chair, one arm poised on its back. "Where did Krael go?"

"Hunting."

"You mean… *wizard* hunting?"

"Yeah."

"So, he can run off, but I can't keep earning us money here?"

"No one can stop Krael from doing it. It's the only thing he cares about, and he lets nothing get in his way. He didn't take an oath or vow; it's something at the heart of who he is."

"Strange," Lorienne said, watching the knife throwers with a disgruntled look on her face.

A silence hung between the two, and the elf-blooded prayed that Lorienne would not break it. When she did, her words surprised him. "Why do you follow Krael, then?"

"I've seen the evils magick can do. If I'm going to live a good life, it would have to be one battling against those dark powers," he answered.

Lorienne raised her eyebrows, surprised at the depth of Darreth's answer. Before he could be asked another question, he stood up, stretched his arms toward the ceiling, and said, "It's been one hell of a day. I think I'll go to bed."

"As will I. Did you get two rooms?"

"No, we're on a strict budget."

"Then I'll get another myself," said the sword-dancer, scraping a handful of silver from the table.

"We're going to need that for supplies!"

Lorienne shot the elf-blooded a deadly glare. "I'll be sleeping in my own room, thank you. Besides, these are my winnings, anyway."

The sword-dancer's hips swayed as she strode to the owner of the Raven's Rest.

"Damn, she's pretty," Darreth muttered.

"A huge man with fangs, eh?"

"And a shorter fellow wearing a headband with dark blond hair," said Garrick.

The old knight stood in the doorway of the roadside inn, envious of the warmth that the small building contained.

The pot-bellied innkeeper scratched his balding head. "No, that doesn't seem familiar either. These men were heading east, you said?"

"I have reason to believe so, yes."

"Then they may have spent the night in Raven's Watch," said the innkeeper, gesturing to the Wylderen Mountains that loomed in the distance. "It's a pretty big town about half a day's travel from here. If these men be fugitives like you say, that town would be the perfect place to hide."

"Raven's Watch," said Garrick to himself, trying to find the settlement on the tree-covered mountainside.

"Just keep following this road here. When it splits, take the one most traveled. It's the largest town in the Wylderens."

"Thank you," said Garrick.

The knight reached into his pouch and produced a coin. "For your troubles," he said, passing it to his informant.

Garrick crossed the road and returned to the encampment, the fires of which barely clung to life in the snowy wind. Tucking his face into his fur-lined collar, he continued along the line of tents until he came to Morgvid's. A verbal call in the howling wind would be futile, so Garrick pulled back the flap of his comrade's tent, carefully shielding the interior from the elements with his own body. He began to say, "The Wizard Slayer may be—"

"Shhh…"

The assassin held a finger to his dark, discolored lips. In his other hand was a pipette, and from its refined end dripped a sickly substance. Drop by drop, Morgvid added the dark liquid to a heated vial. As one chemical mixed with another, a vapor was produced, and the whole tent was filled with an insufferable stench.

Garrick's scarred face wrinkled with disgust. "Damn, that's a foul smell!"

The reek was like a festering mold yet held a peculiar acidic sting. Seemingly unfazed by this, Morgvid answered. "The tools of the Serpent's Hand have no need to be pleasurable to the senses."

"I can tell," said Garrick, trying his best not to dry heave.

"The venom of the black asp is widely known to be a neurotoxin. Its victims will convulse within seconds of a bite. However, if the victim were to have certain antivenoms, this effect is reduced to extreme paranoia."

"So, you're making a fear drug?"

"No. The effect is changed when the black asp's venom is mixed with isolated toxins of the Kihanjiri krait. What is produced is a formidable stimulant indeed. Only after centuries of experimentation did the Serpent's Hand discover combinations such as this, and only by accident. They say the greatest scientific discoveries were made in the torture chambers of my guild's keeps."

The assassin's dark eyes glimmered in the candlelight as he examined his handiwork. Satisfied, he stoppered the vial and placed it in a protective pouch. "Rumor tells that the Wizard Slayers were trained using a similar snake alchemy," he said.

"You know of their training?"

"Only rumors, since they are so few. The Kolgathian slaves were locked in a pit of black asps for days."

"They'd go mad if the snakes didn't get to them first," said Garrick.

"And that's what makes their training so effective. So they would not die from the asps' bites, the Kolgathians were given the antivenom."

"Didn't you mention that it causes paranoia?"

Morgvid smiled, making his pale face seem even more skull-like. "Very astute of you, Sir Garrick. The few who could persevere through the days of fear and agony had their minds... remade. Charms and enchantments have no effect on them. Fear means nothing to them. The Wizard Slayers become inhuman forces of sheer will."

That definitely sounds like Krael, thought Garrick. "Anyway," began the old knight, "the innkeeper suggested we head to Raven's Watch, a town just half a day's travel from here. Krael may be hiding out there."

Morgvid nodded. "Good. I grow eager to meet a Hound of Mog Muhtar in the flesh."

14
THE ENCIRCLING STORM

Galfred reached for the knocker on the door of Artreth's tower. An iron ring hung in the mouth of a face whose bestial features were hidden by new-fallen snow. As Galfred rapped the knocker against the door, its clanging was muffled by the blizzard. Krael, standing next to the guard, looked up at the old structure. The tower's pinnacle was barely visible amidst the torrent of snow. The broken stone and jutting iron beams were repurposed into a makeshift battlement.

The door opened, and after a short greeting with a servant, Galfred led Krael inside. A dying fire illuminated the chamber. The walls were unplastered, and the jagged edges of bricks cast many trembling shadows. In the gloom sat a long wooden table, its empty surface covered with a thin layer of dust. At first, the place seemed vacant, except for the tall and thin servant greeting Krael and the guard. Then, as the roaring winds were shut out with the door closing, they heard the strained breathing.

The babe's breaths were hoarse. His soft little voice seemed to call for help with each exhale. Phlegm choked this sound, and on occasion, the rhythm was broken so harshly that the child went into a fit of hacking coughs. Upon hearing this, Galfred's face immediately grew solemn.

"And who dares to request an audience at such a late hour?"

The voice had come from behind a cushioned armchair, the high back of which hid the speaker. Stepping forward, the old guard introduced himself. "It is I, Captain Galfred, my liege."

"What do you want?" said Lord Artreth, still facing the fire.

"I've brought someone that may be able to help."

The lord sat up and turned from his chair. Atop a head of stringy shoulder-length red hair sat an iron circlet. Artreth's face was gaunt and grief-stricken, sunken eyes hollow with sorrow. "Help?" he said, shaking his head. "Help? Do not torture me with such promises."

Disregarding his visitors, Artreth returned to the hearth, looking down at a small crib. From it continued the weak wheezing breaths.

Galfred limped forward. "But my liege, this man, Krael, is not another herbalist or healer. He can end yer son's curse at its source!"

Artreth stood silent. The only things that moved in the room were the dancing shadows.

Krael, in his slow, awkward dialect, spoke. "I kill users of magick."

As he turned to see the Kolgathian, the spark of fire reflected in Artreth's eye. "Can that truly be done?"

The Slayer nodded.

"Perhaps there is a chance," said the lord, a new vigor in his tone. "Come, sit. I suppose you should hear the whole story from the beginning."

While his lord's newfound optimism was a welcome change in mood, Galfred feared how it could come crashing down if Krael's efforts proved unsuccessful. He sat in a chair, and the Slayer followed suit, catching a glimpse of the child as he passed. He was small, prematurely born, and his head seemed too large for his slender body. The skin was pale and, in many places, bruising a purplish green. What stood out most, though, was how he shivered. Despite being a foot away from the fire, the little arms and legs trembled violently. Anguish showed on the features of the small face, his large eyes closed tight. His breathing was a constant reminder of the agony he endured.

"Caldila and I were wed three years ago, and I'll be the first to admit that I was not a good husband. I wasn't always faithful…"

Artreth choked on his words, but after gathering himself, he found the strength to continue. "But we worked things out. I was eager to sire a child with her, and there's something about being a father and husband that changes a man. I began to see the world differently once little Sebastian came along.

"But one man thought that I could not change. Vornond was his name, and he and Caldila had a short history when they were much younger. But mark my words, there is something different about that man. Kept to himself too much. But you'll know soon enough just how vile that man really is.

"It happened the night when Caldila caught me… being unfaithful. She was so hurt she stormed off into the woods, crying. Of course, it was then that the bastard approached her. Vornond offered his love, saying she deserved better than me. While he may have been right, Caldila spurned him. His pride wounded, Vornond cursed my wife so that any children she would have would be born with a horrible sickness. We thought they were just empty words, but I realized how wrong I was after Sebastian was born. The curse was so fierce that it killed Caldila when she gave birth.

"Somehow, Sebastian survived. When he was born, the poor babe looked as sickly as he does now. He eats little and barely sleeps, yet he lives – if you can call that life."

Artreth's eyes fell to the baby, who seemed to breathe easier, at least for the time being. The hoarse rasps were slower, but they still echoed off the cold stone walls.

"I hear his voice in the night," continued the lord, eyes now staring into the fire. "Whispers come on the midnight wind, mocking me and the remnants of my family."

"Er, my liege," said Galfred, "are ye certain ye ain't just—"

"Vornond speaks!" cried Artreth, lunging forward and grabbing the old guard by the lapels. "On my anguish, that wretched creature thrives. Night after night, he taunts me as if Sebastian's painful cries weren't enough!"

Regretting his outburst, Artreth retreated back to his seat. "I'm sorry," he said.

Sebastian fell into a fit of coughing. The baby's little arms swung as his tongue extended, struggling to clear his airway.

"If I kill Vornond," said Krael, "I cannot promise the curse will be lifted."

Artreth nodded. "I understand. Even if that is the case, his death will bring me a sense of peace."

Galfred asked, "What if Vornond's curse is keeping the child alive?"

"Then he will suffer no more when Vornond is slain," said Artreth.

The lines in the lord's face deepened as he brooded. Outside, the wind whistled and screeched around the buttresses of the tower. At this, the lord tilted his head, eyes wide in fear. "He hears us," he muttered. "He is aware that we plot against him."

"So be it," Krael snarled. For a split second, Artreth thought he saw the Slayer's pupils glow, reflecting the firelight.

Graying brows furrowed, Galfred was astounded by the two men that sat before him. On his right was the hollow husk of a man who had been withered by mourning and desperation. Artreth's mind tortured him, speaking of hearing voices in the night. On Galfred's left sat Krael, the fanged barbarian who seemed unfazed by insurmountable odds. Something dire was about to unfold, or the guard was in the presence of two madmen. Hoping the latter was not the case, he asked, "How will ye find Vornond, Krael? The mountain is vast, and there's no knowing where the bastard could be hiding."

The Slayer looked to the old man and asked, "Any towns nearby?"

Shaking his head, the old guard answered. "Not unless ye count Twin Falls, but that place was abandoned a year ago after the avalanche."

Galfred saw a spark in the Kolgathian's eye, then nodded. "I suppose that'd be the place."

"Tomorrow, I go to Twin Falls," said Krael, rising from his seat.

"Thank you, Krael," said Artreth. "How should I compensate you? Surely, putting your own life at risk is worth a few gold pieces at least."

The Slayer shook his head. "Just enough for a room."

For a moment, the lord was speechless. After examining the far-from-normal man, he realized that such a modest request was not totally out of the question. "Alright, but it'll be the finest room in the Raven's Rest. And, if you are successful tomorrow, I will consider myself in your debt."

As Krael left into the blizzard outside, Sebastian's breathing became even more hoarse.

The storm had not let up at any point throughout the night. What had been dry ground the previous day was now covered in a foot of fresh snow, and the roaring wind made the air feel painfully cold. Bundled in furs and heavy cloaks, Krael marched off into the wilderness despite the atrocious weather. In his gloved hand was a heavy war hammer, gifted to him by Galfred. The four corners of its head stuck out like claws, and the hook on the opposite side tapered to a sinister point. While the weapon was relatively light for the Kolgathian, it would serve its purpose.

Darreth had been irritated by the Slayer's insistence on not being paid, but the elf-blooded was in no position to argue. He and

Lorienne would stay in the warm Raven's Rest, perhaps snagging a small sum here and there. Thinking that no one in their right mind would be out in such weather, Darreth did not feel the urge to keep moving, for if anyone from Saidal was on their tail, they would be slowed to a crawl.

As Krael left the shelter of the walled town, the full fury of the wind crashed against him, piercing the many layers of thick furs. Gritting his teeth, he marched faster, hoping the increased circulation of blood would stave off the cold. This worked for a time, and while his fogging breath left ice on the furs near his face, the pangs of numbness only reached his fingers and toes.

Despite the cold, the mountainside was beautiful. Each of the dark green pines was decorated with a layer of glistening snow, with fine flakes sparkling brightly even in the weak light of the overcast sun. So powerful were the winds of the previous night that wide, sweeping drifts formed beneath the cover of the trees. Walking through this deep snow was exhausting, even to the Kolgathian. The powder was over knee high, and each step meant lifting extra weight. Over countless paces, this weight added up, and before long, the burning of his legs necessitated rest. During one of these breaks, Krael first heard the wizard's voice. As the wind began to whip and howl, all other noise was drowned out. Amidst the deafening wall of sound, a whisper came to the Slayer's ear: "Growing tired already, Krael? I thought you would be tougher than this!"

The Wizard Slayer snarled, raising his hammer as if ready to strike at the wind itself. This resulted in laughter from the disembodied voice. "Go ahead, cling to your weapon. It will not save you."

Ignoring Vornond's taunts, Krael continued forward, walking into the wind that only just then began to blow at his front. Ice and snow scraped at his exposed face, and for many stretches, the barbarian walked blindly, unable to keep his eyes open against the torrent.

Before he had left, Galfred imparted Krael with instructions on how to reach Twin Falls. He would have to head due north from Raven's Watch until he hit the Kirsel River. From there, it would be a climb up the mountain until he arrived at the ghost town itself. The instructions were simple, but as he struggled during the easier half of the journey, Krael realized he would be pushed to his limits even before facing the wizard.

———◆———

"Damn this accursed wind!" hollered Garrick, struggling to hear even himself as the air whipped at his ears, sending the hood of his cloak flying backward and off his head.

Morgvid, who held his own hood with a gloved hand, said, "Take this as a blessing. The Wizard Slayer and his companion would not travel in this weather, would they?"

"No, but neither should we. The men are tired. *I* am tired. You would be tired too if your concoction of snake venoms didn't fuel you."

"Oh, you have yet to see the effect of my guild's alchemy. Trust me, Garrick, I am as sober as anyone else in our party."

The old veteran had trouble believing this since the assassin's skin looked far from ordinary. Allowing his comrade to have the last word, Garrick didn't respond and instead looked ahead to the road. They had entered the pine forest and began making their way up the Wylderen Mountains. The horses, slowing amidst the harsh elements, hated the cold as much as their riders.

After a grueling hour had passed, the two manhunters, along with their twenty-strong regiment of soldiers, rode into the gates of Raven's Watch. The intimidating number of Saidalian soldiers drew many eyes, and doors were barred as they rode through the narrow, snow-filled streets.

An entire drift swept into the Raven's Rest as the front door opened, and twenty-two snow-covered boots only worsened the mess. The snow, in the heat of the fire, quickly melted and made the floorboards a slick, muddy disaster. All eyes of the crowded tavern were on the two men at the company's front, although more so on the hairless, sickly pale assassin than on the scarred knight. Darreth, who sat in the corner of the room, had to suppress a desire to call out a greeting to his friend. Then, a weight dropped in his stomach. *They've sent Sir Garrick after us*, he realized.

The elf-blooded quickly scooted his chair so that Lorienne would block his line of sight with the old knight. "What are you doing?" she asked.

"Don't look now, but the man at the front knows my face."

Disregarding her friend's warning, Lorienne turned her head. "Which one? The scarred one or the ugly one?"

Darreth's voice was muffled by a flagon as he held it in front of his face. "Scarred one."

"Take your headband off. They'll instantly recognize you with that."

The elf-blooded shook his head, hoping he wouldn't have to elaborate. Lorienne shot him a look, but he still didn't budge. "Fine. I'll go and make a distraction," she said. "You go and hide in your room."

"But what if Krael comes back?"

"We'll deal with that when it happens."

Without another word, Lorienne walked straight to Garrick, knocking over a flagon on the way. The contents splashed onto the boots of both the knight and Morgvid. "Watch yourself, ma'am," said Garrick, examining the extent of the damage.

"Sorry," she said, an attractive smile on her face.

While Garrick accepted the apology, the man whose drink was spilled did not. A burly fellow, whose broad shoulders seemed like one with his neck, stood up. His face seemed enormous, and his two wide nostrils resembled a snout. Upon noticing Lorienne's lithe figure, his rage subsided, replaced with devious glee. "Hey, miss, you're gonna buy me another one for that, right?"

Not considering him in her plans, Lorienne turned around, surprised. She apologized to the pig-faced man, curling her hair with one hand while the other deftly reached for the falchion at her hip.

"You know, if you don't want to buy me another drink, we could settle this another way," he said, his fat face sneering.

Before Lorienne could draw her sword, Garrick stepped in, holding the girl back with one arm while the other grabbed the haft of his axe. Unlike Lorienne, the knight did this to threaten. "Sit down!" scolded Garrick. "And consider your next words very carefully."

All eyes were on the confrontation, and the pig-faced man was aware of this. Raising his hands to appear innocent, he said, "There's no need to be violent. I didn't mean it like that!"

"Didn't mean it like that," Garrick mocked. "You know damn well how you meant it."

As Garrick backed away, axe still ready, the large man said, "What's an outsider like you doing here, anyway, getting in our business and all? Do you even know this girl?"

Garrick turned back around. The man loomed over him, chest puffed out and broad shoulders flexed. The veteran knight was far too experienced to fear such a hollow boast and, after a short laugh, said, "I've never met her before in my life."

One of the pig-faced man's companions grabbed him by the arm and talked him down from his temper. Garrick began talking to the owner of the Raven's Rest, not bothering to speak to Lorienne. The sword-dancer herself stood dumbfounded, astonished that her diversion had worked so well. The table she and Darreth had occupied was bare. The elf-blooded assumedly capitalized on the commotion.

As Garrick spoke with the owner, he quickly realized that people from Saidal were viewed with skepticism. Most questions were answered with a single word and often a mumbled one. After five long minutes, the knight slapped two gold coins onto the counter.

"Aye, I suppose I have seen this fanged man. He and..."

The owner's eyes caught Lorienne's face, which had become pale. "He and another guy, a little fellow with a headband, but they both left this morning," he continued, not mentioning Lorienne.

"In this weather?" hissed Morgvid.

The owner shrugged. "They didn't speak much, so I couldn't tell you where they went."

Lorienne backed away, letting out a sigh of relief. Just then, the pig-faced man cried out, "She was with them, too!"

Both Morgvid and Garrick looked to the sudden informant, then back to the owner. Casually shrugging, the owner stroked his beard and said, "She might've been. I've been pretty busy lately and haven't watched too closely who comes and goes. What business do you have with these people you're looking for?"

"Our own," said Morgvid, who then turned to the soldiers and commanded, "Seize the woman. She knows something."

As the men closed in, Garrick scowled. "We have no right to apprehend her! If we must question her, let it not be at swordpoint."

"Your chivalry only aids our quarry," retorted the assassin.

The soldiers stood confused, unsure which of their superiors to follow. Lorienne also stood still, knowing that retreating would only raise more suspicion. Breaking this tension, the owner said, "You and your men are far from Saidal; you hold no authority here. Swordpoint or not, you won't be interrogating that woman."

"What could you do to stop us?" said Morgvid, sunken eyes glaring out from his skull-like head. "We have you outmanned."

From behind the robed assassin, the pig-faced man arose. "Outmanned, sure," he said, "but it'll be a fight to remember."

Garrick's eyebrow raised at the man he had threatened only moments ago. Whether out of hatred for the knight and his party, an attempt to regain the woman's respect, or perhaps even a sur-facing of virtue, the pig-faced man proved to be more than just an instinctual oaf. Following the lead of their largest member, the rest of the patrons arose, one by one. While they were from different families and professions, at that moment, they were all people of Raven's Watch. The Saidalians no longer held the advantage of numbers.

Whispering to Morgvid, Garrick said, "Perhaps my chivalrous approach would aid in our own survival."

The assassin muttered something to himself, but the words were drowned out by Garrick's command. "Stand down, men! We are guests here and have no right to seize anyone or anything. Let us be grateful for this town's shelter and be polite guests."

A few conical helms nodded, agreeing with the veteran knight's approach. Within an hour, the soldiers had driven the chill from their bones and made themselves comfortable in the Raven's Rest. Some even began conversing with the locals.

Morgvid, however, spoke to no one. He sat alone in a shadowy corner of the log-walled room, ears filtering through every con-versation and eyes pinned on the woman who supposedly arrived with the Wizard Slayer.

15

THE WILL OF MOG MUHTAR

The Kirsel River was a dark scar that ran between newly formed snowdrifts. While it was only ten feet wide, the dark color of the ice on its surface hinted at a great hidden depth. The river zigzagged between hills of the mountain, providing Krael with an easy path up the slope. A fall into frigid water would spell certain death, and Krael took extra caution not to step on the ice lest it break. This proved difficult more than once since the Kirsel River tended to skirt around short cliff faces, leaving the barbarian to shimmy along the rock wall or find an alternate route. Numb fingers struggled to find purchase in the granite face, and each time Krael was forced to climb, he found himself out of breath after the endeavor.

One bend was far more treacherous than most. A rock jutted out like the wedge of an axe head on the Slayer's side of the river. Circumventing it would mean climbing through innumerable yards of snow, and Krael reckoned the risk was worth the reward. Tucking his war hammer into his belt, he put his gloved hands to the rock, feeling for anything his fingers could grasp. With one hand securely gripping a recess, the other reached around the rock. It was then when the stone he held broke. The Slayer was helpless to stop his fall, sliding down the jagged edge of the rock. Raw stone tore both pelts and skin, scraping rather than slicing. Sharp pain stung where the crag had left its mark, but that wasn't the worst of his injuries.

As he fell, his feet collided with the thin layer of ice below, and it broke without contest. Within seconds the frigid water had soaked his boots and bit into the flesh of his legs. Krael roared in agony and frustration, knowing the grim consequences of being wet in such a blizzard. As he frantically pulled at the rock, splashing as he struggled, Vornond's voice echoed off the mountains. "Why endure all of this pain for a single child? You should've just put it out of its misery when you had the chance. Now, you will only suffer."

Violently shivering, the Slayer waded through the dark water, shattering the icy surface. As he stepped back onto solid, snow-covered ground, he felt his legs ringing with pain. Vornond continued. "No one can survive this weather. You will die here, alone!"

"Shut up," Krael growled.

He produced a small fire-starting kit from his coat. Inside the tin case was twine, flint, a steel striker, and a flask of oil. The Slayer had meant to save this for disposing of Vornond's body, but the current dilemma required its use. Gritting his teeth, he swept snow off a small patch of ground and placed down a handful of sticks and twigs. They were wet thanks to the snow, but the burning oil quickly dried them. Before long, Krael sat next to a blazing campfire. Finally, he pulled off his boots and thawed out his feet, Vornond's voice mocking him all the while.

The wizard's taunts were wasted. Like the candle in the pit of Mog Muhtar, Krael stared into the fire, honing his focus while Vornond's curses howled about the mountain. Slowly, the feeling came back to the barbarian's feet and fingertips. The fur-lined boots would take some time to dry out, but Krael could wait in the solitude of the wilderness.

———◆———

It was midday when the Slayer first saw Twin Falls, although he couldn't honestly tell. The clouds above had gathered so densely that it seemed like twilight. This was barely enough light to see, yet the Slayer trudged forward, carving a trench in the snow as he went.

The namesake of Twin Falls was a pair of waterfalls that united into the Kirsel River. They were already frozen solid: an occurrence that seldom took place so early in the year. A hundred feet they rose, nestled in a curve of the cliff wall. Their entire height was covered in icicles, tapering down like a horde of jagged fangs. At the base of the two crystalline pillars were the remnants of a small town. Skeletal frames of buildings extended into the air, the roofs they once supported collapsed long ago. Krael walked amidst these, eyes scanning their decrepit alcoves for any sign of a threat. Nothing moved in the ruined settlement, save for falling snow.

There was no sign of Vornond. He had gone silent, and Krael began to doubt his plan. If the untouched blanket of snow was anything to go by, not a soul still resided in Twin Falls. The Slayer knew better than to give up, and he continued to scour the barren settlement, relying on his decades of experience to find his quarry. He looked for someone warped by magick, and to hunt him like an ordinary man would be a mistake.

Vornond underestimated his pursuer. Between the frozen waterfalls was a granite cliff face which immediately caught the Slayer's attention. The wall appeared exactly how the mind would assume it to be. It was strangely devoid of oddities and peculiar features. Krael's honed perception saw this for what it was. Such an illusion may have deceived mortal eyes, but those tempered by the Pit and the Candle would not be so easily tricked. The barbarian approached the wall and strode through it without hesitation.

Just beyond the illusory barrier, a small stone tunnel ran into the side of the mountain. Water froze as it dripped from the sides of the cavern walls, forming icicles and rendering the floor slick. Having to crouch to pass through, Krael moved as fast as he could, desperately trying to fight off the cold gripping his body. His joints ached as he moved, but he did not slow.

The wizard's lair was cathedral-like in its vastness. The erratic walls were coated with a layer of strange ice that gave off a faint blue glow. Held into the walls were shelves containing books and scrolls whose yellowed pages remained dry thanks to the sub-zero temperature. A pedestal of luminescent ice arose in the center of the room, and atop it sat a crystal sphere. Wires and pipes ran from the bottom of the globe like roots, connecting the orb to an unseen piece of eldritch machinery housed in the pedestal below. Images flickered in the crystal ball, and from where Krael stood, these scenes were warped by the curvature of the orb itself. These were not twisted to Vornond, who stood a foot behind the magickal device.

His skin was as pale and withered as a corpse. Sunken eyes glared from beneath a wide-brimmed and pointed hat. His beard was thinning and, in some places, froze to his old gray robes. Staring into the crystal ball, Vornond extended an arm toward the Slayer. A torrent of swirling ice spewed forth.

Expecting such an attack, Krael lunged out of the way. Usually, he would have dodged the volley easily, but the supernatural cold was beginning to sink into his bones. Shards of ice ripped through his pant leg, and the skin on his calf was torn open.

Vornond's mouth contorted into a smile. "You have survived much longer than I expected," he said, "but you are mortal, after all, and you will die here."

From his cloak, the wizard drew a cruciform sword, the blade of which gave off a vapor that drifted to the floor. Holding the brand high, he sent another blast of ice hurtling toward Krael. This second attack was weaker than the first, but the barbarian still struggled to bring his body far enough away from the blast. A sharp chill rang through his back as his coat was reduced to tatters.

The fragments of conjured ice were not as piercing as an arrow, but hundreds could appear at Vornond's whim, and they barreled forth with the force of an avalanche.

Letting out a savage roar and baring his fangs, the Slayer charged forward, his blood freezing as it leaked from his weakening body. Vornond raised the misting sword, but it was knocked away with a mighty swing of Krael's hammer. The wizard, expecting this, reached his left hand toward Krael's face, and another blast of ice was unleashed. In a fraction of a moment, the barbarian lifted the haft end of his weapon and knocked Vornond's arm aside. The ice missed its target.

In his desperation, Krael had left an opening, and the wizard capitalized. The tip of the sword slid into Krael's shoulder, and the resulting cold made all the pain he already felt seem arbitrary. The chill steel scraped against bone, and his whole arm contracted in agony. With one violent motion, he counterattacked. With his unwounded hand, the Slayer swung the war hammer, striking the side of Vornond's knee with a grinding snap. The wizard immediately collapsed and screeched.

Like a wolf hearing the whelping cries of wounded prey, a final rush coursed through the Slayer's veins at Vornond's wail. With one hand, he raised the hammer and brought it back down, crushing Vornond's sword arm. The wizard squirmed away and hid behind the pedestal of the crystal ball. One hammer blow was enough to shatter the orb, sending shards and sparks flying.

Vornond scampered across the floor, worsening his shattered knee in desperation. Whimpering as he crawled, he found himself cornered against the cavern wall. The wizard turned, his wounded body shaking in fear. "This can't be happening!" he cried. "Please, please, please! I'll do anything!"

The Slayer walked forward, teeth bared.

"Name your price. I'll lift the curse on the child! You want me to do that, right?"

Krael's eyes were grim, unforgiving, and filled with hatred.

"Please, no!"

The hammer fell, but thanks to the wizard's squirming, the steel missed its mark and shattered his collarbone with a deep crack. Vornond screamed and thrashed to no avail. His voice became guttural and hoarse, barely understandable amidst his anguish. "The Dark Gods curse you!"

With a roar, Krael again swung the war hammer, using his wounded arm as well. Vornond's skull offered little resistance against the weapon, and gore sprayed on impact as he was silenced.

Upon the wizard's death, the air became warmer. The glow of the cavern walls faded away, and scarce reflections of sunlight were all that illuminated the dim chamber. Krael still shivered, but the pain was bearable. Despite his surroundings of ice and blood, the barbarian felt a sense of serene peace. He took a moment to simply breathe. The teachings of Mog Muhtar were heard in his mind, the litanies from many years ago as clear as ever.

The servants of the Dark Gods cannot be redeemed, for their allegiance cannot be undone. The greatest work of mercy is to destroy them.

Krael looked down at the body that lay before him in a slowly growing pool of crimson. The withered white flesh had regained some color, and the limbs retained a more youthful build. Vornond had not been as old as he seemed, but his descent into magick had twisted his body and mind. As the Slayer pulled the hammer from the concaved skull, the corpse twitched, then remained still.

The servants bear the taint of the Dark Gods beyond death. They must be cleansed.

The tin still contained some tinder and oil, and with this, Krael, shivering and shaking from cold and exhaustion, set Vornond's body on fire. The flesh was hesitant to ignite, but the robes were quickly ablaze. Within minutes, the entire chamber reeked of burning carcass, but the heat it provided was welcome to the Slayer.

Kneeling next to the body, the barbarian basked in the warmth of its acrid flames. The accumulated frost began to melt, and soon Krael was utterly damp. This didn't matter; the cold had been driven from his body.

The secrets of the Dark Gods are a power that mortal men should not possess. They are weapons unwieldy and can never be used for good without working a much greater evil.

As feeling returned to Krael's fingers, he approached the many bookshelves. The tomes were written in an old language and decorated with patterns that twisted into devious, horrible faces. Arcane runes and blasphemous diagrams filled the yellowed pages, and the Slayer spent no time examining them. They were cast into the flames without a second thought, letting out an ethereal hiss as they burned.

Anything less than hatred will fail you.

Krael snarled at the burning corpse. He had heard Vornond's pleas for mercy, but nothing the wizard said could spare him from his fate. The Hound of Mog Muhtar was motivated by something deeper than reason or philosophy. Hatred swelled deep from within his soul, bringing the entirety of his being into his vain crusade against all wielders of magick.

Krael left the smoking cave and found that the blizzard had passed. The sky was blue and dotted with wispy clouds. The sun shone uninhibited. Water dripped from the many icicles of the falls, and the snow became damp and slushy in the heat of the day.

The bloody and beaten Slayer began the march back to Raven's Watch. His fur coat hung in tatters about him, and the exposed flesh was scratched and bleeding. Exhausted, his head drooped, but his eyes still stared forward as he walked, occasionally dragging the war hammer to ease his burden. The return journey was more straightforward than coming toward Twin Falls, as it was mostly downhill. He continued under the pines, occasionally resting in the pools of warm sunlight that broke through the canopy.

The sun had sunk behind the tree line when Raven's Watch came into view, and the sky had shifted from a cool azure to a warm purple. Lights could be seen shining from the few windows that peered above the palisade, and Krael yearned for the warm glow of a hearth that did not reek of death.

Upon reaching the gate, a guard called, "Hail, there! Are you the one that set out to kill Vornond?"

Krael met the man with an irritated scowl.

Realizing that the disheveled, wounded barbarian before the gate had obviously fought something formidable and that he matched the Wizard Slayer's description, the guard cleared his throat and said, "My lord wishes to speak with you at once. It is an urgent matter."

After being ushered through the gates, the Slayer was escorted to Artreth's tower. While waiting for the lord himself, a servant covered the barbarian with a warm blanket and offered a comfortable seat next to the fire. Also sitting in the warm glow was Sebastian. The infant that lay in the crib was different from the ghoulish thing he had been just the night before. Plump pink fingers waved and grasped at little feet. After seeing the child, Krael closed his eyes, worries at rest, and began to doze in the long-awaited comfort.

The Slayer awoke to a gentle tap on his shoulder and the irresistible scent of meat. On a side table was a plate with a glistening leg of mutton and a goblet of wine. Artreth stood, his back to the hearth, beaming.

"Tired after your endeavor, eh?" said the lord, jesting.

Krael, only semi-conscious, looked to the mutton and then to Lord Artreth. After a short laugh, Artreth said, "Dig in! You've earned it."

Fangs sank deep into the dripping meat, easily tearing it from the bone. While the barbarian ate like a wild dog, Artreth said, "I cannot thank you enough. The curse has been lifted, and Sebastian is healthy again. Well, mostly…"

Looking down at the babe, both men saw the icy cataracts that covered Sebastian's pupils. "I fear Vornond's curse will have a lasting effect, but seeing my boy alive and for the first time—"

Artreth's breathing became shallow, and a grateful sob escaped just before he could compose himself.

"I will be eternally in your debt, Krael."

The Slayer, setting down a clean bone, nodded. In his slow, awkward speech, he said, "Don't be. I did what I must. You owe nothing."

"Then perhaps what I am about to do can be considered a favor rather than payment. While you were away, nearly two-dozen men from Saidal arrived, looking for you. They wished to interrogate your companion, but the townsfolk stopped them. We don't take kindly to Saidalians and are even less kind when they order people around without proper authority. Right now, these men are awaiting your return to the Raven's Rest."

The Kolgathian's eyes narrowed as he gulped down wine.

"I will not ask why they seek you out, but I cannot stall them forever."

Setting the goblet down, Krael said, "I leave tonight."

16
A DESPERATE FLIGHT

It was midnight when Galfred crept through the door into the Raven's Rest. Despite his limp, the old man deftly wound his way between the rabble who spilled from their chairs and reveled in drink. Most of these soldiers' eyes were fixated on dice games or wooden *sakhmet* boards, and Galfred passed by without their notice. Unbeknownst to all in the room, Morgvid sat in a shadowy corner, eyes scanning the room from beneath his mail-lined hood. He watched Galfred as he made his way toward the owner and, after a brief word, went directly upstairs.

He did not pay for a room or buy drinks. He's here for something else, thought the assassin. Getting up from his seat, he followed Galfred up the stairs, each step careful and silent. From around the corner came a knock, and Morgvid halted.

"Who is it?" asked a woman's voice, whose accent Morgvid recognized as Valmorian.

"Galfred," answered the old man, "but I come bearing a message from Krael."

The assassin grinned but stayed hidden behind the turn in the hall. He suppressed his breathing to pick up on any minor details of the conversation.

"We don't know Krael," replied the voice.

She's a terrible liar, thought Morgvid.

"From what I can gather, ye do. Do ye want this message or not?"

There was a pause, then the Valmorian voice said, "Alright, come in."

The door opened. Galfred gasped, was pulled in, and the door slammed shut. Morgvid stole a glance from around the corner, and seeing that the coast was clear, he approached and listened.

Lorienne held a sword to Galfred's throat. The old man stood with his back against the door, helpless. "Give me one reason I should trust you," said the woman.

"We be on the same side," said Galfred, trying to ignore the feeling of cold steel on his windpipe. "I was the one that told Krael of Lord Artreth's son and led him to the wizard."

Lorienne cocked her head, confused. After taking a deep breath, Galfred explained the previous night's events. The sword-dancer listened, skeptical the whole time.

Galfred said, "Krael awaits you just past the tree line north of town. He said you will leave behind your cart and ride through the wilderness on horseback."

"That sounds like a trap," Lorienne said.

"It isn't."

At last sheathing her falchion, the woman said, "Perhaps not. We'll see what Darreth thinks of this."

The door opened, and the two approached the room across the hall. The candlelight was dim, and the night sky shed little light through the windows. As they walked, Lorienne sensed an odd gust of wind. "Did you feel that?"

"What?" asked Galfred.

"I don't know. Almost like someone just ran through here, but…"

As she looked down the hall, Lorienne saw it to be empty.

"Yer just jumpy," scoffed the old man. "We would've heard if someone was moving through."

Still not at ease, Lorienne knocked on the door. "Open up. It's me."

Upon no response, she knocked again. "Now."

Darreth's tired face appeared in the entryway as he adjusted his headband. "Good morning," he said, yawning.

The two entered. Noticing Galfred, Darreth fully awakened. "You're the man Krael talked to, aren't you?"

"Indeed I am."

"Didn't seem like it at first," Lorienne remarked.

"Do you take me for my word now?"

Darreth scratched his head, confused. Lorienne nodded.

"Ye two best get movin' soon," said Galfred. "These men from Saidal will notice yer absence in the mornin', and ye'll want a big head start on 'em."

The elf-blooded and the sword-dancer gathered their meager belongings and prepared for their hasty escape. Slinging packs about their shoulders, the two followed Galfred as he took them to a window at the end of the hall. "There be too many men in the common room, so ye'll have to climb out. This window here over-looks the stables. I've readied your horses and filled the saddlebags with enough dried venison and rabbit to last a week."

"Thank you," said Darreth, shaking Galfred's calloused hand.

"Don't thank me; thank yer friend, Krael. He saved Lord Ar-treth's son, ye know. This is my liege's way of saying thanks."

After Lorienne saluted their confidant, she crawled out of the window. With precarious steps, she descended the corner of the building, the logs of which stuck out a foot from the corner and made a nearly ladder-like climb. Darreth followed suit, and the two found their horses ready for the escape.

Morgvid sat in his room, alone. *Damn those men, and damn the knight Garrick*, he thought. *I'll capture the Hound of Mog Mu-htar myself.*

One of his pale arms was exposed, and a belt constricted cir-culation and made his purple veins bulge. In his other hand was a syringe, whose delicate metal pieces were decorated with the runes of the Serpent's Hand. Without flinching, the needle sank into the scar where it had pierced so many times before, and Morgvid injected the dark concoction of venoms.

Within seconds, every nerve of the assassin's body was on fire. Morgvid gritted his teeth as he waited for the pain to pass. It receded like the tide, and a superhuman clarity was left behind. The assassin's pupils dilated. Time stretched and slowed. He could hear the faint wind currents as they crept through the cracks in the wall and underneath the door. His own heartbeat thudded like a drum, and everything felt light. Rising up from his seat, Morgvid grinned. Sheathing a toxin-drenched talwar on each hip, he strode from his room and headed for the stables. While his pace felt casual, the most astute patrons of the common room only saw a black shape dart by.

Snow-covered fields outside of Raven's Watch sparkled in the moonlight. The thundering hooves of Darreth and Lorienne's horses, for a time, were the only noise that echoed through the cold night air. They rode without speaking, scanning the tree line for any sign of the Wizard Slayer. As he searched, Darreth's keen ears picked up noise from behind. The elf-blooded turned, saying, "Who else could be—"

The ghastly visage of the assassin made Darreth choke on his words. Strange black robes billowed as he rode at full speed. His face was gaunt, pale, and sunken, making the figure appear like a specter of death. A curved blade was held in each hand, their razor edges glinting.

"Damn it," cursed Lorienne. "He's following us!"

"Not for long," said Darreth, pulling his bow from its place on the saddle.

Lorienne's eye caught something in the shadow of the trees. Upon a horse sat a hulking figure, black hair waving in the wind. "There he is," she cried. "There's Krael!"

Darreth's horse slowed, and the dark rider gained distance on him, talwars flourishing.

"What are you doing?" Lorienne called back. "We can lose him in the trees! Hurry!"

We won't be able to lose him, thought Darreth. He pulled the bowstring back to his cheek and let an arrow fly. It was a remarkable shot, and the missile flew straight for the chest of the pursuer, but it did not find its mark. Darreth squinted to make out what happened in the feeble light, then fired another shot.

"Get moving!" screamed Lorienne.

Ignoring his companion, Darreth watched his arrow fly as true as the first. In the moment before impact, the robed figure swung his blades and knocked the missile to the side. The elf-blooded whispered to himself, "That's… not possible!"

Gritting his teeth, Darreth readied a third arrow. The nightmarish figure was so close that the whites of his bloodshot eyes could be seen. Even if he wished to flee, Darreth would be overtaken before his mount could get up to speed. Lorienne could do nothing but continue forward, glancing nervously over her shoulder. All the while, the assassin's horse continued to charge ahead, its rider fully confident in his ability to take an arrow out of flight.

Before he let out what might have been his final shot, Darreth whispered, "Try to block this."

The assassin's eyes widened as he realized where the arrow was headed. The steel tip bore deep into his horse's chest, and the half-ton animal toppled forward in a tumult of limbs and snow. Darreth, Lorienne, and Krael saw the explosion of white powder, and they all were surprised when the robed assassin sprinted forward from the crash, unscathed.

Such a fall could be fatal to a normal man, but to Morgvid, who perceived time at a third of its speed, tucked and rolled. In one motion, he came to his feet and charged, fogged breath billowing from his nostrils. It was as if he had not lost any momentum.

With confidence cut short, Darreth whipped the reins of his horse and fled from the superhuman foe. He charged into the trees, head tucked down behind the mount's neck to avoid the frigid cuts of wind and the whipping of needled branches.

Morgvid slowed to a halt. Even with the venom drugs coursing through his system, he could not outrun a horse, and the assassin could only watch the three escape him, galloping off into the depths of the pinewood forest. He let out a vile curse in the Askarian tongue, spit flinging from his hissing teeth. *So be it,* he thought. *You can run for now, but I will follow. Next time, the rest of my company will not be so indolent.*

The fugitives and their sword-dancer companion galloped over a league through the rugged wilderness before stopping to rest. Darreth, despite his excellent shot, was shaken at their pursuer's unnatural dexterity. While he disguised it as a shiver, his feet trembled in the stirrups out of fear.

"Do you think we lost him?" asked Lorienne.

She looked to Darreth, who in turn looked to Krael. The Kolgathian's eyes scanned the shadowy forest. "They still come," he said.

"You see him?" asked Darreth, with more than just a hint of fright in his voice.

Shaking his head, the Kolgathian responded. "No. I know his kind. He will not stop. He is an assassin of the Serpent's Hand."

Seeing his companions tilt their heads in confusion, Krael elaborated. "From Askaron."

"That's it," said Lorienne, crossing her arms. "I won't be chased by an assassin who has come from the other side of the world and can't be killed. The next semblance of civilization we reach, I'm leaving. I've had enough."

Neither Krael nor Darreth spoke. As a gentle breeze came through the trees, snow fell around the silent group. Breaking the silence, the elf-blooded said, "It's probably gonna be a while before we reach another town."

Lorienne scowled at him, and Darreth regretted speaking. "Let's go," said Krael.

The three traveled beneath branches burdened with snowfall. The cold was bearable, but the terrain was irregular and treacherous. No clear paths wound amidst the steep crags, and each step of the journey brought uncertainty. They did not go east and up the Wylderen Mountains but instead traveled north, moving through the uninhabited forests. Before they expected it, the sun's first rays pierced through the trees.

"Should we stop here to rest?" asked Darreth.

Lorienne nodded. "We'll need to sleep sometime."

"No fires tonight," said Krael. "They will know where we are."

Both Darreth and Lorienne grumbled but didn't bother going against Krael's orders. Packing down a patch of snow, they prepared an area for camp. Thick fur bedrolls were unfurled, and while no fire was lit, the sun's light kept them from shivering as they slept.

Darreth, who had slept the most the night before, took the first watch. It was a pleasant time when he could forget those that pursued him. Birds sang, frantically trying to prepare for the early winter. Gray squirrels darted from tree to tree, chittering as they went. As the mountainside warmed up, the air smelled fresher and was easier to breathe. *We may be running for perhaps our very lives*, he thought, *but at least right now, at this moment, I feel at peace.*

***

Rats scampered across the crooked cobbled alleys in the underbelly of Saidal. Beggars and diseased lined the dark stone walls, huddled around braziers to stave off the cold. Their hacking coughs echoed through the narrow, smoky streets, and the stench of mold and feces was inescapable. A tall man garbed in a muddy brown cloak was walking down the center of the lane, giving a wide berth to the sore-faced beggars. Many suspicious eyes glared at the stranger, who was seldom seen in such a wretched corner of the city. Unwavering, the man continued forward, skirting the edges of muddy puddles in the uneven street.

Two men appeared in the center of the alley to meet the intruder. Their pock-marked and weathered skin bore sailors' tattoos, and each carried a makeshift knife. "Whadda you want 'ere?" asked the taller of the two.

"It is none of your business," replied the man, whose voice was much more articulate and proper than that of whom he answered.

The shorter of the two sailors sneered, showing a stub of a tongue in his mouth. The sailor that still retained the ability of speech replied. "Yeah, it is. Yer in our turf, ye gonna tell us what yer doin'."

The stranger was silent. Beaming, the taller sailor said, "Alright, stick 'em."

Brandishing his shiv, the tongueless sailor grinned. He swung his arm, and from beside him came an agonized scream. Both were shocked to see the handle of the shiv poking out from the taller sailor's chest. Choking on blood, the wounded man fell, the spark of rage the last thing in his eyes.

The tongueless man turned to the stranger, trembling. From beneath the heavy mud-stained cloak came a hand with a silver ring glinting on one of its fingers. The remaining sailor could do nothing but scream for help as his own hand reached up and closed around his throat. He kicked and writhed on the ground, but the stranger's bewitchment was more potent than his will to defy it. Within a minute, he lay lifeless in the muddy, bloodstained street.

It seems my power grows, thought Ordric. *Before, such a command could be defied by one's willingness to survive, but it seems that is no longer the case if I truly embrace the ring.*

The beggars, who had since scattered, looked at the strange man from around corners and crooks of the alley, questioning the horrible events they had just witnessed. Ordric paid no mind to them as he continued through the cramped hive of crooked towers and cramped streets. His journey ended when he came upon an alley congested by dozens of irregular leaning shacks. Like rats, the inhabitants of that wretched place built homes from whatever scraps they could find. Rotting lumber, used sails, and crumbled bricks contributed to their construction. Had they not been under the protection of taller and sturdier buildings, they would have been blown apart by the sea wind long ago.

The count curled his lip as he approached the city within a city. Avoiding the glances of those who dwelled within, Ordric weaved his way through the unorganized sprawl of walkways. One shack gathered his attention more than any other. Rat skulls, painted with the dull brown of dried blood, hung from the edges of the conical thatch roof. A thick plume of smoke drifted from the roof's peak, and as Ordric grew closer, the stench of hedge alchemy grew viler.

Upon opening the door, Ordric was met with a snarling hiss. A frail voice spat, "How dare you show your face here?"

"Hold your tongue, witch," said Ordric, glaring at the hag that was Stregana. "What I wish to ask you now does not concern the Wizard Slayer. I have him under control."

The witch cackled again. "Do you, now? Then why haven't you sent him after Stregana?"

"I did not come here to answer your questions. You will be answering mine."

Ordric produced a vial filled with a thick crimson liquid from beneath the muddy cloak. Upon seeing this, Stregana's sunken eyes widened. Like most witches, she had walked the earth far longer than any mortal should, and the preserving power of an elf's blood was one of the few things that could sustain her wretched existence. The blood of children had the same effect, but it was far less potent. "Well then, what must Stregana do?" she said, her tone softening in the presence of the blood she desired.

"Tell me of Prince Eledrith Calidign," said Ordric. "I must know how he can resist my powers without effort."

"Perhaps your powers are not what you think," said the witch, throwing revolting ingredients into her bubbling cauldron.

Ordric, remembering the two wretched sailors he had killed less than an hour before, said, "I doubt it."

The surface of the concoction rippled, then opened up to a fathomless depth below, far lower than what the dimensions of the cauldron should allow. Whispering in a harsh alien tongue, Stregana waved a hand over the brew and looked at Ordric, her eyes totally white. "What do you wish to know, Count Ordric of Saidal?"

"I wish to know of Prince Eledrith Calidign," he repeated.

Upon looking into the cauldron's depths, Stregana let out a horrifying wail. The many jars and containers rattled on their rickety shelves. The candle's flames dimmed to an umbral green. Ordric stepped back, terrified. In his previous visits to the witch, none of her rituals had been this intense.

Stregana spoke. "King Torvaren Calidign has no living heir."

"That's not possible!" said Ordric. "Torvaren's queen died giving birth to Eledrith."

"That child died with her," replied Stregana, "but it was not the Eledrith you know."

"Then who is he?"

The witch's face twisted and strained. Again, she let out a wail. The sickly green of the candles grew back into their original orange hue. Stregana gasped as sweat dripped from her wrinkled face, the cauldron's contents once again appearing as a regular liquid.

"The knowledge Stregana sought has been destroyed," she said.

Ordric shook his head. "Not once this night have your words made sense. I grow tired of your games, witch."

"You don't understand, Ordric. Stregana looked beyond the veil of time to see the true past of who we know to be Eledrith, and there is nothing to be seen."

The count scowled. "What do you mean 'nothing to be seen'? Did he simply appear out of thin air?"

"Someone very powerful wishes for his true lineage to remain a mystery. They are strong enough to hide the astral echoes of prior events."

Ordric cursed to himself. Nothing irritated him more than his questions remaining unanswered, and the dead end he had just run into was an infuriating thorn in his side. "Do you know who may possess such power?"

"Would you think that one with the power to erase memories in time would make themselves known?"

Ordric looked to the floor, fuming, and the witch did not cease in her chastising. "Oh, poor Ordric," she mocked, "even with all of his power and ambition, he pouts like a child when something doesn't go his way."

The count had run out of patience. With a furl of his ragged cloak, he turned toward the hut door.

"One more thing," croaked the witch.

The count stopped and glared over his shoulder.

"Be careful around Prince Eledrith," she said. "Stregana thinks there is a reason someone wants to keep his true birth a secret."

Rolling his eyes, the count passed under the crooked door-frame and into the shadows of the night.

17
LOVE AND WAR

Winter had finally come to Saidal. Snow drifted and swirled amidst the lofty towers, and every roof was coated in a layer of white powder. The cold weather had little effect on the city's inhabitants, who went about their usual business under cover of thick coats and fur-lined caps. Little snow accumulated on the streets that wasn't immediately trampled down by the shuffling traffic of the city.

Prince Eledrith and Lady Morwenna walked along the fortified wall separating the port from the city proper. A statue of Atlor stood atop the battlement, looking over the sea. The maritime god's robes and hair were carved as if flowing in the wind. While the arm that held his spear was intact, the other had broken off long ago. Four bodyguards followed the couple, and per Eledrith's request, they remained just out of earshot. While the circumstances of the stroll were not ideal, the couple's view was breathtaking. The gray sea extended indefinitely, and white-capped waves crashed in the wind. A soft white sky loomed above, and the sun's harsh rays diffused by the snowfall. Massive trading ships appeared like little toy boats from where the couple stood, and a feeling of peace came with being so distant from the chaos of the world below. Morwenna loved this feeling. Auburn hair flowing in the breeze, she leaned against the parapet and took a deep breath of the crisp sea air.

The prince watched his love as she looked to the horizon. They both were entranced by what they saw. It had been a month since Sir Garrick had left, and in that time, Eledrith had spent nearly every day with Morwenna. While Count Ordric and King Torvaren schemed incessantly, their children turned to each other for comfort, and a relationship absent of political motivations grew. The two seldom partook in activities typical of nobles. Instead, they spent every spare moment retreating to the beautiful, isolated places of the city to cultivate what they truly cherished: their love for each other.

Morwenna turned from the sea and looked at her prince. His hair was nearly as fair as the falling snow, and his pale, elegant face made him seem like a figure of legend. Noticing her gaze, Eledrith cracked a shy smile.

"What are you smiling about?" she asked, a coy eyebrow raised.

"I'm just enjoying the view."

Rolling her eyes, Morwenna brushed a lock of hair behind her ear. "The view?"

"Yeah," he replied, a sheepish smile on his face.

"Alright, Your Majesty," she said.

Morwenna looked back to the sea, where a handful of ships bobbed in the turbulent bay. The many oars that extended from the side of each triangular-sailed boat churned and struggled against the currents. "Have you ever wanted to sail?" she asked.

"Of course. When I was a boy, Garrick told me stories of places on the other side of the ocean. Supposedly, there are places like Kihanjir that haven't been touched by men and are total wildernesses. I'd want to go somewhere like that."

"That'd be the worst!" said Morwenna. "You'd be all alone, and you'd be sleeping in a tent every night."

"I'd build my own house, though. Make a little patch of land my own, you know?"

"And what would you eat?"

"Whatever animals I can hunt down and kill."

"You know how to hunt?"

"No, but it can't be that hard."

Morwenna shook her head. "I'd want to go someplace beautiful, like Valmoria. My father told me there are massive statues and white marble cities."

"The last place I want to sail to is another city."

"No, these cities are nowhere near as vast as Saidal. They let trees grow in the squares, and there are no imposing towers."

"It's still a city, though."

Sighing in frustration, Morwenna quietly said, "It's my dream to travel there one day."

"I'm sure I can make that happen," said the prince. "We could say it's a diplomatic errand."

Morwenna smiled. "I think that's the first time you've considered using your privileges as a prince."

"I guess so, yeah."

"Well," she said, pulling Eledrith close, "do you promise you'll take me?"

Her hand was tight around his waist. Putting his arms around her, he said, "Of course I will."

It happened before either had realized. Eledrith could feel Morwenna's warm breath on his cheek, and he turned his head, bringing himself closer. Morwenna did likewise. The two kissed. Eledrith's nerves caught up with him, and for a moment, he considered backing away, but as he felt the warmth of Morwenna's lips on his, he pulled her closer.

The bodyguards, who were thirty feet away, exchanged words amongst themselves, but these were too distant and hushed to disturb the two lovers.

As they finished, Eledrith leaned back. Smiling, Morwenna rested her head against his chest. The prince's nerves were far from subsided. His heart still pounded, for there was a question he knew he needed to ask. Even the battle against Thalnar's wolves evoked less fear than what he was about to do. "Um, Morwenna?" he said.

She looked up, brown eyes warm and inviting. Snowflakes sat in her hair without melting.

"My life," he started, "has been turned around so much lately. With Garrick leaving, the whole thing with Darreth and Krael, and now the Outlaw Kingdoms, I'm just not sure what I am to do. If there's one thing I've learned in the past month, though, it's that I don't want to lose you."

Morwenna looked up to Eledrith, still holding him as she bit her lip. Her beautiful brown eyes were wide in anticipation.

Getting down on one knee, the prince asked, "Morwenna, will you marry me?"

"Yes!" she blurted, joy-filled tears in her eyes.

Ecstatic, the prince arose and kissed Morwenna for a second time. They continued passionately and unashamed, paying no mind to the bodyguards that waited nearby. When they finally ceased, Morwenna leaned her head against Eledrith's chest.

"I love you, Eledrith."

"I love you too."

———◆———

"I must ask, Ordric, how do you feel knowing that your daughter is to be wed to the prince?"

Every face at the table of the High Council turned, awaiting the count's response. Ordric had been staring into space, deep in thought, but as he was brought from his silent planning and into the present, he flashed a warm smile. "I am delighted. It has strengthened the bond between His Majesty and me, but more importantly, my daughter is happy."

The answer was met with a warm lauding and nods from the rest of the council. This was a facade, of course, since most of the counts had hoped one of their own houses would be married into the ruling line. With that no longer a possibility, they settled for the next best thing: being in good favor with the father of the future queen. *And most importantly of all*, thought Ordric, *I now have significant leverage on Eledrith. He may resist my enchantments, but Morwenna is easily bent to my will.*

"I am glad of this as well," said King Torvaren, "but let's not lose sight of why we called this council into session."

"Yes," said Count Gilduin, "the kingdoms ruled by Lidoran Ekbar and Orthil the Skull have forged an alliance and could potentially cut off Saidal from the rest of the Outlaw Kingdoms."

"What motivation would they have?" asked Boridron. "If they were to defy Saidal, the other warlords would be at their throats!"

Gilduin shook his bald and white-bearded head. "Unfortunately, that's not the case. Our latest reports indicate that many other powers are willing to sign on with this alliance. By next year, they would double their export prices."

"Double!" blurted Torvaren. "Our citizens can barely afford the prices they are asking now!"

"Well, they could," said Boridron, "if we subsidized these imports."

"Which would only raise the prices long term," said Ordric. "If it seemed our people had more money to spend, the foreign merchants would charge a higher price. This is why I wish to take territory from the Outlaw Kingdoms. Not only would we punish those upstart warlords, but we would have a permanent foothold outside of the walls of this city."

"We lack the manpower, though," said Countess Sedrana.

"Not unless we employ our Graehalic allies," said the king.

"It would take over a year to muster an adequate army and bring them south," said Boridron. "The ports in that harsh northern land freeze during winter, and it would take a fleet of ships even if the passages weren't blocked by ice."

"There's a solution to this, Boridron," said Ordric. "Your family used to deal with them before."

Boridron furrowed his wispy eyebrows, and then his eyes grew wide. "You don't mean the drenoch?"

"I do."

A wave of murmuring enveloped the circular chamber. While no one openly objected to utilizing the elusive sea nomads, there was hesitation.

"Their iron arks haven't docked in Saidal's port for over fifty years," said Boridron.

"I doubt they have changed much since then," said Ordric. "The drenoch have lived by their machines since before Saidal's founding, and they no doubt still do."

Ordric spoke of a people that few people believed existed without witnessing them firsthand. The drenoch were folk preserved from a different time who roamed the uncharted seas on great metal ships. They raided barbaric lands and enslaved their inhabitants, who were then shipped to coal mines in the far north to dig up fuel for their massive vessels. Great black plumes on the horizon warned of their coming, and sailors from all continents knew to steer clear of their path. The drenoch bore weaponry that few could comprehend and even fewer had seen with their own eyes.

"The drenoch may not have changed," said Count Boridron, "but we of Saidal have. In the past, their services could be bought with a large shipment of slaves, but such a cruel institution has long since been outlawed."

"Outlawed, but not ended," said Gilduin. "You'd have to be a fool to think that slaves are not traded in this city. Sure, they may be under the guise of indentured servants, imported workers, or the like, but when they are pulled off the boat in shackles, it doesn't make a difference what they are called."

Many of the counts shifted in their seats at the mention of this fact. Sedrana's mouth was pulled into a frown. It was because of her much of the trade of humans had waned in recent years. "This is not right," she said. "How dare we sell human lives for expedited movement of soldiers?"

"Think of the consequences," said Ordric, cutting off the countess before she could continue moralizing. "If we do not immediately crush this new alliance, the people of Saidal will suffer."

"But isn't there another way? We could—"

"Ordric is right," said Gilduin. "Time is of the essence, and hindering ourselves to pursue a moral goal of yours would only result in our failure."

King Torvaren said, "The well-being of my subjects is of utmost importance. I wish it could be different, Sedrana, but that is a battle that must be fought later."

Pursing her lips, the countess remained silent.

"Since there is disagreement amongst us, let's call a vote," said Boridron.

Count Ordric rolled his eyes. As the king recited the formalities of the voting process, Ordric drummed his fingers on the table, silver ring in view.

"All those in favor, rise now," said Torvaren.

The majority of the room, Sedrana included, stood up. While some of the counts seemed surprised at the countess's change in opinion, Ordric was not.

"With that matter settled," said Gilduin, "who will lead this force of mercenaries? I'm sure you would hardly trust such an important endeavor to an outsourced general."

"Normally, Sir Garrick would undertake such a task," said the king, "but he is currently unavailable."

Gilduin said, "Perhaps I could lead this force. My knowledge of the Outlaw Kingdoms is unrivaled."

"Why not let Prince Eledrith lead?" asked Ordric.

Clenching his fist, Gilduin said, "He lacks experience! Besides, he has only just made plans to be wed."

"My son will never gain experience if he is kept hidden behind the palace walls for his own safety," said Torvaren. "His journey to Travedd with the Wizard Slayer no doubt proved his mettle. I'm sure he'll excel on the battlefield."

Ordric said, "Perhaps Count Gilduin could serve as a military advisor to the prince?"

Gilduin ran a hand through his short white beard. Resignedly, he agreed. The council continued, and the minute plans of war were made. Their words faded to a distant murmur to Ordric, whose only thought was the capturing of Krael. The Wizard Slayer was a vital piece in the plan for total conquest. While the domains of Lidoran Ekbar and Orthil the Skull could be held for a time, the control over magick users was necessary if a sweeping victory were to be achieved. Ordric stared into the dark, swirling grain of the wooden table as the politicians argued, his mind forming plans greater in scope than any openly discussed by the council.

<hr />

Wedding bells rang in the Calidign Palace, and innumerable lords and counts were gathered to witness the joining of House Maumont and House Calidign. The crowd in the great hall was double the size of the ball just over a month prior, and the checkerboard marble floor was hidden entirely by the mass of people lucky enough to witness the historic moment.

Away from the gathered crowd, Eledrith sat alone in his changing room. A royal servant had fitted him with a white doublet embroidered with the blue, purple, and gold of the Calidign colors. The prince had requested a moment of privacy, and the servant obliged him. In solitude Eledrith sat, waiting for the ceremony to begin. King Torvaren was no doubt mingling with other nobles, basking in the limelight. Eledrith, however, was nothing like that man. If it were up to him, the ceremony would have taken place outside the city with only a handful of guests in attendance.

I wish at least Garrick was here, he thought. Eledrith hadn't received any word from the old knight since he had left Saidal, and his fatherly presence was sorely missed. The prince also mused on the idea of Darreth and Krael attending. *I only knew them for a short while, but I grew close to them. I'd take their company over any of these boot-licking backbiters that carouse about the palace.*

"Your Majesty, the ceremony is about to begin."

Startled, the prince jumped from his chair. After a final smoothening of his hair, he followed the servant through the palace and into the vast arched chamber that was the great hall. Banners of both House Calidign and Maumont hung from the walls, and an altar was placed on the northern balcony. Hundreds of heads, adorned by spectacular headdresses and glimmering circlets, turned to watch the prince as he ascended the stairs and met the High Patriarch at the altar.

Clad in white hooded robes, the patriarch was the head figure of the Temple of Atlor, or whatever was left of it. The faith's inception was a secret lost to time, but after its codification five hundred years prior, it became the official religion of Saidal. Like many things in the old city, the temple waned with time, and little more than scattered texts of the once flourishing faith remained. Marriages were one of the few responsibilities the temple still held.

Also standing at the altar was King Torvaren. Like most public appearances, he wore a long, decorative coat to hide his pot-bellied physique. The patriarch and the king smiled at the prince. Eledrith returned the gesture, bowing, then looked down the carpeted pathway that ran through the masses like a canyon, ending in the door on the far end of the hall. Guardsmen of Saidal, protected by heavy mail skirts and gleaming pointed helms, lined the edges of the walkway.

Just then, a strange face caught Eledrith's attention. Luscious lips smiled beneath two feline eyes. Straight black hair ran around the soft cheeks. The visage held an unsettling aura: a feeling of warm embrace tainted by a sinister luster.

"You seem nervous," said Torvaren, interrupting Eledrith's thoughts.

Facing the king, the groom-to-be said, "No, I'm not. Just, well…"

With a hearty laugh, Torvaren patted him on the shoulder. "It's alright, my boy. I was just as nervous when I wed your mother."

Before the prince could get a better look, he lost the peculiar face in the crowd.

All heads turned when the double doors opened, and even from such a distance, seeing Morwenna's face was enough to drive the melancholy from Eledrith's heart. Her hair was tied up in a lavish style, and excess curling locks drifted past her exposed shoulders. Ordric walked her down the aisle, and before long, they were before the altar as well.

The patriarch raised his hands aloft and began reciting the old matrimonial rites. Eledrith paid little attention to this, instead focusing on Morwenna. She smiled, her eyes filled with excitement.

"With Atlor as witness," recited the patriarch, "I now pronounce you husband and wife."

With a roar of applause, the two kissed.

The couple drudged through the next few hours of formalities and speeches. Faces unknown to both of the young nobles approached as if close friends, offering gifts and congratulations. Morwenna's patience lasted much longer than her husband's, and before nightfall, Eledrith requested another moment of peace.

With Princess Morwenna holding the mass of wedding guests at bay, Eledrith retreated to the garden balcony. A layer of frost had crystalized on the trimmed plants, and snow drifted across the stone tiles in the wind. Wine could only do so much for the prince, and while he knew he should be participating in the celebration, he had grown tired of the small talk and polite smiling.

Looking east, Eledrith spotted massive black plumes tarnishing the distant violet sunset. Such a tumult of dark smoke could not be made if a ship were engulfed in flames. Slowly, the smoke drew nearer, and its source could be seen on the horizon. Instead of sails, four towering columns arose from the floating fortress, from the top of which came the unceasing clouds of choking fumes.

"The drenoch," he muttered, remembering the rumors of war.

With that iron ark came a force large enough to wage war against the Outlaw Kingdoms, and knowing that he would need to lead that force, a sinking feeling grew in the prince's stomach. After brushing snow from the stone railing, Eledrith leaned against it, watching the ship gradually approach across the purple sea.

"Your Majesty," began a voice whose soothing tones came to the prince's ear like a warm embrace.

Hoping the speaker to be Morwenna, the prince turned and smiled. To his surprise, the face he was met with did not have warm, inviting brown eyes. Instead, two predatory yellow ones gazed into his own. Eledrith stepped back, bumping into the railing. Taken off guard, he snapped, "Who let you out here? I demanded to be left alone."

"Shh," said the woman, her lush lips slightly parted.

She stepped forward, her thigh appearing from the folds of a midnight robe. Eledrith was cold in his thick doublet, yet the woman showed no signs of being affected by the icy winds. Her garment was so thin that her figure was apparent, but still, she walked forward without shivering. "Let me look at you."

His hand instinctively reached for his sword, but the prince found his hip bare. "Who are you?" he asked.

The woman smiled. "I'm your mother, Eledrith."

"By hell!" he cursed. "How dare you say such a thing? My mother died in childbirth."

Chuckling, the woman said, "And how do you know that? Can one truly remember the day they were born?"

Eledrith's eyes narrowed. "Stop playing these games."

"Which of your ancestors possessed hair like the silver of the moon? Who had those eyes which burn jade like no other? You certainly bear no semblance to that impotent fool Torvaren."

The prince was at a loss for words, and he could only glare at the stranger. *My mother's hair was said to be blond but not as white as mine*, he realized. "A mutation," he said. "It's not unheard of."

The woman laughed. "Then explain your unnatural intelligence. You certainly didn't inherit it from His Majesty. If you focus, you learn faster than a normal man should."

Cocking his head, the prince stared, confused.

"Don't be so naive. How could a boy best one of the greatest swordsmen in the whole of Saidal's army with just a few years of training?"

Eledrith stammered, but the woman continued.

"How could you beat Count Ordric at *sakhmet* in only your second full game?"

"How do you know about that?"

"I've been watching you for a very long time, Eledrith," she said, pacing toward him with cat-like grace. "I know exactly who you are, and I know who you were born to be. You have inherited great power, even if you do not yet understand it."

As she came within mere feet of the prince, Eledrith put an arm out. "Alright," he said, "if you are my mother, then who is my father?"

"You're not ready to know that."

The prince scoffed and turned his back to the woman. "I've heard enough."

"If I were to tell you, it would bring more questions than answers."

This response did not halt Eledrith as he strode for the door to the palace.

"There will come a time, Eledrith," said the woman, "when you will beg to be free of pain. Accept me, and I will be able to help you. If you do not, you will suffer more than you could ever understand."

A cold sweat beaded on Eledrith's back. Attributing it to the elements, he mustered a laugh before calling the guards. "You really shouldn't say such things to a prince—"

Turning to face the enigmatic woman, he found the whole balcony bare. Only his own footprints lay in the accumulations of snow. Mail clinking with each hurried step, two guards burst onto the scene. "You called, my lord?"

Baffled, Eledrith stared at the empty garden. The frozen skeletal limbs of bushes were not thick enough to offer concealment, and the only exit lay behind him. "She was... ah, forget it."

"Are you sure, sire?"

"Perhaps I've had a bit too much wine," said the prince, hoping his sheepish smile resembled drunkenness.

The guards held enough faith in their prince to go along with his story. Before the three reentered the palace, Eledrith looked to the garden. The only thing that appeared out of the ordinary was the ominous cloud of smoke that billowed from the iron ark on the horizon, blotting out the sun.

That night, Eledrith and Morwenna consummated their marriage. Even while sheltered by the warm embrace of his wife, the prince was troubled. Long after the bedside candles had been extinguished and Morwenna lay sleeping against his bare chest, Eledrith stared into the ceiling, reciting the events with the strange woman in his mind's eye. The truth of her words could not be denied. He clung close to his bride, trying to push that ominous, dream-like memory from his mind.

18
WARRIORS FROM THE SAVAGE NORTH

The iron ark rivaled the height of even the tallest towers of Saidal. Far too large to enter the port, it sat three hundred yards out to sea, unmoving despite waves crashing against its steel hull. Just the main deck was higher than any of the masts of the other ships in the port, and the size of the featureless metal wall resembled the cliffs of an island more than a vessel's hull. Atop the deck sprawled a network of fortifications with countless dark apertures peering outward. Four great cylindrical smokestacks ascended toward the clouds. No smoke came from their peaks, as the ship did not move, but many smaller exhaust ports spewed forth their own haze.

A fleet of ferries, metal like the mother ship, unloaded the drenoch's cargo. The warriors of Graehal were a different breed from the folk of Saidal, as their homeland was a frigid, mountainous realm. If a man did not have a beard, he bore a thick mustache that continued down to his jaw. Instead of cloaks, thick skins were worn on the men's backs, making them seem more like a horde of savages than an organized military. While their corded and muscled arms were exposed, their torsos were protected by a thick vest of scale mail. Most strange of all were their helmets, from which jutted many short spikes.

Count Boridron rode onto the pier as the smaller boats began to dock. His bodyguards would have stood taller than him if he had not been seated atop his white steed. He wore an embellished green waistcoat, and an ornate cruciform sword hung at his hip as more of a status symbol than anything else. Meeting him came two drenoch pilots. Clad in dark robes, they paced forward, the metal clang of their mechanical staves resounding far louder than their feet. Their faces were hidden by masks, and from behind dark rectangular lenses, they watched, motives or emotions indeterminable. In front of the drenoch's mouths were beak-like protrusions, from the sides of which came two pipes. They halted before the count, their breaths sounding like the wheezing of a machine.

The drenoch offered no greeting, and Count Boridron stumbled over his words before managing, "Hail there, friends. It is a pleasure to see you again after all these years."

"Unloading will finish within an hour," one said, its voice more mechanical than organic. "Our payment will be loaded once it is done. Are there any questions?"

Stunned by the strict pragmatism of the faceless pilots, Boridron was slow to answer. "Well, er, no, I suppose."

The count's bodyguards were apprehensive of the drenoch. The men eyed their strange staves, fearful of their true power. While they had the form of a spear, the head was divided into two foot-long blades joined to the metal shaft by a mechanical box. The air seemed distorted in the space between the blades as if there was a great heat between them.

"Excellent," said the drenoch, and without another word, the two robed pilots returned to their ferries.

Boridron exhaled a sigh of relief. Waiting until the robed figures were out of earshot, one of the guards asked, "What manner of men are they? And how can such a mighty ship, made of metal nonetheless, move across the seas?"

"They are the last remnants of a bygone time," answered Boridron. "Let us hope that they never turn their eyes toward Saidal, for I do not think we would stand a chance in open conflict."

The ferries had been empty for only a few minutes before they were again loaded. Hundreds of shackled feet slowly paced onto the metal-hulled boats, tired, sunken eyes staring out of fear at their new drenoch masters. Those people had come to Saidal hoping to find a better life working in the megacity, but like most that pledge their lives to the whims of the aristocracy, they were discarded at the earliest convenience, forsaken to the more openly cruel drenoch. The machine staves pointed ominously at any slave that dared step out of line.

Slowly, the Graehalic army was unloaded onto the pier and began marching through the city's narrow streets, led by Count Boridron. Thundering footsteps echoed through the stone-walled avenues as five hundred warriors marched. Compared to the residents of Saidal, these men were utter barbarians. Cruel axes hung from their belts, and their shields were adorned with spikes not dissimilar to the ones on their helmets. As they marched, the mercenaries chanted a war song in the harsh Graehalic tongue, and the streets emptied before them.

While the bulk of the mercenary force rested in the guard's barracks, their leader was brought into the throne room of the Calidign Palace. He was of terrifying stature. Instead of a helmet, only fiery red hair covered his head and face, the braided locks adorned with animal fangs. From beneath two heavy, jagged pauldrons flexed massive arms decorated with faded battle scars. About him marched a group of mercenaries, who on their own were towering and formidable but, in the presence of the fiery-haired warrior, seemed like children. Their reverence for their leader was apparent on their proud yet fearful faces. It was as if they marched beside a god in human form.

The warrior and his entourage entered the dark marble hall. Upon halting, the soldiers slammed a fist against their scale-covered chests and let out a short guttural yell that continued to echo long after it had ceased. While his subordinates stood at stoic attention, the goliath in their midst dropped to a knee, keeping his eyes on the four figures that waited atop the dais. King Torvaren was on his throne as usual, with Count Ordric lurking behind him. At the king's side were Eledrith and Princess Morwenna.

"Greetings, Your Highness," said the warrior, his Graehalic accent present in his speech. "I am called many things. In my homeland, I am Karag-Viil, meaning Scourgefather in your tongue. You can address me by the name my father gave me: Arngrim. My men and I are eager to fight this war you have planned."

Torvaren smiled at the ferocity of his new asset. "Excellent! I hope your journey here was bearable enough."

"The brig of that vessel was more of a dungeon than a ship, but I never imagined such a smooth and swift journey."

Eledrith watched Arngrim intently. He was ferocious, and while he was still human, his stature rivaled Krael's. Unlike the Wizard Slayer, however, his eyes lacked a certain unyielding conviction, instead housing a dismissive, uncaring stare. Even as he knelt before some of the most influential people in the world, his posture was casual and proud. A hand rested against his knee, and his bearded chin was held high. *He may kneel, but this warrior has no actual respect for us*, thought the prince.

"You will be led by my son, Prince Eledrith, in this campaign," said Torvaren. "While he may seem young, his prowess in both swordsmanship and strategy is admired by many."

Ordric nodded, his dark eyes stealing a look at the prince.

Arngrim furrowed his thick brow. Standing up, he said, "I was under the impression that *I* would be commanding *my* men."

Torvaren, shifting in his throne, said, "Do not fear, you will be leading your men, but you will be fighting under the Calidign colors and in the name of my son."

"I don't want my men being led to their deaths by a young princeling trying to prove himself."

Morwenna grew pale and looked to her husband. However, he was not so surprised and glared at the insolent barbarian warrior. "Do you doubt my abilities?" he asked, jade eyes smoldering.

Having not expected such a controlled, cold response, Arngrim cooled his temper. Smiling, he said, "Perhaps. I have known far too many lords who were coddled by the walls of their castles and palaces. While on the march, they did nothing but complain. On the field of battle, they died, screaming like children."

The princess's hand reached for the prince's, but Eledrith did not acknowledge it. "I've already seen my share of bloodshed," he said.

Arngrim scoffed, then said, "I understand the rulers of Saidal don't concern themselves with the wars in Graehal, so I don't expect you to truly understand who you're speaking to, boy. Hell is flooded with the blood of the men I have slain. I've conquered both their lands and their women. My wives are over a thousand score, and a whole generation will bear my mark. Do you still think your own share of bloodshed can compare to mine?"

Behind pursed lips, Eledrith's tongue itched to chastise him for the boast, but the prince quickly realized that any attempt would only be perceived as weakness. With Morwenna's hand tightened around his own, he said, "I never claimed to have slain more than you. Just know that my mettle has been tested."

After hearing Count Ordric's whisper, Torvaren changed the subject. "Well then, let us discuss the nature of this campaign. How much do you know of the Outlaw Kingdoms, Arngrim?"

"Nothing. This is the farthest south I've ever been."

"They are a collection of warring states. Few maps of the borders are drawn since they change so quickly. Two territories have recently united, blocking off Saidal from its trade routes to the other kingdoms. Our goal is to crush these two warlords."

"Why not sow distrust amongst them?" asked Arngrim.

"Because that is not our end goal. Instead of keeping the Outlaw Kingdoms at bay," said Torvaren, "we plan to conquer them, with these territories being a starting point."

"Ah," said Arngrim, "now we're making sense."

Such a large-scale war will secure my employment, thought the barbarian, *and give me more land to conquer. The peoples of these Outlaw Kingdoms may live under the Calidign banner, but the name of the Scourgefather will be whispered on their lips like that of a god.*

"Our first move will be to take out one of these powers without warning. The keep of Orthil the Skull is little more than two days' march from Saidal."

"Then he will die in three," finished Arngrim, a savage grin on his face.

"Perhaps. Let us not underestimate Orthil's Keep. It is an invaluable defensive position," said the king, "but it will also be difficult to conquer. Still, such a position will be needed to wage the rest of the war."

"If Prince Eledrith is as formidable as you attest," said the Scourgefather, "then victory will be assured."

Eledrith didn't dare betray it while the Scourgefather watched, but in his heart, he felt anxious. He was being sent to fight a war he did not believe in. While Arngrim and the king discussed the campaign's logistics, the prince reflected on the moral ramifications. *Things are only going to get worse when this war begins. I can do nothing to stop it, but I can mitigate the damage. If I'm leading the fight, I can ensure the common folk, those who never asked for any of this, go unharmed.*

Preparing for the march to Orthil's Keep, Eledrith stood in his chamber, arms outstretched as a servant latched together the innumerable plates of his new armor. Fully articulated plate armor was a thing seldom seen, and the one that the prince wore was pristine beyond compare. It was the summit of technological achievement in that age, as the greatest smiths were employed to engineer a suit that offered uninhibited mobility while withstanding the heaviest of blows. The prince's body was covered in over a hundred expertly fashioned steel plates, giving him the appearance of silver scales.

"How does it feel, Your Highness?"

Eledrith waved his arms and lifted his knees. "Are you sure you put it on? It doesn't seem to have any weight at all."

The door at the opposite side of the room swung open, and Morwenna entered. "I hope I'm not interrupting anything."

"No, no, we've just finished," said Eledrith. "Well, my love, how do I look?"

The princess's eyes were wide out of both worry and fear. She ran her hand along the many plates on his chest. "Are you sure this will protect you? It looks marvelous, but wouldn't a normal breastplate protect you better than all of these things?"

"The plates are designed to slide across each other," said the servant, "but when a force strikes them from the outside, they act as one. Have no fear, Your Majesty. The prince will be the most well-protected man on the battlefield."

"I doubt I'll even have to draw my sword," said Eledrith.

"You say that like it's a bad thing," said the princess.

Wishing he had controlled his tone, Eledrith's eyes went to the floor. "I don't really like the idea of telling other men where to go to die while I sit behind, giving orders."

Morwenna tried to comfort the prince, but the touch of her hand could not be felt through the steel plate.

"I know it's necessary," said Eledrith, "someone needs to lead in the fight, but it's not like a game of *sakhmet* where a bad move leads to a loss of a piece. People die. On both sides."

"And you'd rather risk yourself instead of bear that burden?"

"Gladly," said Eledrith, ready to say the word before Morwenna had finished.

The princess swallowed.

Eledrith backed away, testing the mobility of his shoulders. "But Garrick always said that if I don't take my place as leader, burdens and all, someone else will take that place instead, and they usually won't understand the true weight of that responsibility."

"Wise words," said Morwenna.

"Don't worry, I'll be careful," said Eledrith, bringing a gauntleted hand to his wife's cheek.

Tiring of talk, Morwenna pulled Eledrith in, and the two kissed.

———◆———

At the head of the military parade rode Eledrith, a white cape flowing with his hair in the winter wind. Covering the prince's body were the silvery plates of the new armor, and at his hip was his favored swept-hilt longsword. To his side rode Arngrim, the Scourgefather, whose gruff, brutal appearance was far from the prince's near-angelic aura. Peering from hundreds of windows and lining the streets were the civilians. Any sounds they made were drowned out by the marching boots and war-chanting. The Graehalic mercenaries were far more savage than the guards that patrolled Saidal, and their welcome wasn't necessarily warm. Before long, the procession had left the city gates and marched east upon the open road.

"Ah, what a relief it is to leave that godless city," said Arngrim.

Eledrith turned in his saddle. "Godless?"

"Aye," the barbarian answered. "You take offense to that?"

"No, for it bears no truth. Saidal's patron god is Atlor, the Tamer of the Sea," said the prince matter-of-factly.

Arngrim snorted. "Is it really, now?"

"What are you getting at?"

"Many people these days say they follow gods, but it is not faith," said the warrior. "Even in my homeland, many claim they prepare for the great wolf of the underworld, but these are empty words."

"Forgive me, but I'm unfamiliar with the gods of Graehal."

"I speak of Grindenfang, the devourer of souls that waits beneath. We all must face him when we die. He guards the path to the next world, seeking to feast on those unworthy of passing on. A true follower of the old ways will strive in their life to become as powerful as possible in hopes of defeating Grindenfang and reaching the undying paradise."

"Seems barbaric," said Eledrith.

"Coming from the likes of you," Arngrim retorted.

"I struggle to believe that a cosmic dog waits to eat me after I die."

"But you've lived your life in the shelter of your cozy palace, each and every one of your little desires met. Graehal is far different. Little can grow in the frozen soil, and only the strongest stand a chance of surviving the sunless winter months. By knowing that Grindenfang awaits, we have an ideal to strive for that gives meaning to such a painful existence."

Eledrith shook his head. "It's not ideals you strive for, then; it's just survival. Stories of Grindenfang were no doubt conjured up by mortal men to promote a proper way of living."

"Men could merely survive without gods," said Arngrim, "but it is an existence devoid of purpose. Why strive on? The gods answer this question, even if you're too short-sighted to ask it."

Eledrith pondered this answer. *Why does one strive on?* The question had always lurked in his mind, shrouded by the cacophony of more urgent matters. It was then brought to the forefront, and the prince felt a chill in his soul. "To pursue the just and the good," he concluded aloud.

Arngrim broke into condescending laughter. "The just and good?" he mocked. "Such fleeting things."

"What do you mean?"

"It was but a handful of decades ago when merchants of Saidal bought war captives from my homeland to be sold as slaves. Yet now such trade has been banned. What changed?"

"The rulers of Saidal realized it was wrong," answered Eledrith.

"Realized? Or did they deem it wrong? Was it always wrong before, or did it change with time? I don't dare pledge myself to such fleeting concepts, boy."

The prince gritted his teeth and reflected on Arngrim's insight. He had half a mind to end the conversation there, but he couldn't allow someone to simply brush off the idea of good and evil. "I know there is great evil in the world," said Eledrith. "I've seen only a small portion of it firsthand, but I know it exists. Surely then the absence of it must be good."

Arngrim grunted to himself. "It seems we're different men."

They continued to ride without speaking. Close behind was the five-hundred-strong legion of Graehalic warriors, uninhibited by the cold. While the surrounding hills were bleak and white, the low temperature was nothing compared to that of northern Graehal. Even with muscled limbs exposed, the mercenaries marched on with spirits high, following the red-haired figure of legend that was Arngrim.

The crimson light of the evening sky shone across snowy fields, and the massive figure of the Dead Giant lurked in the distance. "Do you think we will reach that by nightfall, Arngrim?"

The fiery-haired warrior squinted into the distance. "Aye, we'll make it, but I'll be damned if I'm going to make camp near such a thing."

Much to Arngrim's discontent, the army made camp beneath the ancient mechanical giant. So high it stood that the camp's firelight only glowed against the thing's knee, and the rest of the body ascended into the starry sky like a titanic humanoid shadow. Arn-grim looked at its ominous heights, a sliver of fear in his otherwise stoic eyes.

"Are you alright?" asked Eledrith, sitting next to him by the fire.

"That thing walked once," said Arngrim. "I do not wish to see it walk again."

The camp was a sprawling mass of tents that extended hundreds of yards. At its center was Prince Eledrith's tent, whose purple, blue, and gold fabrics stood out against the drab, una-dorned brown of the mercenaries'. Inside was the prince himself, accompanied by a handful of royal guards. On a table, illuminated by candlelight, was a topographical map of the region. The map's focus was a dot labeled "Orthil's Keep."

Arngrim had his large hands on the table, resting his weight against it. Cursing to himself in his native language, he stood up, saying, "There's no good way to approach it. The keep has a sight over everything for miles around."

"Assuming we attack by day," said Eledrith.

The fangs that adorned Arngrim's braids clicked together as he shook his head. "Your inexperience reveals itself, boy. Com-manding an army at night is much harder than you'd think."

"Then I must defer to your judgment. I know little of siege tactics."

"Good choice," scoffed Arngrim, eyes scanning the map for any possible vantage point. "If we had more time, we could simply encircle the keep and starve them out, but your father requested an immediate victory."

Minutes passed as Eledrith watched the experienced con-queror strategize, mumbling plans to himself. As he watched, the prince wondered if the tales about the Scourgefather were true. History books held stories of conquerors that took hundreds of wives, but these men often grew fat in their ornate palaces. Arn-grim was not of their stock. Like the prince, he relished in the fight, wishing to lead from the front. While he could have ruled from a throne somewhere in frigid Graehal, he instead chose to risk his life on the battlefield. *His conviction to Grindenfang is admirable indeed, even if it is a barbaric faith*, thought Eledrith.

After Arngrim backed away from the map, Eledrith's thoughts shifted back to the task at hand. "Perhaps we're approaching this from the wrong angle."

Arngrim looked up, a skeptical eyebrow raised.

Eledrith continued. "What if we sent a small force in to assassinate Orthil himself?"

"Do we have qualifying men amongst us?"

"I'd be willing to attempt such a task."

Arngrim laughed. "You really think you could do this yourself, boy?"

Princess Morwenna's warnings came to Eledrith's mind. This plan was precisely what she had told him not to do. *If I am successful, I'll have the respect of these mercenaries*, thought the prince.

"Then again," said Arngrim, "I have seen this done before, and Orthil's Keep is small enough that we could pull it off."

Both Eledrith and Arngrim leaned in toward the map. As the candles dripped wax and burned into the night, they finalized their plan.

"We could keep the bulk of our troops behind these hills," said Eledrith, pointing to a cluster of shaded circles on the map. "And call them in once the keep has been secured."

"I don't care how great you think you are. Nothing short of an army can occupy that fortification. Slaughtering Orthil, however—"

"Would send the defenses into a state of chaos," finished the prince, "which is the opposite of what we want. I'd prefer a clean surrender."

"You'd be surprised at the compliance terror can create."

"I wish to make this whole endeavor as civil as possible."

"This is war, boy. It's going to be anything but civil."

Eledrith released a sigh, then said, "Fair enough."

They continued to scan the map, fingers running over the many inked lines of the parchment. "We could keep the bulk of our forces behind these hills until nightfall, and then once we've taken the keep, we'll give them the signal to approach. They should be given orders beforehand since commanding such a large force is impossible at night."

"If they already have their orders, then there's no need for either of us to be with them."

"Meaning we could both be inside the keep," said Arngrim. "And it wouldn't hurt to bring a few men with us."

"Stealth would be a much more difficult approach the more men we bring."

"Aye, but if it all goes to hell, we can signal for our reinforcements."

The metal plates of the prince's armor clicked as he crossed his arms and took a step away from the map. While his plan seemed difficult at the outset, it was starting to come together.

The door to Orthil the Skull's bedchambers flew open and crashed against the wall, awakening everyone who lay inside. In a rush to move to his feet and draw a bedside weapon, Orthil flung his sheets away, exposing his own bare body and his wife's. The lantern-lit hallway glowed an orange hue, but no light in the chamber revealed the intruder's face.

Orthil stood naked, only protected by a sword. He had always been a well-built man, but as he began to wane past his prime, his body had started to go soft. Regardless, he stood, his gaunt head tilted forward in hostility. His face was gruesomely disfigured, causing those not used to his countenance to gasp in shock. A single sword stroke had cleaved off the tip of his nose along with a section of his upper lip, giving Orthil a permanent sneer and a skull-like appearance that inspired his namesake. "Who do you think you are?" he said.

"Your servant, Romil, m'lord."

"Damn it!" shouted Orthil. "I should have you executed for your lack of manners."

The servant, who was but a boy, averted his eyes. "It's urgent, sir."

"Well then, spit it out!"

"There are intruders in the lower halls. Only ten of them, but they fight without fear. They've killed over twenty men already!"

"No matter," said the warlord, throwing on trousers and a robe. "Send more. They cannot last forever."

Romil stammered, appalled at his lord's disregard for human lives. Before he could question these orders, Orthil commanded, "Send more men now!"

"Y-yes, sire," said Romil, who ran back into the keep to do his master's bidding.

The warlord turned to see his wife cowering amidst the sheets. "Get up, Sarelle!" he barked. "We'll make for the hidden tunnel."

Sarelle pulled herself from the bed and covered herself with whatever clothes were in reach. Then, taking her husband's hand, she followed him through the twisting halls of the keep. She had forgotten to put on boots, and the slapping of bare soles resounded off the unpolished brick floor as she went.

On the first floor of the keep, a battle raged. Soldiers clad in loose rusted mail fell beneath the tide of Graehalic barbarians. At the head of the attacking force was a man whose body seemed to be covered in gleaming silver. From the back of his shining helm came locks of white hair, whipping with grace as he fought. Like a demigod of legend, Eledrith cut down all that charged at him, his technique flawless. At the prince's side fought Arngrim, and while his form was less elegant than his Saidalian ally's, the bodies he sent spattering to the floor rivaled Eledrith's count. Behind them was a small squad of mercenaries, only twelve strong. The quality of the Graehalic weaponry and armor far surpassed the ragged gear of Orthil's men, and the difference in number was not enough to immediately wipe the invading force out.

The spikes of the Graehalic shields tore into flesh. As the victims cried out in agony, swift axe strikes were enough to silence them. Blood pooled on the stone tiles of the floor, coagulating in jagged cracks. While the intruders fought valiantly, the defenders seemed to be innumerable. Many had died, but no ground had been gained. The sound of clashing steel was deafening in the confined space, and only by yelling could Eledrith and Arngrim hear each other.

"There's too many of them," screamed the prince, voice hoarse. "This was a terrible plan!"

The Scourgefather laughed as his axe split the exposed skull of a screaming pikeman. "You best start to revere the gods now, boy," he said. "We'll be meeting them soon enough."

Their plan would have worked if they could have known the sheer number of guards garrisoned in the keep itself. The previous night, a spy had disguised himself and crept into the keep. He had reckoned only a handful of guards protected the front gate (since more could be mustered if an army was spotted in the distance). Instead of a stealthy entrance, a single guard had escaped during the initial entry and sounded the alarm. Thus was their predicament. What could have been an easy assassination had turned into a siege.

Through the fray, the prince watched as reinforcements pooled in from the leftmost of three hallways. "Push right!" he commanded.

Some of the mercenaries obeyed, while others were baffled. "We'll no longer have access to the front gates," said Arngrim.

Eledrith had learned much while playing *sakhmet* with his wife. One lesson in particular applied here. "We don't have many pieces on the board," said the prince. "Defeat is certain if we thin ourselves out. We'll find a defensive position deeper in the keep."

"Pieces?" asked Arngrim, unaware that what Eledrith said was an analogy. "Er, alright, that is a sound plan."

After the red-haired warrior barked orders to the mercenaries in their native tongue, they carved a path in their enemies' weaker, unreinforced side. Fresh troops piled in, cutting off the mercenary force from escape. Shields warding off deadly blows, the invaders shuffled sideways, steadily making their way toward a stone-arched hallway.

A spearhead glimmered as it was thrust toward the chest of one of the mercenaries. A muscled arm strained to lift the spiked shield, but it was too late. The spear's tip had come too close, and the shield's rim knocked the haft upward. Instead of colliding with the hardened scales of Graehalic armor, the spear sank into the eye of the mercenary. Without a scream, he dropped, crimson ichor running down the spear's shaft. With his death, Eledrith's flank was exposed, and the prince then faced twice as many guards.

The flurry of slashes that Eledrith let out was impressive, but they could not fend off all of the encroaching host. A sword made it through the prince's guard, and he gasped, expecting a sharp pain in his chest. Instead, he was pushed back, the enemy's blade glancing off his gleaming plate. With this, a new wave of confidence surged, and Eledrith charged forward. When he had practiced with Garrick, contact with the opponent's blade was considered death, but the prince's new armor changed this. While one hand wielded his sword, the other grabbed and entrapped weapons. No longer concerned with defense, he pirouetted and spun, pulling an axe from one man while cleaving the head of another.

In the face of Eledrith's fighting, the mercenaries backed away. Few had seen such an admirable display, and even Arngrim watched in amazement. For a moment, Orthil's guard looked like they were going to retreat.

"Hurry, Eledrith!" called Arngrim, who had sprinted through the hall and deeper into the heart of the fortress.

Realizing he would soon be left behind, Eledrith offered a final slash to ward off the hesitant enemy before following.

Hidden in the castle was an entrance to a tunnel that resurfaced hundreds of yards away. Dug specifically for hasty escapes, it would allow someone to leave the fortress even if it was encircled by a besieging army. Orthil and Sarelle never made it to this tunnel. As they rounded a corner, they were met with a figure of sheer barbaric ferocity. The red of his hair and beard was interlaced with the white of fangs. While the thick armor and fur cloak contributed to his hulking stature, in that moment, Orthil would have sworn that the man was part bear. Forward the Scourgefather charged, a massive battle-axe held high.

Orthil raised his sword to defend himself, but the weight of the axe came crashing through his defenses. The warlord's skull-like face suddenly lost its grisly aura as his eyes widened and mouth opened in shock. There was a cry of agony, then a screech of horror.

Eledrith, leading the mercenaries, tore down the hall. As the prince rounded a corner, he was met with a sight that made his stomach churn. While there had been no lack of gore that night, seeing the contents of Orthil's chest cavity spattered across his wife's shrieking face made even the hardened warriors leer.

As the limp corpse of the once-warlord dropped, Orthil's wife staggered back, limbs trembling so violently that she could not muster herself into a proper run. Arngrim turned to her, his heavy breaths hissing between gritted teeth. She continued to scream, her voice growing hoarse.

"That's enough!" commanded Eledrith.

Arngrim turned back, scowling at the prince. In the wake of Eledrith's booming voice, even Sarelle went silent. "We should take her prisoner," said Arngrim.

"We could if she doesn't perish from fright."

The red-haired warrior snorted, then turned to the gore-painted widow and grabbed her by the arm. She offered little resistance, and one of Arngrim's mighty limbs was enough to drag her across the newly slick floor.

"Treat her with some respect," Eledrith scolded. "We will hold her for political reasons, to secure dominance over this territory, and nothing else. There's no need to inflict any more suffering."

"Forgive me, Your Majesty," said Arngrim, condescension dripping from every word.

Hoisted upright by the Graehalic man's strength, Orthil's widow stood before the Prince of Saidal, speechless. Turning to his troops, Eledrith said, "Defend this hallway. The enemy has yet to know that their lord is dead."

Passing by Arngrim, the silver-clad prince continued. "This would have been easier if you had let Orthil live."

"In Graehal, armies surrender when they are afraid. Brutality is necessary. If you don't seem like a monster to your enemies, they will still think they have a chance."

I should have expected this would happen, thought the prince as he crouched down beside the fallen lord. His chest was not just cut but torn open by the axe. Cold eyes stared blankly into Eledrith's, and he wondered what Orthil may have done to deserve such a fate. The sounds of battle seemed distant to the prince as the guard clashed with the mercenaries.

With a single slice, Orthil's head went rolling from his body. At that angle, beheading a prone body without striking the floor was difficult, but the prince's skill allowed him to do such a task with ease. Raising the disfigured head high, he paced toward the enemy.

Upon seeing what had become of their lord, the guard's morale was broken. One by one, they ceased fighting and backed away. Between seeing their Orthil dead and recognizing the superior prowess of the Graehalic mercenaries, they saw no point in continuing to fight. With the blowing of a great horn, the rest of Eledrith's force marched onto the town surrounding Orthil's Keep.

19
THE FALLEN RACE

The rugged wilderness proved safer than established roads, and the three fugitives had fared well thanks to Galfred's donation of rations and supplies. Each day that passed, they pressed onward, not knowing how far behind Garrick and Morgvid were.

They had come upon the ruins of what once was a massive concrete fortress. Avalanches had built new slopes over the walls, and only a few fortified corners of the original structure could be seen piercing through the earth and snow. Darreth and Krael got to work clearing an area to make camp. In the shadow of a ruined wall, little snow accumulated, and it made the perfect spot to start a fire and set up tents for the night.

Exhausted by their nonstop flight, the three warmed themselves around a fire in silence. Dark spots had grown under their eyes, and the dried venison considered savory and pleasant a week prior seemed bland. Hoping to break the gloomy mood, Darreth piped up. "Have you guys heard the joke about the man who lost his left arm and left leg?"

Both companions looked up. The elf-blooded finished with, "Don't worry, he's now all right."

Lorienne didn't respond. Krael furrowed his brow for a moment. After struggling with the nuances of the pun, he gave a short grunt. Neither of them were amused.

The smile that Darreth had mustered quickly faded away, and silence once again dominated. Ever since their encounter with the pale assassin, there had been tension amidst the group, particularly with Lorienne. Krael was never the conversational type in the first place, but the sword-dancer was a far cry from the bold, outgoing woman she had been at the Raven's Rest. Her face was fixed into a scowl, and neither Darreth nor the Slayer could tell what she thought. Thinking the group's mood couldn't get any worse, Darreth asked, "So, you still plan on heading your own way once we reach another settlement?"

"Yes," Lorienne said, not bothering to take her eyes off the fire.

"Are you sure?"

"I am," she snapped, glaring at Darreth. "Whatever that thing was that chased us, I don't want to ever meet it again. I'm not bound to you in any way. There's no reason for me to fear those manhunters when it's not me they want."

Darreth started, but Lorienne immediately cut him off. "I don't owe you anything. All my life, I was trained to serve with the sword and my body, and all my life, I hated it. My chance at freedom is so close, and only you two stand in my way!"

Only the crackling of the dying fire echoed off the dilapidated walls, and the whistling of the wind persisted high above. What Lorienne had said was the byproduct of feelings suppressed for far too long, and neither of the men dared comment at that moment. Sensing the weight of her outburst, Lorienne rose. "I'm going to find some wood for the fire," she said.

A stack of firewood sat behind Krael, but regardless, Lorienne left. The sword-dancer's lithe form disappeared behind a snow-covered crag of broken concrete. Reading the anxious look on Darreth's face, Krael said, "Let her go. She's right."

"Wait, what?"

"She doesn't owe us."

The elf-blooded picked up a stick and agitated the orange coals. After a sigh, he said, "Why does this always happen? Whenever we start to find friends, we immediately lose them. Hell, Eledrith was a great man, but you didn't trust his father, so we had to say goodbye."

Darreth's tone grew harsher. Throwing his stick into the fire, he said, "Wait, we couldn't even say goodbye. You demanded we run."

"I'm sorry," said the Slayer.

"What are we even doing? We're just running, but why? Yeah, wizards need to die. Trust me, I believe that with all my heart, but we can't keep doing this forever. We're constantly going on by the skin of our teeth. What's your end goal, Krael?"

The Slayer's eyes grew solemn as he remembered the monks of Mog Muhtar's words: *Your path is one of pain and suffering. You are destined to perish battling the servants of the Dark Gods.* Krael often thought of death as a relief from his duty, and whenever the thought of a peaceful end came to mind, he quickly forgot it. In truth, his end goal was to die, slaughtering as many wizards as he could before that happened.

"Tell me, Krael!"

In his slow, awkward dialect, the Wizard Slayer told his only friend what he was destined for. "I was trained to fight wizards. It is what I must do. If I do not, they commit great evil. I will do this until they stop me. One day, you will find me lying dead by their hand. It must be this way."

Darreth's breath escaped him. He knew the Kolgathian to be grim, but this was something else entirely. Krael had often alluded to this, but the elf-blooded had always figured that one day he would need to peacefully retire. "Listen to yourself! This one-track thinking will definitely end with you dead, that's for sure."

"What else do I do? Let the wizards live?"

"You can't kill them all, Krael."

"I can try."

Clenching his jaw, Darreth knew there was no changing the barbarian's mind.

"Any other life would be wasted," Krael said.

Before he could retort, the ghost of a memory came to Darreth. It was the face of a woman, full of shock and sorrow. A single arrow pierced her and her child, and an empty bow sat in Darreth's cold hand. At that moment, he remembered why he followed the Wizard Slayer.

Lorienne's voice came from out of sight. "Someone's here!"

In an instant, the Kolgathian stood and raised his hammer. His coat slipped from him, and his bare muscular chest was exposed. A rush of blood staved off the cold, and a cloud of fog exhaled from between bared fangs.

"I'll ready the horses!" said Darreth.

The sword-dancer returned to the firelight. "I don't think it was the manhunters," she said.

Krael still glared to the horizon, where orange rays of the setting sun shot between the sparse pines. Darreth, already having unhitched a horse, looked at the woman in confusion.

"I couldn't get a good look at him," said Lorienne. "He didn't seem tall, but I'm not sure. Also, I think he might've been naked."

The elf-blooded's face curled with disgust. Krael tightened his grip on the war hammer. "Dwarves," he snarled.

"Should we camp somewhere else?" asked Lorienne.

"It's no use," said Darreth. "The whole mountain's probably crawling with them."

"So, we're all damned, then?"

"We keep the fire burning," said Krael. "They fear it."

The wet branches of the pines were slow to ignite, but when they were alight, the smoke was choking and the fire blazing. The corner of the smooth concrete wall provided their camp cover from two sides, but the other half was exposed to the shadows of the night. The horses had been hitched inside the wall and occasionally snorted as they slept. Despite its mass of orange tongues, the fire only illuminated the ground but a handful of paces away. Beyond that, unseen shapes shifted about in the mountain breeze.

Taking the first watch was Lorienne. She sat with her back to the wall, her secondhand falchion laying unsheathed across her lap. The disembodied dwarf heads she had seen mounted on stakes had been given new life in her imagination. That pale, knobby form that had scurried behind a tree a few hours earlier was a fleeting image, but its gnarled muscle disgusted the sword-dancer more than any animal. As she stared off into the blackness, she swore there lurked sets of beady, unblinking eyes like those of rats. Sleep weighed down on her eyes, and she allowed them to close for a moment.

When the sword-dancer awoke, the camp was no longer protected by the pillar of orange flame. Smoldering coals were enough to show the twisted body, almost child-like in proportion, with its muscles corded like that of an ox. Outlined by a wispy beard, crooked teeth gaped from a drooling maw. Where eyes should have been, two minute black orbs sat. Where once those organs could have guided careful, crafting hands millennia before, they could now only scowl at the light they had learned to fear. Seeing the troglodyte, Lorienne felt the urge to vomit, but her combative instincts took control. Her fingers delicately wrapped about the hilt of her falchion, she arose in a single bound of grace and lunged toward the creeping dwarf. The thing could do nothing to slow the steel edge from shearing through its barrel-like torso. A pig-like cry of agony came from the dwarf as its entrails pooled beneath him.

Krael was standing in an instant. Darreth was slower to rise but readied his bow without question. Looking down at the dwarf, whose body was now in two, the elf-blooded said, "He was probably trying to grab our rations. Damn good cut, though!"

"Thank you," said Lorienne, struggling to smile in the presence of the slain degenerate.

"You think there's more, Krael?"

His black locks blown out of his face, Darreth could see Krael's bared fangs. Knowing this meant that he did, in fact, sense more nearby, he nocked an arrow.

A horrible battle screech came from the darkness. Amidst its shrill tones was the telltale character of a human-like voice. Bounding through the air came a whole swarm of the dwarves, the largest of them rearing toward the Wizard Slayer. Each of the beasts carried a makeshift tool, but these were not even a shadow of the delicate instruments their race once used. Made from splintered branches and jagged rocks, their shivs would not last after perhaps one use, but their sharp nails and gnashing teeth would be employed at that point.

As the dwarf barreled toward Krael, the barbarian clasped his mighty fingers about the thing's neck. Its painful cries reduced to a hoarse whisper, the cretin dug its fingernails into the Kolgathian's forearm. This did nothing to stop the Slayer from swinging his body around, dashing the dwarf's skull against the jagged edge of the ruined wall. With his free hand, Krael swung his war hammer with ease, knocking back swaths of the oncoming host.

Darreth's fingertips grew raw as he loosed arrow after arrow. His enemies fared far worse as the steel tips of the projectiles bore through flesh and cracked bone. Their bestial fortitude allowed them to often survive the first shot, but they were slowed enough to fall under the wrath of the Slayer's hammer and Lorienne's blade.

Lorienne herself was a spectacle that both Darreth and Krael found themselves admiring. Had she not held a sword and cleaved limbs, her movements would have easily been mistaken for a dance. While desperate in the clamor of the fight, each step had a smooth grace that a layman would struggle to replicate under the best of conditions. With the swiftness of a falcon, she whipped and spun, sidestepping the dwarves' assaults and lacerating their exposed sides.

The three were just barely holding the front lines at bay. The whole of Krael's war hammer was caked with a deep crimson. As Lorienne continued to slash, she noticed her blade begin to dull as it stuck against many sturdy bones. Darreth's hand reached to his hip-side quiver and panicked as he felt it empty. The space between the two front-line fighters began to open without the elf-blooded's volley of arrows. In desperation, Darreth ran to the fire and kicked embers toward the degenerates, who screeched as the coals sizzled against their flesh.

Then, as swiftly as the attack had come, it ceased. The three still stood at the ready, a white-knuckled grip on their weapons. In the distance, beyond the barrier of black shadow, a gibbering chatter came. What little intelligibility that was amongst the dwarves' pseudowords was lost to the Slayer and his companions. A grip of unease was about them as the foul voices receded into the night.

During the relative peace, Darreth rushed to gather as many of his arrows as he could, cursing when he found the shafts to be broken. Krael, regaining his breath, turned to Lorienne and said, "You fought well."

"I'd be dead if I didn't," she said, a sardonic curl forming on the corner of her lips.

Without warning, the Kolgathian's head cocked to the side, whipping his black mane. "They are not finished," he said.

Neither Lorienne nor Darreth knew what caused the Slayer to say this. "Stay here," Krael roared as he charged into the dark.

Minutes passed. The adrenaline began to fade, and Lorienne became aware of the scrapes accumulated on her legs. Stress began to build, and the sword-dancer asked, "Do you think Krael will be alright?"

"He'll be fine, trust me," said Darreth, almost reflexively.

The elf-blooded's confidence waned when he remembered the Slayer's words. *One day, you will find me lying dead by their hand.*

"Not yet, though," mumbled Darreth.

"What was that?" asked Lorienne.

"Nothing."

Behind the encampment loomed the fifteen-foot corner of wall. From its top, unseen by the two below, crawled the body of a dwarf. Fat fingers groped and clutched at the jagged cracks in the weathered concrete. As quietly as it had climbed, it leaped down, reaching stunted arms toward its prey.

Lorienne saw motion in her peripheral vision and, without thinking, slashed. The dwarf would have been wounded by the fall, but it never reached the ground alive. The sword-dancer's slice took off its ear and scalp, and the thing landed with a dead thud. Gray matter spilled from the massive hole in its misshapen skull.

Darreth cursed, then whirled about to fire up at the second assault. Recklessly the dwarves plummeted, urged on by hunger and instinctual malice. The horde then swelled around the encampment, and the two found themselves drowning in a sea of pale, gnarled bodies and screaming bearded maws. Like worms of the earth, their wretched forms scrambled forth, blindly pushing themselves through the chaos. Lorienne hacked and punched, her technique regressing as she struggled to keep the inbred creatures at bay. The horses whinnied as their hooves crushed skulls, and by the stroke of a miracle, their wounds were only superficial.

The elf-blooded fared far worse. He may have proven himself against one of the creatures in single combat, but their crooked hands latched onto him. He screamed as their jagged nails ripped at his skin. Their stubby fingers pushed onto his eyes and teeth. One of the creatures sank its teeth into Darreth's side, and his whole body contracted in pain. *Please, not like this!*

"Darreth!" Lorienne screamed in horror.

Just then, a hulking body fell from the top of the ruined wall. Clinging to it was a mass of pale, sickly bodies, perhaps more densely than that which clung to Darreth. The group hit the ground hard. A crunch was heard, and mutilated dwarves were thrown about the camp. Within the pile, an opposition still lived. Roaring, the Kolgathian pulled the creatures from his gore-painted body.

The ferocity Lorienne then witnessed was a memory that would give her chills until the end of her days. Krael had lost his war hammer, but his killing did not slow. His hands dug into mouths and eyes, ripping flesh apart with brute strength. His fangs sank and crushed, tearing arteries and splintering bone.

Like a hound digging into the earth, the Wizard Slayer dug into the hill of bodies that enveloped the elf-blooded. From one hand, he began to swing the limp body of a dwarf, using it as a flail to punish the vile creatures.

The few dwarves that could still move did so like rats, desperately crawling away from the Kolgathian's wrath. Still, the Slayer gave no quarter. He leaped at the cowering inbreds, crushing a throat with his foot. His hands clutched any enemy within reach, jerking them violently until they ceased to move. Krael's corded, rippling muscles contorted and bulged as he fought; his whole body was a machine designed for slaughter. Dwarves squealed as they were torn open, their tongues curling in agony.

The few cretins that survived died of their wounds in the wretched burrows they retreated to. Victorious, Krael stood in the firelight, blood and entrails dripping from his trembling body.

Lorienne ran to Darreth. He lay on the ground, unconscious, in a pool of blood. While much of the gore belonged to the dwarves, some of it was undoubtedly his, as even in the feeble orange glow, Lorienne could see that he was growing pale. Looking closer, she saw that his headband had been ripped from him, and his ears tapered to peculiar points.

20
WRETCHED LANDS

The entire mountainside reeked of death, and with the coming of the dawn came a swarm of carrion birds. Black beaks and feathers abounded, tearing apart the already mutilated dwarves, and any snow that remained white was then red. For generations thereafter, any degenerates that survived would avoid the area. The grim events were burned deep into their race's subconscious memory.

Krael and his companions slept in sparse bursts that night, save Darreth, who slid on the razor's edge between life and death. Lorienne reckoned that, except for a shiv puncture in his leg, none of the wounds were deep. The elf-blooded was affected by shock. After bandages were tied around nearly every part of his body, he was brought close to the embers of the fire. Even then, his skin was cold and clammy to the touch. He was unrecognizable thanks to the multitude of scratches across his face.

Watching the outskirts of the camp, the Slayer crouched. While he had used a handful of snow to clean himself, dry splotches of dark red still remained. Lorienne called over to him, asking, "What do we do now?"

"Keep moving."

"But Darreth needs to rest."

"He'll die out here. We move. Then he can rest."

Lorienne wished to retort, but she remembered what terrible violence the Wizard Slayer was capable of. The barbarian, moving with the ferocity of a wildcat, eyes wide and teeth bared, was an image that she struggled to drive from her mind. The sword-dancer knew that Krael wasn't necessarily a threat to her, but she was still wary of his presence. She said, "Is Darreth an... elf?"

"None still live," said Krael, keeping his eyes to the dawning horizon. "His ancestors were elves."

"They say Colanthus was built by elves, though they called it a different name. I've always considered them fairy tales, the children of gods and all."

"I know little of them."

"Maybe you should ask Darreth when he wakes up," said Lorienne. "If he wakes up."

"He knows little of them."

Lorienne looked at the wounded youth. His boyish face made it difficult to ascertain his actual age, but the dwarves' scratches made it impossible. "Is it true that people like Darreth are hunted down for their blood?"

"Yes. It's how I met him."

"Really?"

Krael nodded, then said, "A witch wanted his blood. I killed her. Then burned her."

"You mean you saved Darreth?"

The Slayer grunted, and Lorienne assumed it to mean a more humble form of admission. "So he follows you because he thinks he owes you a life debt?"

"He follows me because he wishes to," said Krael.

"Is he insane? I'm sorry, but Darreth's lucky that he survived this long. From what I can tell, you cause trouble wherever you go. Traveling with you is damn near suicide."

The golden sun began to rise into the crimson morning sky, and, for a time, the red gore splattered across the snow was indiscernible amidst the warm light. After struggling to articulate his answer, the Slayer said, "He carries a burden. I do not know what. He knows that a life battling evil is the only life worth living. He forgets sometimes. He often complains. I do not care. I still trust him."

The Slayer's words disturbed Lorienne. Something about the moral obligation of life, at least in the way that Krael alluded to it, scared her. Before she could say anything, Krael announced, "We must leave. Garrick may not be far behind."

"You and Darreth both speak of the knight as if you know him," she said, folding her bedroll.

"We do. Months ago, we traveled with him. And the Prince of Saidal."

"What did you do to make him chase after you? Let me guess, you killed someone you shouldn't have because you thought they were evil."

The barbarian knelt down to his elf-blooded friend and picked him up. "No. Garrick is a good man. The king he serves is evil. The king wished to control me."

"As petty as that sounds, I can respect that," said Lorienne. "I've tried long and hard to be more than just a servant."

Krael shook his head and gave a disapproving grunt. "We all must serve something. If you think you are your own master, you are a puppet of something evil."

The sword-dancer didn't dare question what the Slayer had said since the fanaticism within his tone was something not to be argued with. Giving Krael the last word, she kicked snow into the remnants of the fire.

Gathering what supplies that had not been ruined in the previous night's fight, the two readied their horses for another long day of riding. The black stallions had fared quite well, all things considered. Their coats were riddled with the superficial scrapes that a few dwarves managed, and Krael's mount had lost a bit of its ear, but the beasts had fought just as well as their human masters.

As Krael laid Darreth across the back of his horse, Lorienne asked, "Do these horses have names?"

The Kolgathian's face twisted in confusion. "No," he grunted, "they are horses."

"They're living things with feelings!" said Lorienne. "Since you didn't name them, I will."

After sliding her sheathed falchion into a leather loop on the saddle, Lorienne swung a leg upward. Her body followed, and she was in the riding position with one bound. "I'm going to name you... Eresto. See? I think he likes that name."

Krael rolled his eyes as he saddled his own mount. Holding the reins of Darreth's horse, he began to ride north. Lorienne asked, "What are you naming yours, Krael?"

"Uh... Horse," he said.

"You can't be serious!"

"I think Horse likes his name," Krael said.

Lorienne hoped this was the Slayer's sense of humor talking and not his genuine attempt at language. Krael's back was to her. If he smiled, she did not see it.

As they rode across the mountainside, the sword-dancer kept a nervous eye on Darreth, whose pale bandaged body haphazardly rested against Krael's broad back. With the Kolgathian controlling two steeds, their pace was slow, but onward they went.

———◆———

After a day of riding, they passed over the Wylderen Mountains. As the terrain leveled, their speed increased, and they soon left the pine forest. Before them spread a vast valley, and a shallow, wide river snaked and weaved in its center. The plain was starkly flat, with few trees breaking the monotony of the land. Jutting from the eastern horizon rose the Black Mountains, whose sharp peaks jutted up like fangs of the very earth.

Darreth's condition had not worsened, and both Lorienne and Krael took this as a blessing. He remained unresponsive, and the closest he came to wakefulness was when Lorienne assisted him with eating and drinking. In that time, he mumbled and opened his eyes, but that was all. Darreth had lost much blood, and his body was expending all its energy just to stay alive.

The travelers espied a village on the river's edge. They figured it would be as good a place as any to properly rest and get Darreth the help he needed. No wall or fortification encompassed the scattered cobblestone huts, save for a line of outward-jutting stakes that marked the village perimeter more than anything else. The village was notably distant from the tyrannical civilization of Saidal. Passersby wore garb made from pelts and woolen cloth. Those who could be assumed to be guards lacked any standard uniform and wore loose secondhand mail tarnished by rust or thick plates of hardened leather. Weapons and tools used in the village were of a similar variance in quality. The metal heads of axes, spears, and hammers were rough and unfurnished, made only to serve their functional purpose. At the same time, others fashioned by experienced hands were seen, albeit not without wear and tear. There had not been a specialized craftsman or scholar in this region in over a generation, and the culture they had left behind was more savage than civilized.

As the three trotted between the ring of stakes, many heads turned. The people of that village were homogenous, and the motley band that approached was looked upon with suspicion. Eyes beneath ragged hoods squinted. Crooked teeth sneered. Lorienne could not help but feel to make sure her weapon was within reach.

"Wha' business has ye 'ere?" barked a guard, who spoke a simplistic variant of the High Tongue.

Krael looked down at the guard, whose head was protected by a dented helm. Loose patches of mail covered his crooked frame. In his hand was a spear, although the head seemed to be a repurposed dagger blade. He bore no shield or other weapons, and he leaned on his main polearm like one would a walking stick. However, his stance was far from casual as he leaned forward, imposing on the strangers.

"We come for shelter and healing," said Krael. "We were attacked by dwarves."

The guard gulped upon seeing the massive rider's fangs. "An' why should we let ye stay? We owe ye nothin'," he said, his voice noticeably timider.

A crowd gathered around. While they were not openly malicious, many held weapons and tools in their hands. "Maybe we should head to the next village instead," whispered Lorienne.

"Ye should listen to yer woman," sneered the guard.

Krael looked at the mass about him. Seeing the futility in any other approach, he growled to himself, then turned to Lorienne. "We leave."

At this, the guard spat in laughter. As abruptly as they had arrived, they rode away, the heckling of the villagers still heard from behind.

"Damn them," said Lorienne. "Those bastards."

Turning in his saddle, the Slayer checked on Darreth. His pale, clammy hands still grabbed around the barbarian's waist, and he feebly opened his eyes, the whites of which looked slightly yellow. "Where are we going?" he whispered, and by the way his shallow breaths heaved, Krael knew this was the loudest his voice could be.

"To find a healer," answered the Slayer. "How do you feel?"

"Alive," he said, a faint smirk on his discolored lips.

Krael let out a deep chuckle, relieved at his friend's high spirits. As they rode on, Darreth faded in and out of consciousness.

As they entered each town, the same thing happened. Upon seeing strangers, the native populace grew hard of heart, and the three were forced away each time. Weeks passed, and while Darreth seemed to be slowly getting better, illness had set upon him, and many nights were spent in a sweaty, unsleeping haze. His wounds had begun to fester, and try as Lorienne and Krael might, the best thing they could do was keep the infection at bay.

21
THE COMING OF THE WHITE PRINCE

The throne seemed uncomfortable to the Saidalian prince. Its flat wooden seat was unforgiving, and the back stood at a right angle. Eledrith concluded that it was only for ceremonial purposes, as more than ten minutes in the thing led to backache. As he sat, he constantly shifted, leading Romil to ask, "Is everything alright, my lord?"

Eledrith finally arose and stretched his back. No longer needing the protection of his silvery armor, he wore a fine silk tunic instead. "It's this damn chair," said the prince.

Romil shifted weight between his feet, wondering if this new lord would punish him as the late Orthil had if he interrupted him. Orthil had no problems with the throne, but when he was in the middle of some menial task, he was not to be approached. He had been short of temper, but the new lord from Saidal was much different. Nonetheless, Romil's habits were slow to die.

The doors at the opposite end of the throne room swung open, and through them walked Count Gilduin, accompanied by several Saidalian guards. Bowing before the prince, Gilduin greeted him. "Your Majesty."

"How was the journey here?" asked Eledrith.

"As good as one could expect," said Gilduin. "I look forward to sleeping in a proper bed, although I was hoping for better lodging than this keep. This is certainly a wretched place, isn't it?"

Eledrith's eyes wandered about the cracked masonry and vaulted ceiling. Wooden rafters stretched from the cold stone. A single chandelier hung from an iron chain, its candles dripping wax onto the rough floor. Not a single decoration adorned the place, and no stone was polished. To the prince, it held a rugged, pragmatic aesthetic, but the count missed the carved marble of his home's palaces.

"Congratulations on your victory, by the way," said Gilduin. "Your mentor Sir Garrick would be proud."

A smile came to the prince's face. "Thank you. I owe it to the old man. If it wasn't for his tutelage, I might not have been as successful."

"Count Ordric and your father send their regards as well."

Eledrith only nodded.

"So, I must ask," said Gilduin, "how are the Graehalians? As ferocious in battle as rumor tells?"

Romil gulped, remembering what portion of the carnage he witnessed himself.

"They're quite effective. It's their leader I'm more concerned about, though," Eledrith answered.

"Arngrim?"

"Yes, him. His men practically worship him, and as far as I can tell, the admiration is well earned."

Gilduin nodded his white-bearded head. "Then it's good he's on our side."

"I'm not so sure," said Eledrith. "No ethic guides him other than power and conquest. I fear he'll cause more suffering than the warlords we overthrow."

Gilduin sighed and walked to one of the many windows overlooking the countryside. Below, the settlement around Orthil's Keep was a clamor of peasants and Graehalians. "Perhaps that's for the best, Your Majesty," he said. "If we cannot keep the civilians in check, their uprisings will seriously hinder the war effort. Don't underestimate the value of fear."

"Choose your next words carefully," said Eledrith.

Gilduin froze, then, thinking quickly, turned and said, "Of course, we will exercise prudence and caution. We are here to liberate the Outlaw Kingdoms from tyranny, after all."

Eledrith did not buy it. He sat on the throne, scowling at his new advisor. In order to change the subject, Gilduin produced an envelope. "I almost forgot. Your wife wished for me to give this to you."

Romil took the letter from the count and passed it on to his liege. Grabbing the letter from his servant, Eledrith broke the Calidign wax seal and unfolded the parchment. A delicate script flowed across the page, and the prince did not need to see the signature to recognize it as a message from his wife.

The prince grinned. "She is not happy with me," he said.

Both Gilduin and Romil's curious expressions prompted further explanation.

"Before we left, my wife told me to be careful and not rush into battle. We all know that I didn't follow her instructions."

Gilduin laughed, but Romil shuddered. The events of that fateful night were only a week past, but the carnage that had to be washed from the floor was still familiar in the young boy's mind.

"Well," said Eledrith, preparing to leave the meager throne room, "I suppose I should get to pleading for my innocence."

Everyone in the room chuckled, and Romil asked, "Shall I fetch you a quill and ink, then?"

"No, I think there's some in my quarters."

Eledrith casually strode from his throne and left the room.

"Allow me to show you to your quarters, my lord," said Romil, bowing to Count Gilduin.

"I wouldn't be surprised if my bed is nothing more than a pile of straw," grumbled the count.

Unsure how to take this remark, Romil kept quiet as he escorted the Saidalian noble.

⸻◆⸻

People ducked into the cover of buildings. Instead of passersby crossing the street, they immediately turned around. Like hares, the common folk scattered before Arngrim and his entourage, whose heavy boots trampled the white new-fallen snow into the mud of the street. Rumors spread quickly of Orthil the Skull's death, and such tales inspired justified fears of he that was called Karag-Viil. In the wars of Graehal, the Scourgefather had taken the wives of those he had slaughtered and with them sired children – whether they complied or not. It was the most primal form of conquest. Instead of redrawing borders, Arngrim rewrote bloodlines. That day, he was intent on adding Sarelle to the thousands that felt his libido's sting.

Orthil's widow was kept in the house of her maiden family, the largest abode in the area around Orthil's Keep. The front door came clattering inward with a single kick from Arngrim. The chill winter's wind billowed around the small dining room and extinguished any candles that illuminated it. Servants were struck down before they could reach for a weapon and the blood that flowed quickly soaked into the earthen floor. Arngrim's eyes scanned the meager dwelling. He marched up the stairs, knocking over decorations and keepsakes with a casual swing of his mighty arm.

Alone in her room was Sarelle. The horrors of Orthil's death had taken a toll on her mind and her body. She had eaten little, and an untouched bowl of soup sat at her bedside. As the Scourgefather's visage appeared from the stairway, hysteria overtook Sarelle. In the presence of such a nightmarish warrior, the present blended with memories of the night she first saw Arngrim. Sarelle could feel Orthil's blood on her skin. She could smell the metallic stench of gore. Without thinking, she thrashed, sending the lukewarm soup splashing across the wall. From her came a scream that few in earshot would ever forget. The Scourgefather had heard that scream many times before.

Any fighting Sarelle could muster did little to hinder the Graehalic general as he picked her up with a single arm. The widow in one hand and his axe in the other, Arngrim left the house as suddenly as he had entered it. Unlike before, however, several men stood in his path.

Half a dozen men dared stand against the ten-strong group of mercenaries fully clad in their savage spiked armor. The men had mustered at Sarelle's cries, but they didn't understand precisely how many mercenaries had accompanied the general. Courage withered beneath the ferocity of the hardened warriors. As Arngrim left the confines of the house, the pitchforks and axes leveled toward him began to tremble.

Karag-Viil laughed at the six rag-garbed men who dared threaten him. Instead of raising weapons or charging, the Graehalians simply walked forward without contest.

———◆———

Count Gilduin brought a candle closer to the map. "Our scouts report that Ekbar's forces are heading north in an attempt to cut us off from Saidal."

"So be it," said Eledrith, shrugging. "We have enough men and supplies to endure a full-on siege."

"That is true, but it will make communication difficult. It'd be best if our couriers could ride to and from Saidal uncontested."

The prince nodded. Before he could open his mouth to speak, a knocking came from the chamber's door. Gilduin's bearded face snarled in discontent. The count jerked open the door and said, "I had requested that we are not to be disturbed. This better be important, Romil!"

"It is," said the young servant, eyes nervous but gaze steadfast.

"Let him in," said the prince.

As Gilduin made way, Romil hesitantly stepped into the cramped study. Looking at the prince, he said, "There's something you need to see, my lord."

"If it's so important," scolded Gilduin, "then you can relay it to your master with words."

Eledrith shook his head. "It's alright, Romil. Lead the way."

Gilduin looked as if he was going to chastise the prince, but he only rolled his eyes. Following their servant, the two nobles made their way down the stairs and out through the castle's front gate. A soft blanket of snow had descended in the night, and their steps were the first to tarnish it as they walked in the dawn's light.

When they entered Sarelle's house, Eledrith could instantly tell something was wrong. As Gilduin grumbled about the cold weather, the prince's eyes wandered across the shattered pots and scattered furniture. The quaint abode had been ransacked, but for no reason that the prince could ascertain.

"She is upstairs, my lord," said Romil.

Surrounding the bed was a collection of commoners, solemn expressions on all of their faces. Eledrith was the first up the stairs, and everyone turned to see him. His white cloak was in stark contrast to the drab, roughspun tunics and gambesons worn by the others.

"You should be accompanied by bodyguards," said Gilduin.

Disregarding his advisor, Eledrith approached the group and nodded to them in greeting. "Something has happened?" he asked.

The commoners were hesitant to answer. Before them stood, as far as they could tell, another warlord. Their feet shifted. Most gazes fell to the floor. One man, broad-shouldered and bearded, said, "It's Sarelle. She took her own life."

Shock struck the prince. A body lay on the bed, covered in a white sheet. "What led to this? Were you not taking care of her?"

"We were!" said a youth. By the way he resembled the bearded man, he could have been his son. "But that red-haired northerner took her and had his way with her."

Eledrith's pulse thundered. No curse in the High Tongue could describe his hatred for the Scourgefather; he could only scream in rage. "Why did no one tell me this sooner?"

"We thought you two were on the same side," said the boy's father, a hint of shame in his words.

"He is my enemy," hissed the prince.

"Careful, Your Majesty," said Gilduin. "One should not let emotion overtake reason."

Like a bird of prey, Eledrith snapped his head around and bore down at the shorter count. "Do not speak!" he snapped.

Romil stepped backward, his face pale. In the short time he had known Eledrith, he had seen nothing but kindness from the young prince. As the white-haired warrior looked like he was about to kill Count Gilduin, Romil understood that there was more to Eledrith than what he knew.

Gilduin swallowed and, obeying his liege, did not say a word.

"We tried to stop him," said the young commoner, "but he was too strong. There were ten men with him."

Those words never reached Eledrith's ears. He was already down the stairs and heading straight for the Graehalic war camp. Gilduin and Romil scrambled after him. The prince's long, purposeful strides were difficult to keep up with. As they passed the front gate of the keep, Gilduin motioned for the stationed guards to follow.

"Let us think this through, Your Majesty," said Gilduin, struggling to catch his breath. "The last thing our army needs is infighting."

"He raped someone and pushed them to suicide. The fact that you're not demanding his execution signifies your cowardice, Gilduin."

"In time, Your Majesty. He should be punished by the Saidalian legal system, not killed in a brash confrontation!"

Eledrith muttered, "So it's that obvious I intend to kill him?"

"And what are we to do if he defeats you? You're a prince, not an executioner! We'll have a rogue army on the loose if you are slain!" said Gilduin, his tone becoming more desperate by the second.

While no snow fell that morning, the wind that blew across the fields around Orthil's Keep stoked flurries that scraped across the rawhide tents of the Graehalic mercenaries. Upon hearing of Eledrith's approach, Arngrim had left the comfort of his tent and waited on the open plain. The chill of the morning was nothing compared to that of Graehal, and Arngrim took deep breaths despite the cold biting at his lungs.

Marching through the ankle-deep snow was Eledrith, followed by Romil, Gilduin, and several Saidalian bodyguards. Stopping just out of striking distance of the Scourgefather, Eledrith said, "I'd ask you to explain yourself, but no words can justify what you've done."

"She was a spoil of war," said Arngrim, sneering. "I made use of what was rightfully mine. Hardly the first time I've done so."

"Then why do it behind my back like a coward?" hissed Eledrith, spit flying from his lips.

"We knew you couldn't stomach it."

Eledrith's eyes were ablaze. Despite his seething fury, Arngrim stood calm and collected, a smirk twisting on his bearded face. Eyes burning into the hulking man that stood two heads taller than him, the prince muttered, "I should strike you down here and now."

"Now we're talking," said Arngrim. "A fight to the death will no doubt settle our differences. Don't worry. When you lose, I'll tell your father you fell valiantly on the field of battle."

The wind blew so strong that it moved the sword on Eledrith's hip. Fang-adorned locks of hair whipped across his face, but Karag-Viil stared unceasingly at the jade-eyed boy. Not Romil, Gilduin, or any of the bodyguards dared say a word.

"Meet me in the throne room in exactly one hour," said Eledrith. "If you try to flee, I will hunt you down."

"Don't worry, boy. Grindenfang despises those who run from a fight. I look forward to sending you unto Hell's Wolf myself."

Arngrim then turned his back to Eledrith, but the prince knew better than to strike. What was at stake between them was more than justice for Sarelle; it was for the soul of the war itself. Where Arngrim fought for primal power, Eledrith fought for transcendent virtue.

———◆———

Eledrith waited on the throne, poised forward. His head rested on his fist, and at his side was his swept-hilt longsword. His body, encompassed in the silvery armor plates, glinted in the wintery sunlight that drifted through the arched windows. Had it not been for the grimacing of his rage, he would have appeared angelic.

Lining the hall was his Saidalian guard, their opulent armor more for fashion than function. They waited silently, some eyes watching the door while others looked to see if their lord would break his silence and explain why they had been summoned. Their questions were answered when the double doors burst open. At the head of a Graehalic squadron came Arngrim, whose muscular body was naked save for a loincloth. Red battle paints were smeared across his skin, supplementing the many scars spanning his flesh. Eledrith noticed his physique was healthier than that of the Wizard Slayer's. Where the Kolgathian's muscles were jagged and corded, Arngrim's were proportionally larger, albeit not as toned. He carried his two-headed axe, its curving edge glinting with a razor's sharpness and the wolf visage of Grindenfang etched into the steel head.

With the coming of the Scourgefather, the prince arose. Flooding the back end of the hall were the mercenaries, and a wide area in the center remained bare. Striding into the makeshift arena came Arngrim, who said, "We shall settle this by the traditional way of Graehal. Stop hiding behind that armor and fight me as a true man!"

Eledrith had found comfort in his nigh-impenetrable plates. While he was confident in his abilities, the Scourgefather's reputation was terrifying. After hesitating, he said, "So be it."

At the prince's command, Romil came forward and removed the complex suit of metal and thin linen jack that lay beneath. Wearing nothing but plain boots and pants, it would have seemed to an onlooker that the Graehalic warrior outmatched the prince. Unlike his opponent's bulking figure, Eledrith's build was slim and marred only by a single scar. A number of the Graehalic mercenaries even laughed at his slender, almost boyish physique. Despite this, he walked forward, unsheathing the blade he had practiced with daily for years.

Arngrim smiled. As the two approached, a guttural chanting came from the mercenaries.

"Karag-Viil! Karag-Viil! Karag-Viil!"

The harsh, archaic sound echoed deafeningly through the stone chamber, and many Saidalian guards looked to their prince. He offered them no answer, his jade eyes glaring at Arngrim's. His orders had been simple; they were not to intervene unless the mercenaries drew their weapons first.

No other noble in Saidal would undertake such a primal ritual, but in his justified anger, Eledrith saw that this would be the only proper way to bring Arngrim to justice. The barbarian laughed in the face of civilized laws and morals, but he revered combat. By this, Eledrith would punish him greatly.

"Karag-Viil! Karag-Viil!"

As he approached, Arngrim brought his axe into both hands, readying it for the fight. Eledrith did likewise with his weapon, awaiting his opponent's advance. Soon, the chanting halted, and there was silence.

Uttering a hoarse battle cry, the Scourgefather lunged forward, swinging his axe in a vast vertical arc. With a graceful sidestep, the prince did not even need to use his weapon to parry the blow. The axe head fell forward, and Arngrim's side was exposed. It was too foolish of a mistake, and Eledrith knew better than to capitalize. Without warning, the barbarian shifted his weight and followed up with another wide swing toward the prince. The strike would have cleaved him in two if he had lunged in, and Eledrith was relieved that his cautious approach had paid off.

Advancing with no quarter, Arngrim's axe sliced through the air in a flurry of attacks. None found their mark, and the prince let the more experienced warrior continue forward without retaliating. *He knows his axe is heavy enough to break through any defense I can offer*, thought Eledrith, *so I'll let him waste his breath.*

For a full minute, Eledrith circled around Arngrim's predictable strikes, but the red-haired warrior showed no sign of slowing. His fang-adorned braids whipped about violently as his entire body twisted with each swing. "Fight me, coward!" the barbarian yelled.

He has the advantage of range and power, thought the prince. *If I am to attack, I'll need to make it count.*

The axe whistled through the air, aimed at Eledrith's neck, but the prince did not step back. Arngrim had become used to advancing toward his opponent, but when Eledrith ducked instead of backing away, the brute was surprised. A quick slash to the thigh only left a minor cut but stunned Arngrim long enough for the prince to come in closer. His pommel slammed down on the barbarian's skull.

The Scourgefather let out a yell of both rage and pain. An elbow crashed into Eledrith's forehead, sending him to the floor, his weapon clattering feet behind him. Seeing his opponent prone, Arngrim's muscles flexed as he brought the axe down toward his enemy's head.

Instinctively, Eledrith somersaulted backward. The steel edge of the axe brushed through the prince's silver locks. Instead of finding purchase in flesh, the blade collided with the stone of the floor, cracking tiles and scattering sparks.

Picking up his weapon, Eledrith readied his defense. As he stood up, his surroundings seemed to tilt. Arngrim's elbow had done more internal damage than the prince initially thought, and what should have been a graceful dodge was an awkward sidestep. If Eledrith had time to regain his senses, he might have been fine, but each second was needed to avoid the enemy's onslaught.

The barbarian did not fare well, either. The pommel blow had torn skin on impact and caused blood to run down his face. Squinting through the pouring crimson, he slashed at the staggered prince. A burning ache had swelled in his muscles, and as strong as he was, he was fatigued.

As his opponent slowed, Eledrith took a moment to breathe. Arngrim did likewise, nostrils flaring as he drew in a much-needed breath. Cursing in his own tongue, the Graehalic warrior charged forward. During the fight, Eledrith learned his foe's attack habits. The shifting of feet, the turning of shoulders, and the angle of the strikes had become familiar to the prince, and Arngrim's attack was effortlessly countered.

The weight of his body and weapon brought Arngrim forward, and to his right, the prince was a pale blur. Before he could react, a stinging pain ran through his side. Looking down, he saw a splash of red and entrails. Everything grew hazy. Then, just as the shame of defeat began to swell in Karag-Viil's mind, it was finished.

Standing above the decapitated and disemboweled warrior was the prince, specks of red on his body and blade. No one in the room spoke. No one moved. The mercenaries, seeing the Scourgefather of legend bested, were shocked.

Adrenaline still in his veins, Eledrith spoke. "By your own rituals, your leader is dead. Now, you will serve me. No longer will you cower before your wolf-god. Instead, we will pursue justice in this world. For ages, the Outlaw Kingdoms have been ruled by despotic warlords and power-mad fools. I have been sent to change that."

Something deep within Eledrith's heart burst forward. His words came through before thought, yet he meant them with certainty. "You look upon the future king of not just Saidal, but the surrounding lands. Strength and power mean nothing to me; I despise the vanity and corruption they bring. The higher calling of good and justice urges me forward."

Turning specifically to the Graehalic mercenaries, he said, "If you choose not to follow me, number yourselves amongst my enemies. Karag-Viil devoted himself to aimless strength and dominance, and now he lies dead, no better than those he deemed too weak to live. Choose wisely."

The last of Eledrith's words echoed in the stone chamber. No one dared move.

Then, one of the mercenaries raised his axe. "Hail the White Prince!" he cried.

Another one hollered, "Hail Prince Eledrith!"

The room was soon filled with a chorus of cheering. Eledrith suddenly felt short of breath in the middle of it all. The adrenaline of victory no longer rushed through his veins, and he could reflect on what he had said with a clear mind. He was appalled at his own zeal, but he didn't dare try to clarify anything then. The men in the room were possessed by his words, and their collective will was too ferocious to subdue.

The thought of the strange woman on the balcony then came to mind. He still remembered her sensual feline eyes that watched him intently. He also remembered her ominous words: "You have inherited great power, even if you do not yet understand it."

Eledrith shivered and grabbed his sword with both hands. Even though he was surrounded by adoring followers, he wished more than anything to be reunited with Morwenna.

22
SHADOWS ON THE THRONE

King Torvaren Calidign stammered and swayed through the moonlit hallways of his palace. He held a goblet of wine in one hand, and the other groped at his concubine, using her for stability when his inebriated coordination failed him. The concubine, who considered herself only a servant before that day's events, giggled at the king's sloppy advances. She was drunk as well, perhaps even more so than Torvaren. Together, they zigzagged through the windowed hall, haphazardly stumbling between shadow and moonlight.

No servants paced the corridors that evening, and the two went unheard as they exchanged incoherent conversation. They came to an intersection where a stairway ran down to both their left and right. Confused about which path to take, Torvaren halted and spun. Not expecting this, the servant girl continued forward, oblivious to her liege. His arm slipped from the concubine, and, without warning, he disappeared into shadow. "Your Majesty?" she called out.

There was no answer.

She teetered over to a wall. Bracing herself against it, she called again, "Where did you go?"

The concubine's slurred words traveled through the halls, but if they reached anyone, they did not call back.

There she stood, in an unfamiliar part of the palace, alone. Her shouts became more desperate. "Is there anyone there?"

Still no answer. Unbeknownst to the servant girl, laying at the bottom of a staircase in a puddle of wine and blood, lay Torvaren.

———◆———

Romil presented the message to Prince Eledrith at midday.

The prince had mostly recovered from his ritual fight with Arngrim two days prior, as his wounds were superficial. Still, his head ached from the elbow strike. He looked out of a window into the town below. The Graehalic mercenaries who had sworn allegiance behaved differently since their old leader had died. They covered their faces and gear with smears of white paint to appear more like the White Prince himself. This notion only strained Eledrith's nerves. *They practically worship me*, he thought.

"Urgent news from Saidal," said Romil, gasping for breath.

Taking the letter, Eledrith heeded his servant's urgency and scanned the text. He gasped.

"Bad news, my lord?"

"King Torvaren had an accident."

"Is he alright?"

The prince read the message aloud. "His Majesty was found at the foot of a staircase, unconscious. Since then, he has remained asleep, and no treatment any of Saidal's healers can concoct has shown any sign of awakening him."

"Strange," said Romil.

Eledrith shuddered at the thought of the comatose king. While Torvaren was not a father to him, he was still someone that had been close for the prince's entire life. He was now reduced to what was essentially a living corpse.

Noticing his master's grim expression, Romil asked, "Will you be alright, Your Majesty?"

With a solemn smile coming to his face, the prince said, "Of course, Romil. It's just that these past months have been filled with strange events beyond my control. I should come to expect such things, I suppose."

"Does that mean you'll head back to Saidal and become the new king?"

"No. The laws of succession dictate that the crown is passed on only when the old king no longer draws breath. One of the ruling counts will be elected to serve as the high lord: a surrogate of the king. In the past, a high lord was only needed when a king became senile or overburdened."

"So, one of the counts will be stealing the crown from you," concluded Romil.

"Exactly," said Eledrith, "and it will certainly be Count Ordric."

"You say that as if it's a bad thing."

After a pause, the prince said, "I do not trust him."

Worst of all, thought the prince, *he believes he can use Krael to secure his dominion.*

"Oh, I almost forgot," said Romil, producing another message from his pocket, "Princess Morwenna has written to you."

The gloom that clouded over Eledrith's eyes evaporated, but as he read the letter, an even worse expression came over his face. "No... this isn't right."

Most of the letter was characteristic of his wife, but there was a single paragraph that seemed like a whole other person had written it. *I admire you more and more after hearing of your glorious feats in battle. Commanding an army is a valiant effort, and I am proud to be wed to the man leading that endeavor. I patiently await your return, but I also understand that your duty lies in the Outlaw Kingdoms.*

"She wished for me to never go to war in the first place," said the prince. "These cannot be her words."

Romil stood awkwardly, running a hand through his unkempt mop of hair. "Perhaps you could go to Saidal and ask her about it yourself."

"I would, but I have matters to attend to here," said Eledrith, massaging the temples of his aching head. "Ekbar's forces will attack this keep any day. He wishes to avenge Orthil, and I must be present to lead these men."

"Forgive me," said Romil, avoiding his master's gaze, "but aren't matters of the throne more important? You can always hand off your responsibilities to Gilduin."

Eledrith chuckled to himself, then set a hand on the young servant's shoulder. The prince was barely an adult, and there was a youth's camaraderie between them. "Thank you, Romil," he said. "Everything that has happened has worn down on me. I seldom think clearly anymore."

"It's nothing, Your Majesty."

Heading toward his chambers to prepare for the journey home, the prince said, "I cannot thank you enough. If all goes well, I shall return in a few days. You can tell Gilduin that he'll take over in my absence."

"Yes, my lord."

Eledrith's horse galloped across the snowy plain. The rolling white hills were dotted with twisted metal carapaces of bygone eras. Wasting no time in examining the mysterious machines, the prince rode toward the great black mass on the horizon that was Saidal. A dark smog hung over the city, fueled by the hundreds, perhaps thousands, of fires that kept its inhabitants warm.

Covering his shining plate was a long, billowing black cloak. The armor was so well fitted and light that, from a distance, it seemed that he wore only mundane clothing. There was little traffic that wintry day and the massive arched gate stood empty. Not recognizing the hooded rider, the guards raised their weapons as he approached.

"Halt! State your name and business," barked one of the guards.

"Do you not recognize your own prince?" said Eledrith, lowering his hood.

"Your Majesty!" said the guards, kneeling.

"And my business is my own," continued Eledrith as his horse wove between the men. "You are not to report my presence to anyone. Is that understood?"

"Yes, Your Majesty!" they said in unison.

The thundering of hooves caused the snow to careen about the gate. By the time the cloud dissipated, Eledrith and his mount were nowhere to be seen.

Lady Morwenna sat in her chamber of the Calidign Palace. A flickering candle illuminated the book she read and little else. Her large brown eyes leaped from line to line, totally captivated by the tale the letters told.

Out of the corner of the princess's eye, there loomed a moonlight-silhouetted figure. She whirled in her chair, casting the book aside.

"Eledrith!"

Part of her cry was out of reflex, calling for her beloved. At the same time, it was out of surprise. The candle's orange glow reflected off the prince's pale face. Eledrith doffed his hood to reassure his wife, letting down his unmistakable silvery hair.

"My lady," he said, smiling.

The two embraced each other. No words were needed in that blissful moment.

Clattering against the chamber wall, the wooden door was thrown open, shattering the silence. Morwenna's servant Idda rushed in, saying, "Your Majesty, is there something wrong?"

Upon seeing the prince, the old woman's eyes sparkled. Ever since the wedding, Idda had become like a mother to Eledrith, and seeing him return from the Outlaw Kingdoms made her heart leap with joy. "Prince Eledrith! I..."

"Didn't know I would be returning so soon?" he finished, still holding Morwenna.

He stepped back and leaned against the wall. Only then did the two women realize he was out of breath. "I didn't know I would be back in Saidal until this morning."

Morwenna asked, "Wait, how did you get here so fast? And why was your arrival unannounced?"

"I rode without rest. When entering the city, I disguised my face. If I was discovered by the guards, I ordered them to say nothing of it. I am the prince of this city, after all."

"Soon to be king, perhaps," said Idda. "Have you heard of what happened to your father?"

Eledrith nodded solemnly.

"I don't like it. The whole thing seems, well, strange," said Morwenna.

"Thus why I am here," said the prince. "I am in no rush to secure the throne for myself, but I fear terrible things will come to pass if someone holds that power in my stead."

Morwenna nodded. "The counts already bicker as to who will claim the title of high lord."

Idda said, "And your father is the worst of them all, Morwenna. He has already scheduled the vote for tomorrow morning."

"He assumed I would not be in Saidal? I've heard nothing of this." Eledrith turned to Morwenna. "Save for the letter you sent me."

The princess seemed confused at first, but her face lit up with recognition after some effort. "Ah yes, I had only written that yesterday."

"The courier was swift, and I more so. Upon reading it, I was immediately suspicious. Forgive me, darling, but why do you wish for me to stay in the Outlaw Kingdoms?"

Morwenna pursed her lips, then seemed to be under more strain. What should have been an easy question made the princess grit her teeth in tense confusion. Seeing his wife on the brink of real pain, Eledrith said, "It's alright, Morwenna."

She put a hand to his chest, keeping him from coming closer. "You don't understand! It's like... there are two thoughts in place of one. I want you here with me, but at the same time, I think you should have stayed in the mercenary army."

Idda brought her arms around the young princess. "It's alright, dear. We all sometimes have conflicting feelings."

"It's not just a feeling, Idda. It's something else."

While the old woman tried to comfort the girl she had helped raise since birth, a grim realization came to Eledrith's mind. He remembered the council when the war had first been planned and how a room of squabbling politicians was brought swiftly to Ordric's side. As he backed away from the candlelight, he recalled Thalnar's bewitched minions. The connection was undeniable. Eledrith whispered, "By hell, he's using magick!"

Idda looked up. "What did you say?"

Ordric cannot know I am onto him, thought the prince. *I stand no chance against magick. I need Krael's help.*

Idda waited for an answer. Both she and Morwenna looked to Eledrith. The prince was about to let them in on his revelation but thought otherwise. *If I let them know, Ordric may learn of it, if that's even how his witchcraft works.* Idda still waited for the prince to repeat himself. Frantic for a cover, he blurted, "Perhaps you should relax."

Both women half-bought the lie but were still visibly confused. Eledrith said, "It's my first night back after some time. How about we forget politics until morning?"

"Yes," said Morwenna. "Idda, why don't you fetch us some wine?"

"Certainly, Your Majesty," said the servant, whose eyes still hinted skepticism.

Regardless, Idda left, and by the time she returned with a vintage bottle, Eledrith was out of his armor. After pouring two glasses, she asked, "Is there anything else I can do for you?"

"Please, pour one for yourself," said Eledrith. "I have missed your presence as well."

"You're too kind," said Idda.

Well into the night, they chatted. As the candlelight waned, so did their conversation, and Idda retired to her quarters in time. Finally alone, Eledrith made love to his wife, and they slept in each other's arms.

Morwenna was only semi-conscious the following day when she felt her husband leave her side. He donned his armor by himself, struggling to reach the more secluded latches of the plate suit. The princess poised herself on the bed and looked at Eledrith, confused. Knowing what she wondered without the need for words, the prince answered. "I have urgent business. Very urgent business. I fear I may have stayed too long already."

"Don't go," pleaded Morwenna, the grogginess of sleep in her speech.

A cold, iron-clad finger brushed against the princess's cheek. "I must, but this whole thing will have passed when I return."

After a final kiss, Eledrith pulled his dark cloak about him and left for the door. Morwenna opened her mouth, but she realized it would be futile, and she was helpless to watch as the prince crept into the palace halls.

At dawn, Eledrith was back on the open road. Procuring the correspondences between Garrick and Count Ordric had proven more straightforward than expected, and the letters revealed that the manhunters were as far east as the Black Mountains. They had been snowed in at the small town of Retlaid, and while this information was undoubtedly outdated, it was better than nothing.

Keeping his identity a secret, Eledrith dashed across the Outlaw Kingdoms, resting only when absolutely necessary. The journey was arduous, but the prince relished in the struggle. Fending for himself and not being waited on by a horde of servants soothed his nerves, and even the grave nature of his quest seemed bearable now that he was given solitude. When night fell and there were no settlements to find lodging at, Eledrith slept in the ruined iron skeletons of ancient machines. Their strange shapes and devices were a mystery to him, but even as they lay decrepit, they served as good shelter.

The evils of the Outlaw Kingdoms were present in this journey as well. Far too often, Eledrith beheld corpses staked on the side of the road, the dripping blood reddening the snow beneath them. This sight weighed on the prince's mind, and he realized he may soon meet the same fate if his own identity were discovered. One day, he took the time to dye his silvery hair a muddy brown. This, in addition to furs covering his armor, made him unrecognizable.

Weeks passed, and word spread in the taverns and inns of the small villages. Eledrith overheard rumors of Graehalic mercenaries fighting under the banner of the Calidigns. Supposedly, they had gained much territory and slaughtered many warlords. Rumors also circulated of the ferocity of the Saidalian forces. Those who would not kneel to the throne of Torvaren were enslaved or executed. *I can do nothing to stop this*, thought Eledrith. *Anyone I might call a friend Ordric can subdue on a whim. I must find Krael. He's my only hope.*

23
THE END OF THE HUNT

The host of Saidalian warriors, led by Sir Garrick, rode through the snowy mountain pass. Next to the knight was Morgvid, his strange ring-lined cloak shielding his face from the flurry of ice and snow that blew between the peaks. If the sky were not as blue as it was, the men would've thought they were in the midst of another blizzard. Instead of a storm, only the eastbound wind lapped the many cliffs of the Black Mountains, but the resulting chill was enough to slow the whole company.

Morgvid uttered a curse to himself in Askarian. "If you hadn't acted so soft in Raven's Watch, we'd be back in Saidal by now."

"Enough of your grumbling, Morgvid," said the knight. "If we had intruded any more than we did, the townsfolk would have hindered us further. These matters are far more delicate than you realize."

The assassin scoffed. "It may have been worth it, though. The Wizard Slayer and his companions have eluded us for almost two months. Now, we're following nothing but rumors."

"If capturing the Slayer is so important that His Majesty recruits men like us, it'll surely be worth the wait."

"Or he requested us because he wished not to wait," retorted the assassin.

Their conversation was cut short as they rounded a corner in the road. Before them opened a vast valley surrounded by craggy peaks and filled with dark gray-green pines. At the far end of the dale, a massive face looked out from the mountainside. What once may have been the carved visage of a bearded man was now a twisted effigy of agony. Any sharp features the stone once held had been worn away, leaving behind a nigh-formless mockery of a head.

"The Weeping Mountain," said Garrick, shuddering. "It's hideous."

"Indeed, it is," said the assassin. "Whoever carved that must have been a mighty culture indeed, however long ago they may have been."

"It's speculated that it was made by the dwarves – before their race fell, of course."

Morgvid snorted, then spurred his horse forward down the trail. "Whoever made it, they're long dead now. Come, I'd hate to learn that the Slayer eluded us again because you spent too much time sightseeing."

Damn that assassin, thought Garrick, *and damn this mission. I pray that by the time we return to Saidal, Eledrith will have pulled Ordric from the king's backside.*

In the letters the knight received from Saidal, he learned of Eledrith's victory at Orthil's Keep. He lamented that he couldn't be fighting at the prince's side but was proud nonetheless. Otherwise, everything back in the megacity went as expected, at least according to the reports. *If Eledrith were king, things would be much different*, thought the knight.

Signaling for his men to follow, Garrick descended the winding mountain path and headed toward the valley floor. A small trail of downtrodden snow and dirt wound through the trunks of the pines, and the assassin reckoned that it led to their destination: the city-state of Dron.

A shallow brook ran through the floor of the valley. The springtime melting was still far off, and the banks of this stream were wide, rocky beaches that made traveling easy for the Saidalian manhunters. Ice had occasionally formed, but a steady flow kept the brook unfrozen even in the heart of winter. This ended at Dron itself, where it disappeared beneath a grate in the crumbling masonry of the outer wall.

The stonework of the wall was stout, and thick timbers poised atop it made the fortification impassible save for the main gate. Upon noticing a whole regiment of soldiers approaching, the local guards blocked off the entryway. Their leader, a burly man whose beard extended beyond the confines of his helm, commanded them to halt and state their business.

"We come looking for a fugitive and criminal," said Garrick. "That is all. We have no other business with the people of this city."

The men of Dron spoke out of earshot, then their captain said, "You may enter, but your men may not walk the streets armed as they are now. You'll leave your weapons with us until you leave."

Morgvid whispered something to himself, and the guard captain did not hear exactly what the assassin had said. Hoping to abate any anger, the guard said, "It's nothing personal. There's a ban on weapons within the city. If you have any complaints, you can speak to King Branshar himself."

Hesitantly, the Saidalians handed over their weapons, and most hesitant of all was the assassin. As the captain confiscated the twin talwars, his eyes widened at the exotic blades. "Haven't seen swords like these before."

Morgvid scowled, not bothering to make conversation.

The guard's eyes grew even wider when he beheld the assassin of the Serpent's Hand. His face was hidden under the hood, but what could be seen of the ghoulish flesh silenced the captain.

The streets of Dron were much like most in the Outlaw Kingdoms: muddy and unorganized. Alleys zigzagged between the many log buildings, and the directional signs on street corners did little to help navigate the maze of mud and snow. Adding to this were the tides of passersby whose glares of disapproval made the unarmed manhunters' welcome even colder.

"Should we seek council with King Branshar, then? He may have information concerning Krael," said Garrick.

Morgvid grumbled, "I don't see why not."

Assuming the block of decrepit stone that rose above the lesser rooftops was Branshar's castle, Garrick made his way toward it. The group passed through a small market square where dozens of brightly covered canvases protected merchants' goods from the elements.

Even as he walked, Morgvid felt naked without the weight of two swords pulling on his belt. "Grindenfang damn those guards for taking my weapons," he cursed. "Does this Branshar think he can treat all his subjects like children?"

"We share the same sentiment, Morgvid," said Garrick, keeping a watchful eye on the city guards. "I hate being without an axe at my side, but there's nothing we can do about it for the moment."

The assassin snarled, the purple veins bulging on his bleach-white scalp.

As they rode, he scanned the crowd. The people of Dron were of the fair-skinned race that inhabited the rest of the Outlaw Kingdoms, but none of them seemed familiar, save one. Across the square, perhaps sixty feet away, was the raven-haired Valmorian. The slightly hooked nose and large lips were unmistakable. She was speaking with a rag-garbed herbalist, exchanging coins for a bottle of medicine. She smiled and nodded at the herbalist before leaving the street.

"It seems that fortune smiles on us," said Morgvid, pointing toward Lorienne.

"That's… the woman from Raven's Watch!" said Garrick.

"Seize her before she gets away," ordered Morgvid.

As far as the old knight was concerned, he was in charge, and receiving a command from his subordinate was a shock. He raised a scarred eyebrow.

Morgvid elaborated. "She knows what I am capable of when under the influence of my alchemy, and if she has any wits about her pretty head, she fears me. You're best suited for capturing her."

"Shouldn't we follow her?" asked Garrick. "She could lead us to Krael."

"Without weapons, we don't stand a chance against the brute strength of the Wizard Slayer. If we could lead him from the city, however, things would be in our favor," said Morgvid, a cunning grin plastered on his pallid face.

Lorienne's boots were already caked with slushy mud, but she still tried to avoid the brown pools that riddled the alley. Pulling her cloak closer around her face, she worked to keep out the chill that had come with the sun setting. The sky was primarily purple, though its eastern edge was already a deep bluish black.

In front of the sword-dancer, cutting off the alley from the main street, was a line of Saidalian warriors. Even in the dim twilight, Lorienne recognized the skirts of mail and conical helms. Before thinking, she darted for the other end of the alley. To her surprise, that opening had been blocked off long before, and a grizzled, scarred warrior stood waiting.

"It's no use running," said Garrick. "You're surrounded."

Slowly, the armored men closed in. The alley had been twenty feet long, but step by step, it shortened. With no other options, Lorienne sprinted toward the exit even though it was filled with soldiers. They braced for impact, unaware of the sword-dancer's actual plan. In the murky half-light, her footsteps were a mystery. With the grace of a hunting cat, she bounded off the wall and brought her knee into a guard's face. The blow took him off his feet, and his comrades were splattered with mud as he fell to the ground, unconscious. Their line was broken, and Lorienne stumbled out into the wider street. Her knee throbbed from the collision with the soldier's helm. This was a small price for freedom, and in the heat of the moment, she could ignore the pain. As the sword-dancer dashed across the lane, her boots slid and struggled to find purchase in the slush.

Lorienne's body flew out from under her. As her chest collided with the ground, she let out a hoarse gasp. The mix of dirt and ice scraped at her exposed face. For a time, she saw stars, but when her vision cleared, she saw the manhunters looming over her. Lacking the breath to resist, she was bound, blindfolded, and carried off into the night.

When she could finally see again, the sword-dancer found herself in a cramped cellar. A layer of ice glistened over parts of the stone walls, and large barrels made what would have been a vast chamber something more of a closet. Thanks to the blindfold, Lorienne's eyes had adjusted to utter blackness. Even the feeble candles were blinding. She sat at a table, her hands still bound. Across from her was Garrick, and while Lorienne did not know his name, she recognized him from the Raven's Rest.

The knight began. "Sorry for the trouble, but—"

"What do you want with me?" she interrupted.

"With you, nothing," said Garrick. "I wish only to know the whereabouts of Krael, the Wizard Slayer."

Not knowing what to say, the sword-dancer remained silent, squirming against her binds absent-mindedly.

To ease her nerves, Garrick said, "It's been a while since we last met. About a month now, by my reckoning."

"Yeah."

"Are you comfortable? Need anything to eat or drink?"

Lorienne shook her head.

The old knight leaned back in his chair and said, "All we want from you is information. Once we're done, you'll be free to go."

Garrick watched as the woman's large eyes avoided his, scanning the room in thought. After a short time, she confessed, "I haven't seen him in weeks."

The knight's eyebrows shot up. "What happened?"

"As we rode from Raven's Watch, that ugly pale man you were with had chased after us. Krael said he was an assassin from Askaron, and I didn't want to get involved in the Wizard Slayer's affairs if a man from the other side of the world was going to be on our heels. We continued together for some time, but I bid them farewell a month ago. Haven't seen him or Darreth since."

Garrick couldn't help but smile at the thought of Darreth. It seemed like years ago since he had accompanied the meek, light-hearted boy. Suppressing the urge to ask how Darreth was doing, he asked, "Where did you last see them?"

"One of the backwater towns west of here," Lorienne said.

Scratching his beard, Garrick asked, "Do you remember the name of the place?"

"Not sure it even had a name. It was just a collection of small farmsteads with a roadside inn."

The old veteran was silent for what seemed like a full minute to Lorienne. She leaned forward in her chair and hid her bound hands beneath the table during this time. Gently tugging and twisting her wrists, the binds began to loosen. "What brings you to Dron?" Garrick asked.

Lorienne froze, then said, "My business is my own."

"Don't take offense to this. I only ask out of curiosity."

The woman's jaw tightened, and seeing further questions would only raise tensions, Garrick changed the subject. "How did you end up traveling with the Slayer in the first place? I've journeyed with him myself, and he's strange company, to say the least."

Lorienne stammered, indecisive on how much information to yield. On the one hand, the more she revealed, the more likely she would be let go. At the same time, she was irked at being held captive. She wanted nothing in the whole world more than to be seen as a person with actual agency. Being a sword-dancer carried a reputation of prestige yet, at the same time, a connotation of bodily servitude. In Valmoria, they were guards as well as concubines, used as a means to an end for the highest bidder. Instead of answering Garrick's question, she asked, "Can I leave now?"

After a sigh, the old knight nodded. "I suppose you can."

Garrick rose from the table, leaving Lorienne alone in shock. *Can it be this easy?*

As she got up, a pang of soreness ran in her knee. Her leg gave out, and the sword-dancer had to brace herself against one of the many barrels in the room. Garrick asked, "Is your leg bothering you?"

Lorienne nodded while she grimaced. The old knight continued. "The man you hit with it is faring much worse. You damn near broke his nose. Where'd you learn to fight like that?"

"It was an accident," she said under a facade of innocence. "I was trying to leap over him."

Garrick rolled his eyes. The woman was a closed book, and he had learned all he could. He led Lorienne from the cellar of the inn and out into the streets of Dron. Many still walked about, and the collections of torchlight made the city feel safe and almost cozy. Garrick cut the sword-dancer's binds (while marveling at how close she had come to removing them) and bid her farewell.

During the walk home, Lorienne's nerves were steel trap and hair triggered. Each twisting of shadow caught her eye, and she looked upon all passersby with suspicion. She was sure she was being followed. Twisting and zigzagging between streets, someone openly following the sword-dancer would have lost her, let alone anyone taking a more subtle approach.

It was well past midnight when Lorienne crept through the door to Darreth and Krael's room. The Slayer himself sat against the wall, sleeping. If they had not been forced to yield their weapons upon entry to Dron, the war hammer would've sat within the Kolgathian's reach. Darreth lay on the bed, wounds scattered across his thin body. The remnants of scratches scabbed on his face, and his pointed ears were exposed. As light as her footsteps were, Krael's eyes snapped open upon her entry.

"What took you so long?" said the barbarian in his deep, slow dialect.

Setting the jar of medical herbs on Darreth's nightstand, Lorienne said, "They're here... and they found me."

"They let you go?"

"Yes. I just spent the last two hours wandering the city. If they followed me, I would've realized it by now."

Krael growled to himself. Lorienne removed her coat and pulled a stool up next to Darreth's bed. Placing her hand on his forehead, she said, "He's still running a fever. How long has he been asleep?"

"Since dusk."

"At least he's resting well again. He's healed surprisingly fast, given how sick he was a week ago. There must be something to that elven blood of his."

The Slayer watched as Lorienne administered the medicine. When she had finished, he said, "We must move soon. They will find us."

The sword-dancer nodded. "I know, but let's give Darreth one more night of solid rest. It's a miracle he hasn't died yet, so let's not push our luck."

After a short time, she said, "I need a drink. Want to head down to the common room?"

Krael nodded. "I hunger."

Locking their room, they left for the main dining room, whose crooked tables were still populated by the late-night rabble. Lorienne's nerves needed to relax, and the burn of liquor on the back of her throat was welcome. Krael, gnawing on a hunk of meat, watched the entryway like a bird of prey.

Just outside the window of Darreth's room, in shadows cast by the waning moon, the assassin of the Serpent's Hand grinned.

24
THE SERPENT AND THE HOUND

"Where's Darreth?" the Kolgathian roared.

Lorienne scrambled through the narrow hallway of the inn, paying no mind to the many confused heads that peered from open doors. The sword-dancer was in utter panic. "Did you see him leave, Krael?"

The Slayer ripped apart the cramped two-bed room he shared with the elf-blooded. With one arm, a bed was thrown upward, the dust-covered floor beneath exposed and bare. Krael's head snapped around in a frenzy, searching for any sign of intrusion.

"We locked the door, right?"

Lorienne's words went unheard. Krael darted to the window and threw open the wooden shutters. The morning glow showed footprints in the muddy slush, and the Slayer realized what had happened.

"I should have stayed here," he growled.

"What?"

"They took him. They followed you and found him."

"Oh no." Lorienne sighed, feeling a weight drop on her heart.

"Get your things," said Krael. "We find him."

Garrick waited in the market square, a handful of his men surrounding him. Looking down upon Dron was the horrid, misshapen face of the Weeping Mountain, once honorable features long since warped into a visage of sorrow and pain. Braziers kept the winter's chill from the streets, and the midday sun shone down on the glistening armor of the knight and his fellow soldiers. They attracted many eyes from the crowd of commoners, but none bore on them with such ferocity as the Wizard Slayer. Garrick had seen that look before when Krael had fought Count Thalnar, and the knight was justified in fearing it. While the many fur-garbed passersby did not know why the Slayer advanced with such intensity, they gave him a wide berth, terrified of what his massive build was capable of. Lorienne followed in his wake, though she didn't attract nearly as much attention.

Seeing their quarry approach, one of the soldiers asked Sir Garrick, "Should we capture him now?"

"Try," said Krael, baring his teeth.

In less than a second, the flesh of the Saidalian's face faded to a ghostly white.

"There is no point," said Garrick. "I've seen him fight. Without our spears, we're no match."

The Slayer halted mere feet from the old knight. "Garrick," he said, anger still dripping from his every mannerism.

"You're a sight for sore eyes, Krael," he said. "How I wish our meeting was under different circumstances."

"Where's Darreth?"

Garrick raised his chin, looked the barbarian in the eye, and said, "Come willingly with us, and no harm will befall him."

"No."

"Dammit, Krael," said the knight, shaking his head. "Do you really need to make this so hard?"

"I will not be Torvaren's slave."

Garrick was taken aback. *He knows.*

Lorienne looked at the crowd, which had backed away from the confrontation. Curious eyes stared at the outsiders. Guards of Dron, the only people able to openly carry weapons, closed in, poleaxes at the ready. The sword-dancer opened her mouth to warn the Slayer, but she was cut off.

"Please, Krael. As your friend, I'm begging you to come with us," said the knight.

One of the Kolgathian's hands clasped a fold of Garrick's mail. "Where is he?" Krael growled.

"Let go of him!" came a voice.

Six hide-clad guards surrounded the barbarian and poised their weapons at his head. The guard continued. "Ye be disturbin' the peace of King Branshar's city! We'll kill ye if ye don't back down."

"Do as he says," whispered Garrick. "Not even you can fight them all off."

The Slayer's grip on the mail tightened. "Where is he?"

One of the city guards shouted, "This be yer final warning!"

The sun glinted off all six poleaxes. Even though their tips were tarnished by rust, any one of them could bring a swift end to the Wizard Slayer. Lorienne scanned the situation, panic fueling her thoughts. There was no way she could help other than to cry out, "Please, Krael!"

Garrick tried to pull away, but the Slayer's grip remained firm. *He's willing to die here.*

"Ye had yer warning, big man," said the guard.

"I'll tell you where he is," said Garrick.

As Krael's hand opened, the knight staggered back.

"Don't move," said the guard. "Yer comin' with us."

"I'm sorry, but I think you have the wrong idea," said Garrick.

The leader of the Dronite guards scowled in disbelief, his haggard features twisting beneath a steel cap and hood. "Why should I trust ye, outsider?"

"We're no longer disturbing your lord's peaceful city, are we?"

"He was gonna kill ye! I could see it in his eye."

Krael snorted, then said, "Our business is our own."

Lorienne spoke up. "What charges are you going to press, anyway?"

The guard raised an eyebrow in confusion. "Charges?" he asked.

Lorienne had overestimated the judicial system of Dron. Just like the weathered hide of the city guard was utter rags compared to the ornate Saidalian mail, so was the straightforward law enforcement of the city. The sword-dancer only came to this conclusion after the fact.

After cursing, the Dronite guard said, "Nothing more from you lot. We'll be watching ye."

The six guards dispersed into the wider market square, but their eyes were still fixed on the Saidalians. "Let's not do that again, Krael," said Garrick.

"Tell me where Darreth is," said the Slayer, his eyes glaring back at the guards so close to striking him down but a minute before.

"My associate figured this would happen," said the knight, "you refusing to comply and all. He might actually have preferred this outcome."

"Get to the point."

"Morgvid, the pale assassin, has taken him to that hideous cavern there," said Garrick, gesturing toward the horrible face of the Weeping Mountain. "I will be honest with you, Krael; I lament having to chase you down. I respect your conviction far more than King Torvaren, but it is to House Calidign that I have sworn my loyalty. I'm sure you understand that if I were to break my knightly oath, my honor would mean nothing."

Nodding, Krael said, "I will not hurt you."

"I'm thankful for that. Morgvid is of the Serpent's Hand. Do you know of them?"

"Yes."

"He seems to know much of you and wishes to test his mettle against your own. I suspect this has more to do with personal honor and prowess than following Torvaren's orders, so be on your guard."

"I will waste no more time. I leave for the Weeping Mountain."

Garrick nodded. "I will warn you, Morgvid has coated his blades in a paralyzing venom. One scratch will be enough to render you immobile."

With a snort, Krael retorted, "I do not care. He will kill me if he wishes to leave the cave alive."

"Careful, Krael, he is an expert swordsman, and while you may be a ferocious warrior, his blade skill is unmatched."

"So be it. Farewell, Garrick."

The barbarian gave the sword-dancer one last look. "You come if you wish. This fight will be easier with you. But it is your choice."

She shook her head. "I'm sorry, but I'm scared, Krael. This is your fight, not mine."

Lorienne had expected the Slayer to protest, but without looking back, he strode off to the main gate to reclaim his war hammer.

"I don't know who to worry more for," said Garrick to Lorienne, "Morgvid or the Wizard Slayer."

"They're both monsters," Lorienne said. "I should've left Krael's side long ago."

"But why didn't you?"

Lorienne could not find an answer.

What had been carved in the likeness of a beard long since faded to a mass of grotesque, wrinkled flesh jutting from the side of the mountain. From the two apertures that were the face's eyes, feeble streams dripped, making the Weeping Mountain aptly named. A game trail weaved about the flow, and upon this, Krael tread. Reunited with his weapon, the Slayer was fully prepared for anything the assassin had in store.

Underneath a billowing hooded cloak, Krael wore his sleeveless vest and leather pants but otherwise bore no armor. He was used to fighting uninhibited, and although a coat of mail may have helped ward off the venom of Morgvid's blades, finding a hauberk that fit his large frame would have been an endeavor in itself. Each minute that crept by was one where Darreth's condition may worsen in the wretched cavern, and the Slayer was determined not to let his friend down. Krael seldom spoke of his past, but when he did, the details of his former companions were always omitted.

The Wizard Slayer's path was filled with suffering and destined to end in death. Companionship was something not covered in the teachings of Mog Muhtar, and Krael had allowed friends to follow and aid him. All but Darreth had died. Like the serpents in the trial of the Pit and the Candle, he pushed their deaths from his conscious mind. The pain and tragedy could be taken advantage of by magickal manipulation. Like the haze of a nightmare, the horrid details shifted, but they persisted in his dreams. Every night, his mind was filled with their dying screams and cries for help, thus why his slumbers were always restless.

The mouth of the cave was literally a mouth, as it was the maw of the carved screaming face. Twenty feet in diameter it was, and as Krael stepped into its shadowy depths, he roared, "Morgvid! Show yourself!"

The words, invigorated with inhuman ferocity, echoed throughout the cavern with a deafening strength. Answering it came the assassin's voice. "Ah, the Hound of Mog Muhtar approaches. I have long awaited this moment, Wizard Slayer!"

Morgvid's whispery voice bounced off numerous crags within the cavern, and the Slayer had no idea where his foe waited. Ten paces into the mouth was the farthest the sunlight could reach, and only the faintest of glows reflected off the slick rocks and steel hammer. The assassin had the advantage.

The hiss of a talwar passing through the air served as the first sign of Morgvid's approach, and an ordinary man would have been killed in an instant. Krael's steel-trap muscles contorted and whirled, bringing his hammer across himself to ward off the expert blow. The haft intercepted the first slice, and the second blade came within an inch of the Slayer's shoulder. Even in the blackness, Morgvid's white face could be seen, sunken eyes wide above a ghoulish grin. Worming purple veins twisted like cracks in a bleached skull.

Instead of backing away, the Slayer advanced, pushing the assassin into the shadows. Arcing faster than Morgvid expected a mortal capable of, the steel hammerhead crashed into his shoulder. The Askarian robe-mail offered little protection against a crushing impact. The assassin retreated, relying on his venom-induced speed to evade Krael's torrent of strikes.

As his eyes adjusted, the barbarian found the warm sunlight blinding. At the same time, the formless shapes within the cave became recognizable. With the passing of each second, Morgvid's advantage waned.

"Your reputation does not do you justice," said the assassin, his unplaceable voice seeming to creep from every crack in the rock. "You must be the greatest of the Wizard Slayers, Krael of Mog Muhtar."

"Slayers?" said the barbarian, confused yet ready.

"Your order? You are one of the many Wizard Slayers, are you not?"

"There was only ever me."

Morgvid gasped, genuinely surprised. "You mean to say all those sorcerer-kings and witch-lords fell by your hand alone?"

Krael was silent.

Morgvid continued. "It almost makes me wish I did not have to face you."

From over the precipice of a rock vaulted a whirlwind of strange robes, and amidst this sliced two shimmering talwars. As they sank into the wooden haft of Krael's hammer, Morgvid hissed, "Almost."

The two swung their weapons in a frenzy at each other, each blow narrowly missing. For every great strike the barbarian could offer, Morgvid followed with six. The Kolgathian's might held the assassin's enhanced speed and vigor at bay for a time, but he could not keep it up forever. Krael was on the defensive, backpedaling and parrying through the darkness. Had Morgvid wished to end the Slayer, this battle would have ceased long before. Instead of a killing blow, the assassin wished only to leave the shallowest of scratches. This was a much more challenging feat.

His breathing became heavy, and the Slayer's dodges became ever slower. Morgvid capitalized. As the hammer came within inches of his chest, the razor edge of his left talwar grazed Krael's forearm. At the time, the barbarian did not know why Morgvid had let up in his assault, but as his right arm became numb, the grim realization flooded his thoughts. The hammer dropped, and Krael fell backward, unable to feel his right side.

Morgvid laughed as he watched the barbarian thrash on the ground. "It seems you are larger than most men. The venom that now runs in your blood would normally be enough to paralyze your whole body. Fear not, lone Wizard Slayer of Mog Muhtar, one more cut will keep you from moving."

Amidst the echoes of Krael's enraged roaring, not even the heightened senses of the assassin could hear the approaching foot-steps. As the sword-dancer's shadow fell across his sunken eyes, Morgvid snapped around, but it was too late. With the grace of a diving eagle, Lorienne's sword plunged through the assassin's wrist.

The talwar clattered to the ground. Blood poured onto the cavern rock. Looking down, Morgvid saw that his hand had been completely severed from his arm. The shattering of his own ego hurt him more than the injury, but he let out an enraged hiss nonetheless.

There, wreathed by sunlight, Lorienne stood.

Her proud smirk then faded when the assassin ceased to bleed. Whatever foul concoction of venoms that Morgvid took had caused his blood to instantly coagulate, and what should have been a mortal wound was now a minor inconvenience. He whipped toward Lorienne, his remaining talwar glimmering with the paralyzing toxin, not holding back as he did with the Slayer.

Unlike the Kolgathian, Lorienne was well versed in the finer arts of combat. Her falchion swirled about her body in a strange counterpart to Morgvid's vicious assault. She slipped and pirouetted, making a fool of the assassin in all his rage. The sword-dancer's movements were indeed a dance, yet what seemed to be flourishes were actually deflecting blocks and deft attacks.

As graceful as her movements were, she was no match for her opponent's superhuman strength. With the flat of his talwar, he knocked her weapon aside. She was at his mercy, and seeing the opportunity to take her alive, he forwent a decapitating slash and instead ran the curved blade through her stomach.

Lorienne uttered a short gasp. From the corner of her mouth came a droplet of blood. Smiling, Morgvid said, "A sword-dancer? I've long wished to taste your kind. I prefer a struggle, so perhaps I'll wait until the venoms wear off before I have my way."

Amidst the assassin's taunts, Krael rose to his feet. Morgvid threatened not just Darreth but Lorienne as well. All the screams of his past companions, the incessant torture that haunted his dreams, swelled in his waking mind. In his rage, he fought to answer those long-silent pleas for help. Though his right side was shackled in the grip of the toxins, the barbarian shuffled forward with what muscles he still could control.

The sickly assassin chuckled as Lorienne struggled to protest. She was already paralyzed. Morgvid was surprised once again when he felt the Kolgathian's left hand clamp about his neck. In that short fraction of a moment, which felt like whole seconds to the assassin, he felt the terror of panic for the first time.

Amidst his rage, Krael managed to whisper a single word: "Die."

Like a wolf shaking a hare to break its neck, Krael whipped the assassin's body backward with a single arm. The attack was far from graceful. Morgvid writhed like a trapped animal, scratching at the Kolgathian's thick arm. It did nothing.

The Wizard Slayer loomed atop his prey, and clenching the neck even tighter, he lifted and slammed the pale body. The assassin's enhanced senses were a blur of motion and agony. Over and over again, Morgvid was sent crashing to the hard stone floor.

The assassin lay twitching, but his punishment was far from over. Like a great ape, the barbarian raised his left arm high and brought it down onto the man's shattered body. His fist sank into Morgvid's back like a maul. A minute passed, Krael roaring the whole time. Dark purplish blood oozed from the assassin's mouth, and only when exhaustion overtook the barbarian did he cease.

Marching up the winding path came Garrick and his men, reunited with their spears. Down in the valley, they had heard the Kolgathian's inhuman roars from the cave, and while they didn't know who had won the battle, it was sure to all that it would've been a sight to behold. Slowly they tread, advancing toward the mountain's maw.

Garrick's stomach churned. On the one hand, he wished that Krael was captured, and the whole chase ended. At the same time, he knew his liege's nefarious plans for the Slayer and secretly hoped that Morgvid had been defeated. *I should not think such*

*things, but if Morgvid was killed by the Wizard Slayer, that creep
got what was coming to him.*

The soldiers stopped in their tracks when they saw what carnage lay in the cave. They readied their spears, defending against
whatever savage creature waited within.

Lying in the pale twilight of the cavern was Morgvid, or at
least what was left of him. Death had not overtaken the assassin,
as a hoarse, hate-filled wheezing came from between his black
lips. His left hand was reduced to a bloodless stump, and his chest
seemed concave. The twin talwars were nowhere to be seen. His
two sunken eyes were glaring out in a silent rage, livid with the
vitality that his body no longer possessed.

"By Atlor!" Garrick muttered, then more audibly said,
"Morgvid, can you hear me?"

Only a raspy hiss came from the assassin's mouth, and the
eyes continued to stare.

After scanning the rest of what the light showed, Garrick noticed pools of blood more crimson than the murky purple that was
Morgvid's. Readying his shield, he called out, "Krael, are you
there?"

There was no response.

Garrick continued. "Are you hurt? If you come with me, I can
tend to your wounds."

Like a bear warding off intruders from its den, the Wizard
Slayer's growling voice was amplified by the cavern walls. "I will
die before I serve Torvaren."

"Come now, Krael, we have you cornered and outnumbered."

The Slayer did not respond.

Cursing to himself, Garrick commanded one of his subordinates to light a torch. Slowly, the men tread into the entryway of
the cavern. In the flickering light, the true nature of the cave was
apparent. What had once been the dedicated work of delicate
hands had withered and crumbled. Above them was a carved
vaulted ceiling with many stalactites forming long after it was

chiseled from the rock. Reliefs in the stone had long since been erased by time, but the borders still stood around the oddly textured stone. While most of the cavern could be seen, the far end was still an amorphous blackness in which only a few shapes could be discerned. A gentle breeze passed through, and the men of Saidal realized that the cavern reached far deeper than they had imagined.

"Get Morgvid on a stretcher," said Garrick, "and bring him back to Dron."

While the hands lifting the assassin's body were gentle, a series of sharp cracks were heard as he was raised. His wheezing became more intense, but somehow, he still breathed.

Calling into the darkness, Garrick said, "Where is Lorienne? We saw her approach earlier."

"She is wounded," said the unseen Slayer.

"How badly?"

"Very."

Garrick pursed his lips. After a moment, he said, "There is no need for her to die here – or Darreth for that matter. I'm willing to take them under my care. You have my word that I will not use them as leverage to draw you out – if my word still means anything to you."

For perhaps a minute, no sound came from the shadowed depths of the ancient cave, save for the hints of whispers. Then, slowly, Lorienne stepped into the firelight, Darreth's arm about her shoulder and tawny-haired head lolling from side to side. The hint of paralysis was still shown in the sword-dancer's staggering gait, but the assassin's venoms had otherwise worn off in the time since their battle.

"Aid them!" commanded the knight.

Subject to the whims of whoever guided his semi-conscious body, Darreth immediately slumped onto a stretcher. His face, pale and beaded with sweat, relaxed as he lay down. Lorienne was hesitant to accept help from the men who had chased them across the Outlaw Kingdoms. At their touch, her arm retracted. The wound in her stomach had been covered, but the bandages were soaked with fresh blood. Her struggling didn't make this better.

"Lie down and rest," said one of the Saidalians, "please."

Lorienne eventually complied, and two soldiers picked her up and followed Morgvid and Darreth down the mountain.

Turning to the deeper places of the cave, Garrick said, "I assure you your friends will receive the best treatment available."

After no reply, Garrick continued. "You're totally trapped here, Krael, and not even you can take on over a dozen fully armed spearmen and survive. If you don't come out, you'll starve."

"Then I starve," said Krael.

Sighing, Garrick told his men to set up camp in the shallows of the cave. "We'll sleep in shifts. At least ten of us must be ready at any given time. Hopefully, Krael will see the futility in resisting and come peacefully. If not, stick to your training." He looked to the darkness, wary of the monster that lay within. "And pray."

25
IN THE SHADOWS OF THE EARTH

Time was irrelevant in the utter blackness beneath the mountain, and in that strange dream-like period, Krael experienced only two sensations: the pain of hunger gnawing in his gut and the urge to end that pain. Neither showed any sign of abating. The temptation to resurface into Garrick's captivity was strong, but the philosophy of Mog Muhtar forbade it. In their wisdom, the monks knew the power of what they had created. As clever as Torvaren and Ordric thought themselves to be, their plan of using the Wizard Slayer to threaten magick-users had been predicted decades ago. Their litany had been seared into the Slayer's mind: *You fight in the name of Mog Muhtar and no other. Any other master is a puppet of the Dark Gods.* So there Krael sat, hunched like a lurking ape, resting against a cold, jagged stone. On his hips were the assassin's talwars, and in his hand was the war hammer that Lord Artreth had given him in Raven's Watch so many weeks ago. With unblinking eyes, he stared into the dark.

The Wizard Slayer was in agony. A dribbling, acrid spring had kept him hydrated, but he was drained. Without sustenance, he would die within a few days, or whatever equivalent there was in the sunless realm within the rock, and alone his body would sit to be gnawed on by unseen scavengers. If there was another exit from the Weeping Mountain, it lay beyond a labyrinthian sprawl of twisting half-collapsed tunnels and stygian corridors. To step into it would be suicide, but Krael did not know if he had any other choice.

Each muscle screamed in pain as he moved deeper into the mountain. He ached from the fight with Morgvid. Not even the wounds from the dwarves, Vornond's chill spells, or Amris's bodyguards had fully healed, but the Slayer still crawled through the dark. Whatever humanity that would have convinced him to give up had died long ago in the serpent-filled pits of Mog Muhtar, and only a cold will remained. Like talons, his fingers clung to the rock, cruel stone scraping against tired flesh.

A shadow of a thought passed through the barbarian's mind: giving up and returning to Garrick would end all of the pain. Krael roared at the idea, hating himself for even thinking it. Whether this sound could be heard by any living thing, he did not know. If he still lived and had not gone on to some hellish afterlife, he did not know either.

Blindly he stumbled, falling over ledges and crashing onto unforgiving crags. Sometimes he tumbled more than he willingly continued, but the result was still the same: he moved onward. For all he knew, he may have been going in a circle like a rat unable to understand the confines of its own cage.

The Slayer was not as alone as he thought. In the cavern crept other denizens more accustomed to the eternal night, and their hearing and smell made up for their lack of vision. Krael's grunts and stumblings offended these creatures' sensitive ears. The smaller things crept away, fearful of the clumsy intruder, but this was not the case for all.

As he crawled, the Kolgathian began to tremble from exhaustion. Sweat had formed on his skin, and the pain of hunger swelled into encompassing nausea. Amidst this, he was unaware of the gentle footsteps that crept on the ledge above. It was the soft tapping of a calloused foot against hard stone. The thing approached, and it knew its prey was oblivious. Like a bobcat, it sprang from its high perch. Instinct guided its gnarled hands to where Krael's throat would be, and they clasped like a steel trap upon impact.

Every fiber of the Slayer's body tightened as the clammy fingers sank into his windpipe. Hot, hissing breath preceded the thing's teeth sinking into the back of Krael's neck. He dropped his hammer into the blackness, and the weapon clattered into an unseen abyss, never to be recovered. His body jerked backward, thrashing to reach the unknown horror that leaped onto him. The barbarian's imagination was alight with theories as to what dreadful form the attacker took. His hands clasped around a bulbous head, and with a death grip, he contorted his body forward. Teeth ripped at Krael's flesh as their owner was sent hurtling, naked body clapping against the stone.

With the advantage, Krael pounced, not wasting time drawing a talwar. His hands then fell upon the thing's face, and he felt large orb-like eyes bulging from the irregular skull. Warm, wet gel gushed down the Slayer's fingers as he popped the eyes, and an uncanny shriek came from the victim. Arms and legs thrashed but could do little against the Kolgathian's superior build. Gripping the thing by its empty sockets, Krael smashed its skull against the stone.

After a final bout of twitching, the creature ceased to move. It may have been a variant of dwarf, but there was no way to tell with certainty, and Krael did not care. Like his Kolgathian ancestors urged on by the primal instinct to feed, he hesitantly sank his fangs into the raw flesh. The civilized corner of his mind wished him not to partake of it, but he could not resist. Desperately, he gnawed, and before long, his hunger had finally ceased. The Slayer took no pride in this, but to continue his life's purpose, he must live on, even if it came to eating like an animal.

Sir Garrick stepped into the common room of the inn. The typical evening crowd was scattered about the tables and stools, and the rich smell of greasy meat flooded out all else. The jovial atmosphere was a relief from the dank, dimly lit tunnel he had spent the last week within. Upon noticing their commander, two Saidalian warriors stood up at attention. "Any sign of the Slayer, sir?" one of them asked.

"No, nothing," said Garrick. "I fear that he may have starved, but I'm still hesitant to go in after him."

After a nod, the soldier asked, "What brings you back here, then?"

"Supplies and checking to see if a courier brings news from Saidal. I am eager to know what has happened there in my absence."

"Someone far more important than a courier has arrived. He wishes to speak with you."

Garrick gave a puzzled look and followed the soldier's gesture to a man sitting across the room. He sat next to Darreth, who seemed to be recovering well himself. The figure's hair was a strange, uneven brown, and peeking from beneath a weathered cloak were plates of glimmering steel. The old knight made his way toward him, and upon Darreth's pointing, the mysterious man turned. When he saw the unique jade eyes, Garrick's scarred face smiled. "Eledrith, my boy!"

Bounding from his chair, the prince met his old mentor with a hearty embrace. "I've missed you so, so much, Garrick."

"Have you grown taller in the past months?"

Stepping back, Eledrith answered, "Perhaps."

"You look to be more of a man than when I last saw you, and where did you get that armor? I haven't seen the likes of it before!"

"The latest from the finest engineers of Saidal, but that's a different story. Much has happened in your absence."

"Come, sit!" said Darreth, the sight of an old friend revitalizing his tired body.

"First of all," said the knight, taking a seat next to the elf-blooded, "why in Atlor's name have you ridden all the way out here? These lands are no doubt hostile to royalty such as yourself."

Eledrith nodded. "Indeed they are, hence why I've dyed my hair."

Darreth piped up. "Hey, maybe you could show Garrick how to do that."

The knight scowled and ran a hand through his graying head. Laughing, Eledrith patted the elf-blooded on the back and said, "Oh, Darreth, I'm glad to know you haven't changed much."

"For better or worse," said Garrick with a smirk.

Eledrith pulled a chair out for Garrick. "Come," he said, "I'm eager to tell you everything that has happened."

The three sat together at the table, and amidst the chaos of the evening, they garnered little more than a handful of curious glances. Despite being the heir to the most powerful city-state in the known world, Eledrith went unnoticed. They ordered drinks, wetted their throats, and began discussing what had happened in Saidal. As the firelight waned, the rabble of the place only increased, and the prince's words were drowned by the cacophony of slurred conversations and boisterous voices.

"And now Ordric sits on the throne as High Lord of Saidal," finished the prince.

"In that case," said Garrick, "I am no longer bound to hunting the Wizard Slayer."

The elf-blooded let out a sigh of relief and slumped in his chair. Eledrith had previously told him this would be the case, but hearing the knight himself say it meant much more.

"I serve the Calidign line," continued Garrick, "and since you're the sole living successor to the throne, I assume you wish me to give up this senseless quest, Your Majesty?"

"Of course, I do, but remember my father still lives, be it a frail semblance of life."

"That technicality may keep you from ruling Saidal, but my knightly oath is not so easily manipulated. Still, what happened to your father can be no coincidence. I think Count Ordric has a hand in it."

"And it's something he could do," interjected Darreth, "if he's using magick as you say."

After downing a swig of ale, Garrick said, "That was something I wished to ask you about. How are you so certain that he meddles in the black arts? He is a formidable statesman, and the events you described regarding the changing of minds and such could easily be attributed to his charisma and wit."

Shaking his head, Eledrith's face hardened. "No, I have no doubt that it is magick. The last night we spoke, I knew Morwenna was being bewitched."

"You're still speaking with her?" interrupted the knight. "I'm glad Ordric hasn't come between your blossoming relationship."

"Blossoming?" asked Eledrith.

A cheeky smile came to Darreth's face. "We didn't tell him yet, did we?"

"Tell me what?"

After struggling to find the proper words, Eledrith said, "I married her."

Garrick laughed heartily and put a hand on the prince's shoulder. "Congratulations, Your Majesty! It's a shame I couldn't be present."

"I did miss you, yeah," said the prince.

"Don't worry about it. I'm sure I'll spend many a day at your sides. Well, after this whole ordeal with Ordric is finished. You were saying that he definitely uses magick."

"Yes," said Eledrith, eyes wandering amidst the bubbles that formed in his flagon. "I can't quite describe the sensation, if that's what this feeling even is, but it's the very same that I felt in the presence of Thalnar's thralls. My father-in-law simply has too much control. I don't dare face him myself since I'd be turned into another one of his puppets. I suppose I should thank Atlor that that hasn't already happened."

"So then you've come for the Wizard Slayer," finished Garrick.

After a gulp of his drink, Darreth said, "If anyone can stop Ordric, it's Krael."

For a moment, the three sat in silence. They pondered the ferocity of the man they were about to unleash on the usurper of Saidal. Morwenna, and her inability to stand against the sorcery of her father, then flooded into Eledrith's thoughts. Wishing to waste no more time, he said, "So, was there any sign of Krael? Darreth told me he's hiding in that ugly face on the mountain."

"And as far as I know, he's still in there," Garrick admitted. "He's a cornered animal. I pity the man that dares pull him from that hole."

Eledrith smirked. "I'll then ask that you do not pity me. I can fetch him."

"But, Your Majesty, he could be at his wits' end! He has no reason to trust anything we say."

"I'll come, too!" said Darreth, ignoring the knight's pleas.

The knight's jaw clenched. "If Your Majesty wishes to undertake this task, then I am in no place to stop you." He then turned to the sickly elf-blooded. "You, on the other hand, need to rest. You're as pale as a ghost."

"He can come if he wishes," said the prince. "Some fresh air would do him well."

The knight didn't bother to protest. With a shrug, Darreth arose from his chair and said, "I've rested long enough. The sooner we pull Krael from that gods-forsaken mountain, the better."

The three rushed to the tavern's exit, pushing past stumbling bodies and rowdy tables. Before they left, Garrick asked, "How is Lorienne doing?"

"Well, I think," said Darreth. "She hasn't spoken to me much, but she's alive."

"That's good."

"She wasn't too keen on following us after the assassin attacked in Raven's Watch, but she stuck around to help me after I was almost eaten alive. I was surprised she helped Krael in the cave."

"That woman has true courage within her," said Garrick. "It'd be best for you to keep her close at hand. Friends like her are hard to come by."

Darreth could do little but nod. Lorienne had trouble articulating how she felt, and the elf-blooded was in no place to describe it to Garrick.

"Come on!" said Eledrith, pushing open the door. "Let's not keep Krael waiting."

***

A jutting black void loomed in the tapestry of stars that was the night sky: the Weeping Mountain. Garrick lit a torch to keep them from tripping along the mountain's winding path. In the orange gloom, they marched, unaware of how close they were to the effigy weathered beyond recognition.

In the night, another flame was seen, and Eledrith was relieved that their hike had ended. The prince was met with curious looks from the guards, but as he drew near enough for them to see his characteristic jade eyes, they all dropped to a knee. He recognized some of the faces as men often stationed within the Calidign Palace.

"At ease," he said. "I come bearing dire news from Saidal."

Eledrith gave an abbreviated summary of the events that transpired in the soldiers' home. While he did this, Darreth crept into the shallows of the cave, torch in hand. All around him loomed the forsaken masonry of eons past. He took a deep breath and called out, "Krael!"

Nothing. Even the echo was faint. Praying he hadn't disturbed any other denizens of the subterranean realm, he took another wary step. Just then, a hand fell on his shoulder.

"Fear not, I'm here," said Eledrith.

"As am I," said Garrick.

They had marched twenty paces into the cavern before a dizzying number of offshoots had sprung from the main tunnel and wound in every direction. Long after the ancient passageways had been carved, the stone had crumbled, making new jagged pathways that intersected with the old. As the three continued forward, what they thought were minor recesses in the rock turned out to be more potential paths the Slayer may have taken.

"Let's not go any further," said Garrick. "Even if we find Krael, we won't be any help to him if we can't find our way back."

Heeding the knight's command, they halted. "Do your men have any rope, Garrick?" asked the prince.

The old scarred lip pulled up into a smile. "We have the same idea," he said. "I'll be right back."

Garrick passed through the small pool of shadow between Darreth's torch and the campfire of his men. In the meantime, the elf-blooded eyed the many apertures surrounding him. "He searched for another way out," he said to himself.

Eledrith picked up his friend's mumbling. "All he could do was guess, couldn't he?"

"Yeah. We were in darkness after he fought the assassin, so Krael probably felt his way through the dark."

"Then odds are he stumbled into the biggest holes?"

After considering Eledrith's rationale, Darreth nodded. "Sounds about right to me."

Garrick returned, and carried in both of his hands was a formidable coil of rope. "I'm not sure how much there is here, but it's all we have. Let's hope he didn't stray too far."

The search took hours. More than once, they had exhausted the length of their rope and were forced to turn back. Each time they did so, a weight sank to the bottom of Darreth's gut, and he began to lose hope. On one of these backtracking trips, Darreth heard a curious sound. He raised a single hand, commanding his companions to halt.

"What is it, Darreth?" asked the prince.

The elf-blooded himself did not know for sure. It was like a faint gust of air. If it were not for the echoing effect of the stone walls, the subtle hiss might not have been heard at all. The sound came rhythmically, like the rolling of a distant tide.

"This way," said Darreth.

Garrick struggled with both the rope and keeping up with Darreth. There was a vigor in the young man's stride that ignored caution. Then, without warning, he halted once again.

"I hear it, too," said Eledrith. "It's breathing."

Stalagmites and stalactites loomed like fangs in the cave, but the men pushed past them. So quickly they moved that they did not notice the scratches etched by blind, untrained hands. In the lightless realm beneath the mountain, these served as territorial markers to the semi-intelligent creatures that felt them. Torchlight did little to illuminate their rough textures.

The companions did stop, however, when the tunnel opened to a more expansive cave, the reaches of which were outside the feeble fire's glow. In the recesses of the natural stone floor pooled the dull brown remnants of dried blood. Amidst the gore lay an unrecognizable carcass. Its chest was torn open, and the flesh of its arms was picked clean.

"It's like a pack of wolves set upon him!" said Garrick to his speechless companions.

After a sigh, Eledrith put a hand on Darreth's shoulder. In a hushed tone, he said, "That sound we heard may have been whatever monster killed this… thing."

Darreth had already thought what the prince had said. Brushing the gauntleted hand from his shoulder, he said, "We have to keep going."

"Do you think Krael is capable of such carnage?" whispered Garrick. "He certainly leaves trails of blood, but whoever did this ate this creature."

The elf-blooded looked straight into the knight's eyes. "You pushed him, Garrick. You know he's not like other men who give up when all seems lost. He's accepted that he will die fighting, and he'll keep going no matter how much of a disadvantage he's at. Krael is definitely capable of this."

"We go forward," said the prince, no longer whispering, "but be on your guard. Even if this is Krael and not some subterranean monster, there's no doubt more of these things."

The ripping of dwarves' nails and teeth were all too familiar to the elf-blooded, and heeding Eledrith's command, he drew the dagger from his boot and kept it at the ready. As they continued, Garrick noticed the short steel blade trembling. At the same time, the knight was impressed by the focus in Darreth's eyes. While justified fear wreaked his body, there was a discipline that few men knew how to muster keeping him on the path forward. *That look in his eye is much like that of the Wizard Slayer himself,* Garrick thought. *Perhaps Darreth is taking after him more than anyone has realized.*

Before long, they had found the Wizard Slayer. When his body was first seen, they thought they had come across another corpse. There, splayed on jagged rocks, was the sickly pale flesh of the Kolgathian. His skin was pulled tight across his vascular, corded body. The untamed hair stuck to the cold sweat on his shoulders. Most ghastly of all was the stream of crimson that ran down from his gaping, fanged mouth.

"Krael!" shouted Darreth, running toward him.

The Kolgathian lay unresponsive. What slight motion came from his body was the raising and lowering of his chest with each raspy, strained breath.

"Careful, Darreth!" cried Garrick impulsively.

"By Atlor," muttered Eledrith. "Is that his own blood?"

Darreth shook Krael's body, desperation fueling his movements. The man's head lobbed to the side, and a low growl came from him.

"Krael! It's me, Darreth! We've come to get you out of here."

The Slayer uttered a series of semi-words, but they went unrecognized thanks to his exhaustion.

Sheathing his blade, Eledrith came to Darreth's side and helped lift Krael. Between their strength and whatever remained of the Slayer's, the barbarian was lifted and shuffled through the tunnel.

"We'll have plenty of food for you back at camp," said Garrick. "You'll rest soon, Krael."

The Slayer's eyes snapped open at the sound of the veteran knight's voice. His pupils glowed vibrantly like an animal's. Letting out a hoarse roar, Krael threw both men who helped him forward. Teeth bared, he backpedaled. The barbarian could not continue in his condition, and within seconds he fell to the cavern floor.

"Get... away!" Krael managed, kicking at the air.

Still reeling from his own tumble, Darreth approached the Slayer and said, "Relax, Krael, he's not hunting you anymore."

This proved ineffective, and Krael still lashed at those who sought to help him. He reached for one of the talwars on his hips and drew it, pointing the still-poisoned blade at the blinding torch.

"It is Eledrith. King Torvaren is comatose, and now Garrick follows my orders. He no longer wishes to hunt you down."

The barbarian's knuckles turned white as he tightened his grip on the talwar. Then, as he recognized the prince's voice, Krael let his arm drop. All realized the struggle was finally over.

"What could bring a man to this?" Garrick asked.

Krael did not answer. Only a series of tired, heaving sighs escaped from his lips.

"He wanted to remain true to himself, or more likely whatever higher ideal he pursues," said Eledrith. "Where any other man would give in, he fought on."

Garrick shook his head. "But to this length?"

"He doesn't fear death," said Darreth, "but he fears becoming a pawn of Ordric. He knows that's far worse."

26
REUNION AND RESPITE

Morgvid lay on his back in the darkened room of the inn. His eyes gazed into the graying wood of the ceiling, seldom blinking. At the assassin's request, the windows had been blackened out. Only the faintest glimmers of dawn illuminated his pale, disfigured body. After the soldiers of Saidal had laid him in the room, Morgvid demanded solitude. For all they knew, the assassin was determined to die of his wounds rather than face the wrath of the Serpent's Hand for failing in his quest. Unbeknownst to them, he still drew a feeble, hissing breath.

There came a mechanical clicking from the lock on the door, and Morgvid's eyes snapped toward it. Through the door stepped Sir Garrick, although the assassin could not see his face in the peaceful darkness. He only recognized the knight by the sound of his clinking mail and telltale gait. Not even Garrick knew he walked with a subtle limp, subconsciously keeping weight off a knee injured decades ago. Morgvid had noticed this the day he met the old man. Even when resting, the highly trained senses of the assassin absorbed everything around him. While he may have lay maimed and paralyzed, his predatory mind clung to anything he may one day use to his advantage.

Garrick knew nothing of this. Not even the assassin's faint breaths reached his ears. "Morgvid?" he said.

Mustering his strength, the assassin forced his dry throat to produce a moan.

"So, you are alive," answered the knight.

Morgvid made another noise, this time a more vigorous, hoarse groan.

Straining his eyes, Garrick could make out his associate's pale, shirtless body. What should have resembled a chest was a shapeless mass. The unmistakable white of bone pierced out from the skin in more than one place. A ray of light also fell on the stump where Morgvid's hand should have been. Purple-black muscle showed when white skin ceased. Morgvid's face, however, was concealed by shadow.

Garrick told Morgvid the news of Torvaren's coma and Eledrith's arrival seeking the Wizard Slayer.

"And of our task?" managed the assassin.

"Not my task anymore. I serve the Calidign line, and His Majesty Prince Eledrith has saved me from Ordric's vile plot."

A cry of rage only came from Morgvid as a terrible raspy hiss. Even this wretched sound sent a chill down Garrick's back, and his hand instinctively reached for the empty axe loop on his belt. "You should have let the Wizard Slayer kill me," said Morgvid.

"Why do you say this? Krael must have knocked some wits from your skull."

The assassin coughed up a sardonic laugh, or was it a sob? "I, unlike you, am still sworn to Count Ordric's service. I have failed in this task."

Only then did Garrick remember what those of the Serpent's Hand suffered if they had failed. "Surely your superiors can't find you here. In this backwater town? A whole ocean from Askaron?"

Morgvid snapped upright in his bed using the strength of his maimed arm. Bone-white and claw-like fingers reached toward the knight. A streak of light ran across Morgvid's face, and Garrick could see the genuine terror in his eyes, the whites of which were then red. Whatever injury had caused his eyes to hemorrhage was nothing compared to the fate the assassin feared. "You know nothing of them! Even now, they seek me."

"That's preposterous. How could anyone possibly know what happens out here?"

"The Al'Katiils of the Serpent's Hand possess abilities that make venom alchemy seem like a mere parlor trick!"

The old knight was having none of this. Shaking his head, he said, "Now you're just raving. I knew I should've had my men attend to you."

Garrick turned to leave, but just as he took his first step toward the door, there was a chaotic shuffling from Morgvid's bed. Expecting an attack, the knight raised his fists and whirled back around, fully prepared to worsen every one of the assassin's injuries. To his surprise, the room was empty, and a cold morning breeze slipped through an open window.

Sparing no time, Garrick ran and looked out into the street. There was nothing. No sound. Only staggering footsteps in the snow.

———◆———

Krael sat in the corner of the common room, surrounded by empty plates and friends. The color had returned to his flesh, and as much as a Kolgathian could be, he seemed content and happy. His head rested upon a fist, and a grin lay on his face. At his sides, Eledrith and Darreth exchanged stories and jokes, laughing at each other's immaturity. Lorienne stood amongst them, rolling her eyes at the crudeness (or what some would argue, genius) of the prince and elf-blooded's humor.

"Once, Krael and I stopped to rest at this inn a few days south from Cellenbron. I got to talking with some merchant there," said Darreth, "and of course, I might've been a little tipsy."

Krael raised his eyebrows. "Tipsy" was an understatement.

The elf-blooded continued, ignoring his barbarian friend. "But we were having a good time and all. I was trying to pick up on rumors, but the guy kept bringing up his family. His son was sitting next to him, and I'll admit that when he said he got kicked in the head by an ox, the best response probably wasn't 'I can tell.'"

Eledrith snickered. Lorienne smacked her forehead with her palm, but she nonetheless smiled. The sword-dancer had warmed back up to her companions after Krael returned. In her typical standoffish manner, she grew silent whenever pressed about why she had come to the Slayer's aid in the Weeping Mountain. She said it was because she thought she "owed him a favor," and Darreth and Krael both left it at that.

"I'm glad you're both recovering so quickly," said the prince, "and even you, Lorienne, are doing surprisingly well."

Lorienne said, "That assassin's blade cut clean, but I'm lucky he didn't hit anything too vital."

"He wasn't trying to," said the Slayer.

All eyes at the table turned toward Krael. He continued. "He wished to use the poison on his swords. Not to kill. If he wished to kill me, he would have. I know it."

Hoping to keep the mood light, Eledrith said, "That being said, you have no idea what you're doing against swords. No offense, though. You're a damn great fighter, but I'm sure even Darreth here could beat you in a fair one-on-one duel."

"And that's why he doesn't fight fair," said Darreth, smirking.

Lorienne smiled at Darreth's mannerism.

Noticing her, Darreth said, "What?"

"Nothing," she responded, shaking her head but smiling nonetheless.

"You know who's really good at fighting, though? She is," said Darreth, pointing to the sword-dancer.

"Really?" said Eledrith, raising an eyebrow. "I would never have guessed."

"Most never do," said Lorienne.

"She's a sword-dancer, you know," said Darreth.

"You don't say," said Eledrith, turning his chair to face her. "Garrick told me many tales of your kind. You have my respect."

"Thank you, Your Majesty."

Darreth piped up again. "Hey, maybe you guys could spar. I'd pay money to see Eledrith get beat by a girl."

The prince shook his head. "No. I won't fight a woman, let alone an injured one."

A sly grin came to one side of Lorienne's lips. "What's wrong, afraid I'll beat you?"

There was a glimmer of battle lust in Eledrith's jade eyes. "Alright," he said. "Outside, right now. Darreth, fetch us some sticks. Tool hafts or something."

Just as the group arose from their seats, the armored soldiers of Saidal came hustling through the room and stood guard at each entry. Seeing Garrick come rushing in as well, Eledrith asked, "What's the meaning of all this?"

Upon catching his breath, the knight said, "It's Morgvid. He's escaped."

"Escaped?" asked Eledrith.

"He still lives?" growled Krael, fuming anger more than inquiring.

Lorienne turned pale.

"I do not know how," said Garrick, "but he slipped from his room even with his injuries. He's convinced that others from his guild will hunt him down knowing he has failed his task."

Eledrith narrowed his eyes. "How would they know? Dron is leagues away from even the smallest of towns. Word can't possibly travel that fast."

"That's what I thought, but he seemed convinced. It's the first time I've seen the man show fear."

"Then we should move," said Krael. "Get out of the city. Here he can hide."

Darreth groaned. "Dammit, Krael, I've just started to feel better."

"He's right," said Eledrith. "We need to move. Even without this Morgvid lurking behind any corner, each day that goes by is one where Count Ordric goes unchecked."

"High Lord Ordric," said Garrick, saying the title to himself with spite.

"I suppose I should come with you, then," said Lorienne. "Morgvid knows my face, and the last thing I want is to have any further dealings with him."

Darreth said, "So much for that 'I'll leave once we reach the next town' business, then?"

"Don't push your luck."

Garrick's stern-toned voice brought their conversation to an end. "We leave in an hour. As you gather your things, do not go anywhere alone. Always stay in groups of at least two. There's no telling what Morgvid is planning for us."

⬥

Before an hour had passed, the group, escorted by the small force of soldiers, approached the main gate of Dron. The travelers were relieved to have their weapons back in their possession. Having lost his war hammer in the Weeping Mountain, Krael received Morgvid's talwars from the guards and secured them on his belt. They lacked the mass the barbarian preferred in his weapons, but their curving honed edges would serve well enough.

A layer of snow sat on the branches of the evergreens, causing the great boughs to droop. High above, the pale gray sky threatened more snowfall, but traveling through such weather would not slow the riders' pace. Prince Eledrith was at the group's head, chin high. More than ever, he felt like he was leading an army in a military campaign. No more was he a puppet of Ordric. Now, he fought for the sake of his home. Even more importantly, he fought for his beloved. As the thought of Ordric's bewitchments of her came to the prince's mind, his grip on the reins tightened. If his hands had not been covered with intricate steel gauntlets, the others would have seen his knuckles turn white.

"Is everything alright?" asked Darreth.

Eledrith had no idea that he outwardly showed his anger. "Er, yes."

"Yeah, something's bothering you."

After smiling at Darreth's insight, he said, "I let my thoughts wander to Morwenna. For so long, she's been my refuge, you know? Now, Ordric influences her mind using magick. He's trespassing on what I hold most sacred."

"Don't worry, you have Krael on your side," said Darreth. "Ordric is going to pay."

Eledrith's jade eyes wandered to the Kolgathian. The stern, savage face stared forward as if Ordric stood before him then and there. Even as he gently held the reins of his mount, veins and tendons bulged on his hands and forearms. Then, Eledrith noticed the breed of the Slayer's horse. "Wait a moment, where did you two get those horses?"

"We found them," replied Darreth, avoiding the prince's gaze.

"You stole them, didn't you?"

The elf-blooded froze. They still possessed the steeds they commandeered from the royal stables the night of the ball.

"Those are pure-bred warhorses. They're worth a fortune each!"

"Explains why they fared so well against the dwarves," said Darreth, realizing there was no point in keeping up the charade.

"Krael," the prince called out, "do you know what you are riding right now?"

A fanged smile showed on the Slayer's face. After nodding, he scratched behind the steed's ear and said, "His name is Horse."

Eledrith's face twisted, perplexed. Lorienne said, "He named it himself."

The prince could take no more. He burst out laughing. "Oh, how I've missed you all."

For a time, Eledrith's pain and anger had been abated.

The group made camp underneath a cluster of jagged peaks in the Black Mountains. The masses of solid rock protected them from the whistling winds, and before long, sparks from campfires wound their way into a starless sky. Far from the laughter and stories that accompanied the fire's warm glow, Eledrith had pulled Garrick away from the others.

"What's wrong, Your Majesty?"

After considering the many questions he wished to ask, the prince said, "What do you know of my mother?"

"Queen Elisia," said Garrick, "is a name that has not been spoken of in a long time. Why ask of her now, Eledrith? Your thoughts should be on what lies ahead, not the past."

"It was the day of the wedding. I had left to get some fresh air when I was approached by a woman claiming to be my mother."

"Sounds like either a lunatic or a con artist," grunted the old man.

"I thought it may have been something similar, but I was wrong. She somehow knew of my victory against Ordric in *sakhmet*."

"You've finally learned! I spent months trying to get you to sit down and play that game."

Eledrith shook his head. A gauntleted hand ran through his hair, the dye of which was beginning to fade to a faint reddish blond. "Yeah, I've learned, but there's more to it. I beat Ordric in my second game ever."

"Perhaps he was going easy on you."

"No, it was close until the end. I could see how he was being pushed to his limits."

"Then you must have another natural talent, Your Majesty," said Garrick, a warm smile on his scarred lips.

"Whatever, the game doesn't matter," said Eledrith. "There's no way the woman could have known of it. We were in the privacy of the Maumont Estate."

Garrick crossed his arms. "Then perhaps she's an ally of the count's. Ordric could have told her of the game. Besides, making you question your royal lineage could play to his favor."

Letting out a sigh, the prince looked westward into the black horizon. The expanse was dotted with the fires of small villages but otherwise featureless. Even while covered with white snow, the plains seemed amorphous in the sheer darkness beneath the overcast sky. "Maybe, but she didn't seem like a pawn of Ordric's."

Garrick said, "She wouldn't exactly present herself as one." A chuckle came from the veteran, and the prince knew it was forced. His mentor was trying to keep the mood light.

"Yeah, but as I turned to leave the balcony, she was no longer there. Not even her footprints were in the snow. The whole thing feels like a dream."

"Perhaps it was," said Garrick. "With all the stress you've been through, it wouldn't surprise me if an odd dream was so vivid you've mistaken it for reality."

"It would explain why she could get inside my head so effectively," said Eledrith, finally mustering a smile. "I mean, if she was conjured up there, after all."

"You already seem relieved. It's getting cold. Why don't we head back to the fire? More of Darreth's stories will help keep your mood up."

"There's one more thing," Eledrith said. "She said that one day there will come a time when I'll beg to be free of pain. If I accepted her, she'd help me. If not..."

"The ramblings of a dream, Eledrith," the knight said as he put a hand on the prince's shoulder. "Don't worry, you're surrounded by friends."

Eledrith nodded, avoiding Garrick's eyes. As they returned to Darreth and the others, Eledrith said, "You know, I only have one memory of my true mother."

Garrick raised an eyebrow. "Are you sure? She died when you were quite young."

"It may sound strange, but I remember us on a beach. I couldn't tell you which one, but we made this sandcastle. Perhaps the memory stuck with me for so long because I was heartbroken when it was washed away in the tide. I remember running around it, trying to keep it together, but it fell apart anyway."

"Wait, running?"

"Yeah," said Eledrith. "Why?"

"Your mother died before you took your first steps."

They were silent until they reached the campfire. Neither of them wished to resurrect their ominous conversation. Soon enough, they were laughing with Darreth as he recounted the more misadventurous of his stories. Absent from this, however, was Krael.

Crouching atop a jagged crag of stone was the Slayer, staring across the ill-lit expanse. The time spent talking at the inn had exhausted him, and he found solace in the solitude of the mountaintop. Winds swirled about him, causing his cloak to wave like a flag and his long hair to whip across his face. Even in this, there was a sense of serenity. The howling of the elements drowned out the clamor of the camp below, and Krael was left alone with a singular thought on his mind: Ordric.

Eledrith had described to the barbarian what his scheming father-in-law looked like. The dark hair, widow's peak, full beard, and aquiline nose all seemed familiar to the Wizard Slayer. He recounted the moment at the ball when he first felt the noose of Ordric's plan tighten. The man that Torvaren had looked to and who, in turn, looked at Krael matched the description perfectly. Months later, that image was still vibrant in the Slayer's mind.

Krael took pleasure in few things. Even when he rested with a full belly in a warm bed, he instinctively felt the chain whips of Mog Muhtar faintly lash against his back. The monks of that place were cruel, but so is the truth of life. If Krael was to become more than a barbaric slave, he needed to learn the whole visceral truth. He could take no pleasure in life, for he knew it was all fleeting. No comfort or love could ever sate him. Instead, it was the moments after slaying the wielders of magick where he truly felt at ease. Most would call this a form of madness, and perhaps they were right. To the Wizard Slayer, however, knowing sorcerers still walked the earth sparked rage.

There, on the mountaintop, he thought of battling Ordric. The Slayer knew not of what power he possessed, but then again, he hardly ever truly knew what he was up against. More than ever before, this fight would be personal. The count's plans targeted Krael himself, and the Kolgathian's friends had suffered in the process. As he crouched, the barbarian could feel his heart quicken as he thought of beheading the sorcerer who had wronged him.

27
TO SLAY A USURPER

Gray light did little to illuminate the dark marble of the throne room. The braziers that normally gave off a brilliant orange glow stood cold. In the center of the chamber, raised on a dais, was the comatose body of King Torvaren Calidign. Tended to by a group of hooded servants, the king was covered in lavish robes and blankets. His fat, bulbous neck jutted out farther than his chin as his head was perched atop a lavender pillow.

Upon the throne, thinking in the semi-darkness, sat High Lord Ordric. He was dressed in the old fashion of Ashkazanar, the archaic black robes lacking the refined complexity of Saidal's contemporary style. Still, there was a strange allure to the gold runes that gilded the edges of the many draping frills. While the opinion of Ordric's appearance was mixed, the count still held an inhuman charisma about him. In his study, there were depictions of the ancient lords of Zatraenor, the rulers of Ashkazanar, and it was in their footsteps that Ordric wished to tread. Like the sorcerer-kings of old, this style was meant to appeal to the Dark Gods.

In the past weeks, Ordric's power had grown exponentially. For days he toiled sleeplessly in his hidden study, reading and rereading the blasphemous tomes he had collected. Their ancient letters told of forgotten empires and the fell deities they served.

Most importantly, Ordric had learned of the powers that the ancient rulers used to subjugate their peoples. The ring, whose three-eyed skull signet stared unceasingly, fueled his obsession. No longer resisting the hubris that swelled from the snake-like band, the count had begun to hear arcane secrets whispered to him in his dreams.

With the growth of his power, there came a physical change to the man as well. Silver streaks began to show in his black hair. His skin began to wrinkle, and his dark eyes, while maintaining the glimmer of his cruel intellect, were sunken. It was as if he had aged twenty years in a single month. For this reason, he kept the throne room poorly lit. Rumors would spread like a plague if his condition was known by other members of the ruling class, who had been told that the palace was gloomy in mourning of Torvaren and the missing Prince Eledrith.

A ray of light shone like a beacon as one of the double doors at the far end of the throne room creaked open. The warm glow passed over Torvaren and stopped short of the High Lord, only reaching the bottommost step of the dais. Through the door came the supple frame of Princess Morwenna. Like her father, her appearance had also changed. Stress and grief had taken their toll, and dark spots had formed under her large brown eyes. The princess's face was visibly gaunter as well. "Father?" she said.

Ordric's deep, dark voice had thinned and become raspy. He attributed this to a simple dry throat, a byproduct of long study sessions and forgetting to drink water. This excuse worked for the counts under the sorcerer-lord's sway, but there was a sinister tinge in his speech that a lack of water could not produce. "Yes, my daughter," he said, "what can I do for you?"

Morwenna's eyes had yet to adjust to the dim light, and she struggled to make out the shadowy form that lurked on the throne. She passed Torvaren's body without a second glance. Like a novel piece of furniture or decoration, in time the motionless king became a mundane obstacle. "It's Eledrith," she said. "It has been so long since I've seen him. Has there been any news from the Outlaw Kingdoms?"

"None," said Ordric, shaking his head.

Morwenna approached the throne and sat on the cold marble floor next to her father's armrest. She laid her head against his knee and wept. "I keep having the same dream of him. He returns from the battlefield but then must leave to search for the Wizard Slayer. What does this mean, Father?"

"I do not know," said Ordric.

As his daughter sobbed, Ordric ran his fingers through her dark hair. The three-eyed skull of his signet ring seemed to glimmer, and without effort, he tightened the bewitchment that suppressed the authentic memory of Eledrith's return to Saidal. "It will be alright, darling," he said. "I will always be here for you."

Through tears, Morwenna could see little, and the cruel, twisted expression on Ordric's face was lost to the princess. The sorcerer hated the bond of love that held his daughter, but there was still a part of him who could not deny his fatherly love. *If I could just erase the memory of Eledrith from her mind*, he thought, *this would be so much easier. Yet, if I did, it would complicate matters in a way I could not control. For now, my child, you must suffer. If only there could be an easier way.*

Wiping tears from her face, the princess arose. "Forgive me, Father. I know you value your solitude. I'll be leaving now."

"Thank you, darling," said Ordric.

A spell had caused the princess to leave, not her own will. Thus was a habit for Ordric: manipulating the minds of others, even in small ways, for his own convenience. Shortly after Morwenna left the hall, the High Lord arose from his chair and passed through one of the less grand doors behind the throne. He walked down an unadorned staircase into the depths of the palace. The secret cramped hallway used to be for servants, but the High Lord had adopted it and the subsequent chambers it connected to for his own uses.

After pushing open a heavy wooden door, Ordric stepped into an unused storeroom. No longer housing barrels of supplies, the floor was bare save for crumblings that had fallen from the stone walls. At the far end of the chamber, chained to the wall, was the witch Stregana. About her thin wrists were iron shackles that had left red sores on her wrinkled, leathery skin. Upon Ordric's arrival, she turned her head and scowled, her sunken beady eyes narrowing. Even as his obsession with magick altered his body, the man's tall, broad-shouldered frame was as intimidating as ever. Ordric said, "I require your talents, witch."

A smile revealed the hag's sparsely toothed mouth, each yellowish spike of enamel jutting at a crooked angle. "Stregana can tell you've delved into dark secrets far too quickly."

"Speak for yourself," said Ordric, his lip curling in anger. "As long as I look better than you, I have nothing to worry about."

The witch let out a raspy, cackling chuckle. Captivity and mistreatment had taken a toll on her, and it was present in her laugh. "If you cannot tame your hubris, Ordric, your downfall will be as swift as your rise to power."

Ordric suppressed the urge to bring the back of his hand across Stregana's face. In her current state, such a blow could be lethal. "We'll see," he said.

From his eldritch robes, he produced a small crystalline orb roughly the size of an apple. "Here," he said. "This instrument is far more precise than your cauldron."

"Why not do it yourself if you are so powerful?"

"I have focused on talents other than scrying and soothsaying."

Ordric placed the orb on the floor in front of her. With clawlike nails poised toward the crystal, Stregana began to recite the foul words of a language Ordric was only beginning to understand. Her eyes rolled backward, revealing a web of red arteries on yellowing sclerae.

The orb glowed a dull green, and Ordric stooped forward to see what vision the witch had conjured. "He rides west," said Stregana. "He comes with the Wizard Slayer and Sir Garrick. They wish to kill you, Ordric."

"I never had much faith in the old knight. What of my assassin, Morgvid?"

After uttering another slightly different spell, the witch revealed, "He rides for Saidal as well, although his injuries are grievous."

With a nod, Ordric said, "He wishes to catch them here, then. How many days away is he?"

After twisting her hands and contorting her face, Stregana said, "It is difficult for Stregana to tell. He will certainly arrive before Eledrith."

"Good."

"Do not underestimate the Hound of Mog Muhtar, Ordric," said Stregana. "He has already bested your champion. Do you really think you stand a chance against him?"

"I ask not for your advice. My powers are far from what you imagine."

"It does not matter. The Wizard Slayer will kill you nonetheless. Do you wish for Stregana to show you that premonition?"

"Silence," commanded Ordric.

The High Lord's robes began to blow as if in the wind, and his feet left the floor. He hung suspended in midair, towering over his captive. "Do not question me, foul witch! I have learned to kill with a thought in a matter of weeks."

"That all means nothing," said Stregana. "The Hound of Mo—"

Stregana's words were cut short as she was pushed against the wall by an unseen force, her fragile skull colliding with the hard stone masonry. Then, as Ordric glared, the witch let out a terrible cry.

"Pain is my plaything. A medium at my disposal," he said.

The witch thrashed, screaming for mercy. Then, it became too much for her fragile body. Instead of random thrashing, her thin body began to convulse. Ordric's eyes widened with glee. For a long time, he had wished to see Stregana endure such suffering. Her body continued to jolt randomly. Streaks of blood dripped down from the corners of her eyes, but her torturer continued. Then, a final burst of wet crimson splattered from Stregana's nose and mouth. Her body was then still.

Ordric drifted back to the floor. *Perhaps I shouldn't have done that*, he thought. Regret rang through his heart, and for a moment, the confidence that flowed from his spell-wrought ring was broken. The feeling shook Ordric and sobered him of his power-drunken stupor. All his transgressions were bare before him, and the man was terrified. Instinct drove his will to reach for the ring. As quickly as the regret had come, it was washed away by the three-eyed skull that glinted in the dim chamber's light.

This witch will not be missed, he thought. *Only I knew she had been imprisoned in the palace.*

He picked the crystal orb off the floor and used the witch's ragged clothes to clean its surface of blood. After secreting the ball within the folds of his robes, he turned and left the gore-riddled chamber, leaving Stregana's near-skeletal body dangling from the manacles. One of Ordric's bewitched servants could remove her carcass. That was a task far too lowly for the High Lord to concern himself with, after all.

After reappearing from the small, inconspicuous servant's door at the end of the room, he seated himself back on the throne and schemed in the twilit hall.

———◆———

The Wizard Slayer and his escort had journeyed far in the past weeks. Although they moved with urgency, their travels lacked the frantic nature that their original flight into the Outlaw Kingdoms was plagued with. Seeking shelter was no longer an issue, either, as Garrick's company of soldiers carried enough supplies to accommodate the three once known as fugitives. Over the snowy plains and mountains they rode, and as time passed, green began to show through the white that blanketed the land. Rusted, unidentifiable ruins also pierced the snow cover.

Eledrith espied smoke dimming the evening sun. It was not the plumes from many campfires but massive swirling clouds. As the sun disappeared beneath the horizon, a dull orange glow lit the underbelly of the smoke.

"It seems the fires of war burn brightly," said Garrick, cautious eyes peering west.

Camp had not yet been set, and the group had halted atop a small hill. The ground was dry and covered with dull tan foliage. Soldiers were dismounting as Eledrith commanded, "We must keep going."

"What for?" asked Darreth.

"Ordric wages war in my name, and those fires could only be made by the burning of whole villages. I cannot allow this to continue."

"And what will you do, Your Majesty?" asked Garrick, his horse trotting toward the prince's. "Ride into the midst of Ordric's army and demand they lay down their arms?"

"Well, yes," said the Eledrith. "I am the prince, after all."

Krael watched the two in silence. He held the reins of his warhorse, watching the two argue.

Garrick said, "It's too risky. Besides, why risk being discovered? We have the element of surprise on our side. Let us not forget that Ordric himself is our real objective."

"Ordric knows I come for him," Krael said.

Both Eledrith and Garrick turned in their saddles. "See?" said Eledrith. "He no doubt knows we're coming. He uses magick, after all."

The prince turned back to the hellish glow in the distance. "How can I allow a thing such as this to happen?"

"We don't know the details," said Garrick.

"I captured Orthil's Keep with but a handful of men. I know what war is, Garrick, and as it turns out, I'm quite good at it. Don't try to lecture me about precautions."

"Careful," growled the Slayer.

Not accustomed to being questioned, Eledrith glared at Krael. His expression softened, however, when he realized his mistake. "Forgive me."

"It's alright, Your Majesty," said Garrick. "You have every right to be angry. Let's just not abandon reason at the behest of emotions."

The prince nodded, his eyes on the ground. "I understand, but I still feel the need to intervene. This may be one village amongst hundreds that are being destroyed, but if I can save at least one person, it is my responsibility to do so."

◆

Flames reached from the ruins of what were once homes, the orange tongues reflecting their violent glow in the many puddles of the dirt streets. Only the harshest screams and cries could be heard above the roar of the inferno; countless others were drowned out by the clamor of destruction. Through the streets marched spike-armored Graehalic mercenaries bearing torches and axe alike. Borne high above the soldiers, obscured by the choking smoke, were the Calidign colors.

A Graehalic commander stumbled into the street, his massive axe in one hand and a crate in the other. Even if smoke hadn't been hindering his ability to breathe, he still would have been unable to muster a full run because of his fatigue. Battle lines had been broken amidst the chaos, and it was every man for himself, pillaging and killing as they deemed fit.

A small band of soldiers rounded a blazing street corner. Seeing their commander, they ran to him, sweat pouring down dirt-covered faces. Their dark pike-covered armor had come loose in the struggle, and many tread on without helmets or shields.

"Commander!" yelled one in his native Graehalic tongue. "Should we leave?"

"Not before taking all that you can!" said the superior. "We lost enough men this day. Let's make this worth it."

Suddenly, the tired yet smug grin faded from the commander's face. The mercenaries' demeanor changed as well. At first, they cocked their heads in confusion. Then, they noticed that those who approached were no allies. Through the wavy distortions of heat, the glinting conical helms of Saidal could be seen. At the band's head rode a figure of glimmering steel from head to toe. So perfectly crafted was his armor that it seemed he was a being of pure metal.

The commander raised his axe in defense. Still, the armored leader charged forward, his ornate sword drawn. The pounding of hooves into the earth grew louder than the surrounding roar of flames. Knowing he stood no chance against a mounted rider, the mercenary commander leaped to the side, stumbling forward into the mud.

The steed halted mere feet before where the commander lay. Picking his head up from the muck of the street, the mercenary saw hooves flailing as the horse reared up on its hind legs. After the forelegs crashed back to the ground, the rider removed his helmet.

"It's the White Prince!" cried one of the mercenaries.

The commander gazed in awe. Sitting atop the horse, hair flowing in the smoky wind, was the man that had captured Orthil's Keep and felled the legendary Scourgefather. Rumors and half-truths had spread of what actually caused the prince to disappear, but nothing could deny that he stood before them. In his jade eyes was the cruel strength of a ruler, and seeing this, the mercenaries dropped to their knees.

"This ends now!" Eledrith demanded.

The commander stumbled into a proper kneeling position and asked, "What do you mean? We are following orders."

"When I took Arngrim's life, I demanded we fight not for the vain glory of mere strength and power. Look at you! You are no better than Arngrim himself."

A desperate voice, thick with a Graehalic accent, came from the small group of mercenaries. "Forgive us?"

"Forgive," said Eledrith, anger dripping from his bared teeth. "Aye, I will forgive you, but it will not be free."

Amidst the heat of the razed town, a chill fear came over the mercenaries. Their eyes were wide, hanging on each of the prince's words.

Eledrith said, "I seek to kill the usurper, Ordric. He sits on the throne and prays I do not return. Instead of serving him, you will serve me once again."

From the few mercenaries that knelt before the White Prince came a roar of triumph.

⎯⎯⎯◆⎯⎯⎯

In time, the assault was called off. Eledrith and his companions were brought to the Graehalic war camp. The moon's light revealed a span of countless tents stretching across a low hilltop. Like howling wolves in the night, the mercenaries chanted songs in their harsh tongues. As the White Prince was led through the camp, a weight dropped in his stomach. Countless men indulged in the spoils of war, and more than one Calidign banner was tarnished with blood. Eledrith grimaced at what he saw.

Krael, Garrick, Darreth, and Lorienne followed behind, and the men of Saidal behind them. The sword-dancer kept a weary hand near the pommel of her falchion. She had seen the likes of the mercenaries before, for the bureaucrats of Valmoria reveled in a similar manner, albeit they fought with deception rather than the sword. Still, like the Graehalians, it was for the same end.

Garrick's attitude was similar to Lorienne's. The mercenaries' ferocity made up for their lack of discipline, but both aspects were detrimental off the battlefield. If the veteran knight were in charge, there would be hell to pay as punishment. The encampment was disorganized and in disarray. Instead of resting, the warriors spent energy on their war chants and celebrations. Garrick did not trust them.

The riders were led to the midst of the tent city. Waiting near a blazing bonfire, clad in the scale hauberk, spiked armor, and fur cloak, was a behemoth of a man. In the Graehalic fashion, his dark hair was tied into loose braids, from the ends of which hung fangs. "So, you're the one who killed Arngrim, eh?"

Eledrith's horse stopped in front of the man and snorted. Something about the new general irked the prince, mostly the similarity between his cocky attitude and Scourgefather's, but nothing concrete that Eledrith could point to. As he dismounted from his steed, Eledrith nodded.

"You're smaller than I expected," said the general, looking down at the prince.

Eledrith could only scowl. The general was at least two heads higher than the young Saidalian. Then, a voice came from somewhere in the night. "That's him! That's the White Prince!"

Many turned to see a mercenary step forward, his face covered in white warpaint. Eledrith knew this to be one of the men that witnessed the battle against Arngrim, but his companions only saw a man in ghastly face paint. "If you say so," grunted the general.

"I'll be taking command from here," said Eledrith. "You serve the will of a usurper, and I have come to reclaim my throne."

The general crossed his massive arms and raised an eyebrow. "If you truly are the White Prince, then why is your hair not white as rumor tells?"

"I dyed it to hide my identity."

The general was still skeptical, and a tense silence hung as he judged the slender boy that stood before him. It was in this silence that Darreth's whisper could finally be heard, and many eyes turned to look at the elf-blooded. Amongst these eyes were the general's, and upon seeing Eledrith's companions, he asked, "Krael, is that you? And Darreth?"

"Gazrak," greeted the Slayer.

"I thought I recognized you!" said Darreth.

The general walked past Eledrith toward the Slayer, who dismounted his horse and clasped hands with the hulking man. While Gazrak may have been tall, he was no Kolgathian. Both men utterly dwarfed Darreth.

"You certainly keep good company, White Prince," said Gazrak. "If that is who you are."

"He is," said Krael.

"If I cannot trust Krael's word, I can trust no man's! Come, I'm sure the road has tired you all. There is plenty of food and warm baths already prepared."

Krael sensed an unease amongst his companions. Darreth did not and, without second thought, cried out, "Yes, please!"

"Wait just a minute," said Garrick. "You know this man, Krael?"

Gazrak answered him. "We crossed paths just over a year ago, I reckon. It was back in Graehal where I learned why he is called the Wizard Slayer."

"A tale that can be told over dinner," said Darreth.

As the weary travelers dismounted, they were led into the Graehalic general's personal tent. As they walked along the torch-lit path, Eledrith heard the gruff whisper of his mentor Garrick reach his ear. "I don't like this. For all we know, Morgvid could be behind this sudden change of fortune."

"You mean the assassin plots to kidnap Krael here?" answered Eledrith.

"I'm just saying it's a possibility."

The prince shook his head. "Not likely. Besides, Krael has a history with this man. If the Slayer trusts him, I trust him."

As deft as their conversation was, it had reached nearby Darreth's ears, and he whispered, "I trust him as well."

Eledrith smiled at the short elf-blooded's surprise appearance, then looked to Garrick. The old man pursed his scarred lips, then said, "Alright. I've just been thinking about that assassin. Krael did a number on him, and I'll be damned if he's fully recovered from his wounds yet. I'd wager he'll use others to capture the Wizard Slayer rather than openly engage with him again."

Gazrak's tent and those surrounding it were furnished like palaces. Inside the temporary structures hung pelts of creatures not even the well-traveled Krael recognized. Skulls of many-horned beasts hung, while others housed candles bathing the tents in a warm, if not eerie, glow. Incense wafted through the air, hiding the reeks of war with a calming aroma. It was splendor in the most brutal of senses, and the style would have better befitted a tribe of primitive humans instead of world-renowned mercenaries.

The Saidalian warriors were offered good tents as lodging, but Krael, Eledrith, and their companions were treated like royalty. Each was brought to a separate tent where they were allowed to bathe in relative privacy. The White Prince was led into a huge tent where four of Gazrak's concubines waited to serve him. By their features, he knew that they were natives of the Outlaw Kingdoms, and righteous anger once again boiled from within him. Tempering himself, he found that the women appeared enthusiastic to serve him. Eledrith concluded that the best thing to do was to meet them with genuine courtesy, and he did just that. Awkwardly, Eledrith doffed his garments and stepped into the tub. For a time, he was adamant that he did not need their assistance in scrubbing, but once one began massaging his scalp, he realized how tired his body was. He nearly drifted to sleep as the fading dye was washed from his silvery locks.

Darreth, Lorienne, and Garrick each appreciated the baths themselves. Eyebrows were raised at the elf-blooded's insistence to keep his headband while bathing, but his personality and charm waived the awkwardness of the situation. The sword-dancer, no longer under the hungry eyes of the mercenaries, opened up to the concubines assigned to her. Much laughter came from her tent as she talked and made genuine friendships with the women who scrubbed and massaged her aching muscles. Conversation was made about things that she could not discuss with her male companions, and Lorienne was relieved most of all of the travelers.

Krael, as usual, was difficult. Upon entering his tent, the concubines' faces grew pale. Gazrak was a monster of a man, but the Slayer was truly a monster. As he stripped for his bath, the shadows of wounds he revealed horrified the servants. His form was like the sculpture of a savage god, the corded, defined muscle defaced and maimed by innumerable scars. Krael lowered himself into the tub, and following their master's instruction, the concubines stepped forward to aid the barbarian. Instinctively, he recoiled, sending water splashing from the tub and frightening those around him.

"Don't," he grunted.

He submerged his head and, after resurfacing, shook his hair like a dog. Not even a minute had passed when he stepped out of the tub, dripping suds onto the surrounding pelts.

"Good enough," he said.

With the dirt and grime of the road cleansed from their bodies, the travelers were given fur coverings and were seated in Gazrak's personal tent. Teeth sank into seared venison, and the Graehalic general recounted the tale of his meeting with the Slayer.

"And when Krael finally approached the warlock's cave, he demanded everyone else stay behind, even Darreth here."

The elf-blooded, cheeks full of food and grease running down his chin, nodded.

"That seems to be a common theme," said Garrick. "Only under threat of death did he allow us to accompany him to Thalnar's castle."

"Why are you so adamant you fight alone?" asked Lorienne, looking to Krael.

The barbarian's mouth was full, so Eledrith answered for him. "Magick turns allies into enemies. The last thing you'd want to face in battle is someone you trusted with your life only moments before."

Krael swallowed, then nodded.

"As I was saying," continued Gazrak, "Krael walked off into the tunnel, and we sat waiting for an hour. Darreth just about fell asleep when there was a sound like a thundercrack that came from the dark, then a bear's roar, then silence. Five minutes later, Krael came back dragging the warlock's body. It's a real shame that I couldn't see you fight."

"It would be a sight to behold," said Eledrith.

"Perhaps there's some trade secret Krael doesn't want us to know," Garrick joked.

Krael grunted. Darreth, however, shook his head adamantly. "No. He's just brutal."

"Now I really wish I could've seen it," said Gazrak. "I'm jealous."

The Kolgathian looked down, twisting his knife into the scraps of bone and cartilage that remained of his meal. The attention irritated him, and he was eager for someone to change the subject. Darreth noticed his friend's mannerisms and said, "So, Eledrith, do we even have a plan as to how we're taking down Ordric?"

The prince said, "We'll need to get Krael as close as possible to the Calidign Palace, which will be difficult. I'm sure every soldier in the city is looking for the both of us."

"Not just inside the city," said Gazrak, "but outside as well. The Graehalic forces are just the vanguard. After we conquer, Saidalian infantry is garrisoned in fortifications, and it is up to them to subdue what's left of the populace. Then, we advance once again, and the cycle slowly continues."

Garrick's scarred face twisted in confusion. "Does Saidal have the numbers to continue this?"

"The city itself? No," said Gazrak. "But with more territory comes more manpower wishing to fight for the winning side. Morale may not be at its highest, but I bet that this approach is sustainable across the whole of the Outlaw Kingdoms, at least until us Graehalians tire or die off."

A sly smile came to Eledrith's lips. "So, if your men side with me, the war machine is defanged."

"If we side with you?" said Gazrak. "Of course we will! The legend of the White Prince and his victory over Orthil the Skull is what keeps our morale high, if not the spoils of war as an incentive. Now that you've come out of hiding, you'll give fresh life to our tired armies."

Garrick looked at the boy he had foster-fathered for so many years, wondering how the slender youth could hold sway over such savage warriors. As he sat, he offered a silent prayer to Atlor that he had taught Eledrith well enough to wield such responsibility.

"If the host still loyal to Ordric guards the lands between here and Saidal," said Eledrith, "then that'll pose a problem for us."

After taking a sip from his drinking horn, Garrick said, "Then a stealthy approach will suit us best. If your men come with us, Gazrak, we'll be spotted from miles off. Damn it, even the handful of soldiers we have with us could be too many."

Darreth said, "How the hell are we even going to get into the city? When Krael and I escaped, we got through the gate thanks to luck and the help of a human trafficker."

"It's simple," said Eledrith. "We disguise ourselves as Saidalian footmen."

"That'll work for those of us who can fit into the armor," said Darreth.

Everyone looked at Krael. The Kolgathian could blend in with crowds well enough, but his stature would certainly arouse a suspicion that their mission could not afford to raise.

"We'll sleep on it," said Garrick. "There's no need to sacrifice good rest for a problem that we'll be able to solve in time."

The infinite heavens, dotted with clusters of blue-white stars, were breathtaking. Not even the smoke of smoldering campfires could obscure its brilliance. Both Eledrith and Krael had sought solitude after the meal, and adhering to Sir Garrick's precautions, they stayed near each other. For a time, they simply breathed the cold night air. It was Eledrith who broke the silence.

"I'm scared, Krael."

The Slayer turned his head. In the prince's eyes, there was a genuine, existential fear. Sensing his friend was listening, Eledrith explained. "It was after the wedding. This strange woman approached me, claiming to be my mother. She was very convincing, too. No one discussed why I looked so unlike my ancestors until I met her. She said I inherited a great power, and I'm terrified of what that could be. What am I, Krael?"

As he usually did, Krael took a moment to contemplate his words. Then, in his slow, awkward speech, he said, "It does not matter."

"What?"

"You choose what you do, Eledrith. No one else."

The prince shook his head. He was not frustrated at the Slayer but instead at himself for improperly articulating his feelings. "No, it's so much more complicated than that. Sometimes I feel like a puppet being drawn and quartered by its strings. Regardless of my true lineage, there is still no shortage of people who want to influence me. Every step I take feels like I'm following someone else's command, if not a step into a trap. You can't possibly understand unless you're a prince."

"It is not easy," said Krael.

That comment genuinely irked Eledrith. "Of course it isn't easy!"

Krael was silent, and Eledrith realized his outburst was brash. The prince said, "You know, you accepted that the strange woman I met could be my mother way faster than Garrick."

The Slayer grunted.

"Thank you, Krael. You know, I haven't even told Morwenna about who I saw on the balcony."

With surprising speed, Krael interrupted. "You should."

Eledrith stammered for a moment, then said, "I mean, I haven't yet. To me, she's my refuge, you know, the one person I can turn to when I feel like hope is lost. That's why I'm so eager to bring an end to Ordric; not to take my place on the throne, but to free my beloved from his dark spells. He can keep the throne for all I care!"

Krael met the prince with a skeptical look.

"What would you know?" said Eledrith. "Have you ever even known love?"

The glimmering stars could not illuminate the Slayer, whose jaw clenched and eyes narrowed. "It is not my path."

"See? You wouldn't understand."

"If I give in to temptations, I learn to give in to magick."

"But there is a difference between tempting lust and love, though?"

"Few know that difference."

For a time, the two continued to watch the sky. Occasionally, a glimmering comet could be seen streaking across the blackness, but each time its light faded into the encompassing void.

28
A GRIM HOMECOMING

The purples and blues of the Calidign banner were darkened by ash and dust. Even in the bright rays of dawn, the golden sun on the banner's center seemed dull. As Eledrith watched the tarnished colors flap in the cold wind, he noticed faded specks of blood dot the torn edges of the once-proud banner.

The prince had never liked his house's colors. While the purple and gold represented nobility, the overall banner felt dull. The sun rising from the blue was supposed to symbolize dawn. As he watched the actual sun ascend from behind the distant mountains to the east, Eledrith scoffed. In Saidal, the only time the sun touched an ocean horizon was at sunset, and the prince found it ironic. The dusk of a dynasty was perfectly encapsulated in the impotent Torvaren.

Footsteps approached from behind Eledrith and stopped at his side. "I will create a new symbol."

Garrick, who watched the tired banner like Eledrith, was speechless. Not waiting for his mentor's approval, the prince continued. "That banner there is now Ordric's. It's the setting sun of a dying order forever stained by the evils of that usurper."

"But Eledrith," said Garrick, "that flag has flown in your family's name for countless generations!"

"And look what their efforts have produced: a city in decay and an unwinnable war against a horde of pseudo-states."

"Saidal is the greatest bastion of civilization in the known world, Eledrith. You take your ancestor's achievements for granted while judging them for failures that may have been inevitable."

"Perhaps," said Eledrith, narrowing his eyes and looking skyward. "But still, Ordric and I must not be known for the same colors. While he fights under the setting Calidign sun, I'll fight under the eternal star."

Garrick raised an eyebrow. Then, following Eledrith's eyes, he saw what had inspired him. Piercing the purple-blue blanket covering the sky was a single point of light. Even by day, the brilliance of that star was undeniable. Garrick, with a frown, said, "That star is Carphoras. Those born under it are said to inherit ill fate. Are you sure this is what you want flying above your troops, Your Majesty?"

"I care not for astrological superstition," said the prince. "The stars serve as a guide, a beacon of hope to those that are lost. That is what I want to represent my forces."

The two approached the Graehalic general with this idea. At this, Gazrak ran a burly hand through his fang-adorned beard, weighing the prince's request. "I'm not sure. The design of this new banner will have to be simple if we're to create a large number of them in such a short time."

"But it can be done," said Eledrith.

Few candles illuminated the sketches on the central table of Gazrak's main tent. Many drafts had been scrawled on scraps of parchment, but one stood out from them all: a seven-pointed star, odd point down. The symbol's two top and bottom arms jutted out slightly longer than the others.

"It'll be easy enough to make," said the general, "but finding the dyes will be a problem."

"White on black, just as stars appear in the night sky."

Sir Garrick, who also stood in the tent, seemed perturbed. "Seems rather gloomy, doesn't it?"

"This will only be a temporary design," said Eledrith. "Once the resources of Saidal are again at our disposal, we can change it if need be."

"Then it's settled?" asked Gazrak.

"Aye, it is," answered the prince.

"We best get moving, then," said Garrick. "Darreth may have enjoyed sleeping in, but Krael has been pacing about all morning. He is eager to face Ordric."

A blanket of fog hung amidst the rolling hills, and the spindly limbs of leafless trees reached from the mist like fingers of unseen skeletal hands. Despite the gloomy morning, the group, thanks to Gazrak's hospitality, felt well rested and had no trouble preparing themselves for the final leg of their journey. The two-dozen soldiers that had accompanied Garrick for so many months were free to rest, and their armor was used as disguises. Krael waited at the front of the party, his black hair spilling out from the sides of his hood. As they suspected, no hauberk or helm could properly hide his identity, but the Slayer was not concerned. Gazing to the west, he eagerly awaited the coming battle with the High Lord of Saidal. Even his warhorse seemed restless as it dug at the frozen soil with one of its front hooves.

Gazrak approached to bid his guests farewell. He, and many of his men, wore the pale warpaint in the likeness of the White Prince. Their visages became like that of ghosts, and it only amplified their intimidating presence as savage warriors. "I hate seeing the White Prince leave so soon, but I understand your mission is dire."

Eledrith said, "I hate to leave your hospitality, Gazrak. I speak for my companions when I say what you've done is invaluable. It's been too long since we've had such an excellent rest."

"Are you sure you don't want me to send some of my men with you? They could be extremely useful."

The prince nodded. "Aye, I am. The fewer men, the better."

"As you wish. But, before you leave, one more thing."

One of the white-painted soldiers came forward bearing a bundle. Kneeling, he presented it to Gazrak, who threw open the cloth covers and pulled forth a massive gleaming axe. The terrifying double head was decorated with the likeness of a snarling wolf, and the length of the haft was dotted with carved runes in the old form of the Graehalic tongue. With one mighty arm, the general handed the weapon to Eledrith. "A weapon forged by the greatest smiths in all of Graehal and wielded by Karag-Viil himself. You were the one to strike him down, Eledrith of Saidal, and by right of battle, it is yours to wield."

The prince vividly remembered that weapon slicing mere inches from his head, and it felt strange to be reunited with the visage of Grindenfang carved into the axe. "I am honored," he said.

As Gazrak passed the axe into Eledrith's steel-clad hand, the sheer weight of the weapon became apparent. He was nearly pulled from his mount, and only a last-second grasping of the saddle saved him from a humbling fall. "It certainly is a... heavy weapon. I truly appreciate this, but I'm more accustomed to my own sword."

Gazrak nodded, pursing his lips. There was a hint of disappointment on his whitened face. Eledrith then said, "But I think I know someone who can wield this mighty weapon better than us all."

Without prompt, everyone looked toward the Wizard Slayer. Dismounting, Krael begrudgingly stepped forward.

"Truly, no man could wield the axe better," said Gazrak.

Taking hold of the weapon, the Slayer lifted it with one arm. With such a savage tool of destruction, he could not help but smile, baring fangs that rivaled those etched onto the axe's face.

———◆———

As the Slayer and his four companions rode on, the grim repercussions of Ordric's conquest became apparent. Smoke drifted skyward on every horizon, enveloping the lands in the smog of war. Amidst the haze flapped the dark wings of carrion birds, the sheer numbers of which had never been seen gathered in living memory. Along the road stood the unrecognizable remains of those who stood in the sorcerer-lord's way. Like macabre signposts, naked, staked bodies served as a warning to the Outlaw Kingdoms and a feast for vultures and crows.

The Dead Giant stood as it always had above the scarred countryside. Even as full-scale war wreaked the land, its rusted limbs and aged body did not move. Since there were no corpses within sight of the ancient machine, the group deemed it a good enough place to rest their heads for the night. They set camp out of view of the road and did not dare light a fire in case a Saidalian patrol passed by.

The grisly state of the land had driven conversation from each of the travelers. No words seemed fit in the wake of the day's sights, and only Garrick's cold strategizing was discussed.

"We still do not have a distinct plan on how to enter the city," said the knight, removing the conical, slightly ill-fitting helm from his head.

Eledrith took his own helmet off as well. Beneath a Saidalian hauberk was his slim suit of plate, and light as the latter may be, he still felt fatigued. "I don't dare show my face," he said. "I'm the person Ordric wants dead the most. Darreth, you're good at this kind of stuff. Do you have any ideas?"

The elf-blooded's slightly-too-large helmet obscured his vision. Lifting it up to see the prince, he said, "Nope. It was by the skins of our backsides that we got out of the gates last time. There's no doubt more security now."

"Atlor damn it all!" yelled Garrick, who stood and threw his helmet to the ground. "We should have made a plan weeks ago! How could we be so stupid? It'd be hard enough to get anyone into the city, let alone someone like Krael!"

The entire group was speechless. Garrick seldom lost his temper, and the outburst took all by surprise. The knight was not finished, however. "And you," he said, pointing at Lorienne. "What place does a woman have on the battlefield? We should have left you behind."

"Oh really, you think I can't hold my own?" said Lorienne, her rage rivaling the knight's. "Why don't we find out how good you really are with that sword, old man."

"Quiet," growled Krael, "both of you."

Tempers still fuming, Lorienne and Garrick looked at the Slayer.

"I will enter the city alone," he said.

Not even Darreth was relieved by this. "You can't be serious," said the elf-blooded.

Krael's unwavering gaze told everyone that he meant what he said.

"But it's not possible," said Eledrith. "The walls are impenetrable, save two overcrowded gates that are guarded incessantly. And the port—"

"Is where I will enter," Krael finished.

Once again, the barbarian was met with looks of disbelief from his companions. A cunning smile came to his lips. "It'll be easy."

"It's still too risky," said Garrick. "Even if you did make it into the port, you'd have to pass through the Calidign Palace."

"And that's where we could help," interjected Eledrith. "I know the palace and its seldom-trotted passageways."

"This seems as good a plan as any," Darreth said. "I mean, yeah, it's actually pretty bad now that I think about it, but what else are we going to do?"

This was not the elf-blooded's best use of his silver tongue. Garrick, still unconvinced, rolled his eyes and looked to the Slayer.

"If you get me in," Krael said, "Ordric will die."

Eledrith, putting a hand on his mentor's shoulder, said, "If we don't strike soon, we may never get another chance. Ordric's grip on the throne only waxes with each day. Look what he's done in the short time he has been in control."

After a sigh, Garrick shook his head. "We need to prepare. If we foolhardily charge in and are killed, this will all be for naught."

Krael hurriedly shook his head. "Ordric must die. His power only grows."

"Fine," said the knight, "but by Atlor and whatever gods still watch over this world, we need to be careful."

As the five lay down to rest, the shadow of the Dead Giant loomed above them. The cold nipped at any exposed skin that slipped from the feeble protection of their bedrolls. No one slept well. The ancient metal ruin and the horrors found on the road only inspired nightmares in their shallow slumber.

※

Darreth snapped awake, instinctively reaching for his boot knife. After his initial nerves subsided, he laid still, wondering if it was a dream or reality that stirred him. Then, the unmistakable sound of footsteps came from his right. Knife in hand, albeit still within his bedroll, the elf-blooded turned his head to see who tread so close to their camp. In the faint starlight, he could, if only just barely, make out Lorienne's agile form.

"Lorienne," he whispered.

The sword-dancer offered no response. Instead, she carried a pack and moved toward one of the horses. If Lorienne had heard the elf-blooded, she did not let it be known.

Darreth scrambled out of his bedroll and, after making sure the pointed tips of his ears were covered, chased after her.

"Get back to bed," she snapped, not even bothering to turn her head away from her horse.

"Where are you going?"

Lorienne sighed, then said, "Away."

The grogginess of sleep did not help Darreth make sense of Lorienne's words. "Wait, what?"

Lorienne strapped her pack to the horse's saddle without elaborating.

Only then did Darreth realize what was going on. Eyes wide, he said, "Wait, you're not helping us? But we need to help Krael take down Ordric! You've seen what his armies have done."

"I'm not obligated to do anything," said the sword-dancer, finally turning to face Darreth. "When we first met, we agreed that I didn't owe you any sort of life debt. It was my choice to accompany you."

Darreth stammered, but no words came to him. He was only met with Lorienne's frustrated stare and the chilling night wind. "I'm sorry, Darreth," she said.

"Why didn't you say anything sooner?"

Lorienne turned back to her horse. "What do I even say? You all assumed I'd keep following without so much as asking me."

Even in the faint moonlight, Darreth could easily make out the Valmorian's entrancing features. As he found himself slipping into the depths of her captivating brown eyes, a knot churned within his stomach. He felt as if a family member was passing away, though he had not known any of his biological family or experienced such an event before, save perhaps his traitorous compatriots in the Swamps of Agor. What made his pain worse was that he stood before Lorienne as she prepared to leave him behind. "Why are you doing this?" he asked.

"Because this fight is not mine," she said. "Who am I to care about which man sits upon the throne? They're all the same."

"No, they're not!" said Darreth, whose voice raised and threatened to awaken the other companions. "Eledrith is different. He's a damn good man. At the very least, he doesn't use magick like Ordric."

"He may be, but it's still not my fight. I've made up my mind, Darreth. Don't bother following me."

As she was about to urge her mount into the night, Darreth said, "Before you go, at least tell me why you helped Krael beat Morgvid."

Lorienne froze and averted her eyes.

"That wasn't your fight, either," he said.

"I owed you two a favor. Now we're even."

Darreth shook his head. "You know that's not true. Hell, if anything, we owed you."

"Exactly," she scoffed. "All the better reason I leave."

"It's not about who owes who. You know that, Lorienne. There's something else that kept you with us all this time."

In his desperate negotiating, Darreth had stumbled on the truth. Courage swelled, and he held his chin higher. Lorienne realized this truth as well and, in light of it, flinched to snap the stirrups. Before the horse could break into a trot, the elf-blooded's hand clasped the bridle.

Lorienne glared at Darreth, but he did not back down. The elf-blooded didn't understand the Valmorian curse that came from the sword-dancer's lips, but he did know submission when he saw it.

"You want to at least talk about this?" he asked.

After a sigh, Lorienne said, "Yeah. I need that."

After hitching the horse, the two returned to the encampment. They conversed in hushed tones by the light of the stars. Other than the sound of wind hissing about the Dead Giant and Krael's disturbed sleep, the night was quiet. In the dark, Darreth and Lorienne sat closer than they would in daylight, even resting against one another at times in the name of driving the chill from their bodies.

"I care about you," said Lorienne.

At this, Darreth was stunned. The stoic veil had finally come off the sword-dancer.

"You and Krael, you know. But I suppose I'm just scared," she said. "There's a lot at stake here. If I had my way, I'd wish you, Krael, and I never got involved with this Ordric."

"It's not like we wanted this to happen," said Darreth.

"Well, yeah, but…"

"It needs to be done," he finished. "On the bright side, though, once all of this is over, we'll probably be able to stay in the Calidign Palace with Eledrith."

"That'd be a welcome break from the road."

Darreth said, "Us four get along great when we're not forced to hunt down one another. I'm sure you'd be welcome, too."

A warm smile came to Lorienne's lips, and Darreth felt his heart flutter. As they continued to talk, they drifted from subject to subject, sometimes laughing so loud they threatened to awaken their companions. In time, however, exhaustion caught up to them, and they each retired. As they drifted off to sleep, they reflected on the feelings that were stirred that night. Neither thought it the time to confess, so they were left oblivious to each other's desires.

Long after all had finally faded from consciousness, Krael continued to writhe in his tormented slumber. In the delirium of his dreams, faces of the present were found in grisly memories of the past. One by one, the Slayer was forced to kill Lorienne, Garrick, Eledrith, and Darreth as they fell to the bewitchment of a sorcerer long dead. An onlooker would've heard the Kolgathian growl in his bedroll, but in his nightmare-trapped mind, he screamed.

29
BLOODSHED

The frigid black water of the port swirled and crashed unrelentingly. There were no stars in the sky that night, but the lights in the windows of Saidal brightened the coastline with an astral glow. For Krael, who struggled to maneuver his makeshift raft amongst the four-foot waves, the city's vibrance made the bay almost navigable. None of this light revealed any details in the churning chaos of foam and brine, and in this darkness, the Slayer lurked, approaching the decadent splendor of Saidal like a predator of the sea.

About the Slayer was his cloak, which was thoroughly soaked. The Scourgefather's axe was tied to a strap and slung around his back. His aching, exhausted muscles struggled to pull a large oar through the dark water. Amidst the many waves and currents barraging from all sides, there was no telling if he moved closer to shore or not. Krael growled as near-freezing water splashed into his face. He had entered the city like this once before, albeit under far different circumstances. When he first sailed to the continent from Askaron many years before, a storm had capsized the vessel he had traveled aboard, and he was forced to paddle discreetly into the bay. However, that had been in summer, and he did not have to contend with the heart-stopping cold of late winter. He also did not need to avoid the city guard, whose glinting steel uniforms dotted the concrete piers of the port.

Krael's numb fingers struggled to maintain their white-knuckled grip on the oar. While the cold was nothing compared to Vornond's blizzard he had endured months prior, it still chilled his blood. As he fought to keep balance on the handful of lash-bound logs beneath his feet, each muscle's struggle was not only against the irregular waves but against the cold itself. The Slayer's own cries of exertion were drowned out by the roaring crash of waves. While he was not sure of it himself, slowly and gradually, he approached the massive concrete piers of the port.

The unforgiving onslaught of waves worked to the Slayer's advantage, and soon he was pushed toward the crumbling coastal wall. Splintered boards and other debris lurked within the waves that lapped the concrete barrier, but they were shrouded in darkness with the barbarian. It was well known that corpses gathered in this coastal refuse as well, and images of bloated flesh came to the barbarian's mind as he felt a rubbish-infused wave wash over his body. Before he could collect himself, another wave swelled beneath him. Instead of cold water, the chill of wind whistled over his body. A grim realization then came to the Slayer: he was moving toward the sea wall with terrifying speed.

Forsaking his oar, Krael readied both arms for impact. The crumbling concrete wall, riddled with barnacles and broken rock, dug into the Slayer's body. As the force of the sea pushed him forward, his head collided with the stone, and his hands felt as if they had no flesh left on them. With no time to fret over his wounds, Krael's fingers clutched at anything. He slid down the slime-covered wall, scrambling to find some sort of purchase. As he desperately held on, another wave crashed. Whatever was left of the raft had been sent into his back, and the wind was forced from him. For a full minute, he clung to the wall in a state of half delirium. Sure, he was on land, but amidst the torrent of waves, he might as well have been twenty yards out into the sea.

A single hand reached onto the pier's surface, the scratched, bloodied skin shining in the torchlight. At first, the guard did not notice this. As a hulking shadow fell over him, he raised his spear.

Dripping seawater and blood, a man stood. Clinging to his muscular frame was a black cloak, and from underneath a mask of hood and hair reflected two yellow pupils. The guard held a torch in one trembling hand and a short spear in the other, but this did not deter the Slayer. Sensing the man's terror, Krael strode forward and grabbed the haft of the weapon. Jerking it to the side, the guard's body followed, and the bottom of the barbarian's fist crashed into the side of his helm. There was no rush in this attack, for the guard was defeated by fear before the blow had landed.

Looking back to the water, Krael growled to himself. He remembered how eagerly he volunteered to sneak into the city alone. "It'll be easy," he said, mocking his former self's words.

From there, the Kolgathian slunk into the shadows. Few lanterns remained lit on that windy night, and darkness abounded. Driftwood shacks and other decrepit buildings sat amidst the old stone along the port, but rising above it all, looming in the distance, was the Calidign Palace. Whitewashed walls glowed a dull orange in the brazier light and ascended toward the sky like a cluster of lances. None of the other towers matched the palace in either height or splendor, and even though the city was a labyrinth of streets, bridges, and alleys, Krael always had the towering spectacle in the sky to guide him.

Casting his soaked cloak aside, the barbarian stalked through the city's shadows, axe in hand. Even in the dead of night, the marching of footsteps could be heard echoing in all directions. Ordric's war machine was operating on all gears, and the city was crawling with regiments of soldiers. Evading them was simple, as the tired men cared little more than to continue marching forward. Stopping to look in every alcove was a precaution they did not wish to take.

The streets surrounding the palace were closely watched, and the torches were so numerous that their collective light rivaled that of the day. However, each flaming brand cast a shadow. Only the keenest of eyes saw the barbarian's movement or the trailing end of his axe, and when they did, the sign of the intruder disappeared before the guards knew what to make of it.

It was an hour before dawn when Krael found himself inside the palace. The complexities of the layout were unknown to him, and finding the throne room (the Slayer's mere guess at where Ordric waited) was next to impossible given the sheer number of guards and servants that paced the many winding and crossing halls. As the regimented march of many boots came from around a corner, the barbarian darted to a door. To his surprise, the ornately carved wooden portal led to a mere supply closet. Such was the decadence of Saidalian nobility, but Krael was not one to complain. The door was only meant for access from outside, and with no handle on the interior, Krael clutched at the embossed features of the door to pull it closed. His fingers, still raw if not bleeding from the climb into the port, slipped from the lacquered wood. Footsteps drew closer. The Slayer didn't dare breathe.

A pair of footsteps stopped. Krael retracted his hand and readied his axe. Already, his veins surged with adrenaline. It would be a long, grueling fight, but the barbarian's savage nerves itched for such a conflict. Just as the wolf-adorned axe was raised, the door was pushed shut from the outside.

The footsteps faded. Slowly, careful not to put pressure on the outward-swinging door, Krael brought his ear to the sliver of light from the outer hallway. A sound came to him, but it was not from outside. There was a scraping, like wood against stone, then shuffling of feet. The Slayer whipped around, the instinctual hatred of being taken off guard urging every muscle.

"I figured we'd find you here!" said Eledrith.

As the Slayer's eyes strained against the darkness, he realized that the closet's back wall, which he had assumed to be a shelf at first glance, was actually a secret door. "Come in here," whispered Eledrith. "Our voices won't carry into the hall."

After pulling the sliding shelf shut, a candle was lit, revealing the faces of the Slayer's companions. Holding the candle, Garrick said, "Glad to see you, Krael. You made it in without trouble, I presume?"

"No," said Krael.

Darreth rolled his eyes at his friend and said, "You're here now, and by no shortage of luck, we made it in as well."

"It seems that with all the soldiers moving in and out of the city," said Garrick, "the guards at the gate are far less thorough in their examinations. We stumbled into the back of a formation and marched in through the Eastern Gate. It was disgracefully easy."

Eledrith said, "This whole network of tunnels was once used by servants, but they've fallen out of use. Unless Ordric has found another use for them, they should be safe for us."

Nodding, Krael grunted. "Which way is the throne?"

"Follow me," said the prince with a smile.

The Slayer cringed at how well his group's footsteps echoed off the naked stone walls, but trusting Eledrith, he continued forward. The passageway twisted and wound, haphazardly thinning and looping to accommodate the public halls of the palace.

"I can't take this anymore," said Darreth, pulling the ill-fitting helm from his head.

Garrick scowled. "Keep that on. Your life may depend on it, you know."

"I'd kind of like to see what I'm doing."

The prince chuckled, then said, "I suppose two layers of armor are redundant, aren't they?"

Eledrith doffed the mail-skirted soldier's hauberk. Left in his perfectly fitted plate suit, he hopped and stretched his shoulders. "Much better."

"This never suited me anyway," said Lorienne, letting her mail clatter to the floor.

Garrick said to the Slayer, "And of course, you don't even wear armor."

"It does nothing to stop magick," said Krael.

Disguises forsaken, the group continued through the secret passageways. After minutes of shuffling through the gloom, they came to a small wooden door. Eledrith looked back to his companions. Their steel-trap nerves seemed ready to snap into action, but whether out of fear or confidence, the prince could not tell. "Here it is," he whispered. "Beyond this lies the throne room."

No one said a word. The tension in the air warned them that their quest was nearing an end. Krael pushed through his companions, walking to the front of the group.

"Just like old times, eh?" whispered Darreth, drawing a Saidalian blade.

Garrick raised an eyebrow.

"You know," continued the elf-blooded, "like back when we fought against Thalnar?"

A warm, nostalgic smile came to the prince's lips. That journey seemed a lifetime ago, and the minor scope of it was dwarfed by the vast schemes that Ordric wrought in Torvaren's stead. "Yeah. Old times," he said.

Krael wished to smile, but he could not. The memory of previous companions, now long dead, haunted him. Not even Darreth knew their tales. "Remember, I fight Ordric alone. Magick can turn allies into enemies. You kill guards. I kill him."

"Understood," said Sir Garrick, the soldier's discipline in his aged voice.

Lorienne nodded. In the cramped passageway, she still managed to idly flourish and twirl her sword.

They waited for the Wizard Slayer's command. Cold steel sat in trembling hands. Nerves and battle fury had already begun to swell in their minds.

"He knows we're here," said Krael.

No one had time to ask why or how the Slayer sensed this. With a single mighty kick, the door that should have swung inwards flew out. Splinters fell as the barbarian charged, his axe hewing at enemies yet unseen. The blade found its mark, and within the first second of the battle, an enemy had been felled.

A semicircle of guards had formed around the door, but they, and their sorcerous master, had underestimated the enemy. Expecting the door to swing inward, they poised their weapons close, readying a quick attack. When the door came toppling at them, the guards' polearms were knocked aside, giving Krael a path through their defenses. The barbarian's axe could not cleave mail, but the weight and force behind it crushed bones and organs alike. Instead of a swift death, the first man to fall was left screaming on the marble floor, writhing in vain as his lungs filled with blood.

Eledrith and Garrick followed. Both experienced fighters allowed their armor to absorb hits while they closed the distance. Metal hissed as weapons scraped against each other. The prince was nigh-invulnerable in his plate, and Garrick's shield stopped many poleaxes from finding their mark. Both mentor and apprentice fought with a precision that Krael lacked, blades sliding through gaps and weak points of armor.

Following close behind was Darreth. Never much of a melee fighter, the elf-blooded stood at the ready, holding his arming sword with both hands and hoping that none of the soldiers slipped past Garrick's defenses. When they did, Lorienne's sword whirred through the air, deflecting hafts and crashing into the hands that held them.

Already having pushed past the dozen heavily armored guards, the Slayer sprinted into the gloom-shrouded chamber. Torvaren lay as he had for months in the center of the hall, but it was the man that waited beyond that held the Slayer's attention. Only the twilight that drifted in from the high windows revealed Ordric, clad in black robes and sporting a vile sneer on his shriveled countenance. Krael remembered that face, for those dark eyes had watched him keenly the last time he was in the Calidign Palace. The face, however, was much different than what it had been. While the eyes maintained their cruel intellect, equally cruel shadows deepened underneath them and in the High Lord's cheeks. Most eerie of all was how Ordric laughed. Above the cacophony of shrieking metal and battle cries, Krael could distinctly hear the dark cackle.

What beautiful ferocity, thought Ordric as he watched the Kolgathian charge toward him. The Slayer's garments struggled to contain his muscular form as every fiber of his body contributed to his sprint. The long black locks that flowed from his head bounced like a lion's mane as he moved, and the bared fangs flashed. Most terrible of all was the Slayer's gaze. The cold gray eyes stared with a focus so strong not even magick could break it. In the face of savagery incarnate, Ordric continued to laugh. *He has yet to know Morgvid is here.*

Darreth espied the assassin from across the hall. The pallid skull-like face was unmistakable even in the dim light, and the sunken eyes were pinned on the unsuspecting Slayer. At the sight of Morgvid, a chill pierced Darreth's heart, and he was still. Yet, no one else noticed the assassin creep forward from behind an alcove in the decorative wall.

A spark ignited in Darreth's mind, and the elf-blooded charged through the fray. Only a reckless lunge could bring him to the assassin in time. Poleaxes hissed past his head, but even the guards were surprised by Darreth's sudden assault.

There was an odd manner in which the assassin moved. No longer drifting with ethereal grace, he jutted across the ground as if there was a certain disconnect between how his legs moved compared to the rest of his body. The asymmetrical ringed robes that covered him lashed and jerked about as he ran. Darreth, in the likeness of his Kolgathian friend, let out a battle cry. His vocal cords were incapable of a roar, but the hoarse yell was terrifying all the same.

Morgvid's concentration was broken, and he stared at the new threat with wide, bloodshot eyes. As he turned, Darreth saw that his severed hand had been replaced with a long hooking blade. Dark iron jutted from pale flesh, as it was surgically attached to the arm. The new weapon was raised to strike the elf-blooded's head, but Darreth's courage would not be broken so easily.

Without effort, Morgvid waved his bladed arm across his assailant's face. The young man cried out in agony, blood pouring from his eye. As accurate as the assassin's strike may have been, Darreth's reaction was quicker than any Morgvid had expected. Even as the hooked steel gouged out the delicate tissue, he pulled his head away before the weapon could reach too deep. Nevertheless, the elf-blooded fell to the ground, writhing in a growing pool of his own blood. The assassin couldn't help but smile as he watched the neurotoxins meant for the Slayer begin to paralyze Darreth.

In his victory, Morgvid had failed to see Darreth slip his own sword past his guard. It was only thanks to his enhancing mixture of venoms and toxins that he did not immediately notice the sword's hilt sticking out from his chest. Trusting the alchemy of the Serpent's Hand to keep him alive, the assassin unsheathed the arming sword from himself, wincing. His murky purple blood stained the entire length of the blade.

From across the hall, Eledrith screamed, "Darreth!"

Morgvid had no choice but to give up on his pursuit of the Wizard Slayer. Charging straight toward him was the silver-haired White Prince, the legends of which preceded him.

Krael himself continued his own charge. Ordric, irked by the failure of his assassin, no longer laughed. Rune-embellished robes waved as he turned to flee. The sorcerer's body was not as decrepit as his withered face would suggest, and he maintained a lead on his pursuer with long, powerful strides.

The heels of the Slayer's boots fell like hammers on the marble floor. With one foot, he kicked off Torvaren's dais and flew through the air, his axe falling to the floor just behind the sorcerer. The thick marble cracked beneath the weapon's weight, and while the Kolgathian recovered from the jarring landing, Ordric sped away.

Even as the sorcerer shut doors behind himself, Krael broke their feeble latches without losing his momentum. With a sharp crack, wood burst from nail. Three doors yielded under the weight of the barbarian's shoulder, but the fourth stopped him in his tracks. With a growl, he threw himself on the door again, but to no avail. Raising his axe high, he brought it down on the ornate reliefs of the carved door, reducing the artwork to splinters.

The effects of fatigue had begun to set in. Krael's lungs heaved. From the moment he had first charged into the throne room, he had not slowed to catch his breath. The Slayer was now paying for his recklessness.

◆

In the throne room, Eledrith met Morgvid with a flurry of attacks that the world-traveled assassin had never seen before. The killer had time to become accustomed to his new weaponized limb, and even though it was two weapons against Eledrith's one, the prince was holding his own. Each strike had perfect technique. At no time did Eledrith even come slightly off-balance, and Morgvid found no mistakes to capitalize on. Their exchange was terrifying, with each clash of blades sounding like the crack of lightning. Steel screeched as attacks were parried. Even the assassin's enhanced speed and reflexes could not match whatever gave the White Prince his mastery of swordwork. Eledrith gritted his teeth as strike after strike came upon him. His enemy was not a defensive fighter, instead relying on his speed and a sheer number of attacks to overwhelm.

Morgvid's blade arm swung high, and instead of stepping back like the assassin expected, Eledrith raised his sword, opening his body to a counterattack. Seeing the opportunity, the assassin lunged in, ready to plunge Darreth's sword deep into the prince's chest.

Instead of the satisfying feeling of flesh and bone parting beneath an edge, a vibration rang through Morgvid's arm. The sword's point was halted by Eledrith's plate armor. Before Morgvid could curse himself for this mistake, the prince took advantage of the assassin's overextension. In one swift motion, Eledrith's blade tore through the assassin's wrist.

There was a spray of dull purple blood, but like in the Weeping Mountain months before, the flow was immediately staunched. Enraged, Morgvid lashed at the prince's unarmored head with his blade arm, but this wild strike was also avoided. As far as the prince was concerned, the fight was over, and it was now an execution. With a single stroke, Eledrith sundered both of Morgvid's knees.

The tight, bone-white skin on the assassin's face twisted and contorted in rage. Purple veins bulged, and his bloodshot eyes dripped with hatred. From his mouth came a hissing cry of malice, for Morgvid still had not accepted defeat. Eledrith ended this shrill sound by sending the point of his blade through the back of Morgvid's throat. Blood gurgled as the assassin refused to die, the gore's quick-coagulating properties now suffocating him.

Eledrith burned with anger seeing Darreth lying feet behind him, hands clasped over his wounded eye. Twisting his sword so the blade was vertical, the prince pulled it up through the top of Morgvid's head. There was a deep, sickening crack as the skull was split apart. Morgvid's twitching body thudded against the marble floor, then laid still. No alchemical mixture could help the assassin in his current state.

The door burst open, and Krael charged onto the garden balcony. It took a moment for his eyes to adjust to the morning sun, but as the blinding rays subsided, Ordric's dark robes could be seen. The black, rune-embellished folds billowed in the winds that swirled amidst the high towers of the city. What unnerved Krael, however, was that the sorcerer floated above the leafless branches of the garden's shrubs. His arms were outstretched, palms lifted toward the purple sky, mocking the Slayer.

Krael charged, but as fast as he advanced, Ordric drifted backward effortlessly. There was soon nothing below the sorcerer other than the roofs of the palace's lesser towers. Unmoved by the wind, Ordric stood still in the sky, twenty feet from the balcony's edge. The barbarian slammed against the railing.

"What's wrong, Wizard Slayer?" said Ordric. "Despite all that anger and strength, there's nothing you can do to reach me, is there? It's a shame, really. I had such great plans for you. Together, we could have forged an empire the likes of which have never yet existed in this world. I was hoping Morgvid would have captured you, but I now see he fails to live up to his reputation. No matter, I will just kill you now. In time, I will grow so powerful that I'll have no need for you."

The barbarian's cold gaze did not show the inner workings of his mind. While Ordric gloated, Krael strategized. He wanted to make his move, but he would only have one shot...

"I wonder if, like Morgvid, the legends surrounding you are exaggerated. They say you are immune to the influences of magick."

Still in midair, Ordric's posture changed, and Krael readied himself for whatever spell might be cast. Sinking into a battle stance, he prepared to leap out of the way of some projectile or missile of energy, as his conditioning did not render him invulnerable to such attacks. He was taken by surprise, however, when he felt the sensation of sharp needles within his head. The piercing agony drove out from behind his eyes, and Krael was immediately disoriented and nauseous.

Seeing the Slayer drop to a knee, Ordric cackled. His eyes were alight with a cruel glow, and his body floated god-like in the air. "Even you have a breaking point, Krael. Allow me to show it to you!"

The pain intensified, and the barbarian felt like his skull would split from the inside. Every tooth felt as if it were encased in ice, and the bitter taste of bile swelled in his mouth. With a deep cough, a gush of blood spattered from his nostril. Still, Krael looked at his torturer. The barbarian knew he would not last much longer if he did not make his move, but the circumstances needed to be perfect for his only plan to work.

With a heavy clang, the Scourgefather's axe dropped to the ground. This only fueled Ordric's confidence, and the sorcerer slowed the progress of his spell. He wanted to cherish the sight before him. The famed Wizard Slayer had dropped to a knee and forsaken his weapon. A cold sweat beaded on the Slayer's pale skin, and blood continued to pour from his nostril. Saliva dripped from his trembling jaw. The one thing that tarnished this moment was that the barbarian's head was still high, his eyes still carrying that ever-defiant ferocity. "Before you die, Wizard Slayer, you will bow to me. You must understand that I am the one destined to bring order to the world. Not even you can defy me!"

Everything was almost right. The axe would only weigh Krael down, and the last thing Ordric expected then was retaliation. While the agony may have dulled his senses, Krael was still conscious enough to see precisely where the sorcerer floated. He would only need a second to put his desperate plan into motion, but the usurper lord still watched with intent eyes.

Slowly, Krael lowered his head, and Ordric threw his head back and laughed.

This was the only window the Slayer needed. His head snapped up, feral eyes wide. Like a wildcat, he jumped to the balcony railing, and before Ordric could bring his gaze back to meet him, Krael leaped off the balcony's edge.

The wind truly howled amidst the high towers of the Calidign Palace, and Ordric stood no chance of hearing the heaving breaths or scuffling of the Slayer as he moved. In a fraction of the second that Ordric's eyes had left his foe, Krael had jumped through the air with suicidal fury. The sorcerer could do nothing as he saw the Hound of Mog Muhtar barreling toward him through the air. Spells, incantations, and even the will to physically fight back were absent in the terror-stricken man. The primal fear of predators, bred and tempered for countless generations, took complete control of Ordric. In the face of that fanged mouth, savage eyes, and hands clutching in the likeness of claws, the dark hubris that flowed from the silver ring was shattered. Like a child, Ordric shrieked, but he could not even hear himself over the Slayer's lion-like roar.

In truth, Krael had no idea if he was able to reach Ordric in a single bound. Such thoughts would only dull the viciousness needed to perform such a lofty task. Ordric began to drift back, but the Kolgathian collided with his hip. With all four limbs, the sorcerer tried his hardest to fight his way to freedom. Robes ripped as the barbarian slipped down his enemy's legs, and Ordric again cried out as five vise-like fingers dug into the flesh of his ankle.

No longer merely floating, the Slayer and his prey hurtled through the air with the speed of a diving falcon. Ordric's panic fueled their flight, and both hunter and hunted weaved erratically through the sky. The veins on Krael's forearms bulged as he clung not only for his life but for the death of the wizard as well.

Eledrith wiped sweat and purple blood from his face. Looking back to where they had first entered, he was relieved to see that Sir Garrick had convinced what little of the Saidalian guard that remained to yield. Poleaxes clattered to the floor, and armored hands were raised in defeat. The old knight breathed heavily, but by the way his scarred, gray-haired head was held high, the soldiers knew there was still much more fight left in him.

Lorienne waited with her arms crossed, a smug grin of victory on her face. This faded when she noticed Darreth.

The elf-blooded still lay on the floor soaked in his own blood. He sat paralyzed in the fetal position, both hands clasped to a now empty eye socket. Morgvid may have finally been slain, but the effects of his venom-coated blades outlived him. Eledrith dropped to a knee and held the young Darreth. Even though they had traveled long together, it wasn't until then that the prince realized how small Darreth was.

"You're going to be alright," said Eledrith.

Darreth had lost his ability to move and, by extension, his ability to speak. Struggling, there came a strained gasping sound from his mouth.

"Relax," said the prince. "You've done well."

Turning to Garrick, Eledrith called out, "I'll watch those men. You patch up Darreth."

"Yes, Your Majesty."

The prince carried Darreth to his mentor. While the well-seasoned soldier tended to the wounded elf-blooded, Eledrith kept his eyes on the soldiers. "Do you not know who I am?" the prince asked, anger sneaking into his tone.

The four soldiers' eyes were wide. Hesitantly, one of them shook his head. Eledrith could see the confusion on their faces.

"Ordric's magick, no doubt," said Garrick as he wound a bandage about Darreth's head. "The last thing he'd want would be for you to turn his own forces against him."

Eledrith nodded and thought, *Would he dare do something similar to Morwenna?*

Before the prince could raise the question to Garrick, Darreth again tried to speak, this time mustering, "Dih... Dih..."

"You're going to be alright, my boy," said Garrick. "The wound isn't that deep. You sure are lucky, though."

Then, with muffled enunciation, Darreth managed, "Did I get him?"

Eledrith looked to the body of Morgvid, his skull split open and contents pooling on a formerly pristine floor. While the prince may have dealt the final blow, it was Darreth's selfless charge that allowed Krael to pursue Ordric. Not wanting to dull the elf-blooded's triumph with such details, Eledrith said, "Yeah, Darreth, you got him."

Lorienne's body was positioned to keep watch over their new prisoners, but more than once, Eledrith caught her shooting a concerned glance toward Darreth. Seldom had he seen the sword-dancer with such a grave expression, but the prince knew the time to inquire about it was not the present.

"And now we wait," said Garrick. "And if all goes well, Krael will come back with Ordric's head."

For a moment, Eledrith waited in silence, but the matter became too pressing to him. "I need to find Morwenna and make sure she is safe."

"That can wait," commanded Garrick. "It's best if we stay put. Less chance of something going wrong."

Eledrith scowled. "Alright."

Garrick noticed the prince's features harden. His jade eyes blazed with quiet anger as his slender jaw tensed. "I know you care deeply about her, Eledrith, but we cannot afford to act rashly now."

High above the crooked towers of Saidal, Ordric and Krael flew through the air. Spiraling and spinning, the horizon was a blur for both of them. The only thing that mattered was Krael's grip on the sorcerer, which he threatened to lose more than once. Gritting his teeth, the Slayer maintained his crucial grip as his forearms and fingers felt as if they were being torn apart.

Far below, few bystanders noticed the large black dot zigzagging through the morning sky. Concerned with their own affairs, most eyes were on the shadowed streets ahead. The few who saw the two figures battling in the air could do nothing but watch in utter confusion.

Ordric felt a hand clasp around his knee as the Slayer began to climb. The black robes whipped in both of the combatants' faces as they struggled against each other, but slowly Krael climbed up Ordric's body, struggling to contain the sorcerer's flailing arms. An elbow smashed into the barbarian's face, and since both hands were concerned with keeping him from plummeting to the earth, Krael could do little to stop the elbow from striking again and again. The High Lord's wrinkled face twisted into a sneer as he finally began to gain the upper hand.

Suddenly, Krael turned his head into the sorcerer's body, and the elbow missed its mark. Ordric's mouth was agape in agony as he felt Kolgathian fangs sink into his side. While the pronounced canine teeth were not as sharp as that of an animal whose ancestors had torn flesh since time immemorial, the muscular jaw that supported them drove them deeper than any civilized human could ever manage. Krael jerked his head to the side like a dog, opening the wound even further. Blood was carried on the wind as it sprayed from the sorcerer's side, and Ordric writhed even more.

Out of the corner of his eye, the High Lord could see the massive windows of the Calidign Palace. Knowing he stood no chance in the air, he aimed his flight toward the ornate stained glass panels. Oblivious to this, Krael continued to climb up his enemy's body. Soon, his hand reached around Ordric's shoulder, and Krael pulled himself up for the kill. His neck was exposed, and the Wizard Slayer prepared to sink his fangs into it. Tired muscles strained to pull him fast enough, and just as he was about to hit his mark, both men collided with a pane of glass.

Both fangs and shards tore through flesh, and the men were utterly dazed as they fell to the black and white marble floor of the great hall. The impact of Krael's shoulder against the hard stone drove the breath from him. As he tumbled, glass left hundreds of shallow cuts on his exposed arms and face. Skidding across the floor slowed him to a halt, but even then, the Slayer felt as if the world still moved about him. This worsened as he lifted his head, but he didn't dare relent while Ordric still potentially drew breath.

Glimmering shards of glass were scattered about the room. To the Slayer, it all seemed like a shining blur of color. Straining his eyes, he struggled to bring any details into focus. Things around him sounded as if he were submerged beneath water. Only the lowest tones of voices reached his ears, but he could, if only just barely, recognize what they were saying.

"By Atlor, is that the High Lord?" said one.

"Father!" cried a woman's voice.

"Come quickly, Princess. It is not safe here, either!"

Gradually, the haze that engulfed the barbarian's senses began to lift. The finer details of sounds could be heard, and the Slayer finally recognized the room he had crashed into. To his right, no more than fifteen feet from him, was an auburn-haired young woman being escorted by two armored guards. Decorative polearms were carried by each of them, and given the abruptness of Krael's intrusion, they had yet to lower these in defense.

From the Slayer's left, he heard a deep wheezing voice. "Guards! That man wishes to kill me!"

There, sitting with his back to the wall, was Ordric. The black folds of his robe glistened with crimson, and one of his legs was bent at an odd, jutting angle. His head rested against a pilaster, and if he did not still have the strength to speak, he could have been mistaken for dead. Blood had drained from his already withered face and given him the complexion of a corpse.

"Kill him!" commanded Ordric.

Meeting eyes with the bleeding, battle-raged Kolgathian, the guards raised their weapons, albeit with a hint of hesitancy. Princess Morwenna backed away, knowing she must flee. At the same time, a curiosity overtook the young woman.

Krael did not wish to fight these men. Even with the rush of adrenaline and his own unrelenting will, there was little the unarmed barbarian could do against the two guards. Knowing that he may soon feel sharp steel sink into his back, the Slayer turned and charged toward the defenseless Ordric. The sorcerer raised a hand, upon which glistened the silver of his signet ring. Such a small, insignificant detail meant nothing to the Slayer as he sprinted in what could be his last desperate charge, but that subtle gesture did more than Krael realized. With the bewitching power of his ring, Ordric reached, semi-consciously, toward the mind he had spent countless hours conforming and molding to suit his needs. The barriers of that young, innocent girl had long since worn away, and in his weakened state, Ordric could only control a mind such as hers.

From behind the guards, urged on by supernatural vigor that her own will could not muster, Morwenna also charged toward Ordric. With this new strength, both guards were thrown to the ground, knocked out cold from either the impact of the bewitched princess's arms or the marble floor. Keeping her momentum, the princess leaped onto Krael's back and brought both of her hands to his face.

Before he understood what was happening, the Slayer saw nails reaching for his eyes. Instinctively, his hands went to stop the unseen assailant. The already exhausted barbarian began to stumble, then fell to his knees, but not before pulling his foe's hands away from his face. Morwenna continued to struggle. One of her hands slipped from Krael's grip, and she began to claw at the side of his neck. Nails broke as they tore away at skin, then muscle, then vein. With no other choice, the Slayer grabbed the slim woman and sent her hurtling toward the wall.

The impact was harsh, and Morwenna fell to the ground, unmoving.

It was only then that Krael realized who had attacked him. The princess lay on the ground, her face covered by a veil of flowing hair. At that moment, the Slayer was sobered of all his rage and battle fury. With a hand put to his neck to staunch his bleeding, Krael turned to meet Ordric.

The miserable, broken body trembled. Dark, sunken eyes held absolute fear in their depths, and the hand that bore the signet ring was raised toward the Slayer. Unaffected by the ring's power, Krael stepped forward. There was no victorious execution ahead, only an act of murderous hatred.

Hearing the commotion, more guards and servants piled into the room from all sides, but it was too late. They could do nothing but watch. Ordric flailed his limbs in a desperate, child-like defense, but the muscular freak of a man bent down and pinned the weaker sorcerer's arms to the floor. Like a wild animal, the Wizard Slayer sank his fangs deep into the throat of the High Lord. Ordric's legs kicked in vain. Throughout the hall echoed a scream of agony that ended with a deep, resounding crunch.

Holding his prey down with mighty arms, the Kolgathian jerked his head back. Soft tissue tore apart, and blood began to spray from exposed arteries. Where Ordric's throat should have been was a gaping, bleeding hole. At the sight of this, one of the guards vomited onto the floor. His comrades stormed past him, intent on stopping what had already been sent into motion.

Krael did not bother to run. Instead, he loomed over his prey, blood dripping from his face. Ordric himself began to hyperventilate, the breaths passing through his wound on his neck rather than his mouth. Gradually, these breaths slowed, and the stream of blood ceased to flow. The last thing Ordric saw was dozens of

367

armed guards tackling the Slayer to the ground. Even as he fell to the floor under the weight of countless armored men, Krael glared at the dying sorcerer.

30
THE FRUITION OF DESTINY

Three caskets were marched through the city. From the sky fell a cold rain that forced all who attended to hide under cover of hooded cloaks. Raindrops pattered off soldiers' helmets and collected in the recesses of the unevenly paved streets. At the head of the procession, Prince Eledrith rode upon a white steed. No hood or cloak protected him from the elements, and no one could tell if the widower himself wept or if it was the rain that poured down his face. Wet, silvery locks clung to his slender face as jade eyes stared forward. Whatever thoughts ran through his head were known only to him, and no one dared interrupt his silent reflections.

Following close behind were Sir Garrick, Darreth, Lorienne, and the widowed Countess Camelia Maumont. The knight's proud chin was held high despite the gloomy spring weather, but his fellow riders' heads were low. Camelia was unrecognizable underneath a mourning veil, and her entire body was covered in black. With one eye covered by a patch, Darreth's remaining one looked down. *I wish I could be back on the road with Krael*, he thought.

Winding through narrow alleys came the black coffins, each on their own carriage. One was covered with the rising sun banner of House Calidign, another bore the Maumont colors, and one was draped with a black standard, at the center of which was a white seven-pointed star. Eledrith watched the rain run down the sides of the box holding Morwenna's lifeless body. The last conversation he had with Krael was still fresh in his memory, and as he reflected, the prince's grip tightened on the reins.

"I had no choice," said the Slayer.

"What do you mean?" roared Eledrith. "You're over three times her size! Surely you could have used but a fraction of your brutish strength."

Krael snarled, "She was bewitched. You do not understand."

"Yes, I do! I fended off Thalnar's concubines while they wished to kill me. Not a single one of them died. Why couldn't you fight off just one?"

Krael never answered, only narrowing his eyes.

The funeral procession turned a sharp corner and began to march through a slightly inclined street. Even though it was midday, the sky above only seemed to darken. Towering buildings that leaned on each other in their crooked, decrepit state offered no protection against the incessant rain. Garrick could see Eledrith's clenched jaw. The old knight lamented that he could not help the boy he had raised like a child in his time of anguish.

"You must forgive Krael, Your Majesty," Garrick had said. "He did not mean to do what he did."

"Morwenna was the reason I fought!" said Eledrith. "Ordric could have kept the throne for all I care."

"Don't say such things, Eledrith. I know you feel deep pain, but you must remember that there are more things than just Morwenna worth fighting for."

The prince turned his back to Garrick.

Eledrith had not looked his mentor in the eye since. Instead, his eerie green eyes gazed into depths beyond what he saw, which scared Garrick. That same expression was on Eledrith's face while the entrance to the Great Crypt came into view. Guarded by stone effigies of chimeric gargoyles, the crypt was perhaps older than the religion of Atlor. Scholars knew not which came first, as the origins of both were obscured by the mists of time. The structure's interior was a winding hive of chambers that housed the bodies of rulers whose names were long forgotten. Some of these rulers, whose dynasties were utterly unknown by modern generations, were removed from their resting places to make room for the more relevant dead.

While the ancient structure rose high like the towers of the city around it, a small courtyard at its front allowed the procession to gather. The line of nobles, Darreth and Lorienne amongst them, gathered around the three coffins.

The patriarch of Atlor, who was garbed in soaked white robes, began to recite ancient rites. He stood at the head of the coffin draped in the traditional Calidign banner. Within that oaken box was the body of King Torvaren, who by some circumstance had ceased to breathe the very day Ordric had been killed. Darreth shuddered at the thought of being kept alive by Ordric's magick. He looked at the crypt, whose entire face was covered in snarling, leering gargoyles. Rain poured off jutting horns and curling tongues. *At least this matter of magick is over, for the time being*, thought the elf-blooded, hoping to muster a better mood. The fanged, laughing face of a carved demon stared down at him mockingly.

The brainwashing that Ordric committed ran deep. Upon the sorcerer's death, many minds were swept with nauseating sobriety. Countess Camelia was most significantly affected, as her entire marriage was revealed to be built upon Ordric's dark charms. Many others were stricken by the sudden oncoming of truth, and the whole nobility felt communal guilt over what they had done at the High Lord's behest.

After Torvaren's last rites, the patriarch moved to the next casket. Few knew that Ordric's body had been reduced to ash at the Wizard Slayer's hand. Before he was cremated, the mortician had attempted to remove the ring bearing a three-eyed skull from the High Lord's finger. To the mortician's surprise, the metal had fused with the sorcerer's very flesh, making the ring's removal impossible. When asked about this, Krael was adamant that the ring be destroyed in the furnace along with the body.

Morwenna's last rights began, and if Eledrith wept amidst the pouring rain, he did so with a stoic expression. Her death had been the most tragic of all, and there was seldom an eye that did not shed a tear for the young girl.

In time, the droning recitation of the patriarch had come to an end. The old, robed man turned to Eledrith and asked, "Are there any words you would like to say this day?"

The prince shook his head. "Words will do nothing."

Garrick and Darreth felt a weight sink in their hearts. While the others that stood in the gray rain may not have seen it, all of Eledrith's companions knew that there was uncharacteristic anger that burned. His head was subtly tilted forward, and his lip, if ever so slightly, curled into a malefic sneer.

The caskets were brought into the depths of the crypt. As the ceremony ended, nobles approached the grieving prince offering their condolences. He was due to inherit the crown, and many politicians wished to start their relations with the future king on the right foot. Countess Sedrana's face was unrecognizable amidst the countless others draped in black and streaked by rain. She met Eledrith with a warm, endearing smile. "I know this time can be tough for you, Your Majesty, but if you ever need anything—"

The countess's smile dropped. She almost gasped out of fear as she saw the prince's eyes. "I need nothing," he growled, "save some damn space! Damn it, don't crowd around me!"

Like fish in disturbed water, the nobles scattered away from the silver-haired man. Garrick had half a mind to grab Eledrith's arm and scold him like a child, but such an effort would only stoke the prince's anger even more, not to mention be seen by nearly every influential politician in the city-state. Instead, the knight gritted his teeth.

The elf-blooded went unnoticed, shivering in the downpour. His thoughts were on Krael and the unclear future. Behind Darreth stood Lorienne, and unlike her shorter companion, her expression lacked the sorrowful pain for what the prince was going through. She sensed something dark brooding within Eledrith's mind, and because of this, she did not trust him. If he was unwilling to forgive Krael, Lorienne would be unwilling to side with the prince.

In a cell beneath the Calidign Palace, the Wizard Slayer waited, bound in chains and an iron muzzle strapped around his face. The guards had seen what the Kolgathian's fangs were capable of, and they took no chances. It would have taken a single order for Eledrith to pardon the Slayer and release him, but the prince refused.

No one at the funeral could see it, but in the distant sea, obscured by the towers of the city and downpour of rain, there moved another great iron ark of the drenoch. Even though the orchestrator of the war had died, the momentum of his armies was slow to cease. The massive vessel came through gray, churning waters, bearing another wave of Graehalic mercenaries. Hundreds of those men bore the red hair of their father, Arngrim. They knew the tales of the White Prince who slew Karag-Viil, and like their brethren who had come before them, they wished to fight under Eledrith's banner with the same fanaticism, their own bloodline be damned.

The warm firelight of the hearth illuminated the lounge of the Maumont Estate. The walls were left sporadically bare after the portraits of Ordric were recently removed. While the cozy furniture and bookshelves remained, Countess Camelia sat in discomfort. Her stomach churned as she reflected on her twenty-year marriage and how it was founded on magick and lies. Her arms still bore the bruises and lacerations she received when she first realized the truth. In an outburst, the countess had shattered the mirrors in her chambers. Eledrith, who sat at her side, ran a hand along the bandages about her arm.

"You are welcome to stay at the Calidign Palace if you wish. It's the least I can do for you," said the prince.

"You are too kind, Your Majesty," said Camelia.

Shadows had grown under the countess's eyes. While Eledrith's presence had helped her remain calm, there was still an ever-present wound deep within her mind that threatened to inspire another fit of terror-filled rage. Eledrith knew this, and while he deeply grieved himself, he watched his mother-in-law intently.

"You don't have to make a decision now," he said, "just know the offer is there. I wish only for your well-being."

Camelia's eyes met the prince's. The countess closely resembled her daughter, and while distress had brought out the wrinkles at the corners of her eyes and lips, Eledrith only saw Morwenna's face. Behind a warm smile, Eledrith's own mind screamed in agony.

"Your Majesty, there is something you may wish to see."

The voice came from Idda, the Maumont family's most trusted servant. She stood in the doorway, a frightened look on her tired face. Ordric's scandal and the death of Morwenna had taken a toll on her as well.

"What is it?" asked Eledrith, remaining close to the unstable Camelia.

Idda pursed her lips and gestured for the prince to come closer. When he came within whispering distance, Idda told him, "There's a room behind the wardrobe in Ordric's bedchamber. I think you should see it."

Whispering back, Eledrith said, "I will. Could you keep an eye on Camelia?"

"Yes, my lord."

The prince's footsteps were subconsciously light as he crept into the late sorcerer's quarters. Half of the carpet was covered with shards of mirror, some stained with blood. Camelia's outburst had also wreaked havoc on the bookshelves in the chamber. While Idda had done a fair bit of cleaning, there was still much to be done. Carefully stepping around the debris, Eledrith made his way toward the ajar wardrobe at the other end of the room. About the mahogany furniture was scattered an assortment of coats and tunics, some torn by the countess. From somewhere beyond the back wall should have been, there came a candle's flickering light.

Eledrith stepped into the hidden study. The walls of the hexagonal chamber were fitted with shelves, and on each was an assortment of antique books, strange animal skulls, and other artifacts that the prince did not recognize. As he took another step closer, the candle flickered as if in a turbulent breeze. Eledrith froze.

Then, nothing. The candle burned as it had before, the golden teardrop of a flame pointing upward. With the candle in hand, Eledrith examined the shelves of the hidden study. There was seldom a tome that had not been tarnished by time. Leather bindings began to crack, and edges of pages yellowed and withered. Dust accumulated on the brass metal of astrological models. Upon every one of these things, inscribed even in the exotic skulls, were runes. The strange, jagged lines and odd details wound in ways no contemporary script had, and Eledrith found himself enamored with the ominous letters.

Behind the prince was a presence, and he could only describe it as that. He turned to see the slender, lithe form of the woman who claimed to be his mother on his wedding day. She stood, a sly, almost lustful smile on her large lips. Her eyes, while having typical circular irises, had a feline glare that was unlike any woman's. The black robes that concealed her body did little to hide the curves of her hips and legs as she stepped forward.

"What do you want?" Eledrith said, the candle shaking as he mustered the question.

"I told you this time would come."

The prince narrowed his eyes, trying to hide his fear with anger.

"Do not pretend you have forgotten my words. There is a pain within you that you cannot bear. Do as I say, and it will end," said the woman.

"Who is to say I cannot bear it?"

"Oh, Eledrith," she said, a cruel glimmer in her yellow eyes. "You have imprisoned a man that you once thought of as a friend, perhaps even a mentor."

"He killed the one I love," said Eledrith through gritted teeth. "That's not pain; it's justice."

The woman chuckled. "Then why do you look as if you are in pain now?"

Calming himself, the prince said, "Should a man not be in pain when his wife dies?"

"Any other man, perhaps, but you deserve better, Eledrith."

Hesitantly, Eledrith shook his head.

"But was your love not true and pure?"

The prince did not need to nod. Instead, he only glared, unnerved at his supposed mother's words, for he knew them to be true.

"And if you had the power to bring it back," she continued, "would it not be the right thing to do?"

Eledrith stepped back, stopping when he collided with a bookshelf. The woman paced toward him and moved a hand to his face. Her soft, supple skin brushed against his cheek, then reached for a book above his shoulder. "Such a power is right here," she said.

The prince's eyes grew wide in shock. "But that is magick!" he cried. "It is evil!"

"Says who? The brute who slaughtered your wife? The man who cares for little other than his own religious crusade? His close-minded philosophy brought about the death of the innocent. How true can his beliefs really be?"

For a time, the prince did not speak. The yellow eyes, inches away, stared into his own. After the pressure became too great, he pushed the woman aside and said, "I need time to think."

He left the study and stumbled into Ordric's bedchamber, tripping over scattered clothes. From the darkness of the study, the woman said, "I cannot force your hand in this, my son. The choice is yours."

The air in the depths of the Calidign Palace was cold. Even though he was covered in a thick tunic, Eledrith still shivered. One of his pale hands went to his sword's hilt to soothe his nerves. The shock of the conversation with his mother only a few hours ago had abated his anger, but Eledrith still held a hatred for the Wizard Slayer. He also still missed, and loved, Morwenna.

After taking a deep breath, the prince pushed open the heavy door that led to the palace dungeons. Seldom had those decrepit cells been used, as the numerous prisons around Saidal were better suited for holding criminals and the condemned. Krael's situation was different. Eight guards stood watch in the room, each fully armored and bearing both spear and shortsword in addition to a shield. The many lanterns hanging from the walls drove all gloom from the chamber, and Krael had no shadow to hide in.

Out of the four cells in the room, only one was occupied. The Slayer's corded arms and legs were bound by cold iron chains. A steel mask of a muzzle prevented his fangs from being a threat, and above that sheet of metal bore two deep, gray eyes.

The Slayer's eyes followed Eledrith as he walked into the room. Each guard offered a shallow bow to the prince but kept their attention on the man in the cell. As Eledrith approached the barrier of rusted steel, one of the guards said, "Stay back, my lord!"

A wave of the prince's hand signaled the guard to stand down. If he still held any fear in the presence of the Kolgathian, he did not show it. "Krael," he greeted, his chin held high.

The Slayer only stared at the prince.

"Leave us," commanded Eledrith to the guards.

"But, Your Majesty, he's dangerous!" one protested.

Rolling his eyes, Eledrith said, "Damn it, he's in a cell. I'll be fine."

Reluctantly, the guards marched out of the room, leaving the prince and Wizard Slayer in solitude. After the heavy door slammed closed, Krael said, "I am sorry, Eledrith."

The mask did not muffle the Slayer's words. His deep voice resonated off the metal covering his face. For a moment, Eledrith only stared. He could feel multiple emotions boiling within him, each competing for control. After taking a deep breath, he calmly asked, "Can magick truly be as evil as you claim?"

The Slayer cocked his head, and a deep exhalation hissed through the holes in his steel muzzle. Shifting about in his chains, he said, "Don't."

"Ordric hid a small library within the Maumont Estate. Within it lies the key to bringing Morwenna back."

"Burn it all," Krael growled.

"Really?" said Eledrith, eyes flaring. "I believe it is power, and like any other, it takes responsibility and discipline to wield."

The Slayer began to shout through his mask, "No!"

"You sound like an overprotective mother demanding her child not dare pick up a sword. Like a sword, I can wield magick if I am careful and disciplined in its practice."

"No one has that discipline."

"It was that narrow-minded ideology that killed Morwenna," said Eledrith. "Was it really so important to kill Ordric that you couldn't exercise a little more care? Or is your selfish crusade against magick the only thing that matters to you?"

Even in the best of circumstances, Krael would have struggled to answer that question. While his mind raced with anger, his thoughts were scattered. He could only glare from behind the bars of his cell.

Smirking, Eledrith said, "Besides, wasn't it you that told me it was not what I am but what I choose to do that matters? Through my will, I'll right the wrong that you could not help but commit."

"No, Eledrith. Gods will control you. Dark Gods. Your will won't be your own."

There was a hint of desperation in the Kolgathian's deep voice that the prince had never heard before. Sorrow was what it could be called, and it stirred the same feeling within Eledrith. Not able to bear the burden of more pain, the prince hardened his heart and said, "I have heard enough. I came here to know if there was truth to your zealous philosophy, but now I know it is just narrow-mindedness. The world is not black and white, good and evil. There are shades of gray, and the wisdom to sift through this sea of grayness is something you lack."

"Please, Eledrith, don't."

"You killed the one I love the most. Why should I give what you say any further thought?"

Krael realized arguing was pointless. Anguish twisted the prince's reason. Instead of answering, the barbarian sat in silence.

With a sad smile, Eledrith said, "I consider you a friend. I really do. That is why I haven't had you executed, I suppose. What kind of man kills those he calls friends?"

From behind the mask, the Slayer glared.

"If I go through with this, you will stop at nothing to kill me."

The Kolgathian hesitantly nodded.

"I suppose this is farewell. Goodbye, Krael."

The Slayer rushed toward the iron bars, eyes wild. Chains snapped taut as they prevented him from crashing against the cell wall. Fangs gnashed behind the mask, and Krael's inhuman roars were deafening. Even as the commotion caused the guards to come rushing back in, Eledrith stood without flinching. Remorse filled the prince, but he knew his decision had been made. He left the chamber and made his way back into the upper levels of the palace, the Wizard Slayer's roars echoing off the walls far below.

ABOUT THE AUTHOR

In addition to writing, Franklin Roberts teaches martial arts to students of all ages. Given that most of his writing inspiration comes from heavy metal and weightlifting, he specializes in stories concerning barbaric heroes and blood-stained steel.

Reviews help more than most people realize. If you enjoyed this book, please consider leaving a honest review on Amazon.

Join the Newsletter!   *Review The Wizard Slayer (US)*

 @Franklin Roberts – Author

@franklinroberts4837

CLAIM YOUR FREE SHORT STORY

The time of sacrifice is at hand...

Famine threatens the warlord Alrik's land. Every year, souls are sacrificed to the wizard Morzul to keep the realm's destruction at bay. Recently, the number of people that must die has grown too large for Alrik to allow.

No longer will Alrik give in to Morzul's demands. To face a wizard in battle is madness, so he finds Krael, a savage barbarian who can fight against the power of magick and survive. Though Alrik believes he has found his champion, he may have unleashed something he cannot control...

In addition to getting this free precursor to The Wizard Slayer Saga, you will join Franklin Roberts's monthly newsletter, where the author himself can communicate on a less formal level discussions of fantasy, sword and sorcery, and other miscellaneous musings.

Join the Newsletter!

CONTINUE THE WIZARD SLAYER SAGA

No one can escape the eyes of the Undying Oracle.

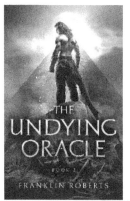

Krael, the Wizard Slayer of legend, is forced into exile by his once-trusted friend Eledrith. Alone in a foreign land, fate brings him into the hands of the Witch Lord of Tyrithel, a towering monster and magick-user that has tyrannized his domain for centuries.

In the Outlaw Kingdoms, King Eledrith must put a swift end to a war that should have never begun. As his dark destiny looms over his soul, the young ruler finds himself committing great evils in the name of saving his own subjects. Burdened with grief, Eledrith seeks the Undying Oracle, a prescient entity that has existed since before recorded history—the very same being controlled by the Witch Lord at odds with Krael.

Grief plagues the Wizard Slayer's heart as well. Not only must he face an adversary who can see events before they happen, but he must also fend off the demons of his own past—both of which threaten to push his indomitable will to its breaking point.

Continue the adventure in book two of the Wizard Slayer Saga, *The Undying Oracle*!

AVAILABLE NOW!

Made in the USA
Las Vegas, NV
12 September 2024

95189297R00229